Wayward Girls

Also by Susan Wiggs

The Twelve Dogs of Christmas
Welcome to Beach Town
Sugar and Salt
The Lost and Found Bookshop
The Oysterville Sewing Circle
Between You and Me
Map of the Heart
Family Tree

Wayward Girls

A Novel

Susan Wiggs

WILLIAM MORROW
An Imprint of HarperCollins*Publishers*

This is a work of fiction. Names, characters, places, and incidents are products of the author's imagination or are used fictitiously and are not to be construed as real. Any resemblance to actual events, locales, organizations, or persons, living or dead, is entirely coincidental.

WAYWARD GIRLS. Copyright © 2025 by Laugh, Cry, Dream, Read, LLC. All rights reserved. Printed in the United States of America. No part of this book may be used or reproduced in any manner whatsoever without written permission except in the case of brief quotations embodied in critical articles and reviews. For information, address HarperCollins Publishers, 195 Broadway, New York, NY 10007.

HarperCollins books may be purchased for educational, business, or sales promotional use. For information, please email the Special Markets Department at SPsales@harpercollins.com.

FIRST EDITION

Interior text design by Diahann Sturge-Campbell

Book part opener photo © arazu/Stock.Adobe.com

Library of Congress Cataloging-in-Publication Data

Names: Wiggs, Susan, author.
Title: Wayward girls: a novel / Susan Wiggs.
Description: First edition. | New York: William Morrow, 2025.
Identifiers: LCCN 2024025125 | ISBN 9780063118270 (hardcover) | ISBN 9780063118294 (ebook)
Subjects: LCGFT: Novels.
Classification: LCC PS3573.I38616 W39 2025 | DDC 813/.54—dc23/eng/20240610
LC record available at https://lccn.loc.gov/2024025125

ISBN 978-0-06-311827-0
25 26 27 28 29 LBC 5 4 3 2 1

To the girls who survived, including Diana, Bonnie, Judith, Patricia, Nancy, Maureen, and so many others. Your stories are more powerful than what happened to you.

Wayward Girls

Prologue

On November 14, 2019, Governor Andrew M. Cuomo signed legislation (S3419/A5494) allowing adoptees to receive a copy of their pre-adoption birth certificate when they turn eighteen years old. The application process began on January 15, 2020.

February 17, 2020
Buffalo

"Evelyn . . . Everly Marie Barrett Lasko," called a clerk from one of the desks in the county records office.

Everly arranged her face in a smile and greeted the clerk, a guy with thinning hair and hands that stayed busy on his ergonomic split keyboard. He glanced up, then did a double take. Even though her modeling days were behind her, she still got that reaction sometimes.

"Unusual name," he commented.

"My mother's favorite group was the Everly Brothers. Her favorite song was "All I Have to Do Is Dream," she said, holding the smile in place.

"Please, have a seat," he said, his voice and his gaze warming. "I've been reading your file, and I want to help."

"Thank you for seeing me." She glanced at the name bar on his desk. "Mr. Harris."

"I'm afraid it's not good news," he said. "There's no documentation of your birth in our state or county records."

Her stomach sank, even though she had been bracing herself for the news. Her own search had been equally fruitless. She'd only been able to access her amended birth certificate, created when Roy and Shirley Barrett had adopted her as a newborn. At that moment, her true origin had been automatically and permanently sealed. Her past was a secret locked in a vital records room somewhere. "Isn't there anything more you can do? Anywhere else you can look? Some other agency, or—?"

"Here's a list of all the inquiries I've made so far. I'm sorry to say, there's no other place to look."

She studied the page-long list of offices and agencies. "I'm already registered in the Adoption Information Registry," she said.

"I understand, ma'am. But that's a mutual consent registry for adoptees and birth parents to facilitate a reunion between registered parties. They can't issue pre-adoption birth certificates."

He pursed his lips and scrolled with his mouse. "Your certificate of adoption is from . . . looks like a girls' home in Buffalo that no longer exists."

"I'm aware of that. I traced the Sisters of Charity to a location in Astoria, New York, but they have no records. They tried to refer me to—"

"Our Lady of Victory in Lackawanna," he said. "Yep, they didn't have anything, either. Nothing from Catholic Charities. Mrs. Lasko, are your adoptive parents still living?"

She shook her head. "They were older," she said. "They've both passed away. And before you ask, they were open about my adoption. But they were not sophisticated people. The nuns told them only that the birth mother was underage and wanted the records sealed. My parents simply accepted the documents they were given when they adopted me. They didn't realize there was supposed to be a pre-adoption birth certificate."

"There were a number of irregular adoptions back in the 1960s," he said. "I wish I could give you more information. I'm sorry."

"I can't get a passport without a pre-adoption birth certificate. Did you know that? I'm fifty-one years old, and I've never left the US."

"Have you applied to the Department of State for a variance?" he asked.

"Several times," she said. "I keep being told my documents are 'irregular,' like you said. They keep insisting I need to produce my original birth certificate."

"Could be you weren't born in this state. It's clear you were adopted here, but this probably means you were born in another state. We can't access records from other states."

"I know for a fact I was born in New York State. Saint Francis Hospital, right here in Buffalo. It was torn down in the seventies when the new medical complex was built."

He tapped his keyboard and wiggled his mouse. "The records would have been moved, then. Could be they were lost, mislabeled, or damaged somewhere in that process."

She struggled for patience. The document she sought was just a piece of paper, but its power was about ensuring equal rights for adoptees—the right to know the most fundamental truth about themselves. "I understand that, but birth records can't just disappear. They can't."

"I've checked and double-checked." He shook his head. "Mrs. Lasko, I've accessed all the records I could find from March and April 1969. But everything's a dead end. I'm truly sorry."

"So, according to your records, I was never born," said Everly. "I don't exist."

BOOK ONE

Then

Part One

Buffalo Daily Republic
Buffalo, New York
Friday, February 19, 1886

WAYWARD GIRLS

Ella Dunn is the fifteen-year-old daughter of John Dunn, who lives on Mechanic Street. Ella has a fondness for bad company and leaves the paternal roof to indulge it. Three weeks ago she ran away from home, and has been a streetwalker ever since. Another fifteen-year-old girl named Minnie Covert, who is without a home, bore Ella company in her street wandering. Yesterday the girls, who had often been observed by the police and warned, were arrested in the evening. Mr. Dunn was notified, and the girls will be charged with truancy...

This afternoon two well-developed and fair-appearing girls were ushered into the police court. They were two truants. Ella told Justice King that she was fifteen years old and two years ago ran away from home and married a worthless fellow named Herth, who afterward deserted her. She has been around to bad houses, living with all sorts of men. Minnie has one good quality, and that is she is unmarried. Both girls were committed for sixty days to the Home of the Good Shepherd.

Chapter 1

The Fruit Belt
Buffalo, 1968

The orchard ladder wobbled on its skinny tripod legs as Mairin O'Hara reached for an apple, deftly plucking it from a branch. With a practiced movement, she slipped it into the long canvas harvest bag slung across her body from shoulder to hip. She felt self-conscious about her faded denim overalls and soft plaid shirt, even though most of the pickers were in work clothes, too. But the others probably weren't wearing hand-me-downs from their big brother. Liam's loose, threadbare shirt was as homely as an old dish rag.

If Mairin complained, her mother would simply respond with her favorite question: "You think we're made of money?" And then Mam's mouth would form its usual sour pucker.

Well, no, Mairin thought. No, we're not made of money. She didn't know anyone who was made of money. That was the reason she and Liam were working in the orchard instead of spending the last of the summer at Crystal Beach on the lake, or going to open-air concerts in Delaware Park. That was what people in the Fruit Belt did.

As one of the smallest on the crew, Mairin was adept at scampering up to the high, slender branches of a tree's crown. She'd only fallen a couple of times, and on each occasion, she got up, ignored the bruises, and kept working. She knew she'd catch holy hell from Mam if she got hurt bad enough to need help. According to Mam, the doctor was expensive.

Not this view, though, Mairin thought, feeling a breeze lift the curls that had escaped from her braid. The lofty perch gave her a bird's-eye view from the shimmering waters of Lake Erie to the patchwork quilt of Buffalo's neighborhoods, made up of clapboard row houses, fading mansions exhausted by time, waterfront smokestacks and church steeples lancing the sky. Way off to the east, the green farmland rolled on forever. The sky today was that perfect late-summer blue, hung with fluffy clouds off the lake, reminding Mairin of that song about looking at clouds from both sides. She loved the song so much she'd practically worn it out on her record player. A moment later, she found herself singing it under her breath.

From the corner of her eye, Mairin saw Kevin Doyle moving his ladder closer to hers. She pretended not to notice, even though she was sure her suddenly burning cheeks would be a dead giveaway. It was the eternal curse of being a redhead, Mam used to say. You wear your feelings like the freckles on your face.

"Hey," said Kevin, his shock of nut-brown hair glinting in the late afternoon sunlight. He had the coolest hair, long enough to brush his shoulders, the bangs angled across his forehead like David Cassidy's. At school, the nuns tended to scold the boys about their long hair, the girls about their short hemlines, and everyone about the music they listened to.

"Hey." She tipped her head in greeting while snapping off another apple. She tried to think of something else to say. It wasn't like Mairin to be at a loss for words, because she was always getting in trouble at school for talking too much. A thrill of nervousness caused her to speed up her picking. Two apples in each hand. Here at Eisman's orchard, speed and efficiency were prized, and you got paid by how much you picked.

Kevin had a transistor radio clipped to his belt. It wasn't very loud, but WKBW came in crystal clear, and the station played all the best songs. When she heard the soft, rhythmic sound of her current favorite, Mairin couldn't suppress a grin. The voices of Simon and Garfunkel melded together with ethereal, breathy perfection. "Mrs. Robinson" flowed from the radio, and the melody filled Mairin with a poignant yearning. She couldn't resist moving with the rhythm as she sang along and descended her ladder.

She knew every single word by heart, even though she barely understood the meaning of the lyrics, like what was Mrs. Robinson hiding from the kids, and why did she need to learn to help herself? And why was Joe DiMaggio called Joltin' Joe?

The nuns at school said this kind of music was forbidden, even though the song mentioned Jesus and heaven. *Girls your age shouldn't be listening to male voices*, Sister Carlotta often said. *And how are you going to explain that in confession?*

"Coo, coo cachoo," Mairin sang along with the radio, hitting every note and catching Kevin's eye.

"You have a good voice," he said, dropping to the ground and tossing his bangs out of his eyes.

"Thanks," she said, feeling the fresh burn of a blush as she climbed down to the ground. She emptied her bag into a waiting bushel. "I love that song."

"Yeah. So . . ." Now he was blushing as he shifted from foot to foot.

"So . . ." she prompted, tilting her head to one side.

He dug the toe of his sneaker into the dirt. "So that movie—*The Graduate*—is playing at the Landmark," he said. "Want to go see it?"

Mairin jolted to attention. What? Go see *The Graduate*? With him? With Kevin Doyle? Was he asking her out? On a date?

She cast her eyes to and fro, scanning the busy pickers up and down the rows of trees. Holy moly, where was Fiona when Mairin needed her? Mairin's best friend would know what to make of this development. Fiona'd had a boyfriend all summer long—Casey Costello, who was going to be a senior this year. She had confessed to Mairin in excited whispers that she and Casey *did stuff*. What sort of stuff, Mairin could only guess at through a gauzy cloud of romanticism gleaned from *Fifteen* by Beverly Cleary. According to that book, dating was all about convertibles, soda shops, sweaters, and boys. According to Fiona, there was a lot more to dating than that.

Mairin tucked her nervous hands into her pockets, wishing that she wasn't dressed like a backwoods hick. Kevin didn't seem to mind, though, as he eyed her with a look that seemed a little bit bashful, a little bit eager. She tried to sound casual when she said, "I . . . um, yes, that sounds fun."

"It's playing through the weekend," he said.

She nodded, her heart beating fast. "I . . . I might, uh, might have to check with my mom. She's strict that way, Mam is."

"Okay," he said, hooking his thumbs into his belt loops. "You can let me know tomorrow, yeah?"

"Okay," she said. "Should I . . . um, want me to call you?" She'd never called a boy out of the blue. What if Mrs. Doyle answered? Or one of his brothers?

"Yeah. Cool," he said.

"Cool," she echoed, blushing again.

"See you, then." He picked up a full bushel and headed for the wagon, where the foreman logged each worker's harvest.

"See you." Mairin watched him go. Did he have a spring in his step? Did he think they were going on a date? Did *she* think that?

Mairin had her doubts about being able to go, on account of Mam. Her mother was Irish through and through, having come from Killarney via Limerick when she was only eighteen. Mam still had the brogue, not to mention the old country ways. Mairin already knew what Mam's answer would be: "Go to the movies with a boy? Ah, sure you can, about ten minutes after hell freezes over, that's when you'll be allowed to go to a filthy dirty movie. With a *boy*."

Mairin didn't think the movie was filthy at all, but the picture in the advertisement in the paper showed a lady's bare leg, and that was all Mam needed to know.

Mairin was sweaty from the humidity off the lake, and probably from nerves over her encounter with Kevin. Afternoon sunlight bathed the orchard in a golden glow upon the fruit-laden trees, alive with the crew of busy pickers. There weren't many orchards left in the Fruit Belt. Folks who had been around for a while said the area used to be a bustling farm community with street names like Mulberry, Lemon, Orange, Peach, Grape, and Cherry. But ever since the expressway had slashed the district in half, things had begun to deteriorate. Old Mr. Eisman's orchard was still producing, though, and he paid a decent sum per bin.

Mairin spotted Fiona at the edge of the main grove, sitting on the ground by a hedge of milkweed that was alive with hovering bees. Fiona was leaning her forehead on her drawn-up knees and rocking slightly back and forth.

"What's up, buttercup?" asked Mairin, dropping down onto the dry grass next to her. She swatted at a bee. The bees didn't worry her, because honeybees were always too busy gathering nectar from the milkweed to bother stinging people.

Fiona lifted her head, and immediately, Mairin could tell something was wrong. Fiona's face was paper white, and there were beads of sweat on her upper lip. "Oh, hi, Mairin," she said in a small voice.

Mairin frowned and studied Fiona's face. With her jet-black hair and pale skin, she looked like Snow White come to life, only instead of singing to the wishing well, she looked miserable. "What's the matter?" Mairin asked. "Don't you feel well?"

Fiona shuddered and nodded her head. "Don't get too close. I'm coming down with something. I puked in the bushes over there." She gestured vaguely. "Twice."

"My gosh, you need to go home." Mairin jumped up and held out her hand.

Fiona waved it away. "Can't, Mair. You know my mom. She'll kill me if I come home without my wages again. I need to pull myself together and pick another couple of bushels at least."

"Your mom'll understand," Mairin said.

"No, I mean, she might, but I *need* the money," Fiona said, a thin reed of desperation in her voice. She braced her hands behind her and levered herself up, staggering a little. She looked chastened, a bit disoriented as she dusted off her dungarees.

"Hey, you can't work like this," Mairin said. "Let me call your mom for a ride home."

"No," Fiona objected again. "I have to get some picking done."

It was never a good thing to come home empty-handed, Mairin knew. Not for girls like her and Fiona. "Tell you what," she said. "I'll give you my bushels today. I filled sixteen. I can fill another couple, real quick. That'll make a whole bin."

"That's . . . Mair, I can't let you give me your—" Fiona made an urping sound and clutched herself around the middle. She leaned over the hedge and made a gagging noise.

Mairin felt helpless as she rubbed her friend's back. Dad used to do that when Mairin was little and sick with the flu. He'd rub her back gently, up and down, and then in circles. It didn't help with the flu, yet his touch always made her feel better. Her dad had been gone for five years, but she would never stop missing him. She would never stop feeling that ache inside her, like a bruise that wouldn't heal.

"Listen, you look really bad. I'm going to call your mom—"

"No." Fiona's voice was sharp. She plucked a black-and-red bandanna from her pocket and wiped her mouth. "I can walk home."

"It's two miles, mostly uphill," Mairin said. "Hey, I'll call one of your brothers to pick you up, okay?"

"I . . ." Fiona swayed a little "Okay, I guess Flynn could come. He's working at the Agway store over on Sandridge."

"You wait here." Mairin noticed a couple of the other pickers eyeing them. "Just have a seat, and I'll look up the number and call, okay?"

She hurried over to the warehouse, a long, boxy building with a loading dock in back. A team of guys in T-shirts and jeans were hoisting bins onto a waiting truck. Their sun-bronzed arms bulged with muscles. One guy, who had big shoulders and a pack of Lucky Strikes tucked into his rolled-up sleeve, saw her staring and gave her a wink and a nod. She quickly looked away, then went inside and paused, letting her eyes adjust to the dim light.

The sweet aroma of fresh apples mingled with the woody scent of crates and pallets. The warehouse buzzed with energy, as if getting the fruit from the farm to the table was a matter of life and death. Workers moved swiftly and efficiently among the bins and stacked pallets; their conversations intermingled with laughter. A portable radio was playing "Harper Valley PTA," and Nadine, the clerk, sang along as she checked the labels on the sorting bins on her clipboard.

Mairin could see her older brother operating a forklift, moving a stack of pallets toward the loading dock. Liam could drive just about anything—a forklift, a tractor, and Colm's Nash Rambler whenever Liam was able to talk their stepfather into loaning him the car. Liam had been teaching Mairin on the sly, because she desperately wanted to pass her driving test the minute she turned sixteen. Her mom and Colm kept saying she didn't need to drive a car when the bus was free with her student pass, but knowing how to drive was important to her. Driving meant freedom and independence and escape.

Sometimes she craved those things so intensely that she couldn't sleep at night. Her chest seemed to swell with yearning. She was filled with a bright longing for everything big—a big adventure, a big love, a big life. She wanted to make her mark. She wanted to build something. She didn't try to explain this to Mam, who would say she was talking nonsense. Her job was to settle down with a good Catholic boy, preferably mere seconds after graduation. But Mairin wanted more. She wanted... just everything.

She went over to the pay phone by the restrooms and time clock where everyone checked in for the day, and dug in her pocket for a dime. Shoot, she only had thirty-five cents, and she'd been saving it to buy the new issue of *Tiger Beat*. But Fiona needed her more.

She leafed through the thin pages of the phone book and ran her finger down the columns. There was a seam of dirt under each nail, and her hands were rough from work. Would Kevin Doyle want to hold hands with her in the movie? Maybe put his arm around her? She shuddered at the thought, wavering between excitement and apprehension. With a will, she focused on making the call.

Fiona had four brothers, and Flynn was Mairin's favorite. He was the kind of handsome you saw on movie posters, with dark hair that tumbled over his forehead and eyes that were as blue as the clear September sky. They were almost—but not quite—too pretty for a guy. Mairin probably had a crush on him, but she knew he was out of her league, five years older and already living in a place of his own up on Huron Street. Plus, he was dating a Protestant girl named Haley Moore, who was as exotic as a bird of paradise in her ragged-edged bell bottom jeans and Indian sandals with a loop around the toe, a fringed halter top and an embroidered band around her forehead, and silky blond hair swinging down to her waist. She lived at something called a commune, where supposedly people hung out naked and listened to acid rock and practiced free love, whatever that was. Mam called them dirty hippies and said Mairin wasn't supposed to talk to them.

Fiona had confessed to Mairin that her mother was so distressed by Flynn's girlfriend that she made the whole family say novenas every day for nine days, and then they had to start the cycle all over again, imploring the saints to intervene and get rid of Haley once and for all, so Flynn could settle down with a proper Catholic girl.

Mairin and Fiona and all their friends at St. Wilda's had been told from the cradle that this was their goal in life—to be proper Catholic girls.

"Come on," Mairin said to Fiona, holding out her hand to help her up. "Flynn will be here in a few minutes."

Fiona nodded, and she leaned on Mairin as they stood in the shade of a sycamore tree to wait. The late-afternoon air carried a hint of autumn's crispness as it rustled through the trees. All up and down the street, the leaves had started to take on their vibrant hues of red and gold. Mairin noticed a ladybug caught in a web on the trunk of the sycamore tree. The little thing's legs were flailing. Even though nature was supposed to take its course, Mairin couldn't help herself. She gently teased the web aside until the ladybug flew free, disappearing on the breeze.

"You feeling any better?" she asked.

"Worse than ever." Fiona lowered herself to an upended crate. "I swear, I don't know what's the matter with me. I can't even puke anymore, but I feel like I need to."

"Put that in your pocket." Mairin handed her a pay envelope. "Don't puke on it."

"Oh, Mair." Fiona's wide eyes were tragic. "I feel so bad taking this from you."

"It's fine," Mairin said. It wasn't fine, not exactly. Her own mother logged every penny Mairin and Liam brought in. But Fiona was one of nine kids. The Gallaghers' noisy, crowded house had leaky plumbing and smelled of onion and boiled cabbage, and sometimes Fiona "forgot" to bring a lunch to school. "Really. You can make it up to me some other time."

"You're the best," Fiona said.

"Nah. Just a friend in deed. Oh, and in need." Mairin's pulse sped up. "I need your advice. Kevin Doyle wants to go to the movies with me."

"What?" Fiona offered a thin, wavering smile. "Did he ask you out? Like, on a date?"

Mairin twirled a finger around the end of her braid. "I think so. I mean, he didn't call it a date, but he asked if I'd want to go."

"Well, that's definitely a date, then. Did you say yes?"

"I said I'd check. Mam will never let me." Mairin pulled a face.

"You'll have to sneak out, then," Fiona said. "Tell her you're going to the library. Parents love it when we go to the library."

"At night?"

"Tell her it's open late."

Mairin frowned. "I'll try asking first. She said I could go to dances at the CYO once I'm sixteen, and I'll be sixteen pretty soon. So maybe she'll surprise me and say yes."

Fiona's brother Flynn arrived in a Fiorelli's produce supply truck with Haley Moore in the passenger seat. Haley looked like a model with her round sunglasses and giant hoop earrings, a long, slender cigarette between her long, slender fingers. She had her bare feet propped on the dashboard and was bobbing her shiny blond head to a song by Jefferson Airplane.

"Hiya, kiddos," she said.

Kiddos. Haley was only eighteen, but she made Mairin feel like a baby.

Flynn jumped out and came around to help Fiona. He wore faded jeans and a white T-shirt that strained against his arm muscles. "Hey, short stuff," he said. "Mairin said you got sick."

Fiona nodded forlornly. "I don't know what's wrong with me," she said in a small voice. "I feel awful."

He stepped back and studied her. "Yeah, you look like death eating a cracker."

She scowled. "Thanks."

"Let's get you home. Get you some ginger ale and soda crackers—Ma's cure-all." He went around to the driver's side and got in. Haley stubbed out her cigarette and sat on a stack of fruit crates so Fiona could have the seat. Flynn caught Mairin's eye. "Thanks for calling me," he said. "You need a ride?"

Mairin shook her head. "I have my bike." She stepped up onto the running board. "Feel better, Fiona. If I don't see you tomorrow, I'll come by."

Fiona slumped in the front seat. "Ma'll make me come to work." She touched her pocket with the envelope. "And thanks for this. I'll make it up to you."

Mairin went back to the warehouse. Since she'd given her envelope to Fiona, she knew she'd better bring something home from the discard bin. There was Kevin Doyle, getting his tally for the day. "Twenty-four bushels," he said with a satisfied grin.

"Impressive. Most I've ever picked is twenty."

"Don't forget to let me know about the movie," he said. "Show starts at seven."

She forced herself to look him in the eye, even though she felt impossibly bashful. No way would her mother let her go, but she'd figure something out. The library excuse might work. She offered a tremulous smile. "I'll call you."

"Okay." He started toward the exit.

"Okay." She ducked into the bathroom, feeling almost light-headed. The idea of going to the movies with a boy was so new, an adventure plopped right into the middle of her boring little life. Bending over a stainless-steel basin, she splashed water on her face and dabbed at it with a paper towel, wishing like she always did that she could dab away the freckles. But all the lemon juice and Noxzema in the world couldn't make them fade.

At the other end of the room, two of the warehouse clerks were leaning toward the mirror, putting on makeup and listening to the radio. Gina and Carla. Mairin didn't really know them because they were older. Warehouse girls. They sat at their stations all day, fingers with polished nails flying over the keyboards of adding machines and typewriters. They were dressed in tight clam diggers and midi blouses, and wore their hair in chin-length flips held in place by clouds of Aqua Net.

"Was that Flynn Gallagher?" Carla asked, glancing over at Mairin. "God, he's so dreamy."

"Total stone-cold fox." Gina flicked a mascara brush at her eyelashes. "Too bad he's going around with that hippie girl." She swayed her hips to "Mrs. Brown, You've Got a Lovely Daughter" and echoed the chorus along with Herman's Hermits, who were almost as cool as the Beatles: "*Daaaaw-ter.*"

Mairin shrugged her shoulders. She wasn't sure what a stone-cold fox was, but it was clearly a compliment. "He came to pick up Fiona. She had to go home sick."

"Sick." Carla scoffed, then traced her mouth with crimson lipstick. "Girl's not sick. She got herself in trouble, betcha dollars to donuts."

Mairin balled up the paper towel and shot it into the wastebasket. She was pretty sure she knew what *in trouble* meant. "Nuh-uh," she said. "She's got a flu or something."

"Right," Carla said. "You wait and see. She's gonna end up with the Good Shepherd nuns."

Mairin frowned. She was only vaguely aware of the gloomy edifice up on Best Street. It was a gray hulk of a building, its brick walls topped by coils of razor wire. She'd heard it was some kind of reform school and workhouse for unwed mothers. When Mam got mad at her about something, she'd sometimes threaten to send Mairin to the nuns if she didn't behave.

Fiona couldn't be in trouble. Not like that. They had been best friends since the beginning of time. They'd done everything together. They were still just kids. Only last week, they had a sleepover, wearing their babydoll pajamas and using their hairbrushes as microphones while belting out "Angel of the Morning" until Fiona's dad begged for mercy.

"You're wrong about Fiona," she muttered, but the very idea gave her a weird feeling in her gut. How could a girl who was a kid only yesterday suddenly be *in trouble*? No one had explained to Mairin exactly how it worked. She knew it was something to do with going steady, riding around in cars, and parking at the spillway. Making out and heavy petting, the progress likened to advancing around a baseball diamond.

It all sounded like too much fun, not *trouble*.

THE SUN WAS beginning to set as Mairin slid into the driver's seat of the old Nash Rambler, which Colm had left parked in the side driveway. Liam had promised to help her practice left-lane turns and parallel parking. Friday was Colm's league night at the Eagles Lodge bowling alley, so he wouldn't be home for a while. It was always better at the house when Colm wasn't around.

She flexed her hands on the steering wheel, her eagerness mingling with a small dart of anxiety. Liam got in on the passenger side. "Okay, squirt," he said with a grin. "Ready to roll?" He tossed the car keys over to her. The keys were on a Niagara Falls key chain, which she had bought for Mam after a school field trip to the Falls last year.

Mairin always felt unsettled when she visited the Falls, a giant raging cataclysm of rushing, tumbling water between two of the biggest lakes in the world. Her dad had worked at the power plant, and he'd been killed on the job. She didn't like to think about that, but whenever she stood staring into the mesmerizing crash of water, she was both repulsed by fear, yet felt strangely close to her father.

She caught the keys, feeling the weight of them in the palm of her hand. She silently went through the checklist Liam had drummed into her, explaining that leaving out any of the necessary steps could lead to failure. Adjust the seat. Key in the ignition. One foot on the brake pedal, the other on the clutch. Gear in neutral. Check the rearview mirror . . . she went down the list from memory.

"Ready to roll," she said, turning the key. The engine grumbled to life. "Where to?"

"Let's go down to Rotary Field on Bailey," he said. "The college has a good parking lot for practicing."

Mairin took a deep breath and nodded, steadying her hands on the steering wheel and gear box as she tried to mask her nerves with determination. She shifted the gear into reverse and eased up on the clutch, hoping it wouldn't pop and kill the engine. It had taken her dozens of tries to figure out just the right move.

"Hey, not bad, sister," Liam said.

"Thanks to you," she said. She checked all the mirrors and swiveled around, then backed out onto the brick-paved street. "I want to get as good at driving as you are."

He laughed, and she could picture his lean, tanned face, although she kept her eyes on the road. Liam was eighteen now, and starting to look like the old pictures of their dad. "You think I'm good?" he asked.

"I know you are." She felt a rush of excitement as she eased along the street. "Can we have the radio on?"

"Nah. One thing at a time. Besides, the dial keeps getting stuck on Colm's crappy polka music station anyway. Nobody wants to listen to that bullshit."

His swearing made her feel grown up. "Okay, stop sign," she said, inching up to the intersection.

"Cool, you're getting the hang of it."

She flicked a glance at him. "You think?"

"I know."

"Mam and Colm don't think I need to know how to drive. They want me to take the bus."

"So take the bus. But learn to drive. You'll be on your own one day. You should know how."

"I think so, too. But Mam thinks I'll find some boy to marry right out of high school, and *he'll* drive me." She maneuvered the car through the Fruit Belt—or what was left of the neighborhood after the expressway had slashed it into two sections.

"That's dopey," said Liam. "Times are a-changin'. You know, like the song says." He sang a few of Bob Dylan's words in his mellow baritone voice. He had always been one of the best singers in the church choir. "Chin up. Don't look at the hood of the car. Look farther ahead. Into the distance."

"Oh, right." She adjusted her gaze. "I'll work on that."

"Just keep doing it, and it'll be second nature pretty soon."

His calm confidence was reassuring. She relaxed, and her driving became more assured as they made their way through the UB area. The college was one of the best in the state, according to Miss Baxter, one of the lay teachers at school. She encouraged all the girls to go to college, even when their parents said it was a waste of time and money. Colm always said the University at Buffalo was a hotbed for a bunch of commies and ought to be shut down. Colm was famous for making broad statements regarding things he knew nothing about.

With remarkable patience, Liam had her spend some time in the empty parking lot, practicing backing up and pulling forward. "Let's try parallel parking," he said after her movements smoothed out. "Head for those two cars over there."

Mairin nodded with determination. She studied the empty space and listened as Liam coached her through lining up with the front car and backing into the space. "I'm horrible at it," she said after the first few tries.

"Take it easy. I had to practice a bunch before I got the hang of it," said Liam.

Eventually, she managed to ease the car into a parking spot without any bumps or scratches. "Just do that a few times every day," Liam said, "and you'll be a pro."

"How'd you get so smart about this stuff?" she asked him.

"When I worked last year at the Kendall station. I wanted to keep working there, but Mr. Banfield put it up for sale." He gestured at the parking lot exit. "Try going toward downtown. Remember where to keep your eyes. And don't hold the wheel so tight." He flexed his hands.

She realized she was tense all over, and she forced herself to relax. As they wended their way through the angled grid of streets toward downtown, he pointed out the signs and signals along the route, advising her to watch for other cars and especially pedestrians. She was getting better at making smooth turns and knowing just the right moment to switch gears.

"Downtown can be crazy," he said. "Take your time."

"Got it."

"You do. I think you're a natural."

Mairin concentrated on remembering everything as she steered the car, stopped at traffic lights, and wended her way through the streets to the lakefront, a jumble of industrial warehouses and silos and shipping wharves, the Cheerios factory emitting a strange, grainy smell. They passed the giant federal building and then the Greyhound bus station on Main Street, bustling with travelers under its curved art moderne awning.

"Where's everyone going?" she wondered.

"Anywhere the road takes 'em, I guess," said Liam. "Take the road east along Buffalo Creek. It's a nice drive, and you can practice getting into passing gear."

It was a quiet, winding stretch of road surrounded by farms and hamlet villages. Even though Gardenville and the towns along the creek were only a few miles outside the city, the farmland area seemed like it was worlds away. Some of the places had quaint names, like Blackberry Ridge and Maple Acres. "I love farms," she said. "Everything seems so peaceful on a farm."

"Farms are a lot of work."

She nodded. "Everything's a lot of work." Something ahead caught her eye—a hand-painted sign with a peace symbol flag by the side of the road. "Oh my gosh, that's Heyday Farm."

"Hey-what?"

"Fiona's brother is going with a girl who lives there. Haley Moore." She slowed down and pulled onto the shoulder. There was an old school bus painted in psychedelic colors with flowers and slogans, like "Mother Earth sustains us" and "Turn on, tune in, and drop out."

"It's one of those communes," Liam said. "I've heard it's mostly a bunch of strays and misfits and runaways." Then he surprised her by adding, "Sometimes I wish I could join them."

"Seriously?"

"Better head back now. Mam'll want help with supper," he said.

She navigated the few miles back to the city. The lowering sun cast a golden glow over the houses and trees lining the street. Parking the car in the side driveway, Mairin felt a sense of accomplishment, but for some reason, she could sense something weighing on Liam's mind.

"It's really nice that you're doing this, Liam," she said. "Thanks."

"Dad would have wanted me to teach you."

Dad. Maybe that was why Liam seemed to be in a strange mood. He had more memories of their father than Mairin did. He'd had a dad for thirteen years, not just ten. Even now, with their father five years gone, Mairin could tell Liam was seized by sad moments every so often, same as she was.

"He'd be proud of you," she said. "And... oh, hey, Kevin Doyle asked me to go to the movies." Just like that, she blurted it out. Probably not a good idea, but she couldn't stifle herself.

"Kevin Doyle, eh? Altar boy. Plays center at St. Joe's. I guess he's okay."

She flushed. "Mam's not gonna let me, but I really want to go."

He shrugged his shoulders. "She might. Remind her he's an altar boy at church. And isn't he in the processional at high mass sometimes?"

"Good point."

"Just make sure he treats you right. And by right, I mean nice. Respectful, you know?"

She nodded, even though she wasn't quite sure she did know. "He will," she said.

"If he doesn't, I'll kick his ass. As long as I'm around to kick his ass."

She heard a strange note in his voice, and she turned to study his face. He wore an expression she didn't recognize. "What's the matter?"

He paused, took a deep breath. "I'm being drafted. Got my induction notice from the Selective Service office in the federal building."

Drafted. Induction. "Liam..." Her voice trembled. They had just driven past the federal building, and she hadn't even realized what went on there. "*Liam,*" she said again. "I don't know what that means." But in her gut, she did. And judging by his expression, it wasn't good.

"After graduation, the draft board changed my status from II-S to I-A."

She pictured the draft board as a bunch of old men randomly picking out young men to explode their lives. "What's that?"

"II-S means student. I-A means cannon fodder."

"What? Liam, I don't get it. Are you really drafted? Like, *drafted?*" She pictured all the raging protests that showed up every night on the news. And the daily paper riddled with terrible images of burning villages and guys on stretchers being rushed off the battlefield.

No. No no no no no. She couldn't imagine life with Liam gone. She had no idea what she would have done without him after their dad had died.

"Drafted," he said with quiet resignation. "Yeah."

"You have to go fight in Vietnam?"

He swallowed, his Adam's apple moving up and down. "I have to report for duty. For a physical and training camp after that. I think I'm being ordered to Fort Dix, New Jersey, for Basic Training and AIT—that's Advanced Individual Training. It's the law. There's no getting around it. If I'm lucky, maybe I won't have to go where the fighting is."

She could tell he didn't believe his own words. There was only one reason guys kept getting drafted into a war nobody understood that was happening halfway around the world.

And that was to go where the fighting was.

Chapter 2

Mairin lifted the lid of the Hills Bros. coffee canister and replaced it, the way she always did at the end of every workday. Only this time, she had nothing to put into the can, because she'd given her wages to Fiona. Mairin just needed her mother to hear the sound of the lid and hope she didn't check.

"That you, Mairin?" Mam called from the basement.

"Yep." Mairin took out a jar of Tang from the cupboard, then opened the fridge and grabbed a pitcher of water. Then she took an ice cube tray from the freezer and stood at the sink, trying to pry some cubes from the battered aluminum tray.

"Get your good self down here, then, and help me with the wash."

Mairin sighed and gulped down a glass of water without the Tang. Mam didn't like being kept waiting. She clumped down the stairs, ducking her head under the rafters. "Hiya, Mam," she said. "How's tricks?"

Her mother flashed a brief, tight smile that didn't reach her eyes. Mairin wondered if she was worried about Liam, but she didn't bring it up. Not yet. Mam was in no mood.

"Let's get the towels pegged out first," Mam said, ignoring the question. "They take the longest to dry." She handed Mairin a wire basket loaded with damp towels from the wringer.

When it came to laundry, Mam was all business. Sometimes Mairin found herself wishing her mother would remember to crack a joke—or even a smile—every now and then, the way Fiona's mom did. But Mam never seemed to have much to smile about. She had married Colm Davis soon after Dad was gone—not because it made her happy, but because, according to Liam, she was scared she wouldn't be able to provide for herself and her two kids. Mam had met Colm at the union hall one night, and he started coming around to check on her.

Mairin still remembered her confusion when Mam put on lipstick and fixed a Sunday roast and told her and Liam to be on their best behavior, because she and Colm were getting married. *Married.* It was weird to see her mother fluttering around as she made room in their lives for a strange man. Colm would give Mairin packets of Sugar Babies, and he'd offer to play a game of catch with Liam, but he would never replace Dad. When Colm came around, Mairin tried to make herself very small. Liam spent more time in his room, listening to records and talking on the new extension phone.

The wedding was a brief, quiet ceremony presided over by Father Campbell on a chilly Saturday morning. Mairin's patent leather shoes slipped and slid on the icy walkway, and Liam took her arm to keep her from falling. Colm's two brothers, who had nine kids between them, drove over from Rochester, and the kids eyed Mairin and Liam suspiciously. Mam's two best friends from the Catholic Women's League did the flower arrangements and dabbed at their eyes when the vows were said. Afterward, there was a fancy meal at the Castle Restaurant, and then they all went home together.

Turned out Colm wasn't such a good provider, either. He went to work most days, but he usually came home by way of Kell's Pub.

Mairin hurried to the yard and pegged the towels, folding the top of each one just so over the clothesline and clipping on the clothespins. Then she hurried down to the basement and touched her mother's shoulder. "Let me," she said, taking a handful of damp clothes from Mam.

Mam stepped back and rubbed her hands on her apron. "You're a good girl, Mairin," she muttered. "I'll go see about supper." Her feet trod heavily on the cellar stairs. Then there was the creak of the swivel rocker and the rasp of a match being lit, and Mairin could exactly picture the flame being held to the tip of a slender white Parliament cigarette.

Mairin and Fiona had tried smoking a time or two but they hadn't liked it. Smoking looked cool when some kids did it, but it made Mairin feel silly and self-conscious, and the smoke tasted like burning leaves.

After her mother left, Mairin switched on the GE radio. Mam always had it tuned to the news reports—war, protests, and politics—but Mairin navigated away from the news, listening to the crackle as she dialed in her favorite station. She took care to keep the volume low so Mam wouldn't yell at her for listening to "that noise." A few minutes later, she was humming along with the Stone Poneys, wondering how Linda Ronstadt's voice could sound like water flowing over rocks, so effortlessly pretty.

She sang softly as she fed the clothes through the wringer, taking care to fold the shirts around the buttons so they wouldn't be crushed between the rollers. She'd learned this technique the hard way. When Mam noticed three broken buttons on her school uniform blouse, it had earned Mairin a smack upside the head and no TV for a week.

Liam's Pink Floyd T-shirt was next. All the older kids were obsessed with Pink Floyd's woozy, psychedelic music, with the haunting guitar riffs and wailing voices. Mam swore it sounded like a plague o' banshees, and she refused to let Liam play the record album anywhere near her. Mairin wasn't quite sure Pink Floyd was her cup of tea, either, but she did like all sorts of music, especially the kind her mother forbade her to play. Now that Liam had to go into the army, he wouldn't be allowed to wear a shirt featuring a rock group. And he'd have to shave off all his nice red hair. Mairin shuddered, fearful that her brother would become a stranger.

Donovan and the Beatles got her through the rest of this tedious chore. She'd never understood why the laundry room had to be in the dank, lightless basement, anyway. Doing laundry was bad enough without feeling like you were being sent to a dungeon.

She brought the next load of clothes up to the yard and finished hanging them on the line. The backyard of the tall, narrow house was small, which Mairin didn't mind, since she was the one who had to mow the grass with the push mower. When she was little, her dad did the mowing, and the smell of fresh-cut grass always reminded her of him. There was an apple tree and a tall sycamore in the corner for shade, making the garden feel like a small sanctuary enclosed by a weather-beaten wooden fence. She couldn't see the McCutcheons or the Spinellis on either side, but she could hear them when they fought.

Tenacious wildflowers and stubborn weeds clung to the edges of the yard. Mairin kept a garden patch, untidy but productive, yielding the beans and potatoes and tomatoes that were part of every meal in the summer, along with sweet corn from the farmers market. She was good at growing things, the way her dad had been. Mam was indifferent, but her dad had taught her to love digging in the soil, tending the crops, and bringing in the harvest.

When she finished, she went inside. Walter Cronkite was on the TV blustering about the election. No one Mairin knew cared much about the election anymore, not since Bobby Kennedy had been shot dead early in the summer. If a Kennedy wasn't going to be president, Mam and her friends swore they wouldn't even bother to cast their votes. Mam was still in mourning for JFK, and now for Bobby. She couldn't seem to get over the destruction of Camelot. Sometimes Mairin thought her mother grieved harder for JFK than she did for Mairin's dad.

Mam was in the kitchen at the table, under the framed portraits of the Pope and President Kennedy. She was busy shucking the sweet corn for dinner. Mairin's mother had never been much of a cook, but it was hard to ruin fresh corn. People said the best sweet corn in the whole wide world was grown right here in western New York. Mairin wouldn't know, since she'd never been anywhere, but she believed it had to be true. At the end of summer, just before the leaves started to turn, a fresh ear of sweet corn was the most perfect food she could imagine eating. That burst of juicy sweetness, enhanced with just a bit of butter and salt, was a pleasure like no other. She sat down next to her mother, set a Loblaws bag in front of her, and got to work, letting the husks and silk fall into the bag.

"Liam told me today," Mairin said, slipping a tentative glance at her mother. "About getting drafted."

"Aye." Mam kept working without looking up.

"Did you know?"

"Of course I know. And amn't I the one who warned that he should enlist before they came for him? But no, he wanted to roll the dice, bettin' his number wouldn't come up."

"I'm scared for him," Mairin said. "Aren't you scared for him?"

"War is a scary business, and that's a fact."

"Well, you're Irish, right? Can't Liam go to Ireland and be Irish until the war's over?"

"There's nothing but trouble in Ireland," Mam said. "Just as much fighting there as there is in Vietnam."

"Is that why you came to America, then?" Mairin asked her. "To get away from the fighting?"

"I came to find . . ." Mam paused, cleared her throat. "I found a better life here, with your da."

Mairin always had a feeling in her gut that Mam kept things hidden, but she couldn't force her to talk much about the old days in Ireland, or to explain why Mam never received letters or long-distance phone calls from any family over there. She went into the living room and turned off the TV. "Enough of the bad news, okay? Sing me a song, Mam. One of the old songs from Ireland."

"Ah, Mairin." Mam sent her a brief smile. "*Is ceol mo chroí thú.*" You are my heart's music.

"Just one," Mairin cajoled, knowing she'd get her way. "We'll harmonize."

Her mother's posture softened, and she hummed a bit, and then sang "Black Velvet Band," a family favorite about a man led astray by a woman.

Good, thought Mairin as they concluded the ballad, their eyes meeting and their lips smiling. Mam's sour mood had turned slightly sweet. Maybe now was the time.

"Mam, I was wondering," she said. "Can I go to the movies tomorrow? I've been saving up," she added before the hard *no* came down like a hammer blow. "And I can work extra next week. Can I go, Mam? Please?"

"And what sort of movie would you be wanting to see?"

Mairin had learned that it was best to stick as close to the truth as possible. If she could get Mam to *yes*, then she could skip the mention of Kevin Doyle.

"It's called *The Graduate*," she said. At least it had a decent-sounding title. Not like demon vampires or something that would immediately send her mother into a tailspin. The song about Mrs. Robinson immediately popped into Mairin's head. It was a fantastic song. It would be even more fantastic in the movie. She just knew it.

"*The Graduate*," Mam said. "And what might that be about altogether?"

"It's, um, it's about succeeding in school, Mam." Mairin was fairly certain her mother hadn't read a review in the paper. Her mother had never been much for reading. With any luck, Mam hadn't seen the ad for the movie, with the woman's sexy leg. "Don't you want me to learn about succeeding in school?"

"Pah. In my day, a girl didn't need school if she had a good head on her shoulders."

Mairin hated it when her mother said her *in my day* things. She was no fan of school, especially St. Wilda's, where the nuns were wicked strict. They spent so much time on Latin declensions and quizzing everyone on the canon of the saints, matters Mairin found totally pointless. Still, between the prayers and assemblies, there were a few lay teachers who taught lessons about nature—the rhythm of the seasons, the habits of birds and wildlife, the wonder of growing things, the science of the stars, the order of the universe, the satisfaction of solving a problem. Mairin lapped up those lessons, and sometimes she even stayed after class to help Miss Baxter, who encouraged her to read books about absolutely everything, and to study the way words worked and how great thinkers expressed their ideas.

Miss Baxter even suggested that a girl who kept her grades up and learned to think for herself could go to college, and not just teacher college or nursing school. If Mairin made good enough scores on the Regents exam, she might be able to get a scholarship to study science or agriculture or meteorology, which would be a dream. Mairin had always been interested in the weather and growing things. The patterns of the seasons held a certain fascination for her, and she tracked the information in the *Farmers' Almanac*. Mam thought it was silly, so Mairin kept the dog-eared paperbound book in her room and studied it late into the night.

"So can I?" Mairin asked, neatly stacking the pale, shucked ears on a tray. "Can I go, Mam?"

"Seems a terrible waste of your hard-earned money," Mam said.

"It's the last Saturday before school starts. Please, Mam. *Please*."

Mam gave a tight smile. "We'll see."

Mairin felt a spike of excitement. *We'll see* was almost *maybe*. And *maybe* was practically yes.

Fiona wasn't at mass on Sunday morning, which totally annoyed Mairin, since she was dying to tell her friend everything about the movie date with Kevin Doyle. Her first date. To a grown-up movie.

She was bursting with the news that she had actually managed to pull it off. She'd worn her jumper dress with the buckle shoulders, which she'd made in home ec. Even though it was homemade, it looked just like the one she'd coveted in the Montgomery Ward catalog, which of course Mam said they couldn't afford. Mairin had also hidden a tube of strawberry-flavored Mary Quant lipstick in her pocket along with her bus pass and a dollar fifty for the movie ticket.

One way she knew she'd gone on a real actual date was that Kevin hadn't been wearing his Yankees baseball cap, and his hair was slicked back with the comb furrows showing the topography of his head. Also, he had already paid for her ticket, so she was able to buy a bucket of popcorn to share. They both blushed and stammered a bit, but during the cartoons that played before the main event, they managed to relax and laugh at the show.

She didn't think any movie could be as good as *A Hard Day's Night* with the Beatles, which of course was the best thing she'd ever seen or heard. But *The Graduate* was just as good in its own crazy way. Crazy, because after spending all that time going to college, the guy named Benjamin didn't seem to have any idea what to do with himself except go back to his parents' California home and float around in the pool and have an affair with the neighbor woman, who drank fancy cocktails and smoked like a chimney. And after all that, he suddenly turned around and fell in love with Mrs. Robinson's daughter. Mairin thought the whole thing was hilarious in a weird way. And the music was phenomenal.

She was still humming "Mrs. Robinson" when she and Kevin walked out of the theater, and Kevin kind of accidentally-on-purpose let his hand bump into hers, and then he held on to it. She'd had to hold in a gasp of excitement, even though it was just two hands with fingers intertwined. He'd walked her to the bus stop, and for a single, breath-held moment, she thought he might kiss her. Fiona once said you could tell a boy wanted to kiss you if he kept staring at your lips. Mairin couldn't really tell whether or not he was staring at her lips. But there was no kiss, just a *goodnightseeyouaround* a few moments before the bus came and the doors opened with a hiss. She wasn't sure whether she was relieved or disappointed about the swift farewell. She was home by nine-thirty, which was the curfew she'd negotiated with her mother.

She probably could have stayed out later, because Mam didn't even stir when Mairin tiptoed through the back door. Mam was asleep in front of the TV, where *Petticoat Junction* was just bleeding into the next show, *Mannix*. Colm was still out, probably over at Kell's, drinking and boasting about something or other.

Good. They always argued over what to watch anyway. Colm wouldn't let them watch *The Smothers Brothers Show* on TV. Even though the comedy team brothers were clean-cut, Colm claimed they were disrespectful, singing about how war was bad and free love was good. Mairin couldn't understand what was so awful about that. Especially since Colm was okay with watching a show about a talking horse, and another about a guy whose mother had been reincarnated as a car.

On most Sundays, Mairin couldn't stand going to church. It was boring and seemed pointless, especially since they did chapel at school, confession every fourth Thursday, and endless catechism with the nuns. Most Sundays, she got up early and rode her bike to St. Mary's for the six o'clock mass. Liam thought she was nuts to get up so early, but she liked getting it over with. Father Campbell, who had a full head of silver hair and a voice like a trumpet, liked to speed through the service, probably so he could go back to bed. He never noticed when she read a library book or paged through *Tiger Beat* hidden within the pages of her St. Joseph missal.

Today, though, she dressed as if it were Easter Sunday—long lace mantilla instead of the usual bobby-pinned doily. She willingly went to high mass, because she knew Kevin Doyle would be there. He'd told her last night he was serving as thurifer, an important role. Mairin made sure she was the last one into the pew, coming in behind Colm, her mom, and Liam, so she could be on the aisle, second row from the front.

Slipping a glance at Liam, she wondered how many more Sundays she'd have her brother by her side. She squeezed her eyes shut and prayed to the Virgin and all the saints for Liam to be okay. She tried not to hear the songs of protest in her head, songs about boys coming home in a box. She made a little gasp that sounded like a hiccup, and Liam gave her a nudge. "Heads up, squirt," he whispered.

She turned slightly as the processional approached, accompanied by the vibrating crescendos of the massive pipe organ playing the opening strains of *O Salutaris Hostia*. The grand chords sounded like thunder from heaven, propelling the tall, ornate processional cross, followed by the candles atop high staffs with banners and icons along the aisle to the altar.

Kevin's job was to go to the sacristy and fill the thurible with lighted coals and incense grains. Seeing him in the processional in his red-and-white, gold-embroidered raiment, swinging the censer with measured solemnity, was strangely thrilling—in a nonreligious way. The cassock and surplice with the long, tunnel-like sleeves made him look like a medieval knight, only with a big brass censer on a chain instead of a flail and sword. The scuffed Chuckies on his feet ruined the effect, but he still looked really cute.

She knew he saw her, because their eyes met, and his lit from behind, as if someone had struck a match. She winked. She couldn't help it. She *winked*.

His mouth went stiff as he tried not to smile, and the tips of his ears turned red. Was he thinking about last night? Did he wish he'd kissed her? The thought caused her to make a soft, involuntary sound, and Liam shifted and sent her a baffled-looking frown.

As everyone sang *O Salutaris*, the servers with the boat approached the altar, followed by Kevin and his thurible. The priest made a great show of adding more incense to the thurible, then he waved the puffs of smoke over the monstrance and handed the vessel back to Kevin.

During the start of the Tantum Ergo, she noticed that something had fallen out of the right sleeve of Kevin's cassock. Craning her neck toward the altar, she could see a black-edged hole in Kevin's garment. Was that a piece of coal? Yes, it was.

The hole was smoldering, but he didn't seem to notice. No one noticed.

Mairin jiggled up and down, trying to get his attention, but he kept his eyes on the priest, getting ready for the second round of incensing.

Liam frowned at her again, but she ignored her brother. She kept trying to make Kevin look at her. When he lifted his arm, she saw that the hole was a red ring, burning in earnest now, and she couldn't keep quiet any longer.

"Kevin," she said in a stage whisper. *"Kevin."*

"What the hell are you on about?" Liam demanded, nudging her shoulder.

Kevin wasn't even her official boyfriend yet. She couldn't let him burn to death like St. Joan before he'd even kissed her.

An older man in the front row turned to scowl at her. The chorus swelled with the strains of the Tantum.

Mairin took a deep breath. *"Jesus Christ, the altar boy's on fire!"* she yelled.

Mam whirled on her, reached across Liam, and gave Mairin's mouth a smack. Holding a hand to her cheek, Mairin scrambled toward the front of the church.

At the same moment, Kevin looked down at his sleeve. He dropped the thurible, rushed over to the holy water font, and plunged in his arm up to the elbow. Mairin was close enough to hear the sizzle.

The entire congregation froze. Even the organ, mid-chord, fell silent. Mairin dashed up the five marble steps to the altar, entering the forbidden zone, but she didn't care.

"Are you okay?" she asked Kevin. "Did you burn yourself?"

Father Timothy, who took his duties seriously, waved Kevin toward a side door, then cleared his throat and resumed the mass as if nothing had happened. Mairin slunk back to her place, her cheek still stinging from the blow. Her mother looked fit to be tied, so there would probably be hell to pay at home. *If* she went home. She dreaded the lecture, which would most likely be accompanied by swats from the paddle.

Maybe her mom just needed a cool-down period. If Mairin could avoid her mother for a while, Mam would find something else to fuss about.

As the chords of the recessional swelled from the organ loft, Mairin dashed away, jostling through the exiting crowd. Keeping well ahead of the family, she rushed over to Fiona's house on Cherry Street.

THE GALLAGHERS' HOUSE always seemed to be in a state of chaos, on account of all the kids. At the same time, it had a peculiar worn-out charm and lived-in character. The chipped and faded paint made the house blend in with the others in the row. It was shaped like a tall box of saltine crackers, with a peaked roof and front porch, some of its balusters gone like missing teeth. A couple of aspidistra plants that refused to die hung from the eaves. A porch swing, empty now except for an abandoned teddy bear, moved lightly in the breeze, its chains clacking rhythmically. Mairin had spent many a warm summer evening here, sitting on the steps and playing Parcheesi and listening to song after song on Fiona's portable record player.

The front sidewalk was chalked with childlike graffiti–hopscotch boards and crudely drawn hearts, flowers, and smiling sun faces. There was an upended tricycle and a pair of flip-flops on the grass. As the third oldest, Fiona often had babysitting duty over the little ones. Maybe that was why she hadn't been at mass today. Or maybe she was still feeling sick.

Mairin snatched off her lace mantilla and crushed it into a ball in her fist. She noticed Flynn's car parked in the side driveway, its front half lifted on two jacks. It was an old heap of a thing, painted half red, half Bondo, and the ground beside it was littered with oily-looking tools. A transistor radio crackled with a hyped-up announcer's voice, calling the Yankees game. A pair of legs in blue jeans and work boots protruded from under the car. According to his sister, Flynn was good at working on cars. Carla and Gina, at the fruit warehouse, had called him dreamy. A stone-cold fox. Seemed like half the neighborhood had a crush on him. They probably didn't realize he was taken. His girlfriend was the gorgeous, Breck-shampoo-ad, blond Protestant hippie, Haley Moore.

Mairin's knock rattled the flimsy screen door. It was a shotgun house, meaning if you shot a gun through the front door, the blast would exit through the back.

No one answered her knock, but Ranger the dog came skittering down the hallway, barking his head off. She could hear voices yelling somewhere in the back of the house. This was not unusual. In the Gallagher house, there was often yelling—the kids squabbling, the parents telling them to pipe down, the dog barking and being shushed, the radio blaring.

This sounded different, though. Mixed in with the yelling, there was crying. Fiona's crying.

Mairin hesitated, then took a deep breath. "Hello," she called through the screen door.

Ranger yapped at her.

"It's me, Mairin. Hey, Fiona—"

"She's in trouble," said Izzy, stepping out onto the porch. Izzy was six and adorable with her dark hair in two ponytails that swung like Goofy's ears. "Shannon heard her talking in the bathroom, and she told Mom, and now Fiona's in trouble."

Mairin felt a thud of concern in her gut. She'd given Fiona her wages to keep her out of trouble. Hadn't it been enough? Or was this the other kind of trouble? "I just came by to see how Fiona's feeling—"

"Get back here, young lady," said Mrs. Gallagher.

Fiona barreled down the hall and burst through the screen door, practically knocking Izzy out of the way. Her face was red with sweat and anger. She grabbed Mairin's hand in passing and towed her down the porch steps to the sidewalk.

"What happened?" Mairin asked, rushing to keep up. "What's going on?"

"They're making me go live with my aunt down in Bradford," Fiona said.

"What? Why?" Mairin gave her hand a squeeze. "That's crazy. What's in Bradford? An aunt? You can't move away."

"It's temporary." Fiona slowed to a walk. Her eyes were puffy and red from crying.

The knot in Mairin's stomach tightened. Apparently what she'd heard at work was true. Fiona was in *that* kind of trouble. She stared at Fiona's completely flat middle, and couldn't force herself to go on.

Fiona placed a hand there and nodded, then gave a shudder that ended in a sob. "I never meant for this to happen."

Mairin nearly tripped over the sidewalk where the concrete had been buckled by a tree root. "You don't look any different at all. Are you sure?"

"My mom took me to the free clinic over on Hawthorn. They did a test." She made a face. "I had to pee in a cup. Have you ever tried peeing in a cup?"

"Uh, no." Mairin blushed. "And that's how they can tell?"

Oak Hill Park was deserted, so they sat on the swings, the rusty chains creaking with each gentle push. The late-afternoon sun cast long shadows, and the air smelled of dry leaves. When they were little kids, they used to play here for hours, spinning on the merry-go-round until they couldn't stand up, giggling as they balanced on the seesaw, and swinging as high as the sky, their laughter floating on the air.

Fiona trailed her foot in the dirt. "Oh, Mairin. I still can't believe this is happening."

Mairin was in uncharted territory. Her best friend—pregnant? "How are you feeling?"

"It's gross. Throwing up and peeing all the time." Fiona hugged her arms across her chest.

"What about Casey?"

"Casey." Fiona rolled her eyes. "It was . . . Well, I'm not going to lie. I really liked him. At first, it was, like, super exciting and romantic, being together like that."

"Like what?" Mairin asked.

Fiona's cheeks lit with a blush. "Like, with nothing between us, nothing at all. Like lovers, you know?"

Mairin didn't know. She had only the vaguest of ideas. "Are you going to have to marry him?" Up until very recently, Mairin hadn't thought it was possible to get pregnant without being married. It was the strangest thing in the world, talking about getting married when she and Fiona had only retired their Barbie dolls a couple of years ago.

"Casey broke up with me," Fiona said. "He told his parents it might not even be his."

"That jerk." Mairin burned with fury for her friend.

"I thought we were in love." Fiona shrugged and looked away. "Last thing in the world I want to do is get married to Casey."

"Then don't."

"Oh, Mairin. What am I going to do? Flynn's girlfriend, Haley? She said there's a way to get rid of it if you have enough money."

"What do you mean, get rid of it?"

"Like, make it go away. Like a miscarriage. My mom had a miscarriage between the twins and Izzy." She sighed. "But Haley said it would cost hundreds of dollars. I'd be scared to do it, anyway. So I guess I'm stuck. It's going to happen. Oh, Mairin. A baby is going to happen. Haley says if somebody has a baby at the commune where she lives, everybody raises the kid together and no one gets in trouble."

"So could you go there?" Mairin pictured the rough-looking farm with the painted bus.

"My parents would never let me."

"But why do you have to go live somewhere else?"

"Oh, come on. You know how people talk. My parents would be so ashamed. Everyone would think I'm going to burn in hell."

"I wouldn't think that," said Mairin.

"Not everyone's like you, Mair. Nobody knows me in Bradford except my great-aunt Cookie. My mom's aunt. She said she'd take care of me. So it's either that, or the Good Shepherd nuns."

"That place over on Best Street?" Mairin shuddered. "No way. My mom would probably do something like that, but not yours." Mrs. Gallagher was loud and strict, but she wasn't harsh like Mam. Mrs. Gallagher didn't threaten her kids with the nuns. "Aw, Fiona. What's going to happen? What about school?"

"I just turned sixteen. I could drop out of school."

And do what? Mairin wondered.

"At least there won't be Sister Carlotta, with her ruler and her bad breath."

Mairin nodded, wishing she didn't feel so helpless. "Well, there's that."

"Maybe I'll go back after this is over and they put the baby up for adoption."

"Wait, you mean that's what you have to do?" Mairin was aghast. "You have to give it away? To strangers? Like you'll never see your own child?"

"They're not giving me a choice," Fiona said, her face crumpling. "I don't have a say."

"Oh, Fiona." Mairin looked at her best friend, feeling a deep, aching helplessness. "I'm so sorry. This isn't fair."

"They said I ruined my life, but at least this way, the baby will have a chance."

A chance at what? Mairin wondered. "I wish there was something I could do. Anything."

Fiona wound the swing up, then let it spin. "Just . . . promise you'll be there. After it's all done."

"I'm not going anywhere," Mairin said. "Where would I go?"

Fiona nodded glumly. "Hey, I'd better get back. My mom's already mad enough at me."

"I'll walk you." They left the park as the shadows grew long across the dying grass, and they slowly began to retrace their steps. "I'm probably in trouble, too, if you want to know the truth. A different kind of trouble." She told Fiona about Kevin's sleeve catching on fire and her outburst in church.

Fiona laughed through her tears. "You're kidding. You went right up past the railing? To the high altar?"

"He was on fire and no one but me seemed to notice." She felt her cheeks color up. "We went to the movies together last night. Saw *The Graduate* at the Landmark."

"Well, well, well." Fiona wiggled her eyebrows. "How did that go?"

It was kind of strange, just talking about normal things, all the while knowing Fiona was going to have a baby. A *baby*. "It was nice, I guess. The movie was really good. Afterward, he walked me to the bus stop. I didn't dare stay out too late."

"Hmm." Fiona seemed preoccupied, and Mairin didn't blame her. "Don't let him . . . you know, go too far."

Mairin understood the warning. She wasn't quite sure what *too far* meant, though. As they arrived back at the house, she wasn't sure what else to say, so she just grabbed her friend into a brief, fierce hug. "Listen, no matter what happens, you'll always be my best friend. Forever. And I'll come to Bradford to see you if I can figure out a way to get there. And

I'll write you letters and save up my money for a long-distance phone call."

Fiona nodded and stepped back. "It just doesn't seem real. It'll probably be scary, but I'm not scared yet."

"Don't be scared," Mairin said. "And remember I'm your best friend."

"You are. Yeah. Anyway, Mom's making Flynn drive me down there tonight."

"Tonight? Jeez Louise."

"I know."

Mairin felt an unexpected lump in her throat. Fiona was going to have a baby. It seemed impossible. She looked the same. Sounded the same. Yet she was going to have a baby and give it away to somebody.

"*Fiona.*" Mrs. Gallagher's voice shot through the hallway.

Fiona glanced over her shoulder. "I better go." The screen door snapped shut on its coiled spring.

Mairin stood on the front porch for a moment, feeling completely disoriented. Then she heaved a sigh. The day was warming up to a blast of Indian summer. She didn't feel like hanging around the house, getting yelled at about church. Maybe she'd ride her bike across the Peace Bridge to Crystal Beach and hang out with some of her other friends there.

She turned to see Flynn rolling himself out from under the car on his mechanic's dolly. She tried not to stare at the long, ropey muscles of his arms, slick with sweat. He lifted the tail of his T-shirt and wiped his face, revealing a ripple of muscle. "Hey, Mairin," he said.

"Hey." Her shoulders slumped with the weight of Fiona's news.

"So I guess my sister told you," he said.

Mairin nodded, knowing her cheeks were touched by fire. She wasn't quite sure why it felt so awkward, talking to Fiona's brother. She'd known him forever. He was the big brother every girl wanted—strong and protective, funny and quick to smile. Mairin's own brother, Liam, was like that, too. They used to giggle about how they would get to be sisters one day if only they would marry each other's brother.

She didn't feel like giggling now. "I'd better get home," she said, wishing she wasn't wearing her church clothes. They made her look, like, twelve years old.

As she turned away, he said, "Hey, Mairin?"

She pivoted back to face him. He had the bluest eyes in the world. "Yeah?"

"Listen, that favor you did for Fiona. Giving her your wages. She told me."

"I'd do anything for Fiona. We're best friends."

"She's lucky to know you. And I'm glad you called me to come get her from work."

Mairin couldn't imagine a world without Fiona. "It just doesn't seem right that she has to go away, like she's a criminal or something."

"There are a lot of things in this world that don't seem right."

"My brother Liam got drafted," she blurted out. "We just found out. I'm really scared for him."

"Oh, man. That's tough." He raked a hand through his hair.

"I'm scared he won't come home."

"Most guys get through it okay."

"I hope you're right. Are you gonna get drafted?" she asked.

He shook his head. "You're looking at lucky number three sixty-six."

"Wow, that is lucky." It was the highest possible number, meaning his chances of being called were nil. "So, do you like working at the Agway?" she asked, not wanting the conversation to end.

"It's all right. I've been driving deliveries for Fiorelli's produce, too. I'm planning to buy his supply truck—you know, the one that makes all the gourmet produce deliveries. He offered me a stake in the business when he retires." He grinned. "I like to eat, and I like to drive. I plan to save up for a place of my own. A farm."

She pictured him with Haley on their fairy-tale farm, surrounded by beautiful kids and growing things. It seemed impossibly romantic, awakening a strange ache of yearning in her chest. "You and Haley Moore?"

He chuckled. "Yeah, maybe not her."

"I thought you were, like, dating her."

"Dating doesn't mean getting married." He laughed aloud and ruffled her curls. "Could be I prefer redheads."

She blushed to her roots, wishing he didn't always treat her like a kid.

He dug in his pocket and took out a coin and placed it in her hand. "Here. Hang on to this. It's just a token to remind you that you can always call me. I know it's not the same as having your brother around, but..."

"It's a Mercury dime," she said, studying the profile.

"Nothing special, but it's from the year I was born."

He was five years older than Mairin. She grinned. "Well...okay, thanks."

"Call anytime you need me." He smiled back. "See you around, Mairin."

Chapter 3

When she got home, Mairin realized with relief that it was fourth Sunday, which was when the Irish Catholic Women's League met in the church basement. Mam never missed a meeting since she was the club's secretary, writing down all the details of their projects, from schoolbag St. Christopher medals to communion stamps. It was basically her entire social life, sitting around with the other ladies, most of them from the old country. They reminisced about Ireland with such yearning, it made Mairin wonder why they had left in the first place. They were all on about the green rolling hills and the old ways, the food and the pubs and the songs everyone sang late into the night.

Mairin had asked about the old country a time or two, wondering what it was really like. Mam had simply brushed away the question as if swatting at a mosquito. "It was a hard place to be" was her vague answer.

Back when Dad was alive, he'd praised Mam's cooking and her singing voice. She never sang much at home anymore. Most of the time, she just seemed to worry about things.

No one was home when Mairin got there. Liam was working at his part-time job as a pinsetter at the Eagles Lodge bowling alley. Colm usually met up with his buddies at Kell's, which was fine with Mairin since she had no interest in seeing her stepfather.

When Mam had first married him, he'd made an effort to be friendly, tossing a baseball with Liam and asking Mairin about her day. Mam had married him in the hopes of filling the void left behind after the accident that had taken Dad from them.

As time went on, Colm lost interest in trying to play that role. Lately, he usually only showed up to nag Liam about changing the oil in the car or to tell Mairin her skirt was too short or her knee socks looked sloppy with her school uniform.

Mairin went to the kitchen and made herself a Fluffernutter, slathering peanut butter and Marshmallow Fluff on a single slice of white bread, folding it over, and taking it to her room. She put on *Bookends*, her current favorite album, and sang along with "Fakin' It," holding her sandwich like a microphone and singing "When she goes, she's gone..." along with Simon and Garfunkel.

Afternoon light filtered through the curtains of the window and fell on a framed picture of Mairin's dad, his head thrown back in laughter as he relaxed in a lawn chair in the backyard. He was so handsome, with his thick red hair and twinkling eyes. He was frozen now, forever young, unreachable, except in her dreams.

She had turned her room into a haven where she could escape and pretend to live a different life. She wasn't always certain what sort of life that should be, but sometimes she was filled with a sharp yearning she barely understood. She just wanted to be a person of consequence living a life that mattered. A person making her mark on the world.

The walls of her room were decked with pictures and posters that told the story of her dreams and aspirations, her yearning to escape one day and find her life. There were faded pennants from St. Joe's—her father's high school—and from her favorite sports team. She was stubbornly loyal to the Buffalo Bills, even though they'd been on a losing streak the past couple of years. Her love of football was all bound up in Mairin's memories of her father. When he was alive, he had been the team's biggest fan. In the dead of winter, when the snow piled up so high it kept them indoors, Dad would make popcorn with melted butter and salt, and he'd let them eat it in the living room with a root beer float. She still remembered the way he would roar with approval when there was a good play, or clutch his chest in despair when the team failed.

Mairin had never been a fan of the wallpaper in her room—fading duck hunting scenes, for no apparent reason—so she turned her walls into a collage of things she hoped and longed for. She put up posters of her favorite musicians and groups, carefully pried from magazines or extracted from the slipcase of a record album.

Even without the music playing, the room seemed to pulsate with the rhythm of her dreams, and the images on the walls transported her to a world beyond the only place she'd ever known. Herman's Hermits, the Beatles, and the Rolling Stones dominated the collection, their handsome faces and shaggy hair making them look as though they belonged to a different species—rare and exotic. Mairin had also pinned up pictures of Linda Ronstadt and Janis Joplin, because she loved their voices and the daring way they dressed, with headbands and beads and fringe, a look that tended to give Mam conniption fits.

Mairin sat on the bed to finish her sandwich while paging through last month's issue of *Tiger Beat*, which she'd already read to death. The pictures and short articles breathed life into a world she could only imagine. She could look at a photo and unleash her imagination, constructing a fantasy world that somehow always involved an achingly cute boy, a beautiful scene in nature, and music coming from some unseen source, far from the neighborhood, and schoolwork, and brothers going to war, and girls getting in trouble.

Mam never wanted to hear about Mairin's dreams of a life beyond the boundaries of the Fruit Belt, where people went to their jobs, yelled at their kids, complained about the heat in the summer and the cold in the winter, and expected every day to be the same as the last. But Mairin was stubborn in her refusal to let herself be defined by her circumstances. Miss Baxter, her favorite teacher, said that the most important steps a person takes in life are the steps in the direction of their dreams. Mairin chose to listen to music that inspired her, and to think about possibilities like going to college, or taking a plane or a bus to the coast to see the ocean.

She finished off her sandwich, and then unfastened the buttons of her Sunday best. She could still feel the weight of the day pressing down on her. What should have been breathless good news to share with her friend had simply shattered into shards of misfortune. She'd wanted to talk about going to the movies with Kevin, but instead, she was worried about Liam going to war, and Fiona going away to have a baby.

Unwilling to let one of the final days of summer get away from her, Mairin picked out a sleeveless blouse and pedal pushers as she made a plan to cheer herself up. A bike trip across the Peace Bridge would take her mind off things. It was a long ride to Crystal Beach, but she was a good rider, fast and steady, because she rode her bike everywhere. She'd probably find some of her friends over on the Canadian side, soaking up the last of summer on the sandy shore and cooling off in the clear blue waters of Lake Erie. Maybe Kevin would be there, although she was too shy to call him and ask. Someone might even spot her an admission ticket to the amusement park, and she could ride the breath-stealing Comet one last time before the park closed for the season.

She heard the front screen door creak open, then snap back on its springs. She recognized the heavy footsteps as Colm's. After he'd downed a few beers, there was a certain leaden cadence to his gait.

"Mairin? *Mairin*. Where're you, girl?" he called. "Your mother's fit to be tied, but me and the guys, we had a laugh over your performance at mass. In fact, I brought you a sugar donut from Sturdy's. You want a sugar donut?"

They were her favorite. Sometimes Colm tried to get along with her and Liam. Maybe this was him, trying. She yanked on the checked pedal pushers and put on the summer blouse. Her fingers fumbled with the buttons. "Thanks! I'm just getting changed," she called. "I'll be out in a minute."

The door opened, and Colm stood there, holding out a white bakery sack, a lopsided smile on his face. "Brought you a little something."

"Can't you knock? I said in a *minute*," she told him, annoyed that he thought he could just barge into her room. She picked up the dress and took her time placing it on a hanger.

"Hey, I was just doing something nice for you."

"Fine, I'll be down in a minute," she repeated.

"Don't take that tone with me. Maybe your mother was right. Maybe that was a lousy stunt you pulled in church this morning," he said.

"You're in big trouble, girlie." His eyes turned dark and filled with something hard and mean. He pushed the bedroom door shut behind him.

A shiver ran down Mairin's spine. The record track switched to "A Hazy Shade of Winter," and Colm reached over and swiped the needle off the turntable of the record player.

"Hey," she said, incensed. "You'll scratch it."

"Buncha hippie noise anyway," he said, dropping the bakery bag on the floor. "Dumbass guys singing la-la songs for brainless girls like you."

Consumed with a mix of fear and confusion, Mairin darted a glance at the door, weighing her chances if she made a dash for it. Lately Colm had been weird around her at odd moments, his attention making her uncomfortable.

Mairin and Colm used to tolerate each other. She'd put up with his teasing, and more or less steered clear of him whenever she could. Now she backed away, edging to the far side of the bed.

"I'm sorry about what happened in church," she said, trying to keep the tremor from her voice. "I'll apologize to Mam when she gets home from her meeting."

"Well, that's more like it," he said. "You know how to be a good girl, after all, doncha?"

"Uh, sure." She squared her shoulders and headed for the door.

"Where do you think you're going?" he asked, blocking her path.

"Out," she snapped. "*Excuse* me."

"Don't you get cheeky with me." He smelled of sweat and stale beer. "And look at you, with peanut butter and crumbs on your face like a baby."

She wiped her mouth with the back of her wrist as she tried to skirt past him. His hand shot out and grabbed her arm. "You don't talk to me like that. You need a good walloping, is what you need. You're not too old for me to show you what for."

"Let go of me," she yelled, trying to twist her wrist from his grasp. "Don't you touch—"

"You're not going anywhere, missy," he said, shoving her back against the bed.

With her free hand, she grabbed the bedpost and clung to it, holding herself upright. "I said I was sorry. Get away from me!"

"You'll talk to me with resp—"

The door burst open and Liam strode into the room. His face was contorted and red as he launched himself at Colm, grabbing him by the back of his collar and yanking him away from Mairin.

"Hey, get off me, you little cocksucker." Colm twisted around, fists flying. Liam was more slender than Colm, and their stepfather was a fighter, always getting in brawls at the pub and at the racetrack.

Mairin froze in shock as blood exploded from Liam's nose. He ducked the second punch and then hit back, driving his fist into Colm's gut. Colm doubled over with a whoosh of air, then rushed at Liam. Liam fought with a ferocity Mairin had never witnessed before, his every strike seeming to be fueled by fury. He drove his fist straight into Colm's throat, and the blow made a sickening sound.

Mairin thought that might be the end of her stepfather. His eyes bulged, and he wheezed and gasped for air. Then came a panicked look and a roar, and Colm charged again. The two crashed into the lowboy dresser where Mairin kept her bottles of cologne, her picture of Dad, and the silver-backed brush and mirror set she'd inherited from Granny O'Hara. Bottles and glass flew everywhere. Colm's fists flailed, and the sickening sound of the punches stirred Mairin into action. She leaped onto the large man from behind, scratching at his face. He reared back, flinging her off. When she hit the floor, all the breath left her, and for a moment, she saw stars.

When Colm whirled back to face her brother, Liam was brandishing Granny O'Hara's hand mirror, broken now, with one slender shard glinting in the light.

"Get out of here, you sick fuck," Liam said, swiping a sleeve across his nose. "If you ever go near her again, I'll kill you. Swear to God I will."

"You hurt?" Liam asked in a hoarse voice after Colm had stormed out.

"I'm okay." The back of her head throbbed, though she didn't recall hitting it on anything. Tears streamed down her face, though she didn't recall starting to cry. Then she realized what he was asking. "You showed up just in time. Come on," she said. "You're the one who's hurt." She led the way down the hall to the bathroom.

The worn wooden door creaked as she held it and motioned Liam inside. The room was barely big enough for the two of them. The walls were clad with cabbage-rose paper, peeling at the edges and faded where the light from the single window struck it. The scent of Ivory soap mingled with the ever-present musky smell of dampness, as if someone had been trapped in the room, crying, for a hundred years.

It was weird to think that a hundred years ago, when the whole neighborhood was covered in orchards, this house had been built to hold someone's hopes and dreams. Or maybe it hadn't. Maybe it had been a slapped-together workers' cottage, meant to shelter the itinerant pickers who came up from the South for the fruit harvest each year.

Sometimes Mairin wondered who else had stood in this spot, staring into the pockmarked mirror. A girl like her, dismayed with her stubborn red curls and freckles, getting ready for a date? A little kid on a stool, learning how to brush his teeth? A man as handsome as her father, lifting his chin to get his shave just right?

Or maybe someone like Liam, glaring at his image—watery eyes, the blood thickening to sludge under his nose.

"Does it hurt?" she asked, grabbing a washcloth from the linen cupboard over the commode. She took one of the more threadbare ones, because it was likely to be ruined by the blood.

"Yeah. But I'll live," he said.

She ran cold water into the sink basin, then stepped aside so he could bend forward and clean his face. Once the stream of water changed from bright red to clear, she handed him the damp cloth. "Do you think it's broken?"

He held the cloth gingerly to his nose. "Nah. Don't think so, anyway."

Fury welled up inside her. "I hate him," she said. "He's the worst."

Liam turned and studied her face. "I need you to be honest with me," he said. "Has Colm ever tried anything like that before?"

"*No.* But he's . . ." She thought about the looks she caught from him when she passed him in the hallway on the way to her room after a shower. "I've never trusted him, not even when he tries to be nice. Honestly, that's the first time he . . ." She wasn't a hundred percent sure exactly what Colm had intended, but it wasn't good. Nothing that made her feel sick inside could be good. "I hate him," she repeated.

"So do I," Liam muttered. He peeled off his shirt, balled it up, and threw it into the rust-streaked bathtub.

She eyed the bruise forming on his rib cage. "What about that?"

He shrugged, glanced in the mirror again. "It's okay." He finished cleaning up, and to Mairin's relief, his nose looked okay. Maybe a little red and tender.

"I sure don't know what I would've done if you hadn't shown up," she said.

"You would've fought like hell, that's what. You're a strong kid," her brother told her.

"Teach me, Liam," she said. "Show me what to do. You know, if it ever happens again."

He braced his hands on the edge of the sink, and she saw his muscles tighten. Then he gave a curt nod. "Let me grab a shirt and meet me out back."

SHE HEADED OUT to the back porch and down the stairs. The late-afternoon sunshine cast a warm glow over the yard and garden, but the serene atmosphere was an illusion. The house didn't seem safe anymore, not the way it had when Dad was alive. When they were younger, she and Liam used to play here every day, even in winter. Dad had built them a tree house in the sycamore, though now only a few broken remnants remained. She could still hear the echoes of their whispered secrets as they played the Swiss family Robinson, surviving in the wild against all odds. She could still feel the release of burdens in tears shed over losses small and large—a pet rabbit, a softball match, a school prize . . . their father.

Now that she and Liam were older, the world felt harsh and unforgiving. Everything mattered more. Especially in this moment, with the threat of war looming over Liam's head, and Colm's temper and creepy ways shadowing Mairin's spirit.

Liam came out to the yard, wearing a fresh T-shirt and jeans turned up at the cuffs, his hair slicked back. She tried to picture him in a soldier's uniform and helmet, but it seemed impossible.

"Are you sure you're feeling okay?" Mairin asked him.

"Fit as a fiddle." He offered her a reassuring grin. "Anyway, first rule is this—don't let it happen again. Not with him, not with any guy. Or any girl, for that matter. Full stop."

"But how am I supposed to figure out—"

"You know more than you think you know," he told her. "Like, trust your gut. Think about it. What'd it feel like when you first saw him in your room?"

She understood what he was getting at. "He brought me a sugar donut." Yet she remembered the slight but palpable inner prickle she'd felt the moment she'd heard Colm's heavy steps. "You know before you know," she said softly.

"Exactly. If it feels wrong, it *is* wrong. So don't let yourself be home alone with him. Or anywhere alone with him. Stick close to Mam, or go see a friend. Go across the street to the Pezzamentis' house. Go to the library. The school gym. The fire station. But if he corners you, then you have to fight back," Liam said.

Mairin felt a ripple of doubt. "I don't know the first thing about fighting."

"You're a smart girl. You're strong. Just remember to respect your gut and act fast. The goal is to defend yourself and get away quick."

"Get away from my own room," she muttered. "That's rich."

"That's reality. I'm going to put a lock on your door as soon as the hardware store opens in the morning." Liam stood across from her, demonstrating a relaxed stance. "Let's work on your posture. Stand with your feet shoulder-width apart. You want to start with a stable base. Plant yourself like this."

Mairin adjusted her stance. Liam continued, "Now, keep your hands up so you're protecting your face. The key is to never stop moving. If some guy tries to grab you, push him away with all your might. Use your knees and elbows. Keep moving. Let's give it a try."

He came at her in slow motion, coaching her through several basic moves, demonstrating ways to use the natural strength of her body to strike and then get away. "Anything is a weapon," he said. "Anything you can get your hands on."

She nodded, remembering the broken mirror. Liam told her to look around the yard and find something to grab—a fallen branch, a rake, a brick or stone.

In the quiet haven of the backyard, Mairin learned how to defend herself when she felt threatened, or worse, when someone like Colm went on the attack. She watched intently and emulated Liam's moves, absorbing the knowledge with a mix of determination and apprehension. Aim for the vulnerable spots—eyes and crotch. Yell at the top of your lungs. Never stop moving. She was glad to be learning these things, but it was scary, too, because it forced her to leave behind her assumptions about the world she lived in.

"This is good," he said, wiping the sweat from his brow. "You're doing good, Mairin."

"How'd you hit him in the neck like that?" she asked. "I thought he was gonna keel over."

"Throat strike," Liam said. "Works good when the other guy's a lot bigger. Make your hand into a cheetah-paw like this. He won't see it coming, and while he's gagging, you can try to get away. Always know where the exit is." Liam's voice softened as he mopped his brow again, studying Mairin. He looked like their father's old high school yearbook pictures, handsome and serious. "Remember, all of this stuff is about getting away from danger. If you ever feel threatened, the main goal is to escape. Got it? Escape and survive."

"Escape and survive," she repeated, and a palpable sense of determination welled up inside her. "You have to promise you'll do the same. I mean, if you get sent to Vietnam and you get captured, find a way to escape and survive."

"Of course. That's what they're going to train me to do."

"Promise, Liam. Swear you'll keep yourself safe."

"Swear," he said, and held up his pinkie finger, hooking it around hers the way they used to do as little kids.

She felt a wave of love for her brother. "What am I going to do without you, Liam?"

"You're going to remember what I taught you today."

She glowered. "I'm telling Mam."

He stood still for a moment, his mouth set in a serious line. "You should. And I'll back you up. But keep in mind, she's pretty damn loyal to the SOB."

"Loyal? Are you crazy? How could she be loyal to a guy who tried to . . . who came into my room? Who practically broke your nose?"

He shrugged. "That's just the way she is. Old-fashioned, letting him be the man of the house."

"Dad bought this house, not Colm," she said. "I wish Mam would just . . . just *divorce* him." She cringed inwardly, saying the word. It was one of the most dreaded words in the world. Mam acted as if it were a swear word. Kids whose mothers were *divorced* were different. She didn't actually know any of them, but she knew they were different.

Liam gave a snort of laughter. "Right. Soon as hell freezes over, squirt. Mam grew up in the Church in Ireland, remember. And divorce is illegal in Ireland. *Illegal.*"

"She's in America now. She can do anything she wants." Yet Mairin felt the hope drain out of her. What their mother wanted was what the Church had taught her to want. Mam's friends in the Catholic Women's League were super traditional, especially the ones who came from Ireland. They believed what the Church taught them to believe—that it was better to hold on to a monster than to face the shame of divorce.

Part Two

Bad girls do the best sheets.
—*Irish adage*

Chapter 4

School was about to start, meaning new notebooks and fresh pens and pencils, classes with friends who'd been apart all summer long, crisp air, and colorful leaves painting the city with warm shades of amber and pink and orange.

On the morning of the first day of school, Mairin pinned up the season schedule of football games. St. Wilda's didn't have a team, obviously, since it was an all-girls school, but the boys' school, St. Joe's, across the road, had a powerhouse of a team. Mairin loved the Friday night games, a chance to wear her favorite jeans and boots and sweaters, and sit among friends with thick plaid woven blankets to cover the bleachers, and cheer the boys on until their throats were hoarse. It wouldn't be the same without Fiona, of course, but there was popcorn and root beer from the concession stand, and a chance to catch a glimpse of Kevin Doyle, who had made the varsity squad this year.

In the days leading up to the back-to-school rush, tension had run high at Mairin's house. At the Catholic Women's League on Sunday, Mam had visited with Mrs. Doyle, and when the two had compared notes, they realized Mairin and Kevin had gone to the movies together without permission from either of them. According to the moms, this infraction was a direct route to teen pregnancy and utter disaster for both families.

And after the Colm incident, nothing seemed to go right. The very night of the fight, Mairin had told her mother everything in a shaking, sobbing voice, certain Liam was wrong to predict Mam wouldn't believe her. "He came into my room when I was changing my clothes," Mairin said. "He tried to . . ." She caught her breath, gagged a little. "He tried to grab me."

"Lies," Colm had said, his voice a low blade of contempt. "Dirty, disgusting lies, and we all know it. I was there to give you counsel about your outburst in church, taking the Lord's name in vain for all the world to hear. And you paradin' around, flauntin' yourself like a damn hussy."

"I was in my own room. With the door closed," she shot back, then rounded on her mother. "My own private room. Liam *said*—"

"Liam lies as bad as you do," Colm said. "Maybe the army'll straighten him out. The two of you are thick as thieves. Always have been. I work my fingers to the bone to keep a roof over your heads and this is the thanks I get. I swear, I don't know why I bother."

There were a hundred things wrong with his statement. He spent most of what he earned at the bar and at the racetrack. He'd made her and Liam work every summer, and after school, too. Mam took in mending and alterations for people in the neighborhood.

The argument had played out exactly as Liam had predicted. Mairin found no sympathy from her mother, because Colm somehow managed to convince Mam that he'd done nothing wrong. He swore on all the saints that his sole purpose had been to talk to Mairin about her outburst in church. He claimed that Mairin had teased him and flaunted herself, and when Liam had arrived, she'd lied to her brother and caused a fight.

Even though Liam had corroborated Mairin's story, saying he'd heard Mairin yelling at Colm to leave her alone, Mam chose to believe her husband, not her own children. She had dolefully shaken her head and said she didn't know what had come over Mairin. She didn't understand why her own born children were being so horrid and disrespectful to their stepfather.

Mairin felt sick with betrayal, because somehow she knew, deep down, that her mother realized what was going on. Mam simply didn't have the courage to stand up to her husband. She was too afraid he might leave her, and if he did, the Church and Women's League would judge her for it.

The only acceptable way for a husband to leave his proper Catholic wife was to die.

In the middle of all this, Liam had to report to training camp. Still bearing the bruises from his fight with his stepfather, he left from the Greyhound station on a bus bound for Fort Dix. At the station, their mother wailed that she might never see him again. Mairin told her brother goodbye in a soft, broken voice, and when she'd watched the bus leave the terminal, she had felt her soul empty out, the way it had when the power company men had come to the house to deliver the news that her father had died.

These days, everything seemed hard. Every. Single. Thing. She didn't even have Fiona to talk to. It would be the first time in history that they didn't walk to school together.

She pulled out her dress uniform—it was always dress uniform on the first day of school. Plaid jumper, crisp white blouse with the Peter Pan collar, navy blazer, knee socks with tabs. And because everything was hard these days, her blouse was hopelessly wrinkled. She'd forgotten to iron it the night before. The nuns always inspected their uniforms, and if the blouse lacked a perfect knife-blade crease down each sleeve, there would be a demerit.

All Mairin could do now was put on the blazer and hope for the best. At the last minute, she noticed one of her penny loafers was missing a penny. She grabbed the only coin she could find—Flynn Gallagher's Mercury dime—and she slipped it into the slot. Maybe it would bring her good luck. She went downstairs and was loading up her backpack when Mam ambushed her.

"No need to bother yourself with all that. You're not going to school today," Mam said, her expression stony. "Not St. Wilda's, anyway."

Colm came striding into the room, coins jingling in his pocket. He wasn't wearing his usual work clothes—gray utility pants, shirt with the power plant logo, keys on a retractable belt clip, and steel-toed boots. Instead, he was dressed as if for church, in a stiff white dress shirt and dark tie, his one good suit jacket, his shoes shined to a high gloss.

"What? It's the first day of school," Mairin said, frowning. "What the—what do you mean, no school? There's never been no school."

Mam cleared her throat. "I had a meeting with Sister Carlotta at St. Wilda's. We've got a different plan for you." The air in the room felt heavy, weighed down by Colm's glowering expression and Mam's resolute certainty. "It's been a difficult decision to be sure, but this will turn out to be for the best," she said.

"This?" Mairin demanded, her brain scrambling to comprehend. "What do you mean, *this?*"

"After sneaking out with a boy, and that outburst in church, and then causing a fight between Colm and your brother, it's clear you need to learn more discipline than St. Wilda's can provide. We can't allow you to—"

"Causing a fight?" Mairin's face, her eyes, her throat, her chest burned with outrage. "*I* caused a fight? Mam, I *told* you what happened. I told you everything that happened." She swung around and threw a furious glare at Colm. "It's the truth, whether you believe me or not."

"We've been through this," Mam said, her voice weary and exasperated. "I've heard quite enough from you." She went and fetched her pocketbook, the good patent leather one with the brass clasp. She was dressed to the nines, in her slingback heels and cloth dress coat from Hengerer's. "It's time to go," she said, and headed out to the driveway.

"Go where?" Mairin demanded, following her toward the door. "I need to get to school, Mam. I can't miss the first day of school. That's when we sign up for teams and clubs, and the cheer squad for St. Joe's, and—"

"Get in the car," Colm ordered, jerking the door open and glaring at her pointedly.

"Go where?" she repeated.

"In, missy," he said, "or I'll shove you in myself."

"Try it," she taunted, her heart racing. Her fists clenched and unclenched as she stared up at him. Her mind raced, reviewing the things Liam had taught her about fighting off an attack. Go for the vulnerable spots—eyes and crotch. A fist-claw to the throat. Could she even? But this wasn't an attack. It was . . . she didn't know what it was. Some kind of ambush. "Mam," she said, turning to search her mother's face for some sign of reassurance.

"In the car, Mairin," Mam said, her gaze darting nervously to Colm. "Right this minute. We'll not be late on your first day."

Mairin flung herself into the backseat, her mind whirling with confusion. What in the world were they up to? She was no fan of school, but everyone had to go to school. "First day of what?" she demanded. There was no answer, so she glared out the window, slathering a layer of resentment over her fear.

In the car, Mam and Colm commented on the morning traffic and quarreled about the election as if it were any other day. Mam had reluctantly settled on Humphrey on account of him being a Democrat like Kennedy, but Colm said she was a damn fool if she didn't vote for Nixon.

Mairin sat with her arms folded, seething. She felt utterly abandoned, with Liam gone off to training camp and Fiona sent to live with her aunt.

Thanks to her driving lessons with Liam, she recognized High Street and a few blocks later, North Street, and then they were headed for the expressway. But instead of getting on the big thoroughfare, Colm trolled along Best Street and then turned into a driveway spanned by a tall iron gate. This was flanked by a brick wall topped by coils of barbed wire.

"This is—What is this place?" Mairin asked, her voice a strained whisper. But she knew. Everyone in the Fruit Belt knew.

The gate rolled open and Colm drove into a parking area surrounded by some kind of yard where the grass had been burned to yellow by the summer sun. Ahead of them loomed a forbidding, stone-built Gothic structure, its somber shadow falling over the landscape like a dark secret. Weathered carvings crouched above downspouts, and intricately figured archways framed thick wooden doors studded with iron hardware. There were more buildings with rows of tall shuttered windows inside the complex.

Colm parked the car, and they got out. Mairin darted a look at the exit gate. It had already closed behind them. "That's called a sally port," Colm said with a self-important air. "A secure gate to make sure nobody gets out."

Mairin scanned the area wildly, wondering if she should make a dash for it. A dash for what? She was all alone. She had nothing, and nowhere to go. The air was heavy with the scent of dry grass. At the top of the wall, a bright bluebird alighted, and then took flight and disappeared.

"This way," Mam said with crisp conviction. "They're expecting us in the office."

"Who's exp—"

"Hush now, and mind your manners," Mam said, cutting the air with her hand. "Aren't you in enough trouble, then?"

They followed a walkway toward the main building. There was a large plaque with a picture of a saintly figure reading an illuminated book to a flock of sheep, and a Latin phrase: *Salus animarum suprema lex.*

"It's quite grand, isn't it?" Mam remarked, studying the old building's peaked windows and pillars.

It was a place frozen in time, an ancient fortress haunted by echoes that whispered against the gray stone in a mysterious, heavy rhythm. Far in the distance, Mairin could see a grove of fruit trees, and adjacent to that, a series of clotheslines hung with linens and towels. The place seemed to be uninhabited. At a school, kids would be spilling out here and there, yet an eerie quiet surrounded the area.

"Come along," Mam said briskly. "This way." The walkways between the various buildings had been swept, the grass clipped short. Mam's heels clicked on the concrete pavement as she led the way to a thick door marked *Office.*

Mairin noticed a flurry of movement at the top of the wall. A bird was caught in the wire there, struggling furiously to free itself. She opened her mouth to say something, but just then, Colm opened the main door and motioned her inside with a jerk of his head. Mairin stepped into a dim foyer with whitewashed walls that seemed to absorb all the light. She sensed an air of dampness and age, as though this place was entirely separate from the rest of the world. There was a bench, and a shelf with religious objects and framed photographs of priests and nuns. In the center was a large yellowed portrait of a nun labeled *The late Rev. Mother Joachim, Prioress.*

A sign by the inner door read *Our Lady of Charity Refuge* and *Sisters of the Good Shepherd.*

"Mam, no." Mairin's breath caught in her throat as comprehension crept over her. This place was the one mentioned in scandalized whispers from the older girls at school. It was the one people gossiped about when a girl suddenly stopped showing up to class. It was the place angry parents—like her own mother—threatened their daughters with. *I'll send you to the nuns, just you see if I won't.* She grabbed her mother's arm. "Mam, please."

Her mother patted her hand. "Go on with yourself now," she said in a soothing voice. "You'll be brilliant here, I'm certain. 'Tis exactly what you need. Things have gotten out of control at home. We can't keep watching you make the same mistakes over and over again. Sister Carlotta agrees this is the best choice for you."

"What about *my* choice?" Mairin demanded. "I don't understand. Tell me why, Mam. Just tell me why."

"Ah, Mairin. We've been over this. The lying and sneaking, keeping company with boys, and now your friend Fiona in the family way. 'Tis only a matter of time until you stray down that path. And we can't have you showing such terrible disrespect for your stepfather. The nuns here will redeem and protect you, because the Lord above knows I've failed at that. You'll get the very best guidance in this place. It's a chance for you to find your way back to the right path. We can't let you wind up like Fiona Gallagher, bringing all manner of shame to her family."

"I'm not going to end up like Fiona," Mairin said, her voice thin with desperation. "I swear, Mam. I swear on all the saints in the canon."

"Stop badgering your mother and show some respect," Colm said.

A searing sense of betrayal ripped through her. Mairin had always been a rebellious spirit, questioning rules, skirting regulations, getting written up at school. She knew she could be exasperating at times—her mother often made that clear. But now, it seemed that the very essence of her identity was being deemed a flaw. A defect that needed to be corrected.

While they waited, Mairin tried to keep her heart from beating out of her chest. She focused on the plaque on the wall. The inscription read: *She is placed in the Home of the Good Shepherd, not as a punishment, but in the hopes that she will mature into all the beauty of womanhood with knowledge, abilities and ideals which evolve into a happy life, and which, in turn, she may share with others.* The text was attributed to someone named Sister Mary William McGlone, Mother Superior and Principal of St. Euphrasia School.

Based on her first impression, this place did not seem like a good prospect for evolving into a happy life.

Beyond the foyer, there appeared to be a labyrinthine network of shadowy corridors. The air was chilly and reeked of cleaning solution. A strange, distant rhythm of machinery penetrated the deep silence. This place was more antiseptic than a hospital, the walls and floors scrubbed spotless. Across from the plaques and portraits was a sign pointing to *Classrooms* and a display of students' work—drawings of rainbows and waterfalls, the flag of Vietnam with a carefully lettered report under it, a childish picture of some saint or other surrounded by small animals. Some of the pages were faded and yellowed, as if they had been on display for quite some time.

From the darkness of a hallway, a tall figure glided toward them like a ghost. Long white habit, blue tassel, black veil over a white cap, the flowing tunic cinched by an oversized wooden rosary, the chunky cross hanging down the front.

The edges of the white cap framed a face of indeterminate age—smooth skin and pale lips, thoughtful eyes that flicked swiftly over Mairin. "I am Sister Rotrude," the nun said. "Welcome to our community."

Sister Rotrude spoke with a pronounced Irish cadence that caused Mam to perk right up, as she always liked meeting someone from the old country. The nun's voice was deep and sonorous, as though she was about to burst into song, like those nuns in *The Sound of Music*, which Mairin and Fiona had seen four times at the theater when they were younger. They'd listened to the record album and memorized all the songs, belting them out until Mr. Gallagher said his ears were bleeding.

Sister Rotrude's mouth curved in a practiced smile, not a movie-nun smile. And for some reason, she terrified Mairin. "You must call me and all the Sisters here 'Mother,' because we are here to guide and protect you."

With her pale, long-fingered hands folded in front of her, she turned to Mam and Colm. "You've made the wisest of choices, Mr. and Mrs. Davis. I myself came up through the system in Ireland, and blessed I am for it."

"Ah, then we have that in common," Mam said. "As a young woman, I was cared for at the Magdalene home in Limerick, just before making my way to America."

Mairin felt a jolt of shock. What? Mam had never mentioned this before. It was true she had little to say about her life back in the old country, but why didn't Mairin know this? Why didn't Mam ever talk about it? What on earth was a Magdalene home anyway?

"Then you know that it's the Lord's work we're doing for these girls," Sister Rotrude said smoothly. "God and the angels only know what would become of girls like Mairin if we weren't here to help."

"I'm not a bad girl," Mairin burst out. "I don't belong here."

"And that"—Sister Rotrude's instant response snapped like the lash of a whip—"is the sort of disrespect we'll be working on while you're with us." Then her expression relaxed into a welcoming smile as she made a graceful gesture toward the inner door. "We'll go in to meet Mother Gerard now."

Mairin balked, struggling to comprehend the magnitude of what was being forced upon her. Tears burned her eyes, and her heart pounded with a mix of outrage and confusion. How could her mother betray her like this? Did she truly believe Colm's story, or was she just afraid to cross him? Did she actually think Mairin deserved to be sent to reform school simply because she had gone to the movies with a boy?

"Mam, I'm begging you," Mairin said. "Let me come home. I'll be perfect, you'll see. I'll do anything—"

"The empty promises come too late," Sister Rotrude interjected, addressing Mam. "This is common among our new girls. You must stand by your convictions."

Mam's eyes flickered with regret, then hardened. "Mairin, you're here because we want the very best for you. We know you're capable of so much more, but we can't do this alone."

Sister Rotrude cleared her throat and pushed open the door to the inner office. Jostled from behind, Mairin entered the room with her mother and Colm. Soft golden sunlight filtered through a film of lace curtains, casting a warm glow upon the scene. The air was heavy with the fragrance of incense and wood polish and old paper files. A line of ledger books on a floor-to-ceiling bookshelf seemed to whisper their stories from the shadows. Under the window was an old-fashioned prayer kneeler with rough ridges where the padding should be.

The decor was a strange combination of austerity and excess. Everything seemed heavy and somber with stern authority. There were numerous gilt-framed portraits on the wall behind the desk. The large oak desk, weathered by years of use and covered with papers, documents, and leather-bound record books, dominated the room. There was a new-looking radio and a few magazines on the desk as well. Next to that was a PA system with a microphone and control panel. A throne-like leather chair with iron studs sat behind the desk, its arms shining from countless hours of use. There were artifacts—a fat Bible bound with brass hinges; a heavy reliquary box with a glass front, displaying a fancy monstrance inside. In catechism, Mairin had learned such things were meant to house a saint's relics. This one was probably dedicated to some obscure dead saint because the famous ones were all taken.

A nun was working at a smaller secretary desk with spindled legs and a slanted top. She looked up when they entered, and Mairin felt even more disoriented. The nun had a face that was as pale and pretty as the moon, with soft cheeks and large, soulful eyes that were the most remarkable shade of deep blue, almost violet. She looked to be about the same age as Mairin, or maybe even younger. Could *this* be the prioress?

"I'm Sister Bernadette," she said, her soft voice lifting, as though she was questioning her own statement. For some reason, she didn't look like a Bernadette. It was true the nuns took different names along with their vows. Maybe this one's real name was Jennifer or Valerie or Rhonda. *Help, help me, Rhonda.* "Mother Gerard will be with you shortly." She offered a brief, shallow bow, sending Mairin a tremulous smile as if to suggest they were kindred spirits. Mairin sent her a hostile glare. Bernadette went back to her labors, sorting a stack of receipts and entering information into a tall, narrow ledger book, using an old-fashioned fountain pen.

Mairin noticed a passageway of some sort at the back of the room. The narrow hall was lined with cupboard doors and recessed alcoves, fading into shadows. The itchy silence as they waited strung her nerves to the breaking point. The young nun's pen scratched away at her task. Mairin kept trying to get her mother's attention, but Mam stared straight ahead, as though expecting the Mother Superior to materialize like the Holy Ghost.

On the desk next to the PA system was a large clock with Roman numerals. The clock hands seemed to stand still, but it appeared to show the correct time. Eight-thirty in the morning.

Time for first bell at St. Wilda's and announcements from the main office. The girls would all be jostling down the hall, slamming their lockers after stashing their things and then chattering in excitement as they made their way to homeroom, then assembly in the chapel.

Mairin should be there, at the school she'd attended since she was a knock-kneed six-year-old eager to learn everything in the world. She should be waving to the friends she hadn't seen all summer, marveling at new haircuts and impressive suntans, discussing who got braces or glasses, whose boobs had grown, who had news to share. She would have told her friends about Liam, and maybe they'd reassure her that he would be all right. She would have protected Fiona by evading the nosy questions about her absence. Now she wondered if the girls of St. Wilda's were asking questions about *her*. Was she in trouble? Was she the girl whose boyfriend had burst into flames during mass?

After a minutes-long eternity, Mairin heard a distant creak and a swish—a door opening, followed by the light tread of footsteps. The Mother Superior emerged from the shadowy corridor, a lithe figure whose tunic and veil fluttered in her wake. She paused at a tiny marble font, like a basin at the dentist's office, that jutted from the wall, dipped her middle finger into the water, then made the sign of the cross. Finally, she stepped behind the desk and pressed her hands on the dark green blotter.

She looked like the nicest nun in *The Sound of Music*. Encircled by the white cap under her wimple and veil, her cheek jowls spilled from the edges, and a seam of gray-and-white hair shadowed her brow. She had eyes the color of an overcast sky.

Please be one of the nice ones, thought Mairin.

"You may be seated." Her voice scratched over the command. As she gestured at three ladder-back wooden chairs, Mairin caught a whiff of cigarette smoke fluttering from her tunic. *The Sound of Music* nuns didn't smoke.

Mairin found herself wedged between her mother and Colm, who held themselves as rigid and unyielding as a pair of stone statues. Mam stared straight ahead, her face as stiff as one of the portraits that dominated the office and foyer. In the stream of sunlight through the window, Mairin could see that Colm's jaw still bore a fading yellowish bruise from his fight with Liam.

Trying to make herself as small as possible, she hunched her shoulders so tightly that it squeezed her chest, making it hard to breathe. Sister Gerard glanced up but didn't seem to see her at all.

"Now then," she said. "You've entrusted the girl to our care. She'll be guided to the right path now."

The girl.

"I have a name." Mairin couldn't stifle herself. "It's Mairin Patricia O'Hara, daughter of the late Patrick O'Hara, and I'm not a bad girl." Her voice was a mix of defiance and fear. "I'm no different from any other girl, just trying to figure things out. I do not belong in this place."

The nun ignored her utterly, as though her voice was background noise. For Mairin, this was more devastating than being lashed with sharp words, or even the back of a hand. It was as if she didn't matter any more than the timid, dewy-eyed Sister Bernadette, laboring away at her desk.

Sister Gerard handed Colm a pen and a folder with some printed form. "You'll sign there, each of you," she said.

Colm swiftly scratched his name. Mam studied the page, her eyebrows drawing together. "I don't see Mairin's name here."

"She's number six forty-seven," said the nun. "That's our system. She'll be assigned a name the sisters will use."

"I have a name," Mairin repeated, more loudly this time. "It's Mairin Patricia O'— *Ow!*"

Mam's fingers dug into her leg. Then she let go and signed the form. Her signature looked more shaky than usual. Mairin tried to guess what on earth her mother was thinking, bringing her to this place.

Sister Gerard handed them a small white printed envelope and a plastic pen. "For the offering box," she said. "It's in the foyer of the chapel." From her tone, this did not sound like a request. They were expected to pay for the privilege of dumping their daughter here. "Sister Rotrude will see you out." Mother Superior didn't bother to stand, but simply flipped open a file and moved on to her next task. Over in the corner, Sister Bernadette looked up from her work and caught Mairin's eye. The young nun's expression didn't change, but there was a brief softness in her gaze, a beat of sympathy, and she shook her head the slightest bit as if urging Mairin to surrender.

Mairin shot to her feet. "I'm not staying here," she said, her voice shaking but clear.

"Sit down, you," Colm ordered.

She ignored him. "What is my crime?" she demanded, swinging to face her mother. Mam's face was flushed red, and the spray of freckles over her cheeks stood out. She flashed on a memory of Dad touching her on the nose. *One day you'll be as pretty as your mama, just you wait and see.* Was Mam pretty? Or had bitterness stolen her looks? "Mam," she said desperately. "How can you do this to me?"

"Now then." Her mother's voice sounded strained, and her cheeks were hard. "Mind your manners and do as you're told, and all will be well."

"It will, and that's a promise," Colm said, his voice smooth with certainty. "Did you know I was one of Father Baker's boys?"

She stepped back and blinked. Why did she never know this? "You were in reform school?"

"Don't you be callin' it that," he said. "It was a home for boys, and a good one, too. Raised me up right when my own mum couldn't care for me."

"Your mother couldn't care for you?" Mairin asked. He must have been awful as a young boy.

"She did her best, but times were hard. Father Baker's home kept me on the straight and narrow, they did. And the good sisters here will do the same for you." He regarded her briefly, and the secret flash of a smile appeared and faded in the blink of an eye.

Bastard, thought Mairin.

"*My* mother can care for me," Mairin shot back. "Mam, tell him. Take me home, Mam. *Please.*"

Throughout the exchange, the nuns waited impassively, as if they'd seen this situation play out a hundred times.

"I'm asking you, Mam," Mairin said. "I'm begging you."

"There, there." Her mother gathered her into a rare hug and held her fiercely with strong, sturdy arms. "Listen, my girl. You'll be perfectly safe here, do you understand? You'll come to no harm. Just be a good girl, none of your pranks and mischief, and all will be well." She stepped back and held Mairin's shoulders, her gaze seeming to absorb every detail of Mairin's face. Mam's eyes shone, and she blinked fast, seeming to struggle with hesitation. "You'll be safe, do you hear me? *Safe*."

Just for a moment, Mairin felt a tiny spark of relief. The house on Peach Street was different now that Liam had gone off to training in the army. And Fiona was away, too, living at her aunt's and making a baby for some childless couple. At least Mairin wouldn't have to live in the same house as Colm Davis. Though her mother didn't say it, that was clearly what she meant by *safe*.

"Come along, Deirdre," Colm said, pulling Mam away from Mairin. "No need to linger and draw this out. The sisters need to get on about their good works."

The look of hesitation and a tiny bit of struggle in Mam's eyes was fleeting. Then she arranged her face into a resolute expression, offered her thanks to the prioress, and turned away.

In stunned disbelief, Mairin stood watching them go—her mother clutching Colm's arm and hurrying along at his side as if they were fleeing a disaster. As if they had left an abandoned parcel on a stranger's doorstep and didn't want to be caught. An Irish goodbye—they went off without a word of farewell.

She was utterly and completely alone now. She didn't know a blessed soul in this place, and there was nothing about these strange nuns that inspired hope or made her feel safe.

The betrayal by her mother moved through Mairin like a sudden frost. In the deep center of her soul, the truth froze into a hard, cold stone of certainty. She wasn't a bad girl. She didn't need to be reformed or turned from a sinful past. They were leaving her at this place because Colm couldn't be trusted to leave her alone.

"Follow me. Make haste, now." Sister Rotrude led Mairin down an echoing hallway with scrubbed walls and floors, and locked doors on either side. A fluorescent light hummed overhead, and once again, Mairin could hear the heavy whir and thud of machinery. "Up the stairs with you," the nun ordered, directing her to an open iron staircase.

Mairin balked. "There's been a mistake, Sister. I can't stay here with—"

A lightning bolt struck her across the face. The nun had moved so fast, it was as if she hadn't moved at all. Her expression didn't change. She calmly tucked her hands into the sleeves of her tunic. "Are we going to have a problem with you, then?" she softly asked.

Mairin's hand shook as she touched her fiery cheek. The lick of pain raised tears in her eyes and she blinked fast, desperate to hold them in. Swallowing hard, she glared at the nun, then climbed the stairs to the third floor. There was an iron gate at the top, which Sister Rotrude unlocked with an old-fashioned key.

"Here's your unit," said Sister Rotrude, pointing out a spotless dormitory room with low ceilings and barred dormer windows. There were a dozen or more cots with thin mattresses, made up with crisp linens and meager, deflated pillows. A wicker basket sat at the foot of each bed.

The nun stopped and unlocked a green-painted door. Her manner seemed different now that Mairin's parents had left. She turned and eyed Mairin from head to toe as if assessing her. Then she took a paper-wrapped parcel from a shelf and thrust it into Mairin's arms. "Your uniform, underthings, shoes, and pajamas. You can leave your street clothes in the changing room."

"This is my school uniform," Mairin said. "It belongs to me."

Sister Rotrude drew her pale lips into a tight bow. "All the girls wear the same uniform here. It's necessary to foster our community bond. You can change in here." She held open another door.

Next stop was a shower room with benches and lockers, and shelf after shelf of folded towels along one wall. Mairin eyed the row of shower heads in the gleaming chamber that reeked of bleach. Rotrude stood by the door while Mairin changed into the clothes she'd been given. The nun didn't stare, but neither was there any private place to get dressed. The parcel contained a kit with a comb and toothbrush and a plain nightgown. The new uniform was hideous—a shapeless, drab shift dress the color of mud, and a pale smock with big pockets to go over it. Lifeless ankle socks and plain canvas sneakers—the cheap kind, not Keds—completed the ensemble.

With a furtive gesture, Mairin placed Flynn's dime in the toe of a sneaker.

Her stomach churned as reality hit home. She was expected to live here in this cold, weird-smelling place full of scary nuns and strangers. The betrayal felt like a physical blow. "Please," she said softly to Sister Rotrude, risking another crack across the face. "There's been a mistake. Truly, I don't belong here. I should be—"

"Your family knows best," the nun said simply. "Come with me." She led the way to a heavy metal door with an etched glass window webbed with metal threads and labeled *Clinic*. Inside was a gleaming metal table and a cabinet on rollers, a desk in one corner. "You're to have an examination to make sure you're healthy," Rotrude told her.

"I don't need an exam," Mairin said. "I'm perfectly health—"

The door slammed with a *thud* and cut her off. Mairin was alone in the room, shivering with pain. The ache deepened, but she couldn't pinpoint the source. Maybe the nurse could help her. She looked around, hugging herself and pacing back and forth. A sharp, antiseptic odor hung in the air. There were instruments laid out on a tray—a mirror, metal picks like she'd seen at the dentist, some kind of scissors with curved blades and pointy ends, and a long tubular object with a handle. The only ornament on the wall was a large crucifix with spiked rays emanating from the Lord's head. On one side of the desk was another door marked *Office*.

Mairin's breathing came in shallow, uneven gasps. Maybe she was ill after all. If she was sick, would they let her go home?

Home... to what? To that house where she'd never feel safe again?

She was still trying to catch her breath when the office door opened and a young man in a white lab coat stepped into the room. He was small of stature and had straw-colored hair, cropped short. He had soft, light gray eyes with long, sweeping lashes. His eyes looked curiously flat, examining her as if she were a cut of meat at the butcher's.

"I'm Dr. Gilroy," he said. "I'll be doing your exam today."

He was dressed like a doctor, but he looked far too young, perhaps only a few years older than Liam. "I don't need an exam," Mairin said. "But... I'm not well. I can't seem to catch my breath. I think I'd better go home."

He seemed not to hear. "Step up and be seated on the table, please."

His manner was strange in some vague way. He asked her a bunch of questions about her life and if she had a boyfriend and how often she bathed. He made notes on a form on a clipboard.

"Are you a virgin?" he inquired, his pen poised over the form, his gaze probing her face, her neck, lower.

"That's personal," said Mairin. Up until recently, she assumed all girls were virgins until they married.

"You're required to answer," he said.

"It's *personal*."

He scribbled a note. Mairin felt a curl of suspicion. This place made her suspicious of everything.

He took a tongue depressor from a glass jar. "Open and say ah."

She tipped her head back and opened her mouth. "Ah."

His breath smelled of tobacco poorly masked by a breath mint. As he peered into her mouth, his thumb touched her lip. "You girls bring all manner of disease here," he said. "It's my job to keep you all healthy." He set aside the wooden stick and slipped the earpieces of his stethoscope into his ears. Reaching around behind her, he murmured, "Deep breath in, please." He brushed her hair out of the way, his fingers flicking her neck. "You're a ginger," he remarked.

Mairin said nothing. No one here seemed to listen to a word she said.

"When was your most recent menses?" he asked her.

She felt a flood of color in her cheeks. "Week before last."

"Lie back, now." He lightly pressed against her chest. "Lie back on the table."

Instinct kicked in. That gut feeling Liam had told her about. *If it feels wrong, it is wrong.* The little weird signals Mairin sensed now added up to a code red. She elbowed the doctor aside and slid down from the table. Her heart was hammering its way out of her chest. "Leave me alone," she said.

His mild, youthful face turned red, and his eyes went hard with fury. "Young lady, get back on that table." He grasped her by the upper arms and hoisted her up, pressing her back against the edge of the table.

She shot her fists straight overhead and then out to each side, and he lost his grip on her. Then, spurred by fear and fury, she drove her cheetah-paw fist into his throat, putting all her weight behind it. He made a gagging sound, his hand clawing at his neck. Mairin lunged for the door, grabbing the handle.

A fist snaked into her hair and yanked her back, slamming her against the wall. He made an angry, gasping sound. His hands pressed against her neck. Mairin couldn't breathe, but a strange, terrifying clarity burst through her panic. She groped blindly for something, anything. The instrument tray—she couldn't reach it. With a sweep of her arm, she grabbed the crucifix off the wall, bringing it down on his head. At the same time, she brought her knee up. She wasn't sure where it landed, but he stumbled back and doubled over. Mairin threw the cross at him. The INRI banner from Pontius Pilate shattered against some part of his body.

Mairin lunged for the door again and yanked it open, bursting out into the chilly corridor. Sister Rotrude waited there, her hands tucked into the cuffs of her tunic.

"Help," Mairin panted. "That man—th–the doctor. He . . . he . . ."

Rotrude gestured toward a double door at the end of the hallway. "That didn't take long. Dr. Gilroy is very efficient. Come along, and let's get you settled in."

Chapter 5

"You'll start in the calendar room. No dallying. There's a lot for you to learn." Sister Rotrude led the way with a dramatic sweep of her robe.

A whole room for a calendar? How could there be that much to learn about a calendar? Mairin was so flustered from the encounter with the doctor that she couldn't think straight. Her skin itched from the new clothes and from her visit to the clinic. Her entire body hummed with the adrenaline rush that had engulfed her as she fought off Dr. Gilroy. Now, as her breathing and heart rate slowed, she started to second-guess herself. Had she misread the situation? Maybe he was only doing his job, and she'd overreacted.

But no. She clung to Liam's advice—*If it feels wrong, it is wrong.*

She had to say something. There might be repercussions. Gilroy might lie the way Colm had. She might get in trouble for speaking up. Then she thought, how much worse could her trouble be than this?

"Sister," she said, "I need to tell you something about the doc—"

"Mother," said Sister Rotrude, her voice a low lash of command as she swung to face Mairin. "You've been told to address us all as Mother. Show some respect."

"Um, I'm sorry. Mother. I think you should know that when I went in to the doctor, he..." She struggled to find the words to explain. "He asked me about personal stuff, and I didn't like the way he touched me." Her own words sounded weak. She didn't know how to describe the ineffable reaction she'd had in the clinic.

Sister Rotrude gave her no time to elaborate. "The man is a doctor. He volunteers his time, doing the Lord's work. We are fortunate to have Dr. Gilroy to keep you girls safe from disease," she said.

"But he was—"

"You do not have permission to speak," Sister Rotrude said. "This is the first rule here at the Good Shepherd. You may not speak without permission. Mind your manners, now." She led the way down another wide corridor with buzzing lights and loud, mechanical noises emanating from the rooms on both sides.

Mairin tried to make sense of this place. There wasn't a desk in sight. None of the rooms they passed even remotely resembled classrooms with chalkboards, books, and maps. There were no students present, not in the hallways or outside in the courtyard.

"That's the host room, down that way." Sister Rotrude indicated a hallway. "We make the hosts for the diocese." A note of pride lifted her voice.

Mairin said nothing. It was weird to think that communion wafers came from a place like this.

At the end of the hall, the nun opened a heavy double door. A massive cloud of steam enveloped her in a wet, intense heat so powerful that Mairin gasped and stumbled back. For a few seconds, she couldn't breathe or speak. She looked around for a fire alarm, certain something was wrong.

After a few moments, the steam cleared, and she found herself in an enormous room that was packed with girls who appeared to be about her age, wearing the same garments as she was. The girls kept their heads down, their gazes averted as they worked. The hum and groan of the gears and the scent of freshly laundered linens filled the air.

A woman in lay garments, with a kerchief on her head and an expressionless, doughy face, motioned Mairin over. "Stand here, and learn how it's done," she said simply.

Engulfed with uncertainty, Mairin cast a glance back at Sister Rotrude. The nun disappeared in a cloud of steam, and when the billows cleared, she was gone like a magician's assistant, and the doors were shut. The room had no windows other than clerestory vents that were cranked open near the ceiling.

Mairin found herself standing next to two other girls. One was Black, with slender wrists and hands that moved with a certain grace as she pulled crinkled pieces of laundry from a large rolling bin. She went about her work with smooth, mechanical movements, and didn't acknowledge Mairin other than giving her a distrustful, desultory glance. The other girl had blond hair caught back in a kerchief, and the prettiest face Mairin had ever seen, with sky-blue, deeply lashed eyes and full lips, and cheekbones shaded the color of rose petals. In any other setting, she'd be the girl all the boys went crazy over. She met Mairin's gaze, and her expression flickered with a sort of helpless kindness.

"I'm Mairin O'Hara," Mairin said.

"Ruth! No talking," bellowed the laywoman.

Mairin snapped her mouth shut. She despised her assigned name. Ruth. Baby Ruth. Ruthless.

The blond girl waited until the woman turned her back. Then she said, "Angela Denny. That's Odessa. Odessa Bailey."

The Black girl gave an almost imperceptible nod of her head, and continued working. "I'd stop and say hello," she said, "but I'd risk getting my ass beat."

Mairin could tell she wasn't kidding. "Who are the women in the gray uniforms?" she asked.

"Consecrates," said Odessa. "Most of 'em started as residents here, and later decided they wanted to stay and support the work of the nuns."

"*Wanted* to stay?" Mairin was incredulous.

"Steer clear of them," Angela warned. "They can be vicious. As bad as the nuns."

"I was told this is the calendar room," Mairin said, keeping her face averted from the supervisor.

"It is," Angela said. "Not the kind of calendar you hang on the wall. This thing is a calendar. It's a roller iron. Nasty machine. Watch your hands and fingers."

"I will. So are you supposed to show me how it's done?"

"Doesn't look like anybody else is going to."

The calendar roller iron was about the size of a kitchen table. It was heavy and unwieldy with a series of heated rollers that would press and iron large sheets and tablecloths efficiently. It seemed to be as dangerous as it looked. One wrong move, and someone's arm could wind up squashed and burned.

"Don't worry, Mairin," Angela said, barely moving her lips. "Everybody starts off the same here, and you just try to make it through the day. You'll get the hang of it. Just pay attention to what we do."

"You're working like rented mules, that's what you're doing. Shouldn't this whole shebang be reported to the authorities?"

Angela's eyes rolled. "What authorities would that be?"

"Like, you know . . . maybe the cops?"

"Cops," Odessa muttered. "Like they give a flip."

"People think the Church can do no wrong," Angela said.

Mairin swallowed hard as the truth sank in. She watched as the girl called Angela took a sheet from Odessa and expertly fed it into the machine, the rollers whirring to life with a soft hum, transforming the wrinkled fabric into a smooth and pristine surface that came out the other side.

"Even the juvenile courts send girls here, right, Odessa?" A tall, big-shouldered girl brought a rolling cart piled with damp linens. Under unevenly cut bangs, her sharp-eyed gaze was direct and challenging. "Didn't you get sent up by the juvie judge?" She spoke with a blunt, lower-west-side Buffalo accent, reminiscent of the dockworkers, the ones Mairin had always been warned to stay away from.

"Knock it off, Denise," Angela said in a warning tone.

"You gonna make me?" The big girl whirled to face Mairin while slowly moving the linens to the table. She had thick, blunt fingers with the nails chewed to the quick. A fading bruise marked her jawline on one side. "Odessa's a straight-up criminal," Denise said.

Odessa pressed her lips into a line and hunched her shoulders.

Mairin had dealt with bullies before. Every school had one. Even this place, apparently. "Yeah?" she said to the girl called Denise. "And what are you?"

"Not a criminal, I can tell you that." Denise jutted her chin out with pride. "Odessa got arrested in that riot last summer, the one around

William Street and Jefferson Avenue where all the colored people started fires and wrote *soul brother* on stuff and broke store windows."

"I think you mean the one where dozens of *Black* people were wounded by police bullets," Odessa said.

The incident had made the news, Mairin recalled. It had shut down the city. She remembered this because work at Eisman's orchard had been called off for three days straight. And the famous Mr. Jackie Robinson himself had visited Buffalo to try to calm things down.

"Police and firefighters were injured, too," Denise shot back. "Just for doing their job."

"Three policemen, one firefighter," Odessa said. "*Forty* Black people."

"Yeah, and *you* were the one who hurt one of the policemen. Broke his face, didn't you?" Denise sent her a challenging glare.

Odessa's hands tightened into fists. "You're just jealous 'cause I'm getting out of this place next summer, and you have to stay."

Angela stepped between them and finished emptying the cart. "Go get us another load." She shoved the cart at Denise, the motion attracting the attention of one of the consecrates. Denise turned on her heel and wheeled the cart away.

Odessa glared after her, then went back to work.

Mairin didn't know many Black people. There were two sisters who attended her school—the Parks sisters—but they were older. They went around with their hair in a neat crown of braids, and one of them sang like a pro in the choir. Some people in the neighborhood were prejudiced against them, but Mairin was never sure why. Now she regarded Odessa, wondering about her family. Where were Odessa's parents? Did she have brothers and sisters? What had her life been like before the Good Shepherd?

"You know what's real cool?" Angela said to Mairin. "Odessa's the best of all of us. Sings in her church choir, does good works. That's how she got arrested, right, Odessa?"

"Doing good works?" asked Mairin.

"Depends on what you think is *good*," Odessa said. "A group from our church went out during the riot to try to help. Thought we could keep the cops from beating up on people. You see how that worked out."

"Did you really break a policeman's face?" Mairin asked.

"Not his whole face," Odessa said. "He was cracking some kid over the head with his baton, and I shoved his arm and he hit himself in the nose. Total freak accident, but the cop didn't take it well. Bled like a stuck pig. He was like a two-hundred-fifty-pound linebacker and I'm this skinny girl. But look who's doing hard time."

Angela clicked her tongue. "Not the giant white cop, no way."

"That's terrible. And the juvie court sent you here?" Mairin's voice squeaked with outrage.

Odessa nodded. "Judge said I was a *wayward girl*. The nuns are supposedly gonna set me on the path to reform."

"You should volunteer to sing in chapel," Angela said, then turned to Mairin. "You should hear her. She's fantastic."

"They don't like my kind of singing here," said Odessa. "Too cheerful, I guess. My favorite is 'Oh Happy Day' but it'd probably get me a whack."

"No talking," barked a nun, raising her voice over the clamor of the equipment.

"Sister Theresa," Angela whispered. "Watch out for her. She pulls hair. Eventually, you'll get to know each one's mean side."

"I don't want to get to know anything about this place," Mairin muttered.

"It doesn't take long. Every day seems the same." Angela's voice trembled over the words. "Rotrude is the worst. She's like the second-in-command to the prioress. When Mother Gerard goes off to a diocese meeting every week, they leave Rotrude in charge."

"There was one in the office," Mairin said. "Sister Bernadette. She seemed . . . maybe not so awful."

"Give her time," Angela said.

"She's so young and pretty. What's she doing here?" Mairin asked.

"I heard she came through Catholic Charities as a child," Angela replied. "Imagine being here as an inmate, and then deciding to stay."

"I can't," Mairin said. "I can't imagine it." She carefully picked up an unfolded sheet from the bin, her trembling fingers gliding over the soft cotton material. Placing it on the gleaming metal table at the lip of the surface, she took a deep breath and fed the sheet into the hungry jaws of the calendar roller iron. The machine roared to life with a rhythmic clanking sound. The rollers spun and pressed against the sheet, their heated surfaces clamping down on the crumpled cloth. As the fabric was drawn into the depths of the machine, Mairin kept her gaze fixed on the rollers. The machine was a beast, devouring the fabric, making a churning sound as it pulled the piece through the heated cylinders.

Then the fabric emerged on the other side, looking brand-new. Odessa brought the pressed goods to a long folding table, and another girl expertly made a precise square of it. The process repeated itself at four other stations.

A lay supervisor instructed Angela to show Mairin the rest of the operation in the adjacent rooms and halls. There, girls were assigned to the various tasks—sorting and then washing in big stationary tubs, followed by a rinse. All the just-laundered pieces were piled in carts and pushed through a low door to the shaking room, where girls operated something called a mangler, which was a commercial wringer. After being run through the mangler, the goods were hung out to dry in a big yard that was webbed with clotheslines.

Each station was monitored by nuns and supervisors who shouted orders and never gave a word of encouragement. It was hot, and everyone was sweating and thirsty, but they were only allowed to go to the drinking fountain with permission. The steam and fumes made some of the inmates cough, earning them a rebuke.

Mairin noticed two girls who were visibly pregnant. The girls looked exhausted, moving slowly through their chores, their protruding stomachs getting in the way. One of them paused to rub her back, earning a cuff from a supervisor.

Angela noticed Mairin's gaze. "Most of 'em go to OLV—Our Lady of Victory—or Father Baker's, but some stay here."

Father Baker's boys. Colm had proudly counted himself one of them.

"What do . . . I mean, what happens when the baby comes?"

"There's a charity ward at St. Francis. That's where they go to have the baby, and it gets placed for adoption. Sometimes the girl's family takes the baby to raise, but in that case, they have to pay a fortune to the Good Shepherd and the hospital to take care of all the expenses. And the girls here come from families that can't afford to do that."

"That's it, then? They simply ... give their baby away?" Mairin focused on the girl with the sore back. She looked like any girl at St. Wilda's, like Fiona or Mairin herself.

"And then they come back here. I saw one girl's boobs leaking milk like a dairy cow. She said it hurt really bad."

Mairin thought of Fiona. At least her friend didn't have to go through the pregnancy in this place.

The workers were hustled out to the yard, where acres of linens and dozens of garments were being hung out to dry. The dry goods were unpegged and gathered in carts for pressing. Mairin tipped back her head and breathed in the fresh air. In an adjacent yard, the orchard looked familiar. There was a harvest ladder. She studied it for a moment, wondering if it was tall enough to get her over the wall.

"Whose things are these?" Mairin asked, taking down a pair of trousers. It felt weird to be handling strangers' clothes.

"Uniforms, mostly," Angela said. "And church garments. A few regular clothes." She hid behind a fluttering sheet and put on a cool shirt. "Look at this," she said, strutting around. "It's from Macy's in New York City."

"You should be a fashion model," Mairin said. "You're really pretty."

"I love clothes," Angela said, taking off the shirt.

"I hate this place," Mairin said, flinging the pants into a cart. "I'm supposed to be going to school at St. Wilda's, but my parents made me come here."

"You mean you didn't choose this place?" someone asked in a darkly teasing voice.

Mairin looked around, fearful of being caught talking. But the speaker was another girl. She was Asian but sounded entirely American, just not with the Fruit Belt twang of the locals.

"Of course I didn't choose it," said Mairin. "What do you take me for?"

"I'm being ironic," said the girl. She wore a kerchief over her glossy hair, which hung halfway down her back like a waterfall. She had an intense, penetrating look in her eyes, as if she was trying to read Mairin's thoughts.

"I don't know what ironic means," Mairin said. "My name is Mairin, by the way. Mairin O'Hara."

"Helen Mei. Is it your first day?"

"It is. I hate it here already. I'm going to figure out how to escape," Mairin said.

"Hmm, good luck with that," Helen said. "I've never seen anyone succeed. The only way a girl gets to leave is if her family fetches her. Some get to leave when they turn eighteen. Or if a girl gets too sick to stay. Last winter, they took one of us away because she was coughing up blood, and she never came back."

"That's horrible," Mairin said. "I can't stay here until I'm eighteen. I won't survive."

"This whole place is horrible," Angela agreed.

"But it's pizza day in the refectory," said another girl in a chirpy, cheerful voice. She was small and awkward, with wide, protuberant eyes and a lopsided grin. Her smock was wrinkled and smeared with food stains.

"That's Kay," said Helen. "And Janice with her."

Janice had a pointy nose and pointy glasses, and she wore her hair in two braids pulled so tight that they stretched her eyes sideways.

"Pizza. Whoop-de-doo," said Denise, wheeling her cart close.

"When do we go to class?" asked Mairin.

The other girls looked at one another. "Ooh, you mean English literature and trig-oh-nometry?" Denise asked. "How about we schedule it between sorting and scrubbing?"

"I guess I know what ironic means now," Mairin said. "The display outside the main office has a sign for classrooms. What's that about?"

Angela and Helen exchanged a glance. "There are a couple of classrooms they have just for show," Helen explained. "Like, to show off when somebody from the diocese or the county social service department comes to inspect. The rest of the time, they're empty. We're allowed to read from the scripture at mealtimes, and if we can get hold of a pencil or pen, they let us draw stuff. The library bookmobile comes once a month. And they let us play games in the yard three times a week."

"And that's all the schooling you're gonna get here," said Denise.

"Can we not write letters to people?" Mairin asked, thinking of her promise to Fiona. She had written down the name and address of her friend's aunt in Bradford, but she'd forgotten it. Maybe she could send a letter to Fiona's house in Buffalo and it would somehow get to her. She wanted to write to Liam, too. He had something called an APO address, and luckily, she'd memorized it.

"Supposedly the nuns encourage letter writing. But who knows if they actually mail them."

"That's nuts," Mairin said. "This is all hunky-dory with the county?"

"A lot of the girls are placed here by the courts." Denise jerked her head in Odessa's direction.

"Is that how you got here?" asked Mairin.

"Piss off," Denise said, and stalked away.

"She seems nice," Mairin said.

"She's a bully," Helen said. "Janice is a snitch, so watch out for her. She thinks the nuns'll be nicer to her if she tattles. And Kay is . . . well, she's sweet. Kind of simple. I heard some of the lay workers gossiping that her mother was a terrible drunk and had too many kids, and Kay was the last of them. Some say all that drinking is the reason Kay turned out like this—undersized and mentally . . . well, also undersized, I guess."

"And what about you?" asked Mairin. "Who sent you here?"

Helen's lip trembled the slightest bit. She shaded her eyes and looked up at the sky. "My parents went to China to see my grandmother because she's sick. They were meant to stay for two weeks, and the nuns here said they'd take care of me while they're away. Mom and Dad didn't know what this place really is. It was recommended to them by someone at my school. I went to Archbishop Walsh."

Mairin knew the school—a sports rival located in a fancy neighborhood near the University at Buffalo. "So are your two weeks up soon?" she asked.

Helen shook her head and looked at the ground. "After they were gone for a month, Sister Gerard had a telegram that said they're being detained on state security charges, and they're under an exit ban."

"What does that mean?" It didn't sound good.

"Means she's totally screwed." Denise had returned with her cart.

"Oh, go chase yourself," Angela said. "Her dad's a professor at the U. He's kind of famous for the books he's published."

"Not famous enough to get home from China," Denise pointed out.

Mairin ignored her. "Whoa, you must be really smart," she said to Helen.

"That doesn't make me smart," Helen said.

"She is," Angela said. "She speaks Chinese."

Helen looked at the stone wall at the end of the clothesline yard. "Mandarin," she clarified. "So anyway. I've been here forever, and there's no end in sight."

"Wow, that's awful," Mairin said. "How will you ever—"

"*Silence!*" A portly nun clapped her hands at them. "You know the rules. One more outburst and you'll be kneeling on corn at suppertime."

Mairin tried not to let fear and confusion consume her as they worked all day, washing and drying and pressing tablecloths, napkins, towels, sheets, and pillow slips. Each piece was marked with an indelible stamp—St. Francis Hospital, the Hotel Lafayette, the Niagara Institute, and several large restaurants and resorts.

With grinding monotony, they gathered the dry items and brought them in rolling carts to the calendar room for pressing. Once folded on the long tables, the laundry was precisely stacked. If it was off even a little bit, one of the nuns or supervisors would force them to redo the stack and make them count it again, because they were paid by the piece, not by the pound.

"That laywoman said 'we're paid.' Are we being paid, then?" Mairin asked Denise, who was working nearby.

"Not hardly. The clients pay the nuns, you dope."

"The clients. You mean like hospitals and hotels and such."

"We service all the fanciest places," said Angela, striking a pose.

Mairin wondered if these businesses knew who was washing their dirty laundry. She wondered if they'd be troubled if they knew it was being done by girls who were being held against their will, girls who should be in school.

According to Helen, the clients were led to believe that the Good Shepherd provided moral education and job training for wayward girls, a worthy service to the community.

"Why doesn't someone tell them what's really happening here?" Mairin wondered. She was quickly learning to whisper through her teeth without looking up.

"Who are they going to believe, a girl arrested for some petty crime, or a nun?" Helen replied archly.

"I didn't commit a crime," Mairin said.

"What, then?"

She felt the burn of a blush. "My stepfather—" She stopped herself. These girls were strangers.

"Creeped on you, didn't he?" Denise passed behind her, wheeling a cart.

Mairin pretended she hadn't heard. "We don't get along," she mumbled, feeling the fire of humiliation in her cheeks, all the way to the tips of her ears. For some reason, every instinct she possessed urged her to keep the incident with Colm a secret.

She kept working until all the neat stacks were wrapped and labeled. She noticed that Helen kept the ends of the wrapping paper rolls and the priest collar tabs, carefully slipping them into her apron pocket.

"Are you going to get in trouble for that?" Mairin whispered.

"Not if they don't see," Helen said simply.

The finished bundles went into enormous Pullman bags that were wheeled to a loading dock behind the main building. Burly teamsters backed their delivery trucks up to the dock and opened the loading doors.

"Out for delivery," Odessa remarked, her gaze soft with wistful yearning. She stood next to Mairin in the chain of girls who were moving the parcels toward the trucks.

"Do you ever think about jumping on board and getting away from this place?" Mairin asked. Her heart sped up at the mere thought.

"Every damn day."

"So why haven't you—"

"You get caught trying that, and it'd be the closet for you," Odessa said.

"What's the closet?"

"Like solitary confinement." Angela shuddered. "It's by Mother Superior's office, and if you make a noise, they make you stay in there longer."

"In a closet?" Mairin asked. "That's nuts."

"Girls who've been there say there's barely enough room to stand or turn around, and it's completely dark."

This sounded like a nightmare to Mairin. She'd never liked dark, enclosed spaces. "Then if I did try," she said, "I'd make sure I didn't get caught."

"You won't give them the slip," Odessa said, indicating the nun and the lay supervisor who scanned the area as if they were armed guards. "Besides, where you gonna go once you're out? Social services'll send you right back."

Mairin eyed the nearly full truck. She pictured herself jumping on board, then waiting for the opportunity to slip away and . . . and then what? She would probably go back home, beg her mother for another chance. Maybe if Mam knew exactly what it was like here, she'd take pity and let Mairin stay home where she belonged.

She might not, though. Mam seemed all too ready to believe Colm, not Mairin.

A nun and a lay worker supervised the loading, pacing up and down the dock. Mairin's pulse raced as her desperation grew. Her thoughts were a runaway train. She had to get out of here.

There was a loud whistle, and the first truck pulled away. Another, larger one backed into its place. The driver was on the young side, slim and muscular in his delivery uniform and cap. He came around to the dock with a swagger and lit up a smoke. His gaze seemed drawn to Angela. Even in her work clothes, she was lavishly pretty, as tall and shapely as a model in *Seventeen* magazine.

He offered a smoke to the nun and the laywoman, producing a Zippo lighter with a flourish. Mairin saw her chance. Quick as a flash, she stepped onto the truck and wedged herself between two tall stacks of parcels. She heard a gasp from Odessa, but sent the girl a pleading look. Odessa's face went blank, and she continued working as if she'd seen nothing.

"Hey, what's she doin'?" asked another girl. Janice. Janice the snitch. "Ow!" Janice said. "Quit poking me!"

A few minutes later, the cargo door rolled shut and Mairin found herself in darkness. A whistle sounded, and the truck lumbered forward.

This was actually going to work, Mairin thought, feeling giddy with relief and anticipation. No one here knew who she was. No one would miss her. All she had to do was slip out of the truck when no one was looking. The scent of detergent and the rhythmic hum of the engine smelled and sounded like freedom to her after the suffocating atmosphere of the laundry. She had no idea where she was headed. *Away* was good enough for her.

The truck seemed to move at a crawl. The bales of laundry rocked with the motion, some of them toppling over. Mairin crouched lower, trying not to panic as she planned her next steps. She was trapped in here, but the door would open at some point. Wouldn't it? She could make a break for it, just run, but what if someone chased her down? Maybe she should wait and sneak out. And then . . . then what?

She curled her toes around Flynn Gallagher's dime, still hidden in her shoe. Yes. She could find a phone booth and call Flynn and beg him to come and get her. She could—

A sharp whistle sounded, and the truck rolled to a halt with a gnashing of brakes.

So soon? They were barely underway. She heard voices—*Gimme a hand, willya?*—and the iron creak of a gate. Then the back door of the truck lifted.

Now what now what now what? Mairin's heart hammered so loudly, she was sure someone would hear it. She tried to force herself to calm down, praying no one was looking at the truck. Traffic sounds on a road somewhere. A train whistle in the distance.

A glimmer of hope ignited inside Mairin. She took a deep breath, craning her neck to peek outside, but she could see only a glimpse of the sky.

Freedom.

All she had to do was figure out where she was, and then find her way home. Except *home* was no longer a place where she was welcome. Maybe she'd run away to the painted-bus commune, smoke dope, and become a hippie.

"Start here," a clipped female voice ordered.

A finger of ice touched Mairin's spine. She held her breath as the truck jostled with someone's weight. The parcels were moved, one by one, and she realized that her refuge was being methodically dismantled. Somehow, the truck had left, then circled back, and had returned to the Good Shepherd. She crouched into a ball of nerves, wishing she could make herself disappear. She held tight to the parcel in front of her, digging her work-chapped fingers into the paper wrapping.

Then, inevitably, a pair of scuffed work boots planted themselves in front of her and the parcel was wrested from her grip. The sound of shattering hope filled her ears as she tilted her head and looked up, up, up at the man towering above her. It was the young driver, the one who smoked and stared at Angela as if she were dessert.

Mairin was so scared that she couldn't move. "Please," she said to the man, her voice shaking and hoarse. "I don't belong here. There's been a mistake. I'm just trying to get home. Please, I'm begging you. I swear, I—"

"Out with you," the guy said, his eyes hard and mean. "Or I'll haul you out myself."

Mairin shot up then, wincing as her knees yelped with pain from all the crouching. Her fear crystallized into fury as she glared at him. The silence was filled with the weight of impending punishment. "I won't forget this," she said, noting the name stitched on the shirt of his uniform. *Clem.*

"Get the hell outta my truck," he said. "C'mon, you're makin' me late."

She ducked her head and lunged for the open bay door, intent on somehow rushing through the gate.

An arm shot out and hauled her back. "No funny stuff."

Mairin wrenched herself from his grip and dropped to the ground, the thin soles of her shoes slapping the pavement. Scanning the area, she saw that the iron gate was closed, so she abandoned the idea of escaping that way. She hadn't even made it out of the parking lot.

"Come with me," said the waiting nun, the breeze causing her habit to billow like the wings of a crow. She turned and marched toward the loading dock. The truck left in a blast of exhaust. The nun stopped and waited, her disapproving eyes fixated on Mairin.

It was a stupid move, Mairin admitted to herself as she trudged back across the compound. She'd let sheer panic cloud her thinking, and she'd acted out of pure impulse. She absolutely did need to find a way to escape this place, but she would have to make a better plan.

Mairin felt a seething defiance. She would not let this place break her.

She followed the nun back to the loading dock area. All the girls were lined up on their knees on the bare pavement, their hands folded and their heads bowed as if in prayer. A few of them were shaking with discomfort. The nun must have recognized the shock on Mairin's face, because she pulled her lips into a sour pucker and gave a sniff. "All the girls had to wait here on their knees until your return."

Mairin's eyes narrowed. "That's ridiculous. They had nothing to do with—"

The nun struck fast and hard. A fist connected with her ear, causing her head to ring and her vision to blur. Mairin gasped, her hand flying to her burning ear. Tears welled up in her eyes, not just from the blow but from the realization that she was now a resident of this place. The nun's cold, unyielding gaze bore into her, and Mairin swallowed hard, the taste of fear bitter on her tongue.

"Girls, Ruth has decided to come back and join us," the nun announced. "You may stand up now and get back to work."

The girls got to their feet, some of them groaning with pain. Several of them shot daggers of fury at Mairin.

"It'll be nothing but bread and water for supper, and you can thank your new friend Ruth for that," the nun added.

Mairin was horrified. "There's no one to blame but me," she said. "It's not fair to punish the others because of what I did."

"When one transgresses, all must suffer. You'd do well to remember that. Come along now." She motioned toward a side door.

"Where are we going?"

"To see Sister Rotrude. She'll be the one to decide what's to be done about you."

Chapter 6

Sister Bernadette savored the quiet of the main office, surrounded by her ledger books, receipts, and records. She felt so very blessed to work for the Good Shepherd order in this capacity, particularly since she had taken her First Vows at such a young age. She was just eighteen, though in her soul she sometimes felt much older than that.

Of course, she had not always been Sister Bernadette. In the Before Time, she was Genesee, named for her birth mother's brand of cheap beer. Perhaps it was a nickname, perhaps not. It was the only name she knew.

When she was little, her first chore of the morning had been to collect the empty bottles strewn around the flat and set them on the stoop for the rag-and-bone man. She used to line up the bottles in perfect formation, like soldiers on parade. Although she rarely attended school in the noisy, trash-strewn neighborhood, she learned to add and keep track of things—how many coins the bottles yielded, how to add and subtract figures simply by picturing the calculation in her mind. She became a champion at skully, and she spent hours customizing her bottle caps for the street game. Ma would jeer at her and maybe give her a cuff on the ear for doing that, but Genesee persisted, and sometimes she won a few pennies off the other kids. Most days, it was the only order she could find in the chaos of her life. Most days, it was all she could do to keep out of sight of Ma's clients, because most of them were mean. And a few were too friendly.

She would always remember the blessed day when the people from Catholic Charities made a tour through the Tenderloin neighborhood on the lower east side, emerging from the looming shadows of the buildings on a rainy afternoon in their perfectly ironed garb, like angels in black, leaving the scent of rain and soap flakes in their wake.

In the poorly heated flat, Genesee had cowered on the bare mattress, her thin shoulders drawn up in anticipation of some kind of punishment. Instead, the nuns had spoken with soft reassurance, and the priest had taken her hands in his and promised they had come to help.

The nuns took note of the bruises that marred Genesee's delicate skin, exchanging sorrowful glances. At the age of twelve, she knew enough to be ashamed of her frailty and ill-fitting clothes. Although the plumbing in the tenement didn't always work, Genesee tried to keep herself clean, and one of the sisters remarked upon the effort. They also remarked on her tangled, lice-ridden hair.

Her mother complained about what a terrible burden it was to raise such a useless daughter, and she readily signed the paperwork presented by the priest. This was followed by a visit to a shelter with showers and a cafeteria. Her hair was shorn; she was given clean clothes and taken to the station for a long and tedious train ride to Buffalo.

Genesee had been one of the girls who entered the Good Shepherd with a feeling of relief, not fear. While so many other girls resisted and rebelled and bemoaned their fate, Genesee held her heart open to this new opportunity. She craved the cleanliness and order of the place, the strict discipline and constant reminders that the way to salvation was through hard work and penitence. At the Good Shepherd, Genesee found the things in life she'd never had—an orderly world, a community, an identity, a sacred purpose.

At first, she didn't understand the building marked *Laundry*. She soon came to understand that it was a way for girls in need of reform or girls who found themselves with child to achieve grace through their hard labor. Bernadette had thrown herself into the work, never uttering a word of complaint. It was soon discovered that she had a gift from God—a mind that was made for memorizing things, whether it be the complete high mass in Latin, passages of scripture, lists from the phone book, complicated calculations, or the lives of the saints.

Her knack for figuring caught the attention of the prioress, who realized that with Genesee managing the bookkeeping, there would be no need for a paid layperson to do the work.

Before long, she became a devoted aspirant, certain she'd been called to serve for the rest of her life. Her postulancy lasted just six months because her mind was so sharp and her devotion so deep, and then she took her first vows as a novice, glorying in the white veil and her new identity as Sister Bernadette. The sense of mission that coursed through her every waking moment assured her that she was doing the Lord's work. Two years from now, she would make her solemn vows, and her commitment would be permanent.

The refuge was a stark place, austere and unyielding, much like the Mother Superior who ruled it with ironclad command. The girls, waifs and strays from Buffalo's harsh streets, labored in the laundry, their youth spent amid steam and suds, their small hands scrubbing away sins as if they could be cleansed with soap and water.

Bernadette didn't understand why so many of the girls who came to the Good Shepherd resisted this way of life. It was a place of cleanliness and order, predictability and security. She wished they knew how lucky they were to be given a chance to redeem themselves, even the ones who had done terrible things—thieving and destroying property, running away, drinking alcohol and taking drugs, getting themselves with child, and falling in with horrible people.

Sometimes a girl who gave birth out of wedlock made a terrible row about keeping her baby, but the nuns always managed to persuade her that the most loving act was to place the child with a caring, two-parent family. Bernadette wished the girls would realize that this was the safest place in the world.

With a sigh and a silent word of praise, Bernadette organized the day's receipts and invoices, glorying in the straight, precise columns of figures in her leather-bound book. When it came to matters of budget, Mother Superior required vigilance and precision. She insisted on making sure the Good Shepherd was self-sustaining, never in need of outside funds. To that end, she had instructed Bernadette to keep a private record of the payments that were made in cash or in silver certificates. These were kept in a hidden compartment under the reliquary dedicated to Saint Apollonia.

When Bernadette had inquired about the practice, Sister Gerard's reply was always veiled in rationalizations. "We prosper as only those do who are resolved to do and dare for God alone," she was fond of saying. The funds were held for charitable work, to support the local community, and for the betterment of the Good Shepherd itself, which was too often overlooked by the diocese. Bernadette was too timid to question Mother Superior, particularly since Sister Gerard had been so supportive of Bernadette's skills.

Bernadette still remembered how she'd been praised when officials from the diocese examined the books, remarking on her accuracy, neatness, and efficiency. Afterward, she'd had to go to confession to disclose the heady rush of pride that had filled her, earning a lengthy but well-deserved penance.

A scuffle from the back hallway interrupted Bernadette's thoughts, and she felt her shoulders contract with tension. She knew what the sound meant.

"Get your damn hands off me." A voice, loud with youthful fury, echoed off the cold stone walls of the corridor. "Don't you touch—"

Bernadette could have predicted the sharp slapping sound. Sometimes a painful blow was the reminder it took to bring a girl to her senses. It was never pleasant, seeing what some girls had to endure in order to realize the error of their ways, but it was a necessary step in their journey toward redemption.

She was quite sure the new girl would turn out to be the source of today's trouble. That one—Mairin O'Hara, who would be known here as Ruth—had an air of trouble about her. Some of the girls brought in were limp with surrender, but not Mairin O'Hara. With her bright red hair and even brighter green eyes, the tilt of her chin, and her defensive posture, she had radiated defiance when she'd arrived. She had even dared to proclaim her name, loudly and with conviction, rejecting the gift of the new name she would adopt here at the Good Shepherd.

In spite of the girl's attitude, Bernadette had felt drawn to Mairin, reluctantly admiring that spark of spirit. But like everyone who came here, Mairin—Ruth—would bend to Sister Rotrude's will. Eventually, everyone did.

"Step inside the closet," Sister Rotrude ordered. "You'll stay until you are cleansed by repentance."

"I will not" came the response. "I swear I'll—"

"You'll swear? You'll *swear*? You'll make no vow except to your lord and savior." There was more scuffling, followed by the thud of a closing door and the iron yawn of the latch slamming home.

Bernadette winced, her concentration flickering away from her chores as the sound of muffled pleas echoed down the hallway.

"You can't lock me in," Mairin wailed. "What if the building burns down?"

"Then you'll know what hell feels like."

Bernadette glanced at the clock. Soon it would be suppertime, and then vespers, the shadowy prayers offered up to welcome the night.

Sister Rotrude swept into the office. There was high color in her cheeks, but her face was soft with serenity. It must be such a relief when a difficult girl finally surrendered, thought Bernadette.

"Don't give her the bucket," Rotrude commanded. "Make her wait."

Bernadette could hear gasps of panic emanating from the closet. Complete darkness tended to do that to a girl. The disorientation and isolation induced anxiety that not even prayer could assuage.

"Will she go to supper, then?" Bernadette asked, keeping her eyes averted and her voice tentative, respectful. Though only a few years older than Bernadette, Rotrude was as hard a fixture here as the marble holy water fonts jutting from the walls. Born and raised in a mother-and-baby home in Ireland, Rotrude had a will of iron. Her unshakable faith gave her the strength to resist the urge to go soft on the girls. Bernadette could only hope she would find that depth of faith one day. She was already regretting her question.

"Bread and water after vespers," Rotrude said.

"Yes, Sister." Bernadette bowed her head in deference. "I'll take care of that."

She tried not to hurry through her supper, which the nuns took on a raised dais overlooking the benches where the girls sat with their tin plates and cups. It was harvest time, and there was food in abundance for the nuns, thanks to Sister Gerard's clever agreement with local farmers. She bartered laundry services for fresh produce. The girls, however, were served their usual soup of potatoes, beans, and greens in thin broth. Sister Gerard claimed that with 116 mouths to feed, it was important to practice strict rationing so they never ran out of food.

Afterward, the girls cleaned and scrubbed the dining hall and dishes, and then evening prayers were offered up. Built in 1888, the chapel's cruciform shape formed a sanctuary that had an intermediary space between the nuns' choir and the transepts, where the inmates were crowded together.

Bernadette's heart swelled as the program moved through the psalms with their chanted antiphons, and the all-important Canticle of Mary, who sang these self-same words when she was filled with the knowledge that she was to bear the Lord's son. Bernadette could only imagine how to aspire to such a state of grace. Tonight, however, she felt distracted, thinking of the girl confined in the tiny dark space behind the office.

She slipped from the chapel and stopped by the kitchen, then made her way through the dimly lit hallways toward the front office. She paused outside the closet and listened. She herself had spent many an hour there, long ago. It had taken several confinements for her to understand the importance of obedience. She could still remember that one time when she forgot herself and yelled one of her mother's crude phrases during a game in the exercise yard. That got her a well-deserved wallop across the mouth. There was another time when she'd spoken out of turn, defending a girl who was being punished for soiling her garments with her monthly flow. That earned her extra hours on her knees, scrubbing the bathrooms. Before long, Bernadette embraced full compliance, and found grace there.

Her hand trembled as she unhooked the latch of the confinement room and slowly opened the door. Mairin O'Hara was crouched on the floor, her head bowed over her drawn-up knees. The closet was too narrow to fully stretch out, one of the many reasons it should be avoided. As the dim light fell over the girl, she tilted her head up, squinting, her face soft and lovely and streaked by tears.

"I've brought you something to eat," said Bernadette.

Bracing her hands on the walls, Mairin stood, wobbling slightly as she came to her full height. "That's just great." She was taller than Bernadette, with an athletic build, and her stance was defiant, matching the glint in her eyes.

"It's true, you could overpower me and try to escape again," Bernadette said quietly, anticipating the girl's thoughts. "It won't work, though, and you'd wind up back here, or someplace even worse."

"What's worse than here?"

Bernadette decided not to tell her about the basement room. Not today. "Someday soon, I hope you'll understand that true freedom lies in repentance and obedience, not defiance."

She stepped aside and gestured at a low wooden bench just inside the office. "You may sit there."

Mairin brushed past her and took a seat. Bernadette handed her the meal she'd brought from the kitchen—a peanut butter sandwich and a cup of broth. Mairin devoured the food without a word of gratitude. As she sipped the last of the broth, she glared up at Bernadette. "The other one—Sister Rotrude—said bread and water."

"And that is what I brought." Bernadette knew she was stretching the rules with the sandwich and soup, but the girl was new, after all.

Mairin stood and stretched this way and that, her body lithe and strong. She stepped into the main part of the office and looked around. "You like working here?"

"I serve where I am called," said Bernadette.

Mairin went over to the radio and switched it on.

"Ruth, you mustn't touch things."

"I'm not going to hurt anything." Mairin frowned as Father Coughlin's voice emanated from the speaker, delivering a sermon in his usual dramatic manner. "Ugh, Catholic radio hour," Mairin remarked. "My mother listens to that." With a deft spin of the dial, she swept through the stations and stopped on one with a cheery beat and a dulcet male voice singing "I Heard It Through the Grapevine."

For a moment, just a thrum of her heart, Bernadette felt a thrill of... something. Excitement. Pleasure. The tune and rhythm were so deeply compelling, they made her want to move in time with the beat. "Stop that," she snapped, reaching over and switching off the radio. "You're not to touch things."

"I like music," Mairin said. "Don't you like music?"

"There'll be a hymn at morning prayers," Bernadette said.

Mairin rolled her eyes. "Not that kind of music. I mean the kind that makes you want to sing along or get up and dance."

"We don't do that here."

"Why not?"

"We do the Lord's work."

"What, this?" Mairin wandered over to the small secretary desk in the corner with Bernadette's ledger books. "The Lord wants you to do this?" She flipped open the top book and glanced at the pages. "He wants you to keep track of all the money you make from forcing us to work?"

"Oh, Ruth. You have so much to learn."

"Yeah? Well, I already know this isn't a school, no matter how much you pretend it is," Mairin said.

"This is a place of learning," Bernadette countered.

"Sure. So, when do we go to science class? Would that be before or after English class?"

"That kind of attitude will get you another visit to the closet," Bernadette warned her.

"So you're going to report me? Send me back in there?"

"I could if you force me to take measures."

Mairin studied her through narrowed eyes. "What's your name?" she asked.

"I am Sister Bernadette. You're supposed to address me as 'Mother.'"

"You don't look old enough to be anyone's mother. How old are you, anyway?"

"That's an impertinent question."

"So what is it?" Mairin persisted. "I mean your real name. Before you came here."

Genesee. "That girl no longer exists." Bernadette would never stop being grateful for shedding the name like an ill-fitting garment.

"Well, *I'm* not going to cease to exist just because I'm forced to be here," Mairin said. "My father chose my name—Mairin Patricia O'Hara—and I mean to keep it proudly all my life."

"Your father brought you here for your own redemption," Bernadette reminded the girl. She felt confident dealing with this strong-willed girl. She'd encountered this scene many times with previous girls. Bernadette had gone down this path before with girls emerging from the closet. She used to be intimidated by the defiant ones until she realized their defiance came from fear.

"That person was not my father," Mairin snapped. "My father was Patrick O'Hara, and he died five years ago. Colm Davis is a creep. He and my mother brought me here because he's too creepy for me to live with."

Bernadette couldn't stifle a sudden sweep of sympathy. In the Before Time, Genesee had encountered the kind of creepy men she knew Mairin was talking about. She wanted to tell the girl that it was pointless to rebel. She wanted to tell her that there was a way to find peace within oneself, as she had done, through obedience and submission. Bernadette was just eighteen, but she had been here long enough to find grace in the hard lessons a girl had to learn at the Good Shepherd. "I'm very sorry for your loss," she said softly.

Mairin studied her with a probing stare. "You know, it's almost worse that you're trying to be nice to me. Why not just be the monster you know you are?"

Bernadette gasped, feeling a flash of temptation to send the girl back to the closet. She closed her eyes and took a breath, reaching for grace and forbearance. Then she opened her eyes and held Mairin's gaze. "Believe me, the monsters are outside," she said. "At least in here, behind these walls, you're safe."

Chapter 7

Angela Denny could have predicted Mairin O'Hara's failed escape attempt. She, too, had once tried to run away from the Good Shepherd, bolting in a blind panic and being reeled in like a lake trout on a fishing line, her fingernails broken and bloodied from trying to scale the wall, her clothes ripped, elbows and ass bruised from the fall. Lots of girls made the attempt, reckless in their desperation to escape. And they all ended up like Mairin—with a stint in the closet and a walk of shame to the shared dormitory on the third floor, where each girl was assigned a cot with a thin mattress on a metal frame. Every night after evening prayers, they were forced to bless their captors; then the lights went out, the iron gate closed, and the shadows rolled in.

Mairin had returned from her confinement more watchful, but not defeated. There was a certain swagger to her gait, and she held her chin high with an air of unmasked anger. She quickly made a presence of herself in the unit, a natural leader. She managed to find ways to distract everyone from their grim reality now and then. She organized kickball games in the yard, and convinced Odessa to teach the girls to sing in harmony when they could get away with it. Odessa's favorite spiritual was "Oh Happy Day," and in the noisy calendar room, they could shout it to the rooftops, hiding the joyful noise beneath the clash of machinery.

Yet no one's spirits stayed lifted for long. Each night, a cloud of whispers bloomed in the darkness, punctuated by sniffles of fear and sorrow.

But the cloud usually dissipated quickly, because everyone was exhausted by the day's toil. Sometimes Janice, who was the worst tattletale in the group, would threaten to take names and tell Sister Rotrude. Or when a girl's muffled sobs could be heard, Denise might tease her, because Denise was just flat-out mean. Sometimes she even teased Kay, calling her a retard and making fun of her speech impediment. Kay had never done anything wrong, yet she would probably spend her whole life here, because she would never be able to live on her own. The nuns of the Good Shepherd were supposed to be preparing the girls for independent living when they reached eighteen, but what they actually did was make them scared to face the world.

Lately, Angela could barely keep her eyes open once her head hit the limp, inadequate pillow. The work was the same, day in and day out, and the stress of ducking the attention of the nuns and the doctor never varied, but the exhaustion seemed to settle into her very bones and muscles with a vengeance, making her feel ill with the yearning for sleep.

And yet she couldn't sleep. The silence of the room echoed with the hushed breathing that sounded to Angela like the girls' collective longing for freedom. She lay still, trying to convince her bladder that it wasn't full yet again. Hadn't she just gone before bedtime?

Scooping her thin nightgown around her, she slipped from the bed and tiptoed to the door, bracing herself for the blast of cold in the long hallway to the bathroom. She passed the stairs, which were closed off at the top by a locked floor-to-ceiling gate. The cold, gray walls of this place looked ancient. She imagined the stones had been silent witnesses to the stories of the broken souls of the girls forced to live here. The wayward girls, they were termed in the printed literature the nuns had given her grandmother. Gran had been promised that Angela would find guidance and solace here. That she would turn from her sinful ways and one day bask in the glow of redemption.

Gran had believed every word of it.

Under the stark glare of buzzing fluorescent lights, the bathroom reeked of harsh, pine-scented cleaner. The girls were required to scrub the toilets and sinks and shower room with the stuff every day. The resin smell assaulted Angela, and she staggered to the john, nearly overcome by nausea. As soon as she sat down to pee, she leaned forward and upchucked her dinner, splattering it on the floor in front of her.

"Oh, shit," she said. "Oh shit shit shit." She went to the cleaning closet, which smelled even stronger of the pine solution, and heaved again, hitting the mop bucket. Jesus, the food here was terrible, but this was the first time it had poisoned her. She rinsed herself off at the sink, then went to clean up the mess. The puke made her want to puke again, and she gasped, trying to tamp down the nausea.

When she was younger and felt sick, Gran would put a cold compress on her forehead and give her soda crackers and ginger ale to settle her stomach. But that was before Gran had caught her and Tanya McDowd, and all hell had broken loose. Gran acted as if Angela had turned into some kind of demon, and she'd dragged her to the Good Shepherd, totally convinced that the nuns would sort her out with their relentless program of work and repentance.

The trouble was the only thing that sorted Angela out was being with Tanya. She craved the quiet acceptance she felt when Tanya was with her. She cherished the feeling that every secret she'd ever had was held safely in a box, and only she and Tanya possessed the key. In those moments, Angela held fast to the knowledge that she wasn't crazy. The rest of the time, she felt like a total freak.

And now she was forced to have those horrible special corrective sessions with the doctor, and she had to do extra penance every Saturday. This failed to sort her out the way the nuns said it would. It messed her up even more.

So no. Gran would probably say that Angela was sick because the devil inside her was trying to get out. She'd relate some old Irish folktale about it. Gran did love her Irish folktales. When Angela was little, she'd snuggle under the covers and shiver with delight when Gran told her the tales of Finn McCool and King Mongan of Ulster, where Gran was from. Gran had never learned to read and write, but she could spin a tale that held Angela in its embrace until she fell asleep.

Angela used to try to do everything right. She got good grades in school. Worked hard in gym class and volunteered at the library. Kept her room tidy, went to mass every Sunday. She did her best at all things, but her best was never enough—not enough for Gran to trust that she wouldn't turn out like her mother, and not enough to quiet the confusing feelings that had started bubbling up inside her.

Before all the trouble started, Angela and Gran would go to the library together, because even though she couldn't read, Gran loved to page through *Life* magazine and look at the knitting patterns in *McCall's*. Angela was allowed to pick out any book she wanted. Miss Rachel Adler, the librarian who had a fancy name plaque on her desk, loved to introduce Angela to new books. When she found just the right book, Angela felt as if she was about to go on a journey to a new world. Miss Adler took her through pioneer days with *Caddie Woodlawn* and *Little House on the Prairie*, to New York City with *Harriet the Spy*, and into the past with *Anne of Green Gables* and *Little Women*.

Miss Adler was observant; she once said she owed her survival to being watchful and being able to read people and see what they were thinking. Angela wasn't sure what she meant by that, but she knew the library was a refuge for her.

Miss Adler had a sixth sense about books and readers. At least that was what Angela believed, anyway. The small, intense woman knew what someone was looking for, sometimes even before they did. That surely was the case when Miss Adler had introduced Angela to a book that had changed everything.

It was a tattered, yellowing paper-bound novel that had been preserved with a special library binding. The cover showed a tall, handsome girl with a suitcase, standing on a street corner. *Beebo Brinker*. Beebo was complicated and funny, brave and bold, a girl who knew what she wanted and found a way to go after it. For the first time, Angela recognized something in herself in the story. It was a revelation to meet a fictional character who reflected her own confusing emotions. Bit by bit, the world came into focus. Eventually, Angela collected all of the Beebo Brinker Chronicles—a world of dark-eyed women with sharp cheekbones and short-cropped hair, and dreamy independent women who discovered that they could survive a broken heart. Angela and Tanya took turns reading the books aloud to each other, and sometimes it led to them fooling around.

She found out something about Miss Adler's history, too, during a special program she gave one night. She announced that it was Yom HaShoah—Holocaust Remembrance Day, which no one in Catholic school seemed to know anything about. Miss Adler stood at the lectern and rolled up the sleeve of her pink cardigan sweater and held up her right arm and showed them a fading bruise.

It wasn't a bruise, she explained.

Then she read an excerpt from a book called *Night* by Elie Wiesel.

That was the day Angela learned that there were harder things in life than being a girl who liked girls.

When Gran discovered the Beebo books under Angela's bed, she'd taken them straight down to the furnace in the basement and tossed them in with the coals.

These days, Angela lived for the visit from the library bookmobile. Once a month, a van with the library logo rolled into the yard. Each girl was allowed to choose one book. The driver would take the books to the main office, where the selections would be scrutinized by Sister Rotrude and Sister Bernadette. The bookmobile wasn't the same as the leisurely hours Angela used to spend at Miss Adler's branch library, but it was a temporary escape from this place.

Moving slowly with a weariness that made her feel as old as her Gran, Angela finished cleaning and rinsed the mop, still gulping air and trying to stave off more heaves of sickness. Losing the battle, she lunged for the toilet and spewed a trickle of fluid, amazed that there was anything left. She'd never puked so much in her life. Maybe she was dying. Maybe she was—

"Hey," said a soft voice behind her. "Hey, Angela."

It was Mairin, the new girl. She held out a wad of brown paper towels, the kind that were so rough they had flecks of wood in them.

Angela shuddered and wiped her mouth, then threw away the paper towels and washed up again.

"Come sit," said Mairin, leading her over to a bench in the locker area. "You want a drink of water?"

Angela nodded. Mairin gave her a Dixie cup and she took a couple of tiny sips. She stared at the floor, feeling the tingle of a tear trying to squeeze out.

Mairin reached out and tentatively stroked Angela's hair. "I love your hair," she said.

"Yeah?" Angela tried to smile.

"It's silky soft. Blond as corn silk, my mom would say. It reminds me of those ads for Breck shampoo, you know the ones I mean?"

Angela felt a nudge of surprise. A long time ago, she'd started collecting the Breck Girl ads from the library's discarded copies of *Ladies' Home Journal*. Angela used to tear them out and keep them in a tattered old school binder, and sometimes she'd sit for hours, paging through the softly drawn pictures, wondering who the girls were, if they were real, or if they just came from an artist's imagination. When she was younger, Angela hadn't understood why she had gotten such a warm, squishy feeling from looking at the pastel-toned, flawless faces and flowing hair.

"Yeah, I always liked those ads." She let a bit more water trickle down her throat and turned to study Mairin. She had the looks to go with her big personality—curly red hair and freckles, green eyes that crinkled at the edges when she smiled. An Irish sprite in one of Gran's folktales.

Mairin tilted her head and frowned a little. "What?"

"What do you mean, what?"

"You're looking at me in a funny way."

"I don't mean to stare. I'm not trying to be rude," Angela said.

"Oh no, I didn't mean you were being rude, but . . . I don't know. I guess, just . . . it's been a long time since I've made a new friend."

"We're not supposed to make friends in this place," Angela said. "But in the middle of the night, who'll know, right? They do bed checks every once in a while, but you can hear when they open the gate at the top of the stairs, because it squeaks." She already knew she and Mairin didn't like each other in *that* way, but in the way of regular friends. "Where're you from? Someplace around here?"

"Fruit Belt neighborhood," Mairin said. "Before this, I never went to any school except St. Wilda's."

"You're a Fruit Belt girl. A St. Wilda's girl. What's that like?"

Mairin described a neighborhood that sounded a lot like the street where Angela had grown up in South Buffalo. Row houses with peeling paint and too many kids, women in kerchiefs and housedresses sitting on the stoop, smoking Lark cigarettes and gossiping.

"None of the girls here come from the rich neighborhoods," Angela said. "You know the area around Millionaires' Row?"

"Delaware Avenue? I used to take walks there with my dad. And when my brother was teaching me to drive, we would go there and check out how the fancy folks live."

Angela did the same thing on her bike rides. A neighbor had given her a hand-me-down Schwinn Panther that she rode everywhere. The bike had a boy's crossbar and a back fender that rattled when she pedaled over the brick streets, but it took her on brilliant rides all over the city. In school, she'd learned that Buffalo once had more millionaires per capita than any city in America, back in the 1800s. Some of the gorgeous stone mansions still stood like monuments surrounded by grand gardens and wrought iron fences.

"You know how to drive?" Angela asked. "How old are you?"

"Not quite sixteen yet, but Liam wanted to teach me before he left. He's . . . My brother got drafted. He's going through basic training now. You have a brother?"

Angela shook her head. "It's just me and my gran. My mom went to California years ago. She keeps saying she's going to send for me, but she never has." Gran had nothing good to say about Angela's mother. Angela had sent letter after letter to California, but the address kept changing. So did the phone number. There had been a phone call last Christmas, but since then . . . nothing.

"I hate it here," Mairin said. "I'm going to run away, and I'll make it this time. Just you watch."

"Sure, I'll watch. Lots of us try to run. It never works. The family always brings them back, or social services gets an order from the juvie court, or they come back on their own because, believe it or not, there are worse places than this."

"Then we just . . . what? Wait here until they let us go? I can't. I absolutely can't." Mairin's chin trembled and her voice broke. She drew her knees up to her chest and dropped her head as her whole body shook with sobs.

"Mairin, shh," said Angela, placing her hand on the other girl's back. It rattled her to see Mairin like this. She was usually the strong one.

Mairin drew in a breath with a shudder and lifted her head. "I can't take it here. I can't. I don't even know where Liam is right now, but pretty soon he'll be in Vietnam. I'm so scared for him, Angela. He's the best brother in the world. What if he gets hurt over there? Or killed?"

"It would be the worst thing ever," Angela said, picturing the lanky young men she used to see in the papers every day, weary-looking guys with peace signs drawn on their helmets and guns slung across their bodies. "I'm sorry he had to go."

"I don't even know what's going on. Another awful thing about this place. They cut us off from the world. We can't even watch Walter Cronkite."

"We're allowed to write letters on Sunday afternoon. Can you write a letter to your brother?"

Mairin wadded up the hem of her nightgown and dried her cheeks. "I suppose it's something. I'll give it a try."

Angela ached for her new friend, but something urgent was happening. She shot to her feet as a fresh surge of nausea erupted like a volcano. She made it to the toilet and sank to her knees, then heaved until the spewing stopped. Mairin gently lifted her hair and held it back.

"Hey, did you eat something bad?" Mairin asked.

"Same as what everyone else ate," Angela said.

Mairin gently touched her forehead. "You don't feel hot. Why do you reckon you're puking?"

Angela shrugged her shoulders. "I don't know. I had the flu last year, but this doesn't feel like the flu."

They sat quietly for a few minutes. "My best friend's name is Fiona," Mairin said. "I miss her like crazy. You got a best friend?"

Angela wiped her mouth and climbed wearily to her feet. "Name's Tanya. I miss *her* like crazy."

"Fiona had to go away," Mairin said. "She's staying with her aunt in Pennsylvania. For a bit."

Something in Mairin's tone caught at Angela. A dull thud of dread started throbbing in her chest. "Had to go away" was code for a situation everyone understood. "Oh," she said. "That's too bad."

"Let's go sit down again," said Mairin, gesturing at the shower bench. "You look really green around the gills." She studied Angela's face with those soft, probing eyes. "Um, when, uh, when was the last time you had your period?"

Angela flinched as if something sharp had poked her. *Nine weeks ago.* Clocks and calendars were forbidden here, but Angela had etched the date on her soul.

"Sorry, I'm not trying to be nosy," Mairin said.

"You're not being nosy," Angela said. "It's . . . I skipped a period."

Mairin pressed her lips together. Her gaze shifted back and forth, then settled on Angela's hands, which were pressed against her stomach. "Could you be . . . I mean, I'm thinking about my friend Fiona. She and her boyfriend went all the way, you know? They did it a *lot*. She got really sick and then . . . I'm just wondering . . . maybe you're pregnant? Maybe you and your boyfriend—"

"I don't have a boyfriend," Angela blurted out.

Mairin's eyes widened, and she studied Angela's face. "You're so pretty. I figured someone as pretty as you would have all kinds of boys to choose from."

"I've not touched a boy," Angela said. *Not on purpose, anyway.* "I've never really been into boys." Her face felt as if it were melting under streams of tears. "But . . ."

"But you missed a period," Mairin whispered, taking her hand.

Angela nodded, unable to speak.

"So if you weren't with your boyfriend, maybe there's some other explanation. And I'm not talking about the immaculate conception."

Angela didn't want to explain. She had spent weeks trying not to think about what was happening to her.

"You don't have to tell me if you don't want to," said Mairin, "and I sure as heck won't snitch on you. But . . . Okay, I haven't said anything about the reason my mom made me come here. It's because of her husband—my stepfather, Colm. He–he tried to grab me—not in a nice way, you know."

Angela did know what *not in a nice way* meant. She flinched, nodding her head.

"I was alone in my room, getting changed," said Mairin. "I hate to think about what might have happened if Liam hadn't shown up and run him off. All I'm saying is that even though you don't like a guy doesn't mean he'll leave you alone." Mairin swallowed audibly. "I know that now. Did some guy ... um ... make you do something, even though you didn't want him to?"

Angela said nothing for a few seconds. She could hear her pulse hammering in her ears, as loud as fear. "It wasn't a boy."

Mairin's eyes flashed with comprehension, and maybe anger. "A man, then? Like, a grown man? You really don't have to tell me, but—"

Angela stared at the tile pattern on the shower floor. "Wh-when you got here, did you have to go to the clinic?"

She saw comprehension dawn on Mairin's face. "Oh, jeez. Yeah. That big nun—Rotrude—told me it was for my own good. In case I have a disease or something. The doctor said he's supposed to do a checkup to make sure I'm healthy, but he was weird, and I wouldn't let him touch me."

Angela stifled a soft gasp. "What do you mean, you wouldn't *let* him?"

"Just that. I shoved him away from me and beat it out of there. I tried to tell Rotrude that he was weird, but ... I don't know. She seemed to think it was just normal, and she refused to listen when I tried to tell her. She whacked me across the face for even bringing it up. So did they make you go to the clinic, too?"

Angela flinched as if something had stabbed her, and turned her head away. "They make everybody go."

"Well, I'll never set foot in that place again, that's for sure," said Mairin. Then she laid her hand over Angela's. "So. The doctor."

"Yes." Angela's lips barely moved. The word was an exhalation of horror.

Mairin's hand tightened around Angela's. "The one here, at the Good Shepherd?" she asked. "Dr. Gilroy?"

Angela didn't answer. She didn't have to. Mairin's expressive eyes darted back and forth with worry.

"That creep," said Mairin. "That horrible, vile creep."

Angela had been told that she needed special help with her situation, and they kept making her go back to the clinic. And she would obey, slinking in shame. Gilroy said he could cure her of her problem. Her mouth felt dry. She took another tiny sip from the little paper cup, which was getting soggy. "Did he try to make you do stuff?" she asked Mairin.

The other girl's expression went hard, and her eyes squinted with contempt. "'Do stuff'? I didn't stick around long enough to find out. He told me to get up on the table. He was going to try something. I could just tell. I told him to leave me alone. He grabbed me, and . . . well, I'm not exactly sure what he was going to do. I fought him off and got the hell out of there. No way I'm going back."

When Angela was at the clinic, she was always too terrified to move. Even to breathe. She just squeezed her eyes shut and clenched her teeth and prayed for it to be over. "You fought him?"

"I did. My brother Liam taught me how to fight." Her gaze went soft again as she studied Angela. "I think that doctor must have . . . He did something to you."

Angela closed her eyes. Nodded her head. "He keeps making me come back. Says he's helping me with . . . He said I have a problem, you know, down there."

"Oh, Angela." Mairin's arms went around her, folding her into a gentle hug.

The sweetness of the hug was searing, almost more unbearable than a slap.

Then Mairin said, "Angela. Did he do . . . I mean, what did he do to you?"

She kept her eyes shut tight, the way she did in the clinic. "He, um, he said he had to do an examination, and he put something up inside me, like an instrument, I guess. And then his—his fingers. And then . . . his *thing*."

Mairin gasped and squeezed her hand. "No doctor would do that. Did you tell someone?"

Angela opened her eyes. "Of course I did. Told Rotrude and Sister Gerard. They gave me extra penance and told me I should be grateful that he's *helping* me."

"Well, now you have to tell them you might be pregnant. Because I really think... that might be the case."

Angela's voice dropped to a whisper. "Oh, dear God, no," she said. "I can't... no."

But she could feel the truth welling up through her entire body, spilling out through her eyes. There was not a *no* powerful enough to make it not be so.

Chapter 8

Dear Liam,

I don't know if you'll ever get this letter, but I hope you do. I memorized your APO address and I'm allowed to write one letter per week. After you went off to basic training, a horrible thing happened. Mam made me come to live at the Good Shepherd down on Best Street, you know the place where bad girls are sent. I always thought Mam was all talk when she threatened to send me here, but here I am.

On the very first day, the nuns gave me a fake name and a number, like they're trying to erase who I really am. It's like I'm nothing. Nobody.

This place is a nightmare. All day long, we're under the eye of the nuns and laywomen (called consecrates, whatever that is) who run the place. I'm either totally scared or totally mad all the time. Every day starts with this really loud bell. The old plaster hallways are like echo chambers, and the noise hurts my ears. We have to get up and go to the shower room, which is just a big room with showers, lockers, and toilet stalls. There's no such thing as a hot shower. The nuns and sometimes the senior girls stand around, giving us no privacy.

The prioress, Sister Gerard, does morning announcements over the PA system, starting with "Blessed be to God." She sounds really nice on purpose, like she's some old-time radio announcer. Then the iron gate at the top of the dormitory unit is opened and we have to go to chapel.

There are more than a hundred girls here. We eat in a big hall at long tables. The food is really bad—tasteless oatmeal, soup, stale bread, mystery meat—but I'm usually so hungry, I eat everything on my plate. Somebody reads scripture from a lectern. No one is allowed to talk unless one of the nuns rings a bell or claps her hands. Think of it, Liam, a bell. Like we're a pack of trained dogs or something. We whisper to each other all the time, but if we get caught, we get a smack with a ruler or rosary belt, or they pull our hair really hard.

I'm getting to know a few of the girls. Some of them are in even worse trouble than I am. We have to be careful about looking like we're friends, because if the nuns suspect anything, they're likely to separate us into different dorm units.

The nuns are everywhere, ordering us around, making us work at the commercial laundry. My hands are all chapped and burned by the steam. We have to stand for hours, and it makes my back ache. When we're not in the laundry, they make us do other chores, like polishing the woodwork, scrubbing the floors, cleaning the halls and bathrooms, weeding or harvesting in the garden. We get kitchen duty on rotation, where we do dishes for hours. There's an altar bread room for making hosts for the entire parish, and a sewing room where we have to work on mending.

Sister R is the worst, but they're all terrible. Sometimes I think the nuns might be from a different species, because they're so rigid. It's like they can't allow themselves to unbend the least little bit, because that might force them to actually look at what they're doing. They might have to realize that they're hurting the girls they're supposed to be helping.

I try to take on the outdoor chores, because just for those few moments, I get to breathe. We grow autumn squash and potatoes and beans. Sometimes I can sneak an apple when no one's looking. Sister T is mean but not too bright, and I figured out that if I pretend to hate being outside, she'll pick me to work in the yard or on the drying lines, pegging out the laundry or bringing it in.

Every once in a while, we get to play kickball in the yard. As you can imagine, I'm always on the winning team. And at night in the shower room we started a club, inspired by you. I've been practicing self-defense, just like you taught me, and I showed one of the girls how it's done. And this other girl—her parents are under arrest in China—is really smart. She speaks Chinese. Are you going to learn the language in Vietnam? Oh, and a girl called Odessa is teaching us to sing Gospel spirituals. She is an amazing singer, and she's teaching us how to harmonize. I wish you could hear us.

I'm learning other things, too, Liam. Like how to be invisible and avoid the darting eyes of the senior girls, the lay workers, and the nuns. How to talk to another girl without seeming to move my lips. How to pocket stray beans and apples and hickory nuts from the garden to eat later.

Now that it's getting colder outside, it's getting worse inside. Cleaning the front office is the best chore in the winter, because at least it's warm there. I'm cold all the time and all I can think about is getting away. There are these high walls topped with coils of barbed wire. It's not actually barbed, but razor wire. The kind that slices your flesh to ribbons if you touch it.

It's hard to believe that outside these walls, it's still 1968 and the world is still turning. Because in here, nothing ever changes.

When there's an infraction, like the first time I tried to run away, they send you to the closet. It's so scary in there, Liam, dark as night. When I'm in there, it feels like I'm living in a nightmare, only I'm awake. My heart pounds and I can barely breathe. It almost feels like drowning. I've been trying to keep my head down and obey—for now. But it's not going to stop me from trying again. I swear it's not.

I hope you get this letter, Liam, wherever you are. I hope you write me back. I miss you so bad, and I pray every day that you're staying safe.

Your sister,
Mairin Patricia O'Hara

Mairin lay on her narrow bed, the weight of the day's labor still pressing on her. The room was filled with the soft sounds of sleeping girls, punctuated by the creak of the old building settling. She stared at the cracked ceiling, trying to steer her mind somewhere else, anywhere but here.

A faint rustling sounded in the next cot. She propped herself up on one elbow and saw Kay crouched beside the wall, illuminated by streaks of light from the stairwell. Kay was often lost in her own world, but tonight she seemed focused, her movements careful and deliberate. She reached into her apron pocket and pulled out a bit of bread. She held it up to a crevice in the wall, her expression mild with gentle anticipation. A few seconds later, a mouse emerged, sniffing the air tentatively before darting forward to grab the morsel. Kay's face lit up with pure, unguarded joy.

Mairin's heart ached at the bond between the girl and the little creature. Moments of happiness were fleeting here. She knew Kay's secret was a dangerous one. The nuns would never allow such a thing, Mairin thought with a quick intake of breath.

Kay glanced up, her eyes meeting Mairin's. For a moment, fear flickered in her gaze, but Mairin gave a reassuring nod and pressed a finger to her lips. Kay did the same, then mouthed a happy "okey dokey." Then she relaxed and continued to offer crumbs to her tiny friend.

Mairin silently vowed to protect Kay's secret. In this place, tenderness was precious and worth safeguarding. She turned over, pulling her blanket tight, and closed her eyes, holding on to the warmth of Kay's small act of kindness.

"RUTH. *RUTH.*" THROUGH the thin blanket, someone gave her foot a shake. "You slept through matins again. Get *up.*"

Mairin had to work hard to remember who she was. That was one of the worst things about this place—it was like they wanted her to forget, with their endless routines and rules. Sleep was her only refuge, the only time she could visit the girl she used to be—Mairin O'Hara, who was good at sports, who liked school, loved her friends, and missed her mother's cooking. She drew up the covers with a quiet "Go 'way."

"Get up," said the voice again. "How can you sleep through the bell?"

Denise. Her blunt voice broke through the last vestiges of sleep.

Mairin pushed herself up. "Don't call me Ruth," she grumbled.

There were some papers on the bed covered in her handwriting. A large red X was marked across each page.

"Hey," she said. "That's my letter to my brother."

"What, you thought they'd let you write the truth about this place?" Denise asked with a sneer. "Fat chance."

"They were supposed to put it in the mail. My brother's a soldier. He's going to Vietnam."

"Try writing about how nice it is here and how you're learning new skills every day and getting closer to God. Try that, and they'll let you send it."

Mairin glared at the other girl. "Thanks for the advice."

Denise glared back. "Anything for a friend."

They weren't friends. But there were little cliques and factions of girls in all the dormitories, same as there were at any school. Denise surrounded herself with girls who egged her on when she was being mean, and snickered at the chosen victim. Janice had a small crew of nosy gossips—the Snitches, Helen Mei called them. Most girls were more like Mairin, wary and resigned, trying to drag themselves from one day to the next while keeping their thoughts to themselves.

To stave off the monotony, Mairin lingered over memories of the ordinary days she'd taken for granted, and the dreams she'd once held. Here, she had no identity other than *Ruth* and some number that had been assigned to her. She was nothing. Nobody. No one cared that she could climb to the top of any tree, or pick a bushel of apples in record time, or grow the best tomatoes of summer, or drive a car with a stick shift. No one cared that she'd read *Johnny Tremain* three times, or that she'd memorized every song on the *White Album*, or that she always passed the Presidential Physical Fitness Test on the first try.

Did she hate her mother for sending her to this place? She didn't. She couldn't. The truth was, she missed Mam in ways that just hollowed her out. She'd give anything to feel her mother's warm touch, soothing her like the heating pad Mam used to bring her when she had an earache.

Mairin and Angela Denny were getting to know each other in bits of stolen moments they snatched here and there. Angela was from the south side, raised by a strict Irish gran who truly believed the nuns could do no wrong. As bad as this situation was for Mairin, things were a million times worse for Angela on account of her being pregnant.

The doctor had targeted Angela, probably because she was so incredibly pretty. According to Angela, Gilroy claimed that he had to monitor some made-up "condition" her grandmother believed she had. Angela had whispered to Mairin that the doctor either didn't know or didn't care that she was pregnant. When Angela told the nuns, they called her a liar. They accused her of sneaking around on high mass Sunday or with the delivery guys.

There was no special arrangement for pregnant girls in this place. If anything, they endured more than their share of teasing from some of the others, and were targets for contempt from the nuns and senior girls. The pregnant ones had to work until they were too big to waddle around the laundry and keep up with the others. Then they went to the charity ward of St. Francis and came back a couple of weeks later, deflated like punctured balloons.

Mairin was working the drying lines near Angela on a cold, blustery morning when Sister Theresa came over, ringing her bell. "Agnes," she yelled. "Agnes, you're due in the clinic right away."

Angela dropped what she was doing, and at the same moment, the color dropped from her face. She pulled in a shuddering breath. "I have to finish my chores, Mother."

"You can make up the work later," said the nun. "Hurry along now, Agnes. Mustn't keep the doctor waiting."

Mairin could feel Angela's anxiety like a blast of cold air. Her gut twisted in outrage. Angela refused to talk any more about what went on during her doctor visits, but Mairin imagined Gilroy forcing her to do things against her will. Until that night in the bathroom, Mairin had not fully understood how a girl actually got pregnant. Angela confessed that she hadn't known, either. It was a terrible way to find out about something that was supposed to be an act of love between a husband and wife.

She couldn't forget the way the strange doctor had looked at her on her first day, couldn't forget his thumb gently pressing against her lower lip, and his expression as he'd instructed her to get on the table. After Mairin had fought him off, she hadn't been summoned again, probably because the doctor was a coward at heart, preying on girls who didn't know how to fight back.

Seized by impulse, Mairin scanned the area to make sure no one was looking. Then, shielded by the long line of bedsheets pegged out to dry, she hurried to the door and slipped through, catching up with Angela, who was trudging along the corridor with her head down.

"I'm coming with you," Mairin said.

"What?" Angela looked around. Her face was nearly as pale as the stark white walls. "Coming where?"

"To the clinic."

"You can't do that. It's not allowed."

"Watch me." Mairin had no idea what she was signing up for, but she had to try to help. She could still picture the expression on Gilroy's face when she'd fought him off. He wasn't used to defiance. She'd resisted him once, and she could do it again.

Angela stopped walking and turned to Mairin, eyes wide and full of hope. "You'd do that? You'd come to the clinic with me?"

Mairin nodded. "Come on. I'll make sure he doesn't force you to have any more appointments with him."

They entered the small office together. It was just as Mairin remembered, stark and spotless, with a tidy desk and exam table. The crucifix that hung on the wall was now chipped, and there were cracks where the INRI banner had been glued back together. The instrument tray was laden with metal objects.

Mairin snatched up a pair of weird-looking bent scissors and slid them into her pocket.

"What are you doing?" Angela asked in a horrified whisper.

Mairin handed her a set of long tweezers. "Hide that in your smock."

"No! I can't—"

The door opened. Angela slid the tweezers into her pocket as the doctor stepped into the room. "Now, Agnes, I—" He broke off when he spied Mairin. She could tell from his expression that he remembered her. "What the devil are you doing here?"

"I am required to come with Agnes to all her appointments," she bluffed, hoping he couldn't tell how fast her heart was racing. "All of them, from now on. It's a new rule."

"That's nonsense. It's preposterous, and completely unnecessary."

"Oh yeah?" Mairin said. "How about we go check with Mother Superior about the new rule?"

"I shall indeed. I most certainly shall," he said, his neck turning red. The deep flush told Mairin exactly what she needed to know. He wasn't about to explain his shenanigans to Mother Superior.

"Okay, good," she said. "Want us to wait here, or are we dismissed?" She stood her ground, looking him straight in the eye.

He looked away first, casting a glance over his shoulder. Then he said, "Get back to work, both of you. Immediately."

The girls scrambled for the door and ran down the hall and out into the yard.

"Oh my God," Angela gasped, practically hyperventilating. "Oh my God, oh my God. What did you do?"

"Hang on to those tweezers," Mairin said. "I'll keep this thing, whatever it is. They might come in handy one day."

"Silence!" scolded a sharp voice. Sister Theresa, shaking her bell and the heavy rosary around her waist, surged toward them. "There is to be no talking! You know the rule."

"Yes, Mother." Mairin and Angela spoke in unison. Sister Theresa was dumber than a box of hair, and she loved it when girls bowed their heads and called her mother. Mairin lowered her eyes in humble deference and closed her hand around the cold metal tool in the pocket of her smock.

She and Angela kept their heads down and continued whispering together. Angela said, "They're going to make me give my baby to strangers."

Mairin gave a bleak nod, thinking of Fiona. "That seems to be how it goes."

"They won't give me a choice. I mean, I can't imagine being some child's mother, but I can't *not* imagine it. The baby is part of me. But they're going to take him away and I'll never see him again."

"It's kind of what girls have to do," Mairin said. "Fiona—I told you about that. Her parents won't let her have any choice in the matter."

"They think a child growing up with two married parents will be better off," Angela said. "But look at me—my own mother was married, but she liked drinking and taking drugs so much that she took off, and I never saw her again. And still I survived that."

"You'd be a perfectly good mother," Mairin said.

"They won't even give me the chance."

Mairin shaded her eyes and watched a flock of migrating birds overhead. The sight filled her with the yearning to be free. This could be her moment to escape, she thought, eyeing the wall beyond the drying lines. She could do it. She could get out of here and not get caught.

Then she looked back at Angela and realized she couldn't abandon her. Angela was pregnant and terrified. No one would send her to a cookie-making aunt. She had to stay here. For now, anyway, Angela needed her more than she needed to escape.

"You shouldn't be talking to that one." Denise approached Mairin, holding a loaded basket from the shaking room.

Mairin frowned, her mouth full of clothespins. "Huh?"

Denise set down the basket with a *thud* and turned to Kay, who was behind her. "Get these things on the line, dipshit," she said to Kay.

"Okey dokey." Kay was almost always mild and compliant, and like most girls, she was afraid of Denise.

"Why should I stay away from Kay?" Mairin asked.

"Not the retard," Denise said, with a toss of her head. She had a presence that commanded attention, and a sneer that could freeze time. "That one." She jerked her head toward the end of the line, where Angela had resumed working.

Mairin folded a towel over the line and clipped on her pins. "She seems nice enough."

"Huh. Ask her why she was sent here."

"It's none of my business."

"I'll tell you why," Denise blustered. "Her nana caught her fooling around with a *girl*."

"I don't get it. What do you mean, fooling around?" Mairin fooled around with her friends all the time, laughing and goofing off. Playing records and arguing about whether John or Paul was the cutest Beatle. She missed those days with Fiona and her other school friends. She missed them like crazy.

Denise shook her head. "You don't know anything. I'm talking about her hugging and kissing and touching *down there*. Making out. Fooling around like normal girls do with boys."

"Oh, for Pete's sake. That's ridiculous." Mairin had never heard of such a thing. However, just because she'd never heard of it didn't mean it didn't exist. Not so very long ago, she'd never heard of a calendar roller iron, and now it was her daily chore.

"It's true. Once Angela got caught, her gran couldn't get rid of her fast enough. They're supposed to set her straight here."

"This place couldn't set anybody straight. Everything here is twisted," Mairin declared. "And so what if it is true about Angela? That's no reason not to talk to her."

"Suit yourself, loser." Denise offered an exaggerated shrug. "Maybe you can be her new girlfriend."

That made no sense at all to Mairin, but she dropped the subject, mainly because she didn't understand it. Kissing and making out with a girl? She couldn't imagine such a thing. But the truth was, she did like Angela. Not in the fooling-around-and-kissing way, but because Angela was sweet and caring and grateful for the smallest gesture. Angela had been the first one to offer a few words of kindness when Mairin had been thrust among them.

"So what are *you* in for?" she asked Denise, wanting to turn the subject.

"Go to hell." Denise stalked away.

I'm already there, thought Mairin, looking around the room.

"What were you two talking about?" Helen whispered, loading up a cart to take outside.

Mairin shrugged. "She's got nothing good to say about anybody. I don't know why we bother with her."

"True. But she's good at stealing from the kitchen, and sometimes she shares."

"Watch out," Angela whispered, coming up behind them. "Sister Theresa's in a rotten mood. Don't let her catch you talking. We've got bookmobile tomorrow, and I don't want her taking away our privileges."

"Thank God," said Mairin. "Being without a book is like starving."

"Don't get too excited," Helen warned. "The books are 'approved literature only' and they're dropped off at the front office. Then Rotrude goes through the material to make sure it's 'appropriate.' Sometimes we don't even get to read any of them. Sometimes we have to read stuff like *The Cardinal Virtues* or Augustine's *Confessions*." She shuddered with distaste.

Denise came out to the lines with another load. "You lot," she said, glaring at everyone. "Could you *be* any slower?"

Mairin wondered what had made Denise so bitter, so quick to say something cruel to another girl or to point the finger of blame at somebody. Denise was a master of deception, always plotting and scheming, and making sure someone other than her got in trouble. She was sneaky, like a shadow in the night, always one step ahead of the nuns.

"Stop talking," squawked Sister Theresa.

"I wasn't talking," Denise said, all innocence. "Ruth here keeps bugging me." She could twist the truth to suit her needs, leaving others in a state of confusion and doubt. "I was just trying to do my work."

"We'll see about that, missy." She grabbed a handful of Mairin's hair and twisted.

Mairin's temper exploded. "Leave me the hell alone, you old bitch." She pulled out the crooked scissors and was about to strike when Kay bustled over and leaped at Sister Theresa.

"Was not Mair'n!" yelled Kay. "D'nise did the talking. D'nise did the talking."

"We'll see about *that*." The nun's hand shot out and took hold of Kay's hair, which was caught back in a ponytail. The nun pulled so hard it drove Kay to the ground.

"Ow, ow, *ow*," Kay yelled, clawing at the woman's arm as she sank to her knees. "Hurts! That hurts!"

Denise melted away, always quick to avoid punishment.

"And what may I ask is *this?*" With one hand still clutching Kay's long, dark hair, Sister Theresa snatched up something from the lawn.

To Mairin's horror, it was the crooked scissors she'd stolen from the clinic. In the scuffle, the instrument must have fallen to the ground. The nun was regarding them with fury in her eyes. "Where did you get this?" she demanded of Kay.

"Dunno dunno dunno," Kay said desperately, her eyes darting in confusion. "Ow. *Ow.* You're hurtin' me!"

Sister Theresa marched toward the door, towing the girl along by the hair. Mairin charged after them. "Sister, it was me," she said. "I swear, Kay didn't have anything to do with this."

Kay was yelling so loudly that the nun didn't seem to hear. She pulled the girl into the laundry building and slammed the door behind her. Mairin tried to follow, but one of the lay supervisors stood in the way.

"Back to work," she ordered.

Mairin planted herself in front of the supervisor, an iron-haired woman with ruddy cheeks and a permanent scowl. "How can you stand there and let her do that?" she asked the woman.

"None of your lip," the supervisor said, "or I'll make a report."

Odessa stepped forward with a huge basket of folded linens. "Ready for inspection," she said, distracting the woman.

Mairin mouthed *Thank you* to Odessa and scurried away.

THAT NIGHT BEFORE supper, Kay was brought back from her punishment. As the girls assembled outside the refectory, Sister Rotrude thrust poor Kay forward. "This is what happens to someone who steals scissors."

In shock, Mairin gaped at Kay, who stood there, hanging her head in misery. Her long, glossy hair had been hacked off. Not cut with any skill, but just chopped haphazardly and probably dumped in the garbage. The back of her neck was starkly white where the shearing had exposed her skin. She looked fragile and diminished somehow, her dignity ripped away along with her hair.

"I'm going to say something," Mairin whispered to Angela as they marched in a line into the refectory. "I took the scissors. I'm the one they should have punished."

"Don't be an idiot," Angela said. "The damage is already done."

Mairin went over to Kay and took her hand. "Come and sit with me," she said.

"Okey dokey."

They set their trays at the end of one of the long tables. Supper was some kind of tasteless stew with bread. Apple cider to drink. It was delicious, but that wasn't the reason the nuns served it. The cider was free, pressed from the apples gathered from the trees on the property.

"I'm really sorry about what happened," Mairin said to Kay. "It's all my fault. I tried to speak up, but she dragged you away so fast. I'm sorry," she said again.

Kay nodded and ate her meal with mechanical motions. Denise sauntered by carrying her tray, her sharp-eyed gaze focused on Kay. Mairin could see that she was about to say something mean. She shot to her feet and planted herself between Denise and Kay.

A few of the other girls nearby stopped eating and leaned forward. No one was supposed to confront Denise.

"Just move along," Mairin said through her teeth, trying not to be intimidated by the older girl's size and presence. "She's had more than enough today."

Denise narrowed her eyes. "She's just a moron. Doesn't even know what's going on. She's stupid enough to be friends with you."

"Listen, it's horrible here for all of us," Mairin said. "What's the point of making it even more horrible?"

"You don't know shit," Denise said.

Mairin's hands hardened into fists. "Are we going to have a problem, Denise?"

"No talking," roared one of the nuns from the raised dais.

Denise curled her lip into a sneer and walked slowly to another table.

THANKS TO KAY'S "infraction," the girls were sent straight to their beds that night. Mairin pulled the coarse blanket around her shoulders and shuddered, hearing Sister Theresa's footsteps bonging on the metal stairs.

Kay was once again kneeling by the wall, offering her tiny mouse friend a stolen morsel from supper. Over time, she had managed to train the creature to crawl into the palm of her hand. She seemed oblivious to the approaching nun, who was armed with a bucket and a broom.

"Heads up," Mairin hissed.

Kay hid the mouse in the pocket of her smock.

"What do you think you're doing, girl?" Sister Theresa strode over to Kay. "I've been watching you, and I know what you're up to. Take that filthy creature out of your pocket right this instant."

Kay froze, and the color drained from her face. "I . . . I . . . I . . ."

Theresa plunged her hand into Kay's pocket. In a swift movement, she seized the mouse and dropped it into the bucket.

"No! No!" Kay's voice cracked with desperation.

"Sister, please," Mairin said, jumping up. Janice did the same, jamming her glasses on her face.

Theresa ignored them both. With swift strides, she went to the bathroom. A moment later, they heard a flushing sound. It was nearly drowned out by Kay's anguished sobs as she collapsed to the floor, her body racked with grief.

Janice rushed to Sister Theresa as the nun exited the bathroom. "How could you?" Janice demanded. "You're supposed to be a woman of God, but all you are is cruel."

Without a word, Sister Theresa grabbed Janice by the arm. Her other hand lashed out, cracking across Janice's face and sending her glasses flying. Then the nun switched off the lights and left the dormitory, causing the gate to clang behind her.

The uneasy quiet was broken only by Kay's muffled weeping.

Mairin seethed. She would never be able to assuage Kay's sorrow, but she thought of something they could do. She passed the word through the unstoppable whispering network that circulated through the halls of the Good Shepherd. The nuns thought they could control every aspect of the girls' lives, but they couldn't control their thoughts. Not everyone's thoughts, anyway. Some girls were inexplicably convinced that the nuns were right—that this was a place where their sins would be washed away so long as they practiced blind obedience.

Mairin would never believe that, not about herself, or about any girl here, even the mean ones, or the ones who came from terrible circumstances.

An hour after lights-out and lockdown, Kay had cried herself to sleep. Mairin went quietly to the bathroom. Helen followed her readily enough. A few others trailed along, tentative and curious—Angela and Odessa. Even Denise and her gang, and Janice, her cheek now bruised from the slap, joined them.

They huddled in the shower room, and Mairin took out a pair of scissors. "I swiped this from the sewing room," she said. "I say we all cut off our hair to protest what they did to Kay."

"No way," Denise said. "You're crazy."

Mairin glared at her. "You ought to go first," she said. "It's your fault they did that to Kay." She noticed a subtle flicker in Denise's hard gaze. "Or are you chicken?"

"Hell, no. It's . . . just a stupid idea," Denise said.

"How many times have the nuns pulled our hair?" Odessa asked. "Think about that."

A few heads nodded. Hair-pulling was a favorite technique of the nuns.

"If we cut off our hair, they won't have anything to yank on," Helen pointed out.

"Exactly," said Mairin. "Besides, it'll mean less time in the cold showers, right?"

That got a couple of nods. There was no hot water for the residents here, and washing in the cold water was excruciating. With that, she grabbed a handful of her own hair and twisted it. Then she took a deep breath and cut it off, letting the long red locks drop softly to the concrete floor of the shower room.

A few gasps rose from the girls. Mairin felt a thrum of defiance in her gut. She used to be self-conscious about her fiery red hair, but her mother had convinced her that it was pretty. Mam used to brush it out in the morning, and she'd say, "The Lord gave you red hair so I could have roses in winter."

It'll be pretty again one day, Mam. Mairin didn't need pretty hair now, not in this place. Not if it gave the nuns something to grab and twist when they wanted to punish her.

"Help me out," she said, handing the scissors to Denise. She knew that if she could convince Denise, plenty of others would go along. "It's hard to do this on myself."

Denise hesitated just for a second, then gave a shrug. "Suit yourself. I have no idea how to cut somebody's hair." Then Denise pushed up the sleeves of her nightgown and brandished the scissors.

"I'm sure you'll figure it out," Mairin said. "You're good at cutting things." As Denise went to work, Mairin noticed a scar on her inner arm. "What's that?" she asked.

"What's what?"

"On your arm. That scar. Are those... letters?"

Denise paused and turned it so she could see. "My name," she said. "They took it away from me when I got here, so I scratched it into my arm with a sewing needle."

Mairin shuddered. "Well, that's ... it's really brave, Denise. It must have hurt like crazy."

Another shrug. "I can deal with that kind of hurt."

"What happened to you?" Angela asked in a low whisper.

"None of your damn beeswax, that's what happened." She snipped off a hunk of Mairin's hair.

"Denise, you can tell us." Angela's voice was gently insistent. "Was it the doctor?"

Denise pressed her lips together. Then she said, "The priest. The one who's supposed to wash away all our sins. And just so you know, I won't speak of it again. Ever." She punctuated the statement with a final snip of the scissors. "Who's next?"

As Mairin fluffed her hands through what was left of her hair, she felt a surge of sympathy for Denise. The girl's hurt was buried in all the things she *didn't* say, and it came out in the urge to lash out at others.

Since there were no mirrors in the building, Mairin had no idea how her hair looked, but the horror on some of the girls' faces was a clue. Without her hair, she felt naked, and light as air. "Come on," she said. "If we get in trouble, I'll take all the blame."

Angela burst out laughing. "You look like a pixie!" She presented herself to Denise. "Here, do me, and then I'll do you." The two of them giggled nervously as they cropped each other close. Angela's long, silken tresses soon littered the floor. She shook her head, touched her fingers to her scalp. "Less time in a cold shower," she said.

Janice studied her in wonder. "Somehow, you look even prettier with short hair."

Angela laughed. "Go on."

"You do. You're like . . . like that famous model. Twiggy! And you're even prettier."

Angela handed the scissors over to Mairin. "You take over now."

To Mairin's surprise, Odessa stepped forward. Her midnight eyes shone with excitement. "Go for it," she said. She turned and presented her long braid, a thick, buoyant twist down her back.

When she wasn't humming or singing, Odessa was usually one of the quietest girls at the Good Shepherd. She tackled all her chores efficiently, her expression neutral, except for the occasional flash of her eyes when something caught her attention. She was tall, with long, slender fingers calloused by work, and she had perfect posture, always holding herself with shoulders squared and her chin held high.

"Are you sure?" Mairin asked.

"I said, go for it." She held the end of her braid, stretching it taut. "Make me look like Nina Simone."

Drawing in a deep breath to steady herself, Mairin gripped the base of the braid. "Here goes nothing," she said. The thick hair took several snips before it came away in her hand. She held it out to Odessa. "Your braid, madame," she said with false formality, dipping into a curtsy. Odessa laughed, and a few of the others joined in.

Within an hour, every girl present had submitted to the scissors. The act of rebellion gave them some kind of odd team spirit, a sense of shared purpose. When the last girl was done, they stood around in the shower room, regarding the pile of hair in all colors and textures, all different lengths.

They gazed at one another. A couple of them fought back tears. Helen put her hand to her head. "How do I look?" she asked.

"Awful," Odessa whispered. "How do I look?"

"Terrible," Helen told her, scrubbing her hand over her freshly shorn head.

"You look like a boy," Denise said.

"Well, so do you," Helen shot back.

"We *all* look awful," Mairin said.

"We're going to be in so much trouble," Janice said, her eyes swimming with regret as her gaze darted from girl to girl. "I can't believe you made me do this."

"Nobody made you," Denise scoffed. "And what are they going to do, pull our hair? Punish us all? If they do that, who'll they get to wash their goddamn dirty laundry?"

Chapter 9

Helen Mei told her mother and father about the hair-cutting incident. Soon after her arrival at the Good Shepherd, she had developed the habit of "telling" her parents everything that happened here. There were a few writing and art supplies around, because the nuns had to pretend they were giving the girls an education.

Helen always noted the date and time, because those details seemed important. They *were* important. There were no clocks or calendars in the gloomy institute, but the days were circumscribed by the rattle of the alarms, the clatter of the chapel bell, and the sharp shake of the nuns' handbells.

There was nowhere for Helen to mail her letters, but one day, she would show her notes to her parents so they would know what really went on at the Good Shepherd. She had to believe her parents would come back for her. The day would come that she would be free from this place. Then her notes would be a tangible reminder of the trials she had endured and the stories she had witnessed.

She had found a way to protect her writings from the nuns' prying eyes. She didn't even have to keep to the shadows the way some girls did, scribbling desperate notes during stolen moments. Helen openly wrote down her observations. So far, no one realized what she was doing, because she wrote in her parents' native language. They had raised her here in Buffalo, but they also taught her to read and write in Han characters. Ever since she was a little girl, her father had worked with her on her writing. It was that important. Everyone thought the small markings were random chicken scratch as she whiled away the time. They had no idea that she was writing down everything she observed about this place—the unpaid labor, the punishments, the deprivation, the cruelty, the lies—so there would be a record of exactly what went on at the Good Shepherd.

She was building an eyewitness chronicle of the girls around her and the bleak world they shared. In the dim light of the refectory, she would capture moments of hope, despair, and quiet rebellion. It was her small act of defiance, a way to preserve her own identity in a place that seemed determined to strip it away.

Helen's father was a professor of Chinese history and culture from antiquity to modernity. He always emphasized the importance of detail in his work and the key role of primary sources in documenting any event, big or small, especially the deeply human stories of the forgotten. She shared her father's love for history, and she emulated his precision and curiosity about the world, past and present.

In her mind's eye, Helen recalled her visits to his office on campus when she was younger. His secretary, Miss Rudolph, always offered her a pink mint from the jar on her desk, and Helen was allowed to use his thick, lined notepads and special stylus pens and ink. Sometimes, she would sit in the top row of a big lecture hall, listening as his animated storytelling brought history to life for a roomful of students. She admired his passion for teaching and the countless hours he spent poring over his students' work or the dusty books in his private office. As she wrote about the hair-shearing incident, Helen found solace in the knowledge that her father's spirit lived on within her.

She had begged to visit China with her parents. Their travel permits had been officially approved, and it was supposed to be a short trip to see her mom's mother, who was ill. They hadn't allowed Helen to come along, saying that travel was too expensive, and they'd only be away for two weeks. Now she understood that the real reason was that a dangerous movement was sweeping through China—the Cultural Revolution. This movement was not kind to people like her parents.

She'd overheard her mother worrying that her father would be deemed a member of the *chòu lăo jiŭ*—intellectuals who were persecuted by the new regime.

When her parents had sent her here, they had no idea that this place would turn out to be a cold labor camp. They had no idea her temporary stay would turn into an indefinite sentence.

Helen had arrived with her bright mind alert and a heart full of dreams. She had expected what her parents had been promised—a safe, temporary residence that would shelter, educate, and nurture her until her mother and father returned from China.

Instead, she found herself in a world that seemed as distant from her aspirations as the moon itself.

While the other girls were lost in their own thoughts or whispered conversations, Helen would keep to herself, taking notes when they had "rec time" in the refectory, which was usually just a pause between laundry and kitchen duties. She chronicled the daily routines, the interactions with the nuns, and the stories of her fellow residents. She captured the anger and tears, the moments of camaraderie, and the silent battles fought, hidden from the world behind the walls.

TODAY SHE INCLUDED every detail she could remember about the night of the hair cutting, from the flash of excitement in Mairin O'Hara's eyes when she'd explained her plan, to the gulp of dread Helen had felt in her throat when her own long, straight hair landed on the shower floor. It had been a moment of rebellion, accomplishing nothing, but it felt important all the same.

Outside the barred windows of the refectory, autumn leaves danced in the crisp air, their vibrant colors a stark contrast to the gray walls of the noisy room where the bad food was served. Even though talk was forbidden until the clap of hands or the ring of a bell, there was a constant clatter of dishes and utensils.

The nuns were strict and unwavering in their beliefs, and Helen was surrounded by a mix of teenagers deemed unfit for society—juvenile delinquents, unwed mothers, truants and petty thieves, and abandoned girls were her companions, each with their own story of struggle and despair.

Helen expected to feel increasingly alien with each passing day, but something more frightening was happening. She was getting used to it. This had begun to feel like her world. The work, the harsh discipline, the isolation, the deprivation felt normal. She was beginning to forget that she loved to learn and strive for high goals, that she dreamed of a life that was expansive and filled with adventure—traveling to far places, meeting fascinating people, doing something that mattered. But these days, all she did was other people's laundry in an endless, numbing routine.

"What're you drawing there?" asked Janice, sidling up to Helen's table in the refectory.

"Just doodling," Helen said without looking up. Great. Sure, she was lonely for companionship, but Janice?

"Doodling seems pretty pointless to me," Janice observed.

Helen didn't think much of Janice, who almost never had anything interesting to say. More than once, Janice had called Helen a Chink and pretended she didn't realize it was offensive. She was one of those girls who thought the nuns would treat her better if she snitched on everyone else. By now Janice should know better. The nuns were equal-opportunity mean.

"My head itches," said Janice. "Does your head itch?"

"No," Helen said, scratching the back of her neck. "Okay, maybe a little, now that you mention it."

"Well, I wish everyone wouldn't have forced me to cut my hair." Janice touched the nut-brown tufts on her head.

"No one forced you," Helen pointed out. "You could have said no."

"Huh. So I would be branded a chicken? No thanks." Janice glanced around the refectory. "I'm still hungry. Are you still hungry?"

"I'll survive," Helen replied. She was no fan of Janice, who was pretty typical of a certain kind of girl here. She was one of the forgotten girls. She came from a big family that couldn't afford so many mouths to feed, so her parents had dropped her off as a charity case, earning her room and board by working in the laundry. Janice always seemed desperate to find her place, but she went about it with clumsy intent, tagging along with the bullies like Denise, and trying to cozy up to the nuns. Her one saving grace was her complete loyalty to Kay. Janice was always around to help Kay when she got confused or flustered.

Helen was acutely aware of the stark contrast between her life's trajectory and those of her newfound companions. While they bore the weight of societal scorn or their own youthful misjudgments, Helen had never committed any of the transgressions that led to a stay here. She'd been caught in a political maelstrom not of her making.

"What d'you s'pose happened to Mairin?" Janice asked, lowering her voice. "Sister Rotrude's face was as red as a tomato when she hauled her off, did you see?" Janice gave a shudder.

"At least she didn't haul her off by her hair," Helen pointed out.

The nuns had been livid when they'd realized so many of the girls in the unit had cut off their hair. As punishment, they'd all been given a meager breakfast of bread and water. True to her word, Mairin had admitted that the shearing was her idea and insisted on shouldering all the blame.

"Rotrude's hands are like claws," Janice said with a shudder. "She's got a grip like King Kong."

"Mairin will probably get a stay in the closet," Helen said. She herself had never earned that punishment, because she kept her head down. And maybe because the nuns were aware that her parents could return at any given moment.

"I hope she survives whatever Sister Rotrude does to her," Janice said.

For that, Helen summoned a brief smile. Janice wasn't so bad.

As she labored over her secret project, Helen wondered what it was like for her parents in China. Were they surrounded by locked doors and high walls and razor wire? Were they forbidden to speak? Forced to work? Was her grandmother all right?

Helen had grown up hearing stories of her laolao, the grandmother she would probably never meet. According to Ma, Laolao was a gifted singer who performed at local teahouses in her Sichuan village of Chengdu.

When she wasn't singing, she liked to relax at her favorite teahouse to catch up on the news and socialize over the májiàng board. The game of mahjong had practically taken over the world, according to Helen's mom. People everywhere were fascinated by the illustrated tiles and the challenge of matching sets and pairs.

History, Helen's father said, was sometimes created by the cruel quirks of politics.

Even the famous pastime of mahjong had been outlawed in China. Expensive tile sets used to be status symbols and a source of pride and tradition. But the burgeoning revolution, incited by Mao Zedong, brought sweeping changes that made their way into even the smallest villages and settlements. Under the new authority, mahjong was condemned as a part of "old culture," and the tiles were confiscated or destroyed—officially, anyway.

Helen's mother told her the tradition was kept alive in secret. Since the prohibition, people fashioned their own tiles from any sort of humble materials—clay or stones, wooden squares, even paper.

Inspired by the story, Helen had decided to create her own mahjong set. A secret one that made her feel closer to her family in China. One that reminded her of the safe, secure world they'd shared before.

Her mother had a special love for the game. When Helen was small, she would watch in fascination as her mother's friends gathered in the living room, slamming the tiles down on the table, constantly laughing and talking, sometimes bickering over a play. Ma often said that an evening of mahjong honored the ancestors who lived inside her. When she closed her eyes, Helen was able to escape to the mahjong table in her parents' living room.

The game required 140 tiles. Helen had been pocketing collar tabs, the kind used at the laundry to stiffen clerical collars. The distinctive Roman collars made the priests look stern and proper and otherworldly. She stole the tabs a few at a time and stored them in a cloth bag under her mattress. By now, she had collected nearly enough for a complete set, and it was time to begin working on the illustrations—stones, characters, bamboos, winds, dragons, and flowers.

Helen's tiles were not as beautiful as the set her mother kept at home, but they meant the world to her. She used a stolen black laundry marker to write her observations and to draw the symbols on the mahjong tiles.

The laundry marker was the perfect instrument for her purposes, because it was indelible.

Chapter 10

Mairin knew she'd get no gratitude for claiming responsibility for the shearing. That was how the act of rebellion came to be known—The Shearing. Like it was the title of some kind of horror movie. The news of the rebellion had rocketed through the halls and dormitories of the Good Shepherd, creating more scandal and outrage than any of the supposed infractions the girls had committed to get them sent here in the first place.

Mairin's entire dorm unit lost one of the few privileges the girls had—their monthly outing to high mass at St. Joe's, over on Franklin Street. Not that the field trip was anything special, but the outing gave the girls a break in routine. The huge sanctuary was dank and cavernous and not terribly interesting except for the sonic boom of its giant organ belting out the "Panis Angelicus," the offertory hymns, and the recessional. The nuns liked to parade the students of the Good Shepherd in front of important parishioners and diocese bigwigs at the cathedral to show the world the good they were doing for the wayward girls of Buffalo. Mairin thought it was totally humiliating, having to appear in public wearing their plain laundry smocks and cheap shoes, but at least there was cider and donuts afterward.

One time, she saw Kevin Doyle by the door to the sacristy, standing tall and solemn in his raiment. Not so long ago he was all she dreamed of. Going to the movies, holding hands while they skated in Delaware

Park. Those days seemed like a distant fantasy now, like something that had happened to someone else. When their gazes caught, she narrowed her eyes. Kevin turned beet red and his gaze darted away. He probably realized his mother and Mairin's mother had discovered that Mairin and Kevin had sneaked off to the movies together. Now Mairin was in jail while Kevin was free. No consequences for him. If he ever caught on fire again, she'd probably let him burn.

This month, however, there was no chance of running into Kevin. The shorn girls would miss out on St. Joe's, thanks to Mairin's rebellious act.

As for Mairin, she endured a harsher fate. She was marched directly to the confessional to give up her sins to the priest, and then pray the act of contrition in a voice that shook with false remorse.

The chapel at the Good Shepherd contained a set of old-fashioned confessional booths, the kind with the priest hiding in the middle and the sinners in separate chambers on either side. The ornate door handles lined up in a row. In catechism class, kids called it a sinner sandwich.

The anonymous priest behind the screen listened in silence as Mairin owned up to what she had done. When she finished her confession, he gave her a perfunctory penance that consisted of some ridiculous number of Hail Marys, and dismissed her with a terse *Go and sin no more.* Then he shut the privacy screen in haste, as if bored by his duties.

Mairin took her time emerging from the confessional, because she knew what was coming next. She stood and rubbed her sore knees, then pushed against the door of the booth. The handle was stuck, and she realized she was trapped in the tiny cubicle. Panic flared in her chest, and she nearly called out for help. Then, remembering where she was, she rallied and took a deep breath, nudging the sticky handle until the latch finally clicked and the door opened.

Under the fiery glare of Sister Rotrude, Mairin shuffled over to the hard wooden kneeler below the altar.

She didn't bother to count her prayers. Instead, she pretended to bow her head in sorrow while letting her mind wander. She and Fiona used to go to confession together each Saturday in preparation for receiving Eucharist on Sunday. "You have to do it on Saturday," Mam would say, "so there's no spare time to sin before receiving communion on Sunday."

The girls would walk slowly to church as they planned out the transgressions they were willing to own up to—telling a fib, playing a prank, disobeying one of the nuns at school. During penance, they would make a game with their rosary beads, racing through the prayers to see who could finish first, both girls cheating with a *hail Mary hail Mary hail Mary* and leaving out the rest of the prayer. Sometimes they would hum "Midnight Confessions" by the Grass Roots under their breath until one of them burst into giggles.

Now Mairin wondered what had become of her friend. It was still impossible to imagine Fiona, her lifelong friend, having a *baby*.

When she stood and turned to exit the chapel, Mairin noticed the nuns waiting to make their own confessions, which they did every week without fail. All in a line in the front row of pews, they knelt in prayer, their faces illuminated by flickering candlelight. Shadows danced on the colored panes of the barred windows. The carved bas-relief scenes depicting the stations of the cross had just been given a polish by the senior girls, and the scent of lemon oil mingled with frankincense and dank stone.

Mairin wondered what sort of sins these veiled women copped to, week in and week out. Did they seek penance for the lies they told themselves—that they were helping the girls in their charge? Did they seek absolution for hurting people in the name of the Lord? Or did they harbor secrets like anyone else—impure thoughts? Self-aggrandizement? Evil intent? Their own shortcomings? She tried to picture Sister Agatha sneaking sips of sacrament wine when no one was looking. Maybe Sister John whispered rude thoughts about her fellow nuns behind their backs.

As she walked past the nuns, Mairin could read nothing but chilly disdain in their glances. Only Rotrude and Bernadette were absent. They made their confessions at a different time, because they had to serve in the front office when the prioress went to her weekly diocese meeting every Thursday afternoon.

Now Sister Theresa gripped Mairin's arm, her fingers digging in painfully as she delivered her once again to the closet. Mairin said nothing to object, because by now, she knew exactly how the nun would react—by doubling down on the punishment. Mairin struggled to keep her expression neutral as the stone-faced woman held the door open and gestured into the dark room.

"Inside with you, then. You'd do well to spend the time here thinking about what you've done, missy."

Mairin kept her eyes cast down and stepped inside the space. She loathed and feared the dark isolation of the closet, but she had learned to keep her emotions tightly locked away. The door shut and the latch fastened with a decisive *click*, and darkness swallowed Mairin.

Alone and surrounded by blackness, she groped for the door and jimmied it, but it was latched from the outside. She ran her fingers around every corner and crevice. Overhead, she found a grill or vent with a small lever that opened and closed. It didn't let any light into the space, but she felt a rush of fresh air, and she could hear sounds from the hallway outside. That was something, at least.

Her spirit flickered like dim embers struggling to survive, and she lost track of time. To keep herself from going mad, she filled her mind with dreams of home. Not the home dominated by Colm and his dirty looks, but the place where she'd felt safe with her dad before the accident at the Falls. The nuns might control every aspect of her life, but not her thoughts. Not her imagination. Not her fondest memories.

Mairin found solace by retreating to a time when her world was filled with love and warmth. Back then, life revolved around her father, who shone like the sun.

Patrick O'Hara was a tall, gentle man with twinkling blue-green eyes and a booming voice that could effortlessly turn gentle enough to soothe even the deepest wounds of her young heart. She and Liam and their dad used to spend countless hours together. Even now, years later, Mairin could still smell the faint scent of her father's shaving soap and feel the rough texture of his calloused hands. He was her hero, her source of comfort and protection.

Strolling hand in hand as if they were the only two souls in the city, they would meander along the waterfront, taking in the sound of gulls echoing in the distance, their laughter mingling with the lapping of the waves against the shore. He taught her to see the beauty in the simplest things—the flash of sunlight dancing on the water, the twinkle of a single snowflake on the back of her mitten, or the way a smile from a stranger could brighten even the gloomiest of days.

Dad encouraged Mairin's love for growing things in the garden. He believed that the garden was a great teacher. One story he loved to tell was about artichokes and dandelions. He said if you're born a dandelion, you are naturally robust, able to tolerate any kind of growing conditions. But if you're an artichoke, you're highly sensitive to cold temperatures and pests and bad soil. You need more sunlight and water in order to thrive. "It's just the way you came to this earth," Dad used to say. "One's no better than the other, but it's a lot easier to be a dandelion. The artichoke has a harder path."

When she closed her eyes, Mairin could almost hear his voice again, filled with pride and tenderness. She held on to his words like some girls held on to a locket, securely closed around the memories.

He worked long hours for the power plant, but whenever he had time off, he would spend it with her and Liam, teaching them how to ride a bike, fixing their broken toys, and telling them stories. His laughter was infectious, and his love for her and Liam and Mam felt like the safest place on earth.

On hot summer afternoons, the whole family would escape to the lush countryside, heading up toward Niagara Falls to cool off in the mist and hike the river isles. Mairin recalled the feel of the soft grass tickling her bare feet as they lay beneath the shade of an old maple tree, gazing up at the cotton candy clouds drifting lazily across the sky. Her dad would point out the shapes they formed, creating stories that only the two of them could understand.

It was on a blustery November day, five years ago, when Patrick O'Hara went to work the way he did every day. As she sat there in the closet, Mairin could still see him in his crisp, gray uniform and waterproof parka with his name stitched above the badge with the New York Power Authority insignia, his steel-toed boots polished to a sheen. As he did each day, he told his wife and kids goodbye in his big, jovial voice. He always said *See you when I come back around* with the same grin on his face, and his lunch bucket in his hand.

It was Thanksgiving week in 1963. Mairin was a ten-year-old girl full of dreams and innocence. On that particular day her life changed forever. Everything changed. The universe changed.

And not because President Kennedy had just been assassinated. While the entire world was reeling from that event, something worse happened to Mairin.

That afternoon, the phone rang. Liam scrambled for it, because he had recently discovered girls, and sometimes a girl named Dodie Watson called him and made him blush scarlet. That day, the call was not from Dodie.

"Mam," Liam called. "Dad says don't wait dinner tonight."

"Whyever not?" asked Mam. She and Mairin were snapping the green beans for supper.

Liam had shrugged and relayed the question into the receiver. "He says there's an Ontario hydro boat caught in the fog on the upper Niagara. They're taking an icebreaker out to haul it to safety."

"Sure the Canadians ought to be hauling their own boats to safety," Mam said, annoyed. "I've a roast in the oven that'll be dry as shoe leather if he's late."

"Says they might be awhile," Liam related. "He doesn't know when he'll be home."

"Tell him to get back in time for *Dobie Gillis*," Mairin had yelled. It was her favorite show to watch with her dad, even in reruns.

Mairin got busy on her homework—a letter of condolence to the First Lady and her two tiny children. The nuns at school said such letters might bring them comfort after their terrible loss. Mairin couldn't find the words, because she couldn't imagine how it would feel for a family to suddenly lose their dad.

She dawdled through the homework, stealing glances at the clock and the darkening skies outside the window. She ended up watching the program by herself—Dobie and Maynard playing the bongos and serenading a girl outside her window—but it wasn't as funny without Dad.

The show was over by the time she heard a car door slam ... and then another. Maybe her dad was bringing someone home. She remembered noticing her mother's brow quirked in a frown as she went to the door. Mairin looked outside to see a strange car parked out front. The car door bore the insignia of the power authority, same as the one on Dad's uniform.

Two men in heavy, somber overcoats and hats and skinny ties came to the door.

"I'm Leaving It Up to You" by Dale and Grace was playing on the radio.

To this day, Mairin couldn't stand to hear that song.

She closed her eyes, trying to turn off the memory, but here, in the closet, memories were like a ride she couldn't get off.

The story made the front page of the *Buffalo Evening News*. The Ontario hydro boat got caught in a blinding fog on a shoal near Tower Island. In order to rescue the boat and its crew, a helicopter was brought in to drop a lifeline to the stranded vessel. It was then able to be towed to safety by an American icebreaker employed by the New York Power Authority. During this phase of the rescue, a wall of water crashed over the deck of the vessel.

Patrick Michael O'Hara, age thirty-nine, was swept by a torrent of water, mud, and rock into the wild, churning waters of the Whirlpool Rapids, which attained a speed of approximately thirty miles per hour. He was the only fatality among the forty men who had been swept up in the maelstrom. The somber recovery crew had found his broken body caught in a snare of rocks and fallen trees.

The darkness in the closet didn't care if Mairin's eyes were open or closed. The news that day had shattered her young heart beyond repair. Nothing would ever fill the void her father's absence had left behind. Now she was trapped here like some kind of criminal, where work and punishment replaced the warmth and love she had once known.

As tears welled up in Mairin's eyes, she knew that even though her dad was gone, his love would forever be engraved in her heart. The pain of his loss was still fresh, but it was also a reminder of the deep connection they had shared. Mairin whispered, *I'll always love you, Dad*, her words evaporating into the darkness. In that fleeting moment, she felt a gentle presence, as if her father was there, watching over her.

Now, with an impatient swipe of her hand, Mairin wiped away her tears and vowed to honor her father's memory. Though separated by eternity, the bond between father and daughter would never be broken.

She would find the strength to endure the hardships of the present and carry his love with her into the future. She vowed to be a dandelion, not an artichoke.

The scent of musty old wood filled her nostrils, mingling with the lingering fear that clung to her like a second skin. She must have dozed off, and somehow managed to sleep in the small, dark space. Yes, she must have slept, because a noise awakened her. Voices, and the acrid reek of cigarette smoke, trickling in through the vent she'd opened earlier. It was coming from Sister Gerard's office. The prioress, and some of the other nuns, loved smoking and somehow rationalized that it wasn't a sin.

Mairin clenched her fist in readiness to pound on the door of her dark prison, demanding to be let out, but something stopped her. There was a certain tone in Mother Superior's voice that made Mairin hesitate.

"... must show better judgment in the future," Sister Gerard said. Her harshness made Mairin flinch.

"And I shall, Mother," said the other voice, pitched high with contrition. Sister Bernadette. Mairin recognized the young nun's plaintive tone. "I am heartily sorry for the mistake. I am covered in shame."

Shame? What in the world could Bernadette be ashamed about? She was a mouse whose entire purpose was to serve the order.

"... make amends immediately," Bernadette was saying. "I shall prepare a written apology to the diocese to explain—"

A slapping sound interrupted her, and she fell silent.

Whoa, thought Mairin. She shouldn't be surprised that even when you try to be the perfect nun, you get walloped.

"You'll do nothing of the sort, you foolish creature." Sister Gerard's voice cut like a knife. "I thought you understood that all cash donations are to be recorded separately and kept right here in this office."

"Understood, Mother. But I'm confused. The code of canon law requires that *all* revenues are the Temporal Goods of the Church," Sister Bernadette said, her voice shaking.

"And so they are," snapped Sister Gerard. "That's why we separate the payments made in cash and silver certificates, to make sure the Good Shepherd can be self-sustaining, instead of being a drain on the resources of the diocese. I thought you understood that."

According to some of the other girls, the prioress was obsessed with money. Supposedly she had some kind of cozy arrangement with certain judges, encouraging them to place girls here and pay for their keeping. But hiding cash transactions didn't sound quite right.

When Colm was treasurer of the Eagles Lodge, he had pulled a stunt like that. Instead of reporting all the revenue to the club, he undercounted the cash money and kept it for himself. For a couple of years, there had been nice things for Mam and even a trip to Montreal last summer to see Expo 67, the World's Fair. Then Colm's scheme was discovered. He would have gone to jail, except that he promised to pay back every last cent.

Mairin wondered if Sister Gerard might be up to something like that. She pressed her ear against the closet door, straining to hear more.

Sister Bernadette's voice, filled with uncertainty, trembled as she asked, "But Mother Superior, is it right to withhold this information from the diocese?"

"There's no need to burden the diocese with the petty revenues and expenses generated by our hard work and devotion, Sister Bernadette." Something about Sister Gerard's false piety sent a shiver down Mairin's spine. "We're responsible for so much—charitable work, support for the local community, and the betterment of the Good Shepherd itself. The diocese is so vast and complicated, our work is too often overlooked."

"Of course you're right, but according to my reading of canon law—"

"Enough!" A scoff echoed through the air, followed by the sound of papers rustling. "The diocese has enough money, but we must provide for the needs of our charges, and for that matter, our own needs. If we fail to secure our future, what will become of us? Of our elderly sisters who depend on us to care for them in their old age? Do you think they should live in poverty just because they are nuns?"

"I should hope not, Mother." Bernadette sounded contrite.

"Exactly. When we're old, no one will take care of us unless we act now to plan for our future. And consider the girls who depend on us—those who seek to wash their sins away, the unwed mothers, the wayward souls, and those poor babies who need homes. How do you imagine we pay for all the good we do?"

As she stood in the darkness, Mairin was pretty sure she had stumbled upon something sinister.

"We'll continue to leave the cash gifts to St. Apollonia for safekeeping," Sister Gerard stated.

St. Apollonia? Who was that? Maybe a code name for the nuns' private fund.

"Yes, Mother." Bernadette's voice was soft with remorse. The young nun was smart about math and bookkeeping, but she seemed to totally fall for Sister Gerard's veiled rationalizations, and too timid to challenge the corrupt practices.

Mairin's mind raced, her thoughts colliding like leaves in a whirlwind. It was bad enough the nuns were so cruel to the girls here; they were also helping themselves to the money they earned from forced labor. Hidden funds and secret dealings. Mairin didn't quite understand the process, but she wasn't stupid. She knew it was wrong. It seemed that the prioress, the very person trusted with the well-being of supposedly troubled girls, was not so high-minded as she wanted people to think.

As she crouched, forgotten, in the dark closet, Mairin's resolve hardened. Not only was she determined to escape this place. She was going to find out what kind of secret dealings Sister Gerard was involved in.

As the minutes passed, silence closed in, and the smell of cigarette smoke dissipated. Sister Gerard had left. Mairin could hear rustling papers and the occasional heavy sigh, so she assumed Sister Bernadette was still in the office. Spineless Sister Bernadette.

Mairin closed her hand into a fist and knocked on the door, hard. "Someone help," she called in a pathetic voice. "Please, I'm desperate in here." She knocked some more.

Footsteps hurried close. "Who's that? Ruth, is that you?" asked Bernadette, her voice hesitant.

"Yes!" Mairin cringed as she owned up to the false name she'd been given. "Yes, please help me."

After a few beats of hesitation, there was a shuffling sound. Then the latch clicked, and the door opened up, just a crack.

"Ruth! I didn't realize you were here. What is it, child?" Bernadette asked, her voice laced with caution.

Child. As if. Mairin figured Bernadette was maybe three years older than she was. *Child.* It was ridiculous. But Mairin had a larger purpose, so she didn't make a federal case out of it.

"I'm desperate for the restroom," Mairin whispered. "It would be an act of mercy. Please, it's an emergency."

"Ruth, you're meant to stay here," Bernadette objected. "I'll find a bucket."

"Oh, no, I beg you. I'll be quick, I swear. And I'll come right back. I swear on all that's holy, I will." She gasped with a fake sob.

More hesitation. Framed by her wimple, Bernadette's face looked flat and mild, like a child's drawing of the moon. "Hurry, then." She stepped aside and gestured toward a door marked *WC*.

"I will. Bless you, Sister Bernadette. You are truly the soul of kindness." Spots of color dotted the nun's cheeks, and she ducked her head.

Mairin used the tiny, austere bathroom, sighing with relief. She hadn't been kidding about the need to pee. She came out of the washroom, blinking at the light and looking around the office. Bernadette was absorbed in her work at the spindly secretary desk, and didn't seem to notice her. Mairin couldn't stop thinking about the conversation she'd overheard. Everything about this place was a facade of faith, a front for Sister Gerard's corruption—the massive, ornate desk, the Bible on its stand, the floor-to-ceiling shelves filled with books and journals, the reliquary on its shining silver legs, lavishly ornamented in tribute to some forgotten saint. There was an extensive PA system for issuing commands to the girls.

"You need to go back in," Bernadette said, noticing her at last.

"I will, but... I'm not well." Mairin pressed her hands to her middle. "I have a bad stomach. Please, can you leave the door open, just a crack?"

"Of course not. Locking you in is the whole point of the punishment."

"Don't you remember what it was like?" Mairin persisted. She summoned a smile at Bernadette's startled look. "You told me that you were sent here yourself, and this is where you found your spiritual path," she explained. "The girls all talk about it."

"The girls should be minding their own paths to redemption." The red spots returned to Bernadette's cheeks.

"You should be flattered," Mairin said, sensing the nun's weakness.

"You're an inspiration to us all. Your devotion to the reformation of wayward girls is so admirable."

"It's the Lord's work," Bernadette said, "to be a beacon to those who have lost their way. That is the mission of this place—bringing you girls real hope for a brighter future."

Mairin tried not to gag. "Do you truly believe that?"

"With all my heart."

"You're the real thing, aren't you?" Mairin asked. "Just like that song by Marvin Gaye."

"Who?" Bernadette frowned, regarding her with a mix of suspicion and curiosity. "What in heaven's name are you talking about?"

Mairin sang a few lines of "Ain't Nothing Like the Real Thing." She noticed that Bernadette seemed intrigued. "I bet we can find it on the radio." She flipped it on and turned the dial to the Top 40 station. Mick Jagger's voice drifted from the speaker.

"Goodness, Ruth, you mustn't—"

"Oh, Sister, we must! Music is good for the soul. Everyone knows that. Let's just listen for a few minutes. This is such a good song. It's a huge hit."

"But . . ." Sister Bernadette hesitated, her gaze shifting uneasily from the main door to Mairin. "Rock music is the devil's work. It's a corrupting influence that has no place within these walls. Why, the very idea of young girls listening to male voices is an abomination."

"Shh, wait for the chorus," Mairin said, noting that Bernadette was in no hurry to turn off the music. "It's so beautiful. This is a really good radio," she added. "The sound is clear as a bell."

"Sister Gerard insists on the best equipment," Bernadette said. "She wants all the very best for the girls here."

I'll just bet she does, Mairin thought. She did love the crystal sound of the music, even though it caused an ache in her heart. She missed listening to music with her friends, whether it was on a crackling record player or a hi-fi stereo in some of the rich kids' living rooms. She looked over at Bernadette and was surprised to see the nun's eyes closed, and a tear slowly tracking down her cheek. In the same moment, she saw an opportunity. Her hand shot out and flipped the broadcast switch on the PA system. Now the entire place would hear the Rolling Stones belting out

"Let's Spend the Night Together." Male voices, singing a rock and roll song about sex. Mairin savored the thought of the girls at work, suddenly hearing Mick Jagger like the voice of God through the speakers.

The song seemed to transport Bernadette to a place far away. She hugged herself and swayed gently to the music. Mairin took advantage of the lull to ease open a drawer under the radio. Nothing much of interest except ... a rusty iron key of some sort. Like an old-fashioned skeleton key, maybe. She snatched it and hid it in her pocket.

She was casting about for other treasures—maybe more clues about Sister Gerard—when the next song came on—"Sunshine of Your Love" by Cream.

Bernadette seemed to come to her senses. "Enough, then," she said, flustered. "God forgive me for indulging you. I must remember to say a novena for both of us."

"Please. Let's just listen to this one last song. I'm begging you, Sister. It would be such a blessing to hear some music, and a way to connect me with the family I wronged so grievously," Mairin said.

Bernadette's gaze went soft with sympathy, but then she pursed her lips and glanced at the clock. "I have work to do. I cannot neglect my duties here in this office."

"You must be quite proud to have such important responsibilities." Mairin watched her face change. Among the nuns, pride was a terrible transgression.

"It's not that," Bernadette insisted. "It's ..."

The song crescendoed, and she seemed caught up once again. Her shoulders slumped, and she nearly swooned through the chorus. She didn't even seem to hear the sound of running feet in the corridor leading to the office, although Mairin did.

Sister Rotrude and Sister Gerard arrived, nearly collapsing from exertion, their faces red and sweating. "What ..." Rotrude wheezed and tried again. "What in the name of all that's holy is the meaning of this?"

Bernadette let out a squeak. "I'm sorry, Mother! Heaven forgive me, but the girl needed the bathroom."

Sister Gerard snapped off the PA system and then the radio. Still red-faced, her eyes swimming with fury, she stared at Mairin as though she were on display in a window. "You're quite the troublemaker, aren't you?"

Mairin knew it wasn't a question, so she didn't answer.

"We were really worried about you," Angela said as Mairin made her way through the dim evening light to her cot, moving slowly, aching with the stings and bruises from Sister Rotrude's penance stick. "We thought we might never see you again."

"I had to do time in the closet, and after that, they made me clean out the senior girls' unit," Mairin said. "The senior girls are totally mean and rude."

"Oh my gosh, your poor face." Angela stared at Mairin's cheek. Mairin hadn't seen a mirror, but she probably looked like Frankenstein. "Are you okay?"

"Right as rain," Mairin said, her mouth twisting in an ironic smile. She winced as she gingerly sat down on the cot.

A few others came over to welcome her back. "Whoa, you got it bad," Janice said. "Which one beat the crap outta you?"

Mairin waved her hand dismissively. "So did you hear the music?"

"It was incredible," Angela said, her eyes lighting up.

"Fantastic," Odessa agreed. "When we heard it coming over the speakers, we thought there were ghosts in the building, and then we realized it was *music*. Oh, man. Real actual music. Like the kind we used to listen to on the radio."

The girls all started chattering at once, telling Mairin about the brief, magical moments when the music had suddenly come drifting through the PA system. It was amazing, how a song could just fill you up. Even Angela joined in the conversation, seeming to set aside her worries for those few precious minutes.

"When I heard the Rolling Stones, I was, like, *whoa*," said Denise.

"A bunch of girls got up and started dancing," Odessa said.

"*Dancing*, can you believe it?" Kay showed off her wide, goofy grin.

"Totally," said Odessa. "We couldn't help ourselves. We all just jumped up and started dancing around. The nuns couldn't stop us."

"I bet some of them wanted to join in," Janice crowed.

Mairin looked around as if to make sure no one was watching. "I found something." She took out the rusty iron key and held it up. "It's a skeleton key."

Kay looked horrified. "A *skeleton* key? I'm skeerd o' skeletons."

"For opening a lot of different locks. I pilfered this one from Mother Superior's office. It opens the gate at the top of the stairs. I just tested it, and it works." She sent a hard-eyed look at Janice. "And if anyone says a word, you're dead meat."

Janice made a zipping motion across her lips.

"So if the key works in the upstairs gate, then we don't have to be locked in at night," Denise said.

"Exactly," Mairin said. "I bet it works on some of these other doors, too. First chance I get, I'm going to try the main gate."

She saw a glimmer in Angela's eyes. A glimmer of hope, maybe. "Anyone wants to come with me, you just say the word," Mairin said.

Angela's expression quickly dimmed. "Even if I got away from this place, then what? My gran would simply send me back. There's nowhere else for me to go."

Mairin shifted her gaze back and forth. "Maybe we'll figure something out. Oh, and I learned something else, too. You know all the money the clients pay to have us do their laundry? The hospitals and hotels and stuff? Sister Gerard's hiding some of that money. I heard her telling the young one, Sister Bernadette. There's a stash somewhere in her office."

"Seriously?" Helen asked. "How'd you figure that out?"

"They don't realize you can hear them from the closet. I found a vent in the ceiling."

"If they're doing something wrong, they should get in trouble," Odessa said.

"In trouble how?" Mairin scowled. "They'll just call me a liar and cover their tracks."

"She's right," Denise said. "Who would we tell? The family court judges and social workers who sent us to this place? The diocese? They'd never believe it."

"When my parents get back, I could tell them," Helen suggested.

"And when are they coming back?" Denise snapped, her mean streak showing. "They're in jail in *China*."

"Are not," Helen shot back. "They're under an exit ban, but it's not forever."

An awkward silence fell over the room. After a few minutes, Janice said, "Man, we went crazy when the music came on. Oh my gosh, I wish we could do that every day, Mairin. When can you sneak down to the office and play the music again?"

"It's risky," Mairin said. "But . . . yeah. Maybe another time. What did I miss while I was gone?"

"Helen's teaching us a secret game." Janice leaned forward and lowered her voice. "Ever hear of marchong?"

"Mahjong, Ding Dong." Denise poked her in the ribs.

"Hey!"

"Hush," said Helen. "We have to keep it on the down-low. You're supposed to name the tiles you play, and call an action based on what someone else just played—but be quiet about it. If we get caught, they'll take away all the tiles I made." She, too, sent a warning glance at Janice.

"Well, I want to learn, too," Mairin said. She had never heard of the game, but maybe it would take her mind off her troubles even for a little while.

"We'll have to take turns," Angela said. "We can only play four at a time."

Mairin was too keyed up to sleep. "Show me."

"Tell you what," Helen said. "I'll teach you to play mahjong if you'll show me how to fight."

Mairin glared at Angela, whose cheeks turned red. "I'm sorry, Mairin. I know it was supposed to be a secret, but I told them about what you've been teaching me."

"We want to learn, too," Janice said, looking at the floor. "We want to learn to fight."

"Seriously?" Mairin's spirits lifted. Just for a moment, they felt like a team instead of a band of lost girls. "It's risky. If we get caught . . ."

"If that happens, we'll *all* be in trouble," said Odessa.

Denise aimed a glare at Janice. "Fine. Then let's make sure we don't get caught."

Chapter 11

Angela sat on a hard bench outside Mother Superior's office, shivering with fear, and with the chill of winter seeping through the tall, wavy-glass windows of the hall. The weak, cold light added a somber blue tint to the austere space. She eyed the array of pictures and icons on display, most of them depicting the Virgin Mary.

Now that she herself was unmarried and unexpectedly pregnant, Angela was skeptical of Mary's story. What had Mary said to convince her critics that what had happened was not her fault? Did they believe her when she said that she'd seen visions? Did they agree that her pregnancy was a miracle?

Angela could claim neither. She knew that what had happened to her was definitely not a miracle. Unlike Mary, Angela would never be the subject of praise and prayers, hymns and tributes, and timeless art treasures. She could only hope there was a way out of this horrible situation.

Gran had arrived on the city bus from the south end, but her purpose was not to pay a visit to Angela. She had come to meet with Sister Gerard and Sister Rotrude. Angela could hear them talking at length, the conversation punctuated by Gran's Irish outbursts, most of them sounding like a cross between a curse and a wail.

Stepping carefully so as not to cause the floorboards to creak, Angela pressed her ear to the door.

"What am I to do?" Gran begged. "Her own fallen mother was a floozy who never wanted her, and now this."

A searing pain ripped into Angela's heart. She was never wanted. Never.

"Whatever in all that's holy am I to do now?" Gran continued.

"There, there," Sister Rotrude said. "'Tis not your fault the girl has fallen pregnant."

Fallen. Angela grimaced. Fallen. As if she'd tripped and got knocked up by some freak accident. She kept listening, waiting for her grandmother to demand to know who had caused the pregnancy, who had caused her to *fall*, but the question was not asked. Gran didn't seem to concern herself with that.

After she'd caught Angela and Tanya together, Gran had wrung her hands and lamented that Angela would never have babies of her own until the nuns at the Good Shepherd "fixed" her. And once she was cured, Gran was absolutely certain that she would want to marry and have babies one day. As if a girl's sole purpose was to marry and have a baby.

Well, apparently the baby-making part of her had been "fixed." But instead of being overjoyed, Gran was clearly mortified by the news. When she'd arrived this morning, she could barely look at her granddaughter, although she'd done a double take when she noticed Angela's shorn blond hair.

After the shearing, Angela had studied her image in the dormitory window at night, which was the only thing that approximated a mirror. She wasn't so sure she looked like Twiggy, although that wouldn't be bad at all. She thought the short hair made her look vaguely like Mary Martin as Peter Pan. Angela had seen the movie when she was a little girl, and she had been utterly enchanted by the sprightly, boyish girl leading a group of kids to Neverland.

The nuns spoke in low tones, their voices meant to soothe. Angela couldn't quite make out what they were saying. Then there was a footstep, and she jumped out of the way just in time to pretend she hadn't been eavesdropping. The door swung open, framing the imposing office of the prioress.

"Inside with you, Agnes," Sister Rotrude ordered, gesturing at a ladder-backed chair.

Angela sat and held herself rigid, hands clutching the seat to still their trembling.

Gran rocked back and forth on a cushioned chair. Lines of hardship and uncompromising faith etched her face, and she clutched her rosary, the beads slipping through her fingers as if seeking absolution not only for Angela but for her own shame and devastation.

The nuns, in their habits as dark as secrets, stood like silent sentinels, their faces shrouded in shadow. Then Sister Gerard took a seat at her massive desk and regarded Angela with a look that was soft but unyielding, weighted by a decision that had already been made.

As the Mother Superior began to speak, her voice was quiet, yet it carried the irrevocable force of conviction. "We've made a plan for you," she said. "Your baby will be blessed to find a home with a family of faith, one that will raise him—or her—in the grace of our Lord."

Angela's gaze darted around the room, searching for an ally, a reprieve, something to hold on to. But all she saw were the hard-eyed expressions of the three women, the gilt-edged tomes on the bookshelves, the crucifixes that hung heavily on the walls, and the massive reliquary on its four silver claws, reputed to house the very teeth of St. Apollonia, or so said one of the senior girls in the laundry.

She swallowed past the knot in her throat and tried to breathe past the panic rising in her chest. "Don't I get to have a say in this decision?" Her voice was so soft that she almost couldn't hear herself.

Sister Rotrude fixed her with a heated glare. "You're a child, still, and this is your chance to find redemption. For you, and for your baby."

"You just said it," Angela said, her voice sharpening with anger. "*My* baby. *My* child. I'm the one who gets to decide—"

"Nonsense," Gran cut in. "The good sisters' offer is a vast and sacred blessing. 'Tis a chance for you to do what you must for the love of the Lord and our family honor. One day, you'll have the chance to continue your life as though this . . . as though you had never made this terrible mistake."

Mistake. *Mistake.* Angela wasn't sure what her grandmother was referring to. Was it a mistake to want to be close to Tanya, or was her mistake in getting caught? Was it a mistake to do as she was told by the doctor, a man who claimed he knew the way to "heal" her? Should she have fought him the way Mairin had?

"What of the doctor?" she demanded, emboldened by anger and fear. "*He* is responsible for making me pregnant."

The word *pregnant* was forbidden, and when she said it aloud, all three women reacted, stiffening and gasping. Then she looked at Gran's face, and realized her grandmother had no idea what she was talking about. Angela turned to address the prioress. "Did you not tell her, then? Didn't you explain that I'm pregnant by the doctor?"

Gran fanned herself with her neck scarf. "That cannot be so."

"Can't it?" Angela demanded. "I got pregnant *after* you forced me to come here. How do you suppose that happened? Was it an immaculate conception?"

Rotrude struck her on the ear so hard that her head rang with the blow.

"Lies and blasphemy," said Sister Gerard. "You'll do penance for a week, girl. Longer, in fact." The nun regarded Gran with a deeply pious, sincere expression. "Mrs. Denny, I'm very sorry to tell you that your granddaughter brought this upon herself with her seductive ways. A temptress, a seductress, sneaking off with a man she refuses to name, perhaps a delivery driver or layman who works around the place. She could have been with a boy during social time on cathedral Sunday."

"I did no such thing," Angela shot back.

"'Tis the work of the devil," her grandmother said. "I shall pray for your eternal, misbegotten soul every day of my life."

Angela knew she would never get them to admit the truth. When she'd finally found the courage to tell the nuns she was pregnant by the doctor, their denial had been so swift and practiced that she got the impression she was not the first—nor the last—of his victims.

She yearned for this whole episode to be erased from her memory. From her soul. She wished it had never happened. But it *had* happened, and there would be a child, and she was expected to surrender it to strangers. It was the only option presented to her. And despite the fact that she was pregnant due to a hateful act by a hateful man, she felt a sense of grief so profound that she fought an impulse to scream, to plead, to clutch at the life within her and declare it her own.

Still, she didn't know if she could ever separate the life inside her from the man whose seed had planted it there. The baby would come, and she would always know it had been caused by a crime. Her mind twisted around the situation. Ready or not, she would become a mother. And as a mother, she would see her child as a part of her heart. At the same time, she was terrified that one day she might see her rapist in the face of that very same child. Would she be able to separate the child from its paternal side?

She was expected to comply with this plan. Refusal was not an option. But in the smallest corner of her heart, she made space for a silent vow to remember, to hold on to the memory of the innocent person she would never know. And then, in another corner of her heart, she harbored the hope that she would find a way to keep this child, to raise it in a world of love and acceptance, not fear and intolerance.

As tears burned her eyes, she fought for breath. The room felt as if it were closing in, the very air heavy with expectations and silent judgment. Angela had nothing more to say.

Gran promised to pray endless novenas, begging for the child to be given a proper home. The nuns were businesslike but reassuring, letting her know that they had decades of experience with the sort of tragic circumstances that had befallen Angela. They promised Gran that this "unfortunate situation" would fade into a dark and distant memory, as if it had never happened.

LATER, ANGELA LAY on her cot in the dormitory, staring at the ceiling. Her stomach churned with a life of its own, except it wasn't her stomach. The terrible sensation occurred lower down, where she used to get period cramps. Only this didn't feel like period cramps.

"What's the matter?" Denise plunked herself down on the edge of the cot. "You don't look so good."

Denise had been a bully when Angela had first arrived, prodding her about her princess looks and timid ways. Lately, as Angela's belly swelled along with her misery, Denise had softened, admitting that her own parents had not been married, and that she herself had been born at Father Baker's, over in Lackawanna, a reformatory for some of the worst cases. And then she said, "You're not the only one, you know. But you're the only one that got pregnant."

Angela gasped. "You too? Did he... did that doctor do things to you?"

"Nah, he only likes the pretty ones. But I've heard other girls say he did stuff."

"Why does he keep getting away with it?" Angela shuddered.

"Because we're here. Because he can. Because we're nobody."

Janice joined them, sitting cross-legged on the floor, ignoring Denise's scowl. "Angela, are you sick?"

"She's pregnant, moron," said Denise. She turned to Angela. "Maybe being pregnant is supposed to feel like... well, however you're feeling. But, holy shit, what if it's some horrible disease? Should we tell someone?"

"No," Angela said with crystal clarity. "Absolutely not." No disease could be as bad as the thing she feared the most—that if she got sick, they would make her go back to Dr. Gilroy. When that thought crossed her mind, Angela knew without a doubt that she would rather die than visit the clinic. "I'm just so... so scared. I have no idea how to do this. Maybe I'll feel better in the morning."

She didn't feel better. She felt sick and tired all the time. Her stomach churned in horrible knots and she constantly had to pee. She was terrified, because she didn't know what was happening to her. Before Gilroy stuck his thing in her, she hadn't even known how a baby was made. She didn't know what was going on inside her, and she had no idea how a baby would get out.

Yet when her entire world felt as though it was about to collapse, it was Janice, of all people, who helped her solve the mystery. She was a snitch, but she had a kernel of decency.

"I brought you something," Janice said, scooting next to her in chapel one morning.

"What?" Angela glanced to and fro, making sure the nuns weren't watching. Talking during chapel brought on swift punishment—a lashing with someone's heavy rosary, or extra duties scrubbing floors.

"You know how you've been saying how scary it is, bein' pregnant and all?"

"I guess I'd know that," Angela whispered with a grimace.

Moving as one, they knelt after the Lamb of God. Janice slipped something into the pocket of Angela's tunic. "It's a book," she said, giving Angela's arm a squeeze. "Maybe it doesn't have to be all that scary."

After the recessional, Angela grabbed Janice's hand and ducked into a shadowy corner. She took out the book and squinted through the dark to read the title: *Nine Months' Reading: A Medical Guide for Pregnant Women.*

"What the heck, Janice?"

"I thought it might help," whispered the other girl. "You got to read it fast, because it goes back to the bookmobile on the next run."

The bookmobile. "How'd you manage that? The nuns have to approve every single book we choose." Angela knew it was one of the most cherished duties of Sister Rotrude and Sister Bernadette. On bookmobile day, the driver brought the girls' selections to the office so the two nuns could make sure the material was "appropriate," which everyone knew was code for boring.

Janice gave a knowing look. "There's a way around it. I figured out that Rotrude and Bernadette go to confession right when the bookmobile comes. So I wait until the driver goes to the office with the books all piled in a crate. Sometimes she goes to the refectory for a cup of tea. Then I go to the van and grab something off the shelf." Her gaze shifted as she looked from left to right. "Is it stealing? Am I gonna burn in hell for stealing?"

Angela gave her hand a squeeze. "Maybe you'll go to heaven for helping a friend."

ANGELA COULDN'T WAIT until nightly lockdown, when she could study the book Janice had slipped to her. By the weak glow of the bare bulb in the dormitory, she eagerly studied every page of *Nine Months' Reading.* It was written by a doctor named Robert Elliot Hall. She could tell right away that it was an actual science book. And she knew it was the kind of book that would have the nuns hauling everyone into confession if they discovered it.

Gran never talked about sex at all, not one word. Angela's ignorance had made the doctor's attack even more horrifying. When she told the nuns she believed she was pregnant, they tried to send her back to Gilroy, but she refused to go, so they took her to a woman called a midwife whose clinic smelled of carbolic soap and cigarette smoke. She was an older woman with a brusque manner who clearly disapproved of unwed mothers. She performed a painful internal exam and gave Angela a tarry concoction to drink each day, saying it would help the baby grow. Angela was too frightened to ask the woman for more information.

The *Nine Months'* book included hand-drawn pictures, which shocked Angela, since she'd never seen a picture of the human body, inside and out. One of the early illustrations showed something called the fetus, which started out as a negligible dot like the spot on an egg yolk. According to the book, the fetus progressed week by week, month by month, until it resembled a seahorse curled into an egg, only the egg was the mother's womb. Or the uterus, which was the proper term for it.

Over the next few nights, Angela read the book in secret as fast as she could, studying and sometimes marveling over every word and illustration.

She learned that the terrifying, fluttery movements inside her were normal. All the peeing and exhaustion and aching back and fat ankles—normal.

It was not the first time a library book had saved her sanity. Thanks to *Nine Months' Reading*, Angela understood a bit more about what to expect. She was still scared out of her gourd but at least she had a better understanding of what was happening to her. It was pretty overwhelming knowing she was in the process of growing a whole person, sharing her blood and nutrition with it while her belly grew as round as a hot air balloon. She was apprehensive about the actual process of giving birth. Previously, she'd known nothing about how a baby got from inside its mother to the outside world. It was shocking to realize that she would have to push it out through the birth canal between her legs. The doctor might have to go in with something that looked like giant salad tongs, using the tool to pull the baby out.

Yet, as the stages of gestation progressed, something else was happening inside Angela. She started to think of the baby as a human being, someone who would emerge from her body as a helpless, tiny infant, needing the love of a mother. Angela was going to be a mother. The thought filled her with a sweet-sharp stab of emotion. Yearning. Fear. Anticipation. She was carrying a baby in the comfort of her own body, and it was some kind of miracle. Those first flutters she felt were a comfort now that she understood. This child had nothing to do with the person who'd made her pregnant. It was hers and hers alone.

Was the baby a boy or a girl? Angela daydreamed, picking out names. She might name a boy Paul or Sidney, after the most handsome movie stars she could think of. If it was a girl, she'd call her Alice, like *Alice in Wonderland* or maybe Alice B. Toklas. Growing up alone with only her grandmother, Angela had been lonely all her life, but with this baby, she was never alone. She loved that.

She tried to commit each page of *Nine Months'* to memory before the book had to be returned. In the middle of reading it one night, she heard a noise in the hallway. It was the sound of the gate at the top of the stairs closing with a metallic clang.

Mairin was back from her latest punishment. She kept getting in trouble for sassing the nuns or trying to run away. This time she had a bruise on her cheekbone, her lips were blue with cold, and the neckline of her tunic was torn, but she entered the dorm with her head held high in that cocky way she had. Proud. Undefeated. The way Angela always wished she could be.

"Hey, are you all right?" Odessa ran over to Mairin and put her arm around her. "I swear, some days we don't know if you'll ever come back. What'd they do to you this time?"

"Dungeon," Mairin said with a weary voice. She was referring to the shower room in the basement—a cavernous, cobwebbed place that some girls said was haunted by a trapped woman who shrieked during storms. "It was wicked cold and there were rats, but at least I could move around down there. I'm up to a hundred push-ups, easy."

"Oh boy," said Kay. "Boyo boy!"

Mairin's mouth trembled with the effort to smile. "Anything to forget about this place, even for a little while."

"Amen to that," Angela said.

"How're *you* doing?" The iron cot squeaked as Mairin sat down next to her.

"Still pregnant," Angela said. "I can't *not* be pregnant no matter how hard I wish and hope and pray."

A tear must have slipped out, because Mairin patted her arm and gentled her voice. "Try to take it easy," she said. She looked around the circle of eager faces. "We can't stay here another minute. Swear to God, we have to get out of here."

"You know that's impossible," Denise said. "Nobody gets out of here. I reckon you're proof of that."

"There has to be a way. I've been studying the situation."

Angela could practically see her mind working. If there was a way out, Mairin would probably find it.

"The situation is, we can't get out," Denise said. "And if by chance we do, they'd bring us right back."

"In case you haven't noticed, I've had a lot of time to think," Mairin retorted. "The laundry carts—"

"You already tried the laundry carts," Denise pointed out.

"Okay, so I could tie some sheets together and climb right over the wall."

"The top of the wall has broken glass set in it. And razor wire, remember. You'd be sliced to ribbons."

Angela shuddered. She couldn't stand the sight of blood. Still, the prospect of getting away made her ache with yearning. Away to some fantasy place, where she could take care of her baby and forget how that child had been made.

"It's too cold out now, anyway," Odessa said. "Where would you go? Who would you call? You said your own parents made you come here."

Mairin studied the rough, planked floor. "I still have his dime," she said softly.

"Whose dime?" asked Angela.

"Um, this guy I know. He once gave me a Mercury dime to remind me I can call him anytime."

"Ooh, a guy you're sweet on?" Janice leaned forward.

Angela felt Mairin tense beside her. "No, not like that," said Mairin. "He's my best friend's big brother, is all. Someone I've always been able to count on."

"Well, you're going to need a lot more than a dime if you manage to get to the outside," Denise said. "Fine, escape if you want, but then what? Will your family welcome you home? Where'll you go? How will you live?"

"We've just got to stick it out," Odessa said quietly.

"Easy for you to say. Your sentence is up next summer. The only way out of here for the rest of us is to wait until we're eighteen."

"That's a hundred years from now. I'm not waiting," Mairin insisted.

"You won't make it," Helen warned.

"Will too," Mairin said. "You watch me."

AND THE GIRLS did watch, some with skepticism, some with dark amusement, all with grudging respect. They watched Mairin try to escape by pulling a fire alarm and then begging the first responders to take her with them. The men laughed her off, telling her she ought to be grateful to the Sisters of Charity for giving her a roof over her head.

Another time, she hid in one of the big Pullman bags, but was found out when the bag turned out to be too heavy to lift. One blustery day, she did try to scale the wall by bringing out the orchard ladder. She managed to get over the wall, and she went from door to door, asking for help. Someone in the neighborhood was so alarmed by all her cuts and gashes that she called for help, and Mairin had to return once again.

Some of the girls even put wagers on how long it would take before Mairin was caught and brought back in. In one attempt, she nearly froze to death waiting for a bus that never came. Once, she did manage to board a city bus, but was ejected because she couldn't come up with bus fare, and someone recognized her Good Shepherd uniform.

When the all-girl choir came from St. Mary of the Sorrows to sing Christmas carols, Mairin tried to slip out with them, but they were terrified of her and told Sister Rotrude that some tough-looking girl was hanging around them.

Angela felt exhausted just watching Mairin's efforts, but she felt inspired as well. Mairin paid for each attempt with penance and punishment, but it didn't hold her back from trying again. Mairin never stopped believing in possibility.

Chapter 12

Fiona Gallagher's school uniform didn't fit. On a cold March morning, she put it on for the first time since returning from Aunt Cookie's down in Bradford, and it was too tight in all the wrong places. A part of her wished she could have stayed with her aunt, even though there was no pregnancy to hide anymore.

Cookie was actually her mother's aunt, and she was more like a grandmother, with a face like risen dough and kind eyes that didn't judge. Aunt Cookie—her real name was Corrine, but she was known for her jam-filled cookies—used to come to Buffalo for a stay each time Ma had another baby.

A godsend, Ma called her, looking after all the other kids so Ma could give her full attention to the new little one.

Now that Fiona herself had gone through the ordeal, she understood why her mother needed help. Having a baby was the biggest, scariest, most mind-blowing thing in the world. It took over every part of your body, your mind, your heart, and your soul. No one had ever explained to Fiona that having a baby would change her forever in ways she couldn't imagine.

Still, it would have been nice if someone, somehow, somewhere had told Fiona how easy it was to get pregnant, and how hard it was to understand what would happen as a result of all the sex that brought every cell in her body alive. When she first started having those warm, yearning feelings, the sensation was so powerful that she actually thought it was true love. Now she knew it didn't work that way. She wished someone had explained how awful it was to stand before your mother, eyes on the floor, face on fire with shame, and admit to her what had happened. It would have been nice if someone had told Fiona that the hardest thing in the entire universe was to push a baby from your body. And that the most holy thing in the universe was to be flooded by the purest, most intense, and sweetest love you'd ever felt.

Her labor had been agonizing, but the pain had felt strangely cleansing. The love itself wasn't hard at all. It was as natural, beautiful, and eternal as breathing the air. No, the difficult, impossible part was the goodbye. That was the thing that killed Fiona—saying goodbye to the glorious, fully formed, beautiful child she had grown under her heart for nine months.

She had been allowed to hold and cuddle the tiny, sweetly breathing bundle of perfection for only a day and a half. Despite her exhaustion from the hours of labor, she had not slept for a single moment. She simply stared at the little miracle, pressing her lips to the warm, delicate forehead, inhaling a scent so sweet and unique that it pierced straight through to her breaking heart.

Seated in Cookie's new wooden Kennedy Rocker, Fiona had parted the striped hospital blanket to study every inch of the new little life she'd created. She smiled at her baby, made a memory of her face forever. She tried to fold every detail into her heart—the sweet, slender limbs; the face of an angel; the starfish hands and seashell ears. Fiona had pressed her mouth to the baby's delicate ear and whispered, *Your name is Ruby*.

Yes, Ruby. A precious gem that was the color of life, the color of blood, the color Fiona could see when she squeezed her eyes shut to hold in the tears.

Of course, the new parents would pick a different name for the little girl, for the child Fiona had made, for the person she would never see again in this life.

The idea of losing her child made Fiona want to die so she could get to the afterlife sooner and then wait in paradise for Ruby to join her when the time came. That was a bad idea, though, since it obviously wouldn't work. Because Fiona would never get to heaven. She was going to hell. She'd had sex with a boy. She had given birth out of wedlock, and she'd blown her chance of avoiding eternal damnation.

Aunt Cookie said maybe she might be able to redeem herself if she became a nun and devoted her life to serving the Lord, but Fiona couldn't imagine taking such a step, even to save her own soul. The very thought of taking vows for life and living in a faith community sounded like a jail sentence.

An officious, intimidating woman had made Fiona sign papers and certificates, surrendering her rights as Ruby's mother. She had begged to keep her, but was told it was impossible—and dangerous to the child. A baby born out of wedlock bore the stain of original sin, and without proper parents, she was bound to suffer eternity in purgatory.

After the strangers arrived to take Ruby away in their gleaming Chrysler, its trunk filled with shiny new baby gear and pink blankets and stacks of diapers, Fiona had cried for days. Milk filled her breasts like a hot tidal wave, turning them into rock-hard volcanoes that spurted thin, blue-white lava, and the searing pain caused the world to tilt on its axis.

Aunt Cookie brought warm compresses for her boobs and a cool cloth for her face, and somehow, Fiona's breasts stopped trying to produce nourishment for a baby that had been snatched away. The heat and hardness slowly subsided. Fiona imagined the milk turning to tears and flowing out through her eyes for hours and hours and hours.

Now she was home and nobody talked about where she'd been and what had happened. Fiona was an invisible mom, a girl who had created life inside her body, yet had no baby to hold in her arms. Ma gave her a pad and a belt and told her to get some rest. Her kid brothers and sisters regarded her with wide eyes, and then Izzy flung herself into Fiona's arms, clinging for dear life. *Don't ever leave me again*, she wailed over and over. *It's awful without you.*

The other kids either ignored her or tiptoed around her, treating her like something fragile that would break at the slightest pressure. Her father could barely look at her, and when their eyes met by accident, she saw a deep and painful sadness reflected back at her.

Her brother Flynn was an unexpected ally—kind and matter-of-fact, making her feel like she might have a shot at not being miserable forever. He had a place of his own and was still dating Haley, even though their parents disapproved. He told Fiona that she needed to get back to normal. Reenter the flow of her life, reconnect with her friends, rediscover her goals and dreams. Then everything else would fall into place.

That was the idea anyway.

But her school clothes didn't fit. The blouse smashed her boobs, and she couldn't get the skirt zipper past her waist. She inched it up as far as she could, and then put on a cardigan to hide the gap. She studied herself in the closet mirror. She looked like herself, but different. The cloth St. Wilda's badge on the sweater added a note of familiarity. Yet there was something different about the shape of her face, and maybe the way she held herself, tiny details she hadn't noticed before. Having a baby had changed her from the inside out. Fiona knew that now. Cookie said she'd get her figure back, but no one explained how Fiona would get *herself* back. She would never be that girl again. She would never get herself back. She would get a different girl, put together in a totally different way.

With a worried sigh, she moved through her morning routine of breakfast, schoolbag, bus card, library card. Her next step in reclaiming her life was to drop by Mairin's house. She and her best friend always walked to the bus stop together. They'd been doing it since first grade, when their mothers deemed them old enough to cross the street by themselves, holding hands.

Truth be told, Fiona was mad at Mairin, even though she yearned to see her friend. Mairin had promised to write every week. But she had not sent a single letter to Aunt Cookie's in Bradford. Not one.

Fiona had written to Mairin a few times, describing life in the small Pennsylvania town, taking classes at a school where no one knew her, but she gave up when she didn't hear back. Mairin's silence troubled and confused Fiona. It wasn't like Mairin to go back on a promise. But then again, it wasn't like Fiona to get herself in trouble and give away a baby and then come back home like a flat tire.

Maybe the two of them could talk about it on the way to school, Fiona thought. She grabbed her schoolbag, which she'd filled with supplies she'd bought last fall, never realizing the long gap that awaited her. Then she stepped out into the brisk morning.

A chill wind, scented by the lake water, chased her down the block to Peach Street. When they were little, Fiona and Mairin used to run back and forth to each other's house, slamming in and out without knocking, calling each other's name. This morning felt different, though. Time had passed. She and Mairin had never been apart for so long.

Fiona cleared her throat and knocked on the front door. Usually Mairin would come clattering down the stairs with her fabulous curly red hair tumbling past her shoulders and her socks slumped down around her ankles, a piece of peanut butter toast clenched in her teeth, because she was always rushing around, running late. Her big brother, Liam, would often be eating cereal out of a mixing bowl because he had a huge appetite, and the radio would be on, adding to the noise and energy of a busy morning filling the house.

This morning, the storm door opened, and there was Mrs. Davis in a threadbare bathrobe and plain gray scuffs, her hair caught back in a plastic barrette. Fiona's heart pounded with dread. She hoped she wouldn't have to explain too much to Mairin's mother.

Obviously, the whole world knew why a girl went away for a certain number of months and then came back deflated and brokenhearted. But Fiona didn't really want to talk about it.

"Hiya, Mrs. D," she said brightly.

"Fiona! And here you are entirely, dear girl." She stood aside, motioning Fiona into the foyer. Mrs. D was the same age as Fiona's mom, but she seemed older. Wearier. As if life weighed heavier on her shoulders.

A hacking sound came from the back of the house, and Fiona pretended not to hear it. She'd always thought Mairin's stepdad was kind of gross. A drinker, she'd heard her own mom whispering to Flynn.

"Yep, that's me," Fiona said, forcing a smile. "Mairin ready?" She glanced around the foyer, which was once as familiar to her as the one in her own home. This was a lot less cluttered than the one at Fiona's. With eight kids in the family and seven still living at home, the Gallaghers' place was always filled with coats and boots, sports equipment and schoolbags.

By contrast, this place looked spare, almost empty. There was a hall table with a mail tray, and an umbrella stand in the corner.

Mairin's mother was studying Fiona with an odd, unreadable expression on her face.

"Mrs. D?" Fiona prompted.

"Oh, Fiona. How are you, dear?" Something in her tone dipped into the deep well of sadness that lived inside Fiona.

She waved her hand and meant to say everything was fine, but what came out was a broken whisper. "I'm not okay, Mrs. Davis."

Mrs. D took her hand, then ever so slowly and gently gathered Fiona into a cushiony hug. "I know, dear. I know it's hard. It's just so very hard. I know, dear Fiona."

She didn't know, thought Fiona. She couldn't. No one could ever know what it was like to push a living, amazing baby out into the world, to watch her draw her first breath and take on the color of life and let out a sweet bleating cry, and then to tell her goodbye forever. It was a kind of pain that nobody had ever found a word for. It was something dark and cold, taking up residence in her chest like a disease that had no cure. Still, the embrace felt nice, and Mrs. D's lilting Irish voice was soothing.

As she pulled back, she was surprised to see tears in Mrs. D's eyes.

"Um, everything okay?" she asked the woman.

"Certainly, dear. Of course."

Fiona felt a flicker of concern. She recalled that Liam O'Hara had been drafted last fall. Maybe he was already fighting over in Vietnam. Maybe something had happened to him, and that was why his mother was upset. Fiona looked around the foyer and down the hall toward Mairin's room. She focused on a handful of envelopes that lay in the mail tray. To her surprise, she recognized the Paula Paper stationery Aunt Cookie had given her when she first arrived in Bradford, urging her to stave off the homesickness by writing letters to her friends.

"Are those my letters to Mairin?" she asked Mrs. D. "Did she not even open them?"

Mrs. D took an unsteady breath. "Ah, that. Well, as it happens, Mairin is away, dear. I've been saving the letters for her when she gets back."

"Away?" Fiona frowned. "I don't understand. Away where? For how long?" A thought crossed her mind. Girls going away usually meant one thing. "You can't mean—"

"Of course not," Mrs. D said hastily. "Certainly not. It's—" She paused, glanced over her shoulder, and then gestured at the door. "Come out on the porch, Fiona dear, and I'll see you off to school."

"Hell's bells, Mrs. D." Fiona followed her out into the chilly morning. She was worried now. "Where did Mairin go?"

"She's gone to stay at the Good Shepherd Institute," Mrs. D said, her voice thin with tension. "Maybe you know it? Over on Best Street."

Fiona was vaguely aware of the old stone buildings that covered a city block. It was some kind of orphanage or reform school, something like that. "I don't understand at all, Mrs. D. What's she doing there? And when's she coming back?"

"Ah, well, then. It's . . . a difficult thing, it is," said Mairin's mother. "You see, she became troublesome, don't you know."

"Mairin? Troublesome?" Fiona gave a snort of disbelief. Her best friend was loud and energetic and irrepressible, but never troublesome. She had a heart as big as the world. "What on earth did she do that she's been sent away?"

Mrs. D rubbed her hands down the front of her bathrobe. Up and down, up and down. "Well, the sad truth is, Mairin and Colm—Mr. Davis—don't entirely get along. The two of them are like oil and water, truth be told. And with Liam away in the army . . . It was decided that Mairin would be better off staying over at the Good Shepherd. The nuns there will keep her safe."

Safe. Was Mairin not safe in her own home, then?

"I see," Fiona said. But she didn't see at all. "I'll go pay her a visit after school."

"Ah, no. You mustn't do that," said Mrs. D. "'Tisn't allowed. The nuns there are very strict about the rules."

"Is it some sort of prison, then?" Fiona asked. "She's not allowed to have visitors?"

"The nuns are very strict," Mrs. D repeated. "Very strict indeed. It was a hard choice that was made, but it's for the best—"

"Deirdre," called a rough male voice from inside the house. "Deirdre, *coffee*."

Fiona cringed a little at the sound of Mr. Davis's voice. And she was reeling from the news about Mairin—her best friend, the sister of her heart. *Gone*. The neighborhood, the whole world just didn't feel right without Mairin. Fiona looked up at Mrs. Davis, who used to have two kids and now had none. But at least she'd been allowed to be a mother to her children.

"I should get going to school," Fiona said. "So long, Mrs. D." She hurried down the front steps, chased by the sound of Mairin's stepfather yelling for his morning coffee.

It was kind of freaky, thinking about Mairin with the nuns. No, not just freaky but infuriating. Because Fiona knew Mairin didn't belong in some walled institute run by nuns. She deserved to be running around the neighborhood like always, waiting for the spring snowmelt and hanging around with her friends.

Fiona could guess at the real reason Mairin had been sent away. It wasn't because she was bad or in trouble. It wasn't because she had done something wrong or terrible.

It was because of Mr. D. Fiona knew it. She had never liked the guy.

DEIRDRE DAVIS WATCHED Mairin's friend hurry along the sidewalk in the direction of St. Wilda's, off to school like any girl in the neighborhood. Then, feeling the chill through her threadbare robe, she went inside. She paused at the antique hall table, where Fiona's letters to Mairin lay unopened in a tray.

Letting out a sigh, Deirdre slid open the drawer of the hall table, a repository for odds and ends. At the very back was a tiny parcel wrapped in layers of tissue. She took it out, parting the paper, and stared at the contents—a small white candle and a single baby's bootie made of snow-white knitting wool. She ran her thumb over the bootie, touched it to her cheek, and then put the keepsake away.

She lifted the loose end of her cloth belt and dabbed at her eyes, then let out her breath with a shudder. A sadness filled her, prompted by a wave of nostalgia. Seeing poor Fiona Gallagher at the end of her ordeal dredged up memories in Deirdre that popped up like sucker roots under the apple tree. Memories that refused to stay buried.

"Deirdre, goddamn it, where's my coffee?" Colm's bellows made her grimace.

"Coming," she yelled back peevishly. "Give it a rest, already. I'm up to ninety doing my morning chores, while you're in there faffing about, giving out orders when you could come down and make your own damn coffee." She stalked into the kitchen to find him already seated at the Formica table. He was scowling at the lottery numbers in the morning paper.

Feck. The man couldn't even be bothered to pour his own coffee. The percolator was finished on the stove. She turned off the flame, then picked up the carafe and filled a thick porcelain mug, adding a scoop of sugar just the way he liked it. She set it before him and spun away to pour a cup for herself.

"Who the hell was that?" he asked in his grainy post-drinking voice.

"Mairin's friend Fiona," Deirdre said curtly. "She came by looking for Mairin. Fiona's been away and didn't know Mairin's been sent up to the nuns."

"Fiona? Oh, the dirty one that got herself knocked up, then?"

There was so much wrong with his question that Deirdre almost laughed. Almost. "Fiona's not dirty, but decent," she retorted. "She's a sweet-natured girl I've known since she and Mairin were tiny."

"So sweet-natured that she got herself knocked up," Colm insisted.

"She didn't get herself knocked up. It took the willing participation of a boy, for Christ's sake."

"She's a filthy chit," he continued, steamrolling over the point she was trying to make. "The Gallaghers went too easy on her, if you ask me."

"No one asked you, and it's none of your business anyway," Deirdre retorted. Her husband was always so ornery after a night at Kell's. She leaned against the counter and sipped her coffee, letting the hot, bitter taste of it slip over her tongue.

"She should have gone to the nuns," Colm pontificated. "That'd be the way for sure. Then the girl would get what she deserved."

Deirdre lost herself in thought, unable to bear listening to more of his rantings on things he knew nothing about. Every word he said regarding unwed mothers and babes out of wedlock was a stab to Deirdre's heart, even though no one in this life would ever know why that was.

When Fiona showed up at her door this morning, Deirdre had been taken aback by a flood of unexpected emotion. She had recognized Fiona's sadness as if the girl were holding up a mirror.

The stark recognition reminded Deirdre that she, too, had once known the heat of teenage passion. Back in her day, in the Irish town of Limerick, she herself had been that girl—a pretty, promising youngster full of youthful energy and impossible dreams. But oh, so naive and careless.

Her mum had figured it out in the first three months, noting Deirdre's frequent trips to the loo, her sudden aversion to cabbage-laden colcannon, and her bouts of weepiness for no apparent reason. Mum had hauled her off to the midwife's for a test.

And then it was away to the Clare Street laundry with her, where the Sisters of the Good Shepherd would help her wash away her shame. She took up residence in a hulking, joyless place where she was forced to work, punished and humiliated by the nuns and supervisors.

And that wasn't even the worst thing that had happened to Deirdre. The worst occurred after the baby came—a perfect little angel of an infant with lovely round cheeks and the softest bow-shaped lips she'd ever seen. The worst occurred when he was taken from her.

When they took the baby from her arms, she tried to hold on, but the infant whimpered, and she didn't want to hurt him. He was whisked away. She had looked down at her hand. In it was a tiny knit bootie, made of local wool, white as new-fallen snow.

The nuns made her go to the church and light a candle and say a prayer of farewell. She didn't light a candle that day. She slipped the unlit votive into her pocket along with the snow-white bootie, and she'd kept both tokens ever since. She just wanted some kind of reminder that she never willingly gave her baby away. That she would never say farewell.

The Justice Minister of Fianna Fáil had a policy that favored the sending of children to America for adoption in suitable homes. This was deemed a far kinder alternative to life in an institution in Ireland. Deirdre was told nothing except that Catholic Charities had given her son to a prosperous couple in a city called Buffalo in America.

The grief that had descended on Deirdre was a kind of madness. She had wailed for weeks until the sadness nearly killed her. She knew it would kill her entirely if she didn't find her child. She seized on the mad notion that she must reclaim him and keep him forever.

Driven by that singular impulse, she had raised money by doing the things she'd learned at Clare Street—laundry and mending. The moment she'd saved enough to buy a one-way ticket to Buffalo, New York, in America, she had secured a travel passport and went without her parents' consent. They wouldn't miss her. Ever since she'd had the baby, they treated her like a leper.

Back then, Deirdre had known nothing about the world. She knew only that her baby had been sent to the Archdiocese of Buffalo. She'd memorized the information on the papers she'd been forced to sign. For the sake of her child, she had endured a frightening, bumpy flight to America, and then an endless ride by coach from New York City to Buffalo, a frigid, windswept city by a lake that was as vast as the sea.

She never found him, of course. The records were sealed. No one at the archdiocese would speak to her, and when she persisted, they even threatened to bar her from the offices, which were adjacent to the huge church of St. Joseph. She would never know the name of the couple who had taken her baby. The adoption was shrouded in secrecy.

To make things worse, Deirdre's pocketbook was as empty as her heart. She had no way of getting back to Ireland, not that her family would welcome her home after what she had done. Swamped by failure, she had stood at the river's edge above Niagara Falls, mesmerized by the power of the raging water cascading between the two Great Lakes. One step was all it would take. One step and she would be gone forever. Just. One. Step.

She had swayed toward the surging, foaming water, weirdly drawn to the unending motion of the current. In that moment, she felt a gentle touch on her arm and turned to see a young man next to her. Later she would learn that the reason he had been so gentle with her was that he didn't want to startle her and send her plunging into the river. But his unseen fist was firmly clutching the belt of her coat just in case. One day, he would tell Deirdre that he had sensed exactly what she was contemplating, as if he could read her thoughts.

"You look like you could use a bite to eat," he said in an affable American voice. "Ever try a beef on weck?"

The young man had brilliant red hair and kind, soft eyes. He was wearing a shirt with a power company badge on it. "I'm Patrick O'Hara," he said. "I'd like to buy you a beef on weck."

"Sorry, what?" Deirdre asked, blinking as though his face were the sun. "And why?"

"It's a local specialty—roast beef on a kummelweck roll, with salt and caraway seeds. And it's delicious. I bet they don't have such a thing in Ireland." He grinned at her expression. "I knew you were Irish," he said. "Not just because of the red hair." He gestured at her travel case, which still bore the tags and stickers of her journey. "Come on. There's a diner over on Ferry Ave. My treat."

Patrick O'Hara saved her, and not just because of his good timing. He saved her by giving her something to live for. He told her she was pretty, and he courted her with respect and unwavering devotion. He told her he loved her, and when she broke down and confessed about the lost baby, he said it made him love her even more because of the ordeal she'd gone through to try to find her child, her own flesh and blood.

He said that when the moment came, she would love their own precious babies with that same devotion. In almost no time at all he won her heart, and she married him, and that was what had saved her altogether.

They did have two kids, three years apart, first Liam and then Mairin. Only two, because Patrick was a second generation American, and he practiced birth control just like the Protestants did. At first, Deirdre had been certain that using birth control would brand her a sinner. But she couldn't deny feeling relieved that there was a way to avoid having baby after baby, year after year, like so many of the harried women in her club.

Deirdre and Patrick had thirteen hard, joyous years together, building a life in their snug little house on Peach Street. They should have had decades more, but the accident at the Falls took him, and it sucked all the joy from her life.

Deirdre was left to raise two kids on her own meager earnings gleaned from a commercial laundry where she worked eight hours a day. She was terrified that she would lose the house she and Patrick had bought with the bright, soaring hope that at last, they were achieving the American dream.

Colm Davis worked at the power plant, too. He was supposed to save her the way Patrick had. But he didn't save her, and by the time Deirdre realized her mistake, it was too late. She was naive, and had sunk into a deep hole of grief, and she was desperate for someone, anyone, to hold out a hand to her.

That hand happened to belong to Colm, and she had held on tight. What she hadn't understood was that just because he worked at the plant didn't mean he was the man Patrick had been. She hadn't seen that at first. All she'd seen was a big, broad-shouldered, good-looking guy who talked with confidence and went around with a swagger as if he owned the world. Terrified of falling destitute, she'd put her trust in him. Before long, she learned that all jobs at the plant were not equal, and all men who worked there were not equal. Colm was a maintenance specialist, which Deirdre later learned was just a janitor making an hourly wage. And the wages tended to shrink dramatically thanks to Colm's frequent stops at the corner bar after work. He had a fondness for playing the lottery, which never did him a lick of good, but he still kept trying, certain that easy street was just around the next corner. When Colm got in trouble for taking money from the Eagles Lodge, the only thing that kept him from jail was that he agreed to have his wages garnished until he paid them back.

They tried for more kids—Colm wanted to match his brother's six—but it was not to be. As the years passed and she failed to conceive, Colm was convinced there was something wrong with her. She even saw her doctor about it, and the doctor suggested the trouble might be with Colm. That simply made him furious, and he refused to see a doctor himself. With a sense of relief, Deirdre contented herself with Liam and Mairin, who both had their father's fiery red hair and adventurous spirit.

Now Deirdre grieved every day over Liam, who had gone into the army and was stationed in Texas, waiting to be shipped out to a place she couldn't even fathom, it was that foreign. He almost never sent letters home. Her son was mad at her for sending Mairin to the nuns.

Deirdre felt guilty about making her daughter live with the harsh, humorless nuns over on Best Street, but she felt she had no choice. As Mairin grew from coltish little girl into a willowy young woman, Deirdre had noticed Colm eyeing her like a lamb chop. At first, Deirdre hoped Colm would obey his better angels, but after the incident last fall, she couldn't ignore it. Mairin was safer with the nuns.

Deirdre truly believed that. She had to believe that. And she prayed her daughter might forgive her one day.

She looked out the window over the kitchen sink in time to see poor little Fiona turn the corner toward St. Wilda's. There were many ways to lose a child, Deirdre thought with a shudder of sadness. Far too many ways to lose a child. She let out a sigh that turned into a sob.

"What are you on about, then?" Colm demanded, glancing up from the sports pages.

"Ah, I just... It was a wave of sadness. Seeing Fiona reminds me of how much I miss Mairin." She twisted her hands nervously together. She'd underestimated how much she would miss her lovely sprite of a daughter. Perhaps she could bring Mairin home and still manage to keep her safe. Yes, she could find a way to make sure her daughter never found herself alone with Colm. "Hasn't she been gone long enough?"

Colm gave a snort of contempt. "She's not welcome in this house, not after what she did. She'll stay her full term, and make her own way in the world once she turns eighteen. I won't have it any other way."

The ache in Deirdre's heart was unbearable, each painful beat a reminder of the impossible choice she'd had to make. It wasn't fair—none of it. Mairin was only fifteen, her childhood innocence turning into vibrant beauty. It wasn't her fault that she'd become a dangerous magnet for her stepfather's gaze.

Resentment boiled inside Deirdre, not toward Mairin but toward the man they had once trusted. She'd hated sending Mairin away from the familiarity of home, yet a fierce sense of protectiveness had demanded it, even if it meant breaking her own heart in the process.

Chapter 13

Sister Bernadette prayed long and hard for Mairin O'Hara—or Ruth, the Magdalene name that had been assigned to the girl. She truly didn't seem like a Ruth—a symbol of loyalty and devotion. She was definitely more of a *Máirín*. The name meant "star of the sea," bold and fearless. It would take more than a name change to rein in her spirit.

Bernadette had been spending extra time in the chapel, murmuring urgent supplications and seeking guidance on behalf of the girl, because despite all her flaws, there was something about her that sparked a glimmer of sympathy. Bernadette prayed that Ruth would come to accept her place at the Good Shepherd. The girl wasn't just wayward. She was incorrigible. She kept trying to leave the holy refuge as though this place was some kind of prison.

Her dogged persistence was troubling, as it highlighted a flagrant disrespect for the rules. Mairin didn't seem to be deterred by the usual methods—Sister Rotrude's leather-tipped baton or heavy wooden rosary beads, a day of bread and water, or hours in the closet or basement. The dark isolation of the closet was the most feared and effective punishment, but even that didn't keep Mairin from scheming about escape and hurling herself from one reckless attempt to the next.

After the fiasco with the PA system, Bernadette had every right to be cross with Mairin, but that would be uncharitable. Besides, it was like being cross with a puppy. The girl was irrepressible and unapologetic. She simply could not resist the impulse to flee.

One night at bedtime, Bernadette was concluding her prayers when she heard urgent whispers sweeping through the hallway. She opened the door to her spare, painstakingly neat chamber, and immediately sensed a stir in the air. A flurry of excitement. Mairin again? Another escape attempt?

Clutching a shawl around her, Bernadette stepped into the hallway to see Sister Rotrude and Sister Gerard rushing toward the dormitory wing. "Is something the matter?" Bernadette whispered. "Can I help?"

Sister Gerard paused. "Thank you, Sister. All will be well. Agnes's baby is coming. We'll be taking her to St. Francis."

"How exciting," Sister Theresa whispered, joining them in the hallway. "Please wish her godspeed."

"Say a prayer for the little one," Sister Rotrude said. Then she and Mother Superior were gone, their tunics swishing as they hastened down the hallway.

Bernadette whispered a string of prayers for Agnes and the baby, hoping they would be all right. Although most of the unwed mothers went to Father Baker's, and the babies to Our Lady of Victory, there were a few births each year right here among the girls of the Good Shepherd. Mother Superior was diligent in arranging just the right match, making certain the couple was prepared—not just spiritually, but financially. Sister Gerard was adamant that Angela should stay here, getting the care she needed and guarding the privacy her grandmother insisted on. Whenever a girl arrived who was expecting, the prioress had many private meetings with married couples who yearned for a child. Childless mothers, their hearts aching for a babe of their own, placed all their hopes and dreams in the process.

For Bernadette, pregnancy was a deeply mysterious process, and childbirth, a miracle. Of course, when she was very young and living in the big city with her drunken, sin-stained mother, she had not been shielded from the mechanics of copulation. But she knew virtually nothing about how a birth actually happened. And a special mystery surrounded Agnes, because she'd been a resident here for a year, which meant she had fallen pregnant while under the care of the Good Shepherd. Bernadette believed Sister Gerard was particularly protective of Agnes due to the unanswered questions that shrouded her pregnancy.

In the manner of the Holy Virgin herself, Agnes refused to speak of the mysterious conception. After the tumultuous meeting with Agnes's grandmother, no one had mentioned it. Some of the nuns speculated that she had slipped away on high mass Sunday in the city. Others suspected that Agnes, with her angelic looks, had tempted one of the delivery truck drivers. Yet in her heart of hearts, Bernadette yearned for the birth to be an actual miracle. A gift from God. Agnes was exceptionally beautiful, and would surely produce an equally beautiful infant.

Bernadette had heard many times that a girl would be better off saying she'd murdered someone than admitting she was unmarried and pregnant. Sister Gerard insisted that the only way for such a girl to find redemption and a future for herself was absolute secrecy, because it was a well-known fact that no decent man would ever have her if he knew what she'd done.

For the fallen girls here, the birth was a bittersweet event—the sweetness of a new babe taking its first breath on God's green earth contrasted with the bitterness of the young woman whose shame could never be washed off or prayed away. Still, that didn't keep Bernadette from praying the Lord would lead Agnes to redemption and the baby to a proper family. Adoption would be mandatory, of course. A girl who tried to keep her own baby was told in no uncertain terms that she was being selfish. She would be heaping a lifelong stigma on an innocent babe. Every child had the right to grow up with two parents.

Some girls—including Agnes—claimed they wanted to keep their baby, but that was impossible. A teenage girl with no education or job skills, whose character would be in question because of her sin, had no way to earn a living and care for a child. For an unmarried girl with a baby, the world was a grim and dangerous place. She might find herself having to wander the dark tenements of the waterfront, doing unspeakable things just to keep food in her belly.

It was a blessing, then, that Agnes's ordeal would soon be over, and the babe placed with a family that could give it a better life.

The next day, however, the news came back, and it was not good. A somber Sister Rotrude reported that Agnes's baby had been declared stillborn.

On hearing this, Bernadette felt a shudder of pure shock, and then she wept real tears. The babe—a wee, perfect girl, as pretty as her mother, according to Sister Rotrude—was gone even before she'd been shriven, which made the situation even more tragic.

In the office, Sister Gerard handed Bernadette a packet of papers to file in the special safe that was used only for the most sensitive and important documents, such as birth, death, and adoption records. To protect the records from being destroyed or lost, they were kept in a large, immovable safe behind a bookcase that swung outward like a door. Sister Gerard claimed the hidden safe was meant to protect the records from the elements and from prying eyes. "People's private lives are at stake and we must guard their privacy with all vigilance," she'd told Bernadette.

The safe was a relic from the last century, with ornate flourishes on the corners and a combination lock. There was a verse from the first book of Samuel, chapter one, verse twenty-seven, engraved on the top of the metal safe: *I prayed for this child, and the Lord has granted me what I asked of Him.*

The verse seemed so poignant now, in the face of such a heartbreaking tragedy. Bernadette knew better than to question the mysterious ways of the Lord, but this situation brought more tears to her eyes. She clutched the thick folder to her chest as Sister Gerard spun the lock. No one but the Mother Superior had the combination.

Now Bernadette stood back while the prioress dialed the combination. She inadvertently saw the first digit—a seven—before looking guiltily away.

A page slipped from the folder and wafted to the floor. Bernadette picked it up. A glance revealed an official-looking document with the heading *New York State Department of Health Office of Vital Statistics Certificate of Birth Registration.* There were two tiny footprint stamps, like parentheses around a phrase, at the bottom of the page. Was it common to make a footprint impression of a stillborn child? She knew better than to ask. But she also wondered if such a document was needed for a stillbirth. She quickly replaced the page and put it out of her mind.

"Mother, I was wondering," Bernadette said as she helped move the bookcase back in place. "Regarding poor Agnes's baby."

Sister Gerard eyed her sharply enough to make Bernadette wince. "How's that?"

"Have arrangements been made for the little one?" asked Sister Bernadette. "Will we attend services?"

"Under the circumstances, that would not be called for," said Sister Gerard. "The arrangements are the purview of the family, and not for us to decide."

"Oh my goodness." Bernadette felt a beat of distress. "Surely we must go to Agnes, and to her grandmother, Mrs. Denny."

"Agnes is to stay in the hospital on complete bedrest until she's better. Mrs. Denny has the support of her community over at Our Lady of Victory. You'll recall that Mrs. Denny's greatest wish is for this never to have happened."

"But—"

"We'll not torment the poor woman further over her granddaughter's shame. We shall offer our prayers right here in our own community. Let us light a special candle at prayers today." The mother superior's reply was swift and firm. "In some ways, it's a blessing altogether," Sister Gerard said. "The poor girl can now lay the past to rest. She won't spend the rest of her life fretting over what's become of the babe. You'll recall the girl last year who was so desperate over the fate of her baby that she had to be taken to the State Asylum."

Bernadette nodded, staring at the floor. She could still hear the poor girl's screams as the ambulance crew escorted her out. She was transported to the terrifying fortress in the north of the city where not even prayers could save her.

Now Bernadette wondered if this was the Lord's plan—to spare Agnes from the pain and uncertainty of knowing her child was out in the world somewhere, unknown and unreachable, in the keeping of strangers.

Bernadette herself had been born to an unwed mother who had no way to look after her. As Genesee, her childhood had been nothing but misery and danger until the people of Catholic Charities had stepped in. She still remembered the cold apartment and the noise and the smells, the gnawing hunger and uncertainty she faced every day, even as a tiny child.

Would it have been better for her not to have been born at all? Or did the Lord have a larger purpose in mind for her?

"And when Agnes heals," she asked the prioress, "will she return to her grandmother's, then?" Bernadette asked.

"Certainly not. She is still afflicted with the French vice. Her education is far from complete." Sister Gerard shut the safe and spun the dial.

THE EAR-GRATING BELL for lights-out sounded, and the girls were supposed to kneel in prayer beside their cots. Mairin assumed the position and closed her eyes, but she didn't pray. Prayer had never worked for her. Instead, she imagined a life beyond these cold walls, where freedom was not just a distant memory but a reality she craved with every cell in her body.

She missed almost everything about her former life, even school, and having to shovel the front walk after a big snow, and her mother's endless soap operas on TV. Most of all, she missed the comfort and privacy of her own room, hanging out with her brother and her friends. She missed Fiona and Liam so much that it hurt.

By now, Fiona would have had her baby. Was she okay? Was the baby? Did they really make her give it up for adoption?

And Liam—how could her big brother, who had the best laugh and the kindest eyes, be expected to fight in a war nobody wanted? What if she never got to see him again? It was too unbearable to think about, but she didn't know how to stop her racing thoughts.

She even missed her mother these days. Yes, she'd been furious with Mam. But she couldn't forget the way her mother used to whisper her name in Irish—*Máirín*—and sing songs at bedtime, and how her buttery scones were the best in the world.

As the girls were rustling and sighing, trying to get comfortable in the chilly dorm unit, Mairin noticed a silhouette crossing the room toward her.

"*Lún dào ni zhuā le,*" Helen whispered, passing close to her cot. That was the phrase Helen had taught the girls—an invitation to a game of mahjong. Despite her exhaustion, Mairin flung aside her blanket, welcoming the distraction. The game was a secret rebellion, a way to do something normal in this awful place. They tiptoed, along with Odessa and Denise, to the end of the dormitory, where light from a caged bare bulb fell across the floor. Moonglow filtered through the barred windows, casting eerie shadows across the rows of beds.

The girls huddled together, sitting cross-legged on a frayed woolen blanket around the mahjong set Helen had made. Her markings were beautiful and delicate—the stones, characters, and bamboos, the winds and dragons, the daintily drawn flowers.

Odessa's nimble fingers arranged the tiles into a precise array. "Think there'll be a bed check tonight?" she asked.

"Nah. They never do," Denise pointed out. "The old biddies are too lazy to climb the stairs."

"Want to hear something crazy?" Mairin said. "Something I found out last time I was in the closet. I overheard them talking about birthdays and stuff. Guess how old Sister Rotrude is. Just guess. You'll never guess."

"We can't guess if you don't stop talking," Denise said.

"She's probably in her fifties," Odessa said. "Am I getting close?"

"I bet she's older than that," said Denise. "Older and meaner."

"Nope, guess again," said Mairin.

"Maybe she's like, ninety, and she's just freakishly well-preserved." Helen set out her little makeshift bettor, a wind indicator to help players keep track of the prevailing wind during the game.

Mairin shook her head. "You're all wrong. Rotrude is twenty-four. Can you believe it?"

"No way," Odessa said.

"Impossible. *Twenty-four?* That old hag?" Helen looked aghast.

"Swear," Mairin said, holding up her hand. "She's only nine years older than me. Crazy, huh?"

"Being a bully ages you, I guess." Odessa cut a quick glance at Denise.

"Who you calling a bully?" Denise scowled at her. "Come on. Forget the nuns, already. We're going to play just like free girls."

The game began, the soft clicks of tiles filling the air as they drew and discarded with growing expertise and confidence.

"This is nice," Odessa said. "Gives us a chance to forget where we are."

"And who they're trying to force us to be," Mairin said.

The night wore on, and just for a while, the intricate game play transported the girls away from the cold dormitory, offering a brief escape into a world of camaraderie and freedom. Even though friendships were forbidden here, the girls grew close, giggling and groaning as they competed for the tiles they needed to match.

Suddenly, the door at the head of the stairs creaked open, and the room fell into an oppressive silence. "Shit," whispered Denise. "Someone's here."

The girls dove for their beds. Helen scooped everything into the blanket and rushed away with the bundle just as a shadow darkened the doorway. Mairin squinted at the figure, then leaped from her bed. "Angela!" she said. "Hey, Angela!" Her heart flooded with gratitude and relief. To her surprise, she felt a lump in her throat, and she realized how much she'd missed her friend.

The other girls stirred and murmured. Angela moved into the room slowly and cautiously, her shoulders hunched. Feet shuffling along the floorboards, she made her way to the bed that had been empty since the night she'd been taken away to have her baby. She looked different, somehow. The big belly was gone, but it wasn't just that. Her hair was longer. The blond swirls framed her somber face.

"Oh my gosh, you've been gone such a long time." Mairin sat next to her on the bed. "We've been wondering if we'd ever see you again. How are you doing?"

"I'm . . . not really doing very well." Her gaunt face was as pale as the moon.

Mairin's stomach twisted. A few other girls gathered around. "Tell us everything. That is, only if you feel like talking about it."

Angela expelled a tremulous breath. "It was awful. I puked all over the station wagon on the way to the hospital, and got yelled at for making a mess. They put me in this iron bed on wheels . . . nuns all around, telling me I was bad and that the pain was my punishment."

"Fuck them," Denise snapped.

Mairin had never used that word, but she repeated it now. "Yeah, fuck them. You didn't do anything to deserve what happened to you. Please say you know that."

"I . . ." Angela nodded weakly. "It hurt so bad. I felt as if I was being torn apart. And then they did stuff."

"What kind of stuff?" asked Odessa, leaning in to stroke Angela's hair.

"Like, they herded me around like I was an animal. They shaved me *down there*. They said they had to give me an enema."

"What's an enema?" Janice asked, offering Angela a cup of water.

"I didn't know, either," Angela said. "And then . . . I did." She described the process, which sounded humiliating and unnecessary. "I freaked out. I was wailing and screaming and crying, and nobody moved a muscle. It was like they were used to it. Nobody asked how I was feeling. It was like I was invisible except for down there. It hurt so bad. I thought I was dying. In the middle of everything, they shoved a bunch of papers at me and made me sign them. But I wouldn't. I refused. So my gran signed them instead, because I'm not eighteen yet."

"What kind of papers?" Mairin asked.

"Just . . . hospital papers, I guess. It's all a blur now. Then they put a gas mask on me, and after that, I don't remember a thing. Not a blessed thing. One of the nurses—the nurses there are all nuns—said I was lucky to get the gas at all. Most girls don't get a painkiller because the pain is part of their punishment." She took a sip of water.

"Angela, what a nightmare," said Odessa. "I'm real glad you're back with us now."

"I have no idea how long I was unconscious. I woke up in a different bed in a different part of the hospital, and I was sick all over again. Puking, with a massive headache and a raging thirst, but they wouldn't give me any water. I had a heavy pad in my underwear because I was bleeding. There was some kind of tight band around my middle. They made me wear a bra with pads to soak up the milk."

"You had milk?" asked Janice. "In your *bra*?"

"For the baby, moron," said Denise. "Don't you know that the milk comes out of your boobs?"

Janice recoiled and wrapped her arms around her chest.

"Did you get to see the baby?" Helen asked, leaning forward. "Was it a boy or a girl? Did they let you hold it?"

Angela finished her water. Then she hugged her knees up against her chest. The look in her eyes was so sad that Mairin had to look away for a moment. "It's... it was a girl." Angela's voice trembled. "She was stillborn."

The word hovered in the silence that followed. *Stillborn* sounded like an old-fashioned term, something Mairin remembered from the *Little House on the Prairie* books she'd read when she was younger. Angela took in a breath and exhaled with a broken sob. "I wish *I'd* been stillborn."

"Don't be dumb," Denise said.

"Maybe it's the will of the Lord," said Janice, but her voice wavered as if she didn't believe her own words.

"And you're even dumber," Denise snapped at her. "Now, shut up and let her talk." Denise's voice was uncharacteristically soft when she turned to Angela. "If you feel like it, I mean."

Angela rested her chin on her drawn-up knees. In the silvery moonlight, her face was as beautiful as ever, but she looked older, somehow, her eyes haunted. She looked like a ghost—insubstantial, fragile, as though all it would take was a breath of wind to blow her away. "I never even got to see her. I mean, I didn't really want to have a baby, but... she was mine, I guess, for a while. I carried her inside me. I even thought of what I would name her. I thought about keeping her for my very own. When she came out, I was unconscious. They said she was still. Didn't take a single breath. That's all they told me. They never let me see. I slept through the whole thing, and I never got to see."

"Not even... well, was there a service or something?" Helen asked. "Where's the baby now?"

"My gran said there wasn't any money for a funeral. The truth is, Gran didn't want a funeral. She was ashamed, on account of me not being married."

"Well, then..." Odessa touched her hand. "Who took care of the baby?"

Angela brushed away a tear. "The nuns said she was laid to rest in consecrated ground, courtesy of the diocese."

"You didn't get to have a service?" Mairin felt terrible for her. The funeral for her father had been unbearably sad, but it was important, honoring and acknowledging that Patrick O'Hara had been in the world. Even a newborn deserved that.

"I was sick in bed," Angela said. "They kept giving me painkillers. I couldn't go anywhere. I couldn't even walk to the bathroom on my own for days and days. I had lots of stitches, and there was a lot of bleeding." She let out a sigh that turned into a sob. "She was mine for nine months. I felt her inside me. I wanted to name her Alice. I wish I could have seen her. Just once."

"Let's tell them you want to visit the grave," Mairin suggested. "We could all go."

Angela shook her head emphatically. "They wouldn't allow it, anyway. It's . . . complicated, I guess."

"Because of the pervy doctor who got you pregnant?" asked Denise.

Angela shuddered. "Sister Rotrude says I have to go back for a checkup."

"We'll protect you," Mairin said. "We have to protect each other. I'm just glad you're back with us."

"How can we help?" asked Odessa. "We want you to be all right. All right?" She patted Angela's knee and hummed a familiar tune, then began singing softly. "Oh Happy Day" was one of the songs Odessa had taught them, even the descant part, a favorite the girls liked to sing when no one was watching them. A few of the others joined in, tapping their feet and trying their best to cheer Angela up.

Mairin sang along, snapping her fingers to the beat, hoping her friend would join in. An idea struck her. "I'll be back in a jiff," she said.

She slipped on her shoes and retrieved the skeleton key from a high ledge above the only window in the dorm, then unlocked the iron gate at the top of the stairs. The gate was a fire code violation, but the nuns didn't care.

A while back, one of the new girls had asked, which had earned her a dozen pops with Sister Rotrude's penance stick. "You'll take the fire escape like anyone else," the nun had said. Then she'd punished everyone by having a fire drill in subzero temperatures, forcing the girls out the window onto the rickety exterior stairs made of rusty iron. The stairs ended ten feet above the ground, so they had to dangle and drop to the frozen earth.

Mairin made her way to the office, giving a little shudder of remembered fear as she passed the closet. If she got caught tonight, it would probably mean more time in confinement, but she had to risk it for Angela's sake. For all their sakes.

In the main office, she flipped the switch to open the PA channel to the dorms. Then she turned the radio dial to the top 40 station. "Twist and Shout" was playing. Perfect. By the time she ran up the stairs to the dorm, it was "Happy Together" by the Turtles, and the girls were already dancing. Even Angela was up on her feet, practicing her go-go girl moves. Exuberant laughter and song filled the room.

"We're screwed if we get caught," said Janice. "Rotrude'll go ballistic."

"Let her do her worst," said Angela, her cheeks finally showing some color. "I just had a baby that died. Nothing worse can happen to me, ever."

Chapter 14

In June of 1969, a miracle occurred. Niagara Falls, one of the mightiest waterfalls on the face of the earth, one of the seven wonders of the world, went bone-dry. The water stopped almost completely. A mere trickle leaked over the lip of the cliff.

It was such a singular wonder that the Sisters of Charity organized a field trip to take the girls to see the miracle. It was like a second miracle that the nuns were actually taking the girls on a field trip.

On the Fourth of July, everyone was instructed to make sure their uniforms were spotless, their hair neatly combed, their faces scrubbed, and their teeth cleaned. In the kitchen, they put together sack lunches—slabs of white bread, government cheese, plums that were not quite ripe, and as a special treat for the holiday, a Little Debbie cake in the shape of a star. The girls buzzed with excitement as they filed onto the bus. Normally they only ever got out for high mass once a month, so this was a rare opportunity. The nuns harangued them with dire warnings about their behavior, and of course everyone solemnly promised to follow the rules.

Mairin's excitement was edged by a sense of urgency. This could be her chance to escape. It was Independence Day, after all. As the bus drove north to the Falls, she stared out the window, sizing up the situation and looking for opportunities to get away. Maybe she could get someone to see her situation. Or maybe she could slip away into the crowd.

The bus pulled into the parking lot, and the girls chattered and prodded one another as they got off, blinking in the summer sunlight. The chaperones made them line up in front of the bus for another lecture about their conduct in public. Mairin hunched her shoulders and pretended to listen, feeling the heavy cloak of shame settle over her. The whole world could see that the side of the bus was marked with large letters spelling out *Good Shepherd Refuge*. She hated the stares of curiosity checking them out as the girls, in their drab uniforms, formed two lines flanked by vigilant nuns.

"Stay away from that lot," a pinch-faced woman in a mod minidress cautioned her children, guarding them like a hen with a clutch of eggs and drawing them away from the girls. Her hands closed like talons on the handle of her pocketbook. "They're from that reform school down in Buffalo." The information only made the kids gawk harder, turning back toward the girls even as their mother towed them in the other direction.

Teenagers nudged one another and snickered, pointing at the Good Shepherd girls. Denise shot them the bird, and one of them called, "Ooh, I'm so scared."

"Look at their weird hair," said a girl with a waist-length ponytail and a top that showed her bare midriff.

Mairin exchanged a glance with Odessa. Everyone's hair had actually grown out quite a bit since the shearing. Odessa was cultivating an impressive Afro style, which the nuns hated, but Mairin thought it looked cool. Her own hair was a curly mop, like Orphan Annie in the comics.

Helen walked along with her gaze on the ground, looking as if she wanted to fling herself over the falls. Janice hovered near Kay, who hunched her shoulders and kept her hands in the pockets of her smock. Angela glanced around, her eyes bright with excitement. Ever since she'd returned from having the baby, she seemed different. Bolder and angrier, and grown up in a way the others could only imagine.

The nuns herded the group along a walkway to the viewing area where tourists and summer camp groups milled around, taking pictures and staring at the giant pit far below. "Little Deuce Coupe" by the Beach Boys streamed from speakers at the WKBW booth, the upbeat music lifting everyone's spirits. Almost everyone. Sister Rotrude bridled and wrinkled her nose as if she detected a bad smell.

Standing at a railed viewing station, Mairin surveyed the pile of rubble at the base of the falls—where the thundering water should have been, anyway.

"Girls, this is a place no creature has ever stood before," Sister Gerard intoned, raising her voice to be heard over the music and crowds. "You are looking at a place the sun has never touched, nor ever will again, once the Lord God Almighty reopens the floodgates."

Like our lives, thought Mairin, lifting her face to welcome the midday heat. We live in a place the sun never touches. She knew the sun would darken her freckles, but she didn't care because it felt as sweet and warm as summer itself.

Sister Gerard preached with grand authority, telling the girls that before the miracle, sixty-five and a half billion gallons of water used to flow over Niagara Falls every twenty-four hours. "That works out to seventy-six thousand gallons that spilled over every second," she said. "Now the Lord has pulled back the protective curtain, exposing all to the world."

Mairin wondered what it would be like if the protective habits of the nuns were stripped away, if the constant rush of scripture and discipline and cruelty were shut off in one motion. What debris and remnants would be exposed for all to see?

"We are privileged today to witness such a never-before-seen spectacle," the prioress said.

"Yeah, sure," Denise muttered.

"It's been seen before," Helen said. "The falls stopped like a hundred years ago, when there was an ice jam. I read about it in *National Geographic*." Helen seemed to have read and memorized all the *National Geographic*s in the world. Maybe that was what brainy kids did when their parents were college professors.

"But an ice jam could never happen in the middle of summer like this," Janice said, pressing her hands to her heart.

Mairin looked down into the dry chasm, where she could see all sorts of debris—broken trees and pieces of metal among a big pile of jagged rocks. Her father had worked here for his entire career, until the Falls took him. She leaned against the railing and stared out over the cliff, wondering if any part of him remained. *Dad, are you there?*

She could still hear his daily farewell, called over his shoulder as he left for work: *See you when I come back around.*

You never came back around, Dad. You never did.

"Hey, are you all right?" Odessa's brow was puckered with concern.

Mairin brushed at her cheeks. She was supposed to be the tough one. "I'm okay," she said hurriedly.

"Were you overcome by the miracle, Ruth?" asked Sister Bernadette in a tremulous voice. "This hallowed miracle?"

"What?" Mairin scowled at her. "Jeez. It's not a damn miracle."

Bernadette winced as if stabbed by pain. "We've all seen the divine power of the water," she said. "Nothing short of a miracle could possibly stop Niagara Falls."

"So I guess they're gonna rename the Army Corps of Engineers the Army Corps of Miracles," Mairin said.

"I don't understand." Bernadette glanced nervously from side to side. A tiny bead of sweat escaped her veil. "You mustn't blaspheme, Ruth."

"Turning off the falls has been talked about for a long time," Mairin said. "Even six years ago when my dad was still alive. He worked for the power company."

"Your dad's dead?" Odessa asked. "You never told us."

"That's really sad," Helen said. "What happened?"

Mairin pulled in a shaky breath. This would always be hard. Always. This would never not be sad. She had to simply resign herself to that reality. The sadness would continue for as long as she lived. "He was killed right near here, down in the Whirlpool Rapids. He and his crew were trying to rescue another boat that was in distress, and he went under and drowned. It was the worst day of my life," she added, her voice cracking like the rocks over the cliff. Maybe, she thought, this was the reason she was able to tolerate all the punishments the nuns doled out. There would never be anything worse than that day.

"Oh, jeez, that's really awful," said Janice. "About your dad, not the water being turned off."

"They didn't exactly turn off the water," Mairin said, wanting to change the subject. "The army engineers made a dam to divert the flow of the river away from the American Falls."

"Why?" asked Kay. "Why'd they do that?" She stared down at the pile of rocks.

Without the water, it was just a cliff, thought Mairin. It wasn't much to look at—a big pile of rubble.

A man in a park ranger uniform came over, tipping his cap respectfully to the nuns. "I overheard your question, young lady," he said to Kay.

Kay clutched at Janice's arm. Kay was afraid of the outside world. She shrank and shivered from strangers, and was currently regarding the ranger in horror. The fact that he was a man in uniform, crisp and authoritative-looking, only added to her fear.

Janice stuck to Kay like glue and kept her calm. "Don't freak out or they'll make us go back early," she said under her breath.

"I wonder if they found buried treasure down there," Odessa speculated.

The ranger winked at her. "So far, we've only found random coins, bike parts, and junk, but nothing of value."

"Then why'd they stop the water?" asked Denise.

"The idea was to find a way to move the boulders piled up at the base of the falls so the cascade would have a longer fall," the ranger said.

"So did they figure out a way to move the rocks?" asked Helen.

"They did not. Human mastery over nature doesn't always work out. It was a grand experiment, though. The dam will be dismantled soon, and the flow will be restored."

"Thanks be to God." Sister Bernadette made the sign of the cross.

He tipped his hat again. "You have a good day, ma'am. Girls."

A daring impulse seized Mairin, and she hurried after him. "Sir! Sir, wait a minute, please."

He stopped and turned with a wary frown. "What is it, young lady?"

Mairin slipped a glance over her shoulder. "I'm . . . We need help. The girls and I." She gestured back at the group. Lowering her voice, she said, "We're prisoners, sir. We're being held against our will at the Good Shepherd."

"Uh-huh," he said, lifting his eyebrows in bafflement. "Is that so? Well now, listen. You girls ought to be grateful that the good sisters are looking after you. Run along, now."

Mairin felt her face fill up with a furious blush. She sounded completely hysterical. Outsiders believed the nuns were saints, trying to rescue the poor wayward girls of Erie County from perdition. She should have kept her mouth shut. A park ranger had no power to help her, anyway.

"Ruth!" Sister Rotrude came bustling over. "Goodness, Ruth, you must learn to stay with the group. God bless you, sir," she said to the ranger.

With a bemused frown, he touched the brim of his hat and moved on to the next group. Rotrude's fingers bit into Mairin's arm as she marched her back to rejoin the group. Mairin would have been subjected to a tongue-lashing, except for the presence of a tour guide, who was lecturing about the subjugation of natural forces to the service of man.

"So we are the forces of nature?" Denise whispered. "And we're subjugated to the service of man?"

"Of nun," Mairin said, glowering at the chaperones and rubbing her arm where Rotrude had grabbed it.

They went to view the statue of Nikola Tesla, which was a tribute to the man who had designed the first hydro-electric power plant near the Falls. There was a park nearby with picnic tables and some carts and kiosks that were swarming with people buying souvenirs, taking pictures in photo booths, and posing in front of the jagged cliff. More pop music played from the radio station's pavilion, and little kids ran around, laughing and dancing. The nuns said the girls could have their lunch in the picnic area before boarding the bus back to the Good Shepherd.

The girls took their time eating their borderline-stale cheese sandwiches and tart plums. For a short time, it felt completely normal to be having a picnic with friends, enjoying the sunshine and chatting together. For the first time in weeks, Angela looked happy and relaxed.

Denise went to the bathroom and came back in a rush of excitement. "Hey, you guys," she said. "Look at this!" She held out her hand, palm up. "I found four quarters in the restroom!"

"Ooh, lucky you," Janice said. "You could get an ice cream or cotton candy."

"Nope, we're sharing. And I know just the thing." Denise glanced over at the nuns, who had found a table in the shade and didn't seem to be paying attention. "Let's go to the photo booth!"

"What's a photo booth?" Kay asked.

Denise rolled her eyes, then glanced over at the nuns. "Come on, there's no line. We have to be quick."

Giggling and shoving one another, they went into the booth two and three at a time. One quarter was good for a strip of four black-and-white photos. They made a different face for each shot. Then they waited impatiently for the fresh pictures to emerge from the slot.

"It's a miracle!" Kay crowed.

"Look at us! Just look," said Janice. "We look totally groovy."

Leaning their heads together, Mairin and Angela studied the pictures quietly for a moment. Since there were no mirrors at the Good Shepherd, they hadn't seen themselves in ages. "We look like any other girls," Mairin said.

"We do," Angela agreed.

"Except you're way prettier," Mairin pointed out.

"Stop it," Angela said. "If these were in color, you'd be the pretty one, with all that red hair."

The other girls exclaimed over the pictures, and Mairin hid them from the nuns in her jumper pockets. They walked around the park area, soaking in the festive sights and smells. To everyone's delight, a marching band started playing patriotic songs. People sang along and waved flags.

"Wow, they sound really good," Mairin said. "Way better than any band I've ever heard."

"It's the West Point marching band," Helen said, pointing at the printed drum. It read *U.S. Military Academy Band, West Point, NY.*

"They're great," Odessa said, bouncing up and down with excitement. "So completely great!"

"I play clarinet," Helen said. "Maybe I'll go to West Point."

"Right," Denise scoffed. "Girls can't go to West Point. It's not allowed."

"Well, it ought to be," Helen retorted.

While the band played on, a group of hippies in flowing tops and bell-bottom jeans and bare feet swirled around the band, holding signs demanding peace—*No More War. Drop Acid Not Bombs. Make Love Not War.* Yelling over the music, they chanted anti-war slogans. Some of the spectators yelled back, calling them commies and telling them to go take a bath.

Mairin watched in fascination. A war she barely understood had taken her brother away. She pictured Liam as one of the weary, sweat-stained soldiers on Walter Cronkite, his head covered by a helmet that didn't seem like it would be much help against a bomb. "No more war," she yelled in unison with the protesters. "No more war!"

Janice grabbed her hand. "You're gonna get us in trouble!"

"What, like we're not already?" Mairin asked bitterly.

A squad of police officers arrived to break up the crowd, brandishing their batons. Odessa shrank away from them. "Watch out for those guys," she said.

Mairin used to feel safe around policemen. But knowing what they'd done to Odessa made her cautious. "Let's get out of here," she said, taking Odessa's hand. She scanned the area, wondering if there was a chance to run away, but Sister Theresa came bustling over.

"Where do you think you're going?" she demanded.

"Just over here to the exhibit booths," Angela explained before Mairin could say something. "Can we, Sister? Please?" She batted her eyes at the nun, and Sister Theresa relented.

Some of the exhibitor booths were giving out penny candies. Mairin hadn't tasted a Bit-o-Honey or a Sugar Daddy in months, and she wished she could gorge herself.

"The library's here!" Angela practically squealed, rushing over to a table with a county library banner. The volunteers invited them to apply for library cards and to join the summer reading program. Mairin grabbed a form and filled it out. At the bottom, she wrote, "The Good Shepherd Institute is a prison! Send help!"

A rickety-looking table caught her eye. *Heyday Farm Commune. Work for Us. Work for Peace.* That was the place with the painted school bus where Flynn Gallagher's girlfriend, Haley, worked. Someone handed her a flyer, and she folded it and slipped it into her pocket with the photo strips.

"I wish we could stay for the fireworks tonight," Helen said. "I love fireworks."

"We'd never be allowed," Janice said. "Not in a million years. The nuns'd probably say it's the work of the devil."

"We should make a pact so we never lose each other," Angela said. "I mean, once we're free. We could stay friends forever."

Janice sent her a skeptical frown. "Who knows where we're gonna be? We'll just lose each other."

"Well, that's why we should pick a meeting place, something that'll never change. And a date that'll never change. We can make a pact to meet right here on the Fourth of July." Angela gestured at the Tesla monument. "That thing's never gonna move."

"Hey, it might work," said Mairin, warming to the idea. After all they'd been through, they shared a bond no one on the outside would understand. "Fourth of July, high noon."

Odessa folded her arms and faced them with a resolute expression. "I don't know about you guys, but I plan on being a million miles away."

"Yeah? Where's that?" asked Denise.

"California." Odessa's dark eyes turned dreamy.

"Why California?"

"Because... California. I mean, come on. Who *wouldn't* want to live in California? It's got beaches and freedom, and the sun shines all the time. I'm gonna get into the music business."

"Yeah, aren't we all?" Denise regarded her skeptically.

"You've heard her sing," Angela pointed out. "And just look at her."

"I can definitely picture you in the music business," Mairin said. Odessa had a fantastic voice and an unforgettable face, now dramatically framed by her Afro hairstyle.

"I got connections," Odessa said. "My mama's got this cousin, Bobby Freeman, out there in San Francisco."

"Never heard of him," Denise said.

"Ever heard the song 'Do You Wanna Dance'?"

"Everybody has," Angela said.

"It's an oldie," said Denise.

"Well, that's Bobby Freeman, my mama's kin. And I'm gonna meet him."

"Wow, that's cool. But how're you gonna get all the way out to California?" Janice asked.

"I'll get a job and save up for a ticket," Odessa said.

"Cool that you have a plan." Janice shrugged. "I never been anywhere. Never had a home of my own."

"We'll be your home," Kay said with a bashful smile.

Mairin patted her arm. "I still think it would be a good tradition to meet back here every Fourth of July at noon. Or whenever we can on the Fourth. It's a day of freedom, after all. Freedom and independence."

As she spoke, a group of teenage girls went by, carefree in their colorful outfits of bikini-cut shorts and halter tops, beads, and hipster sandals. Some of them wore headbands and wire-rimmed sunglasses with round lenses. Mairin felt a tug of yearning as she watched them laughing and jostling one another. People who took their freedom for granted were going about their day. Heading off for picnics, meeting up to watch the fireworks. Families and groups of friends. She spotted a girl with red hair who was holding hands with a guy, and felt a spike of envy. Oh, to be free again. What would that even feel like?

The sound of a backfiring engine made Kay jump, emitting a squawk of alarm. Then she started rocking back and forth and hugging herself. Poor girl was scared of her own shadow. Janice put her arm around Kay and patted her shoulder.

The backfire came from a big panel van backing up to the busy hot dog stand. The rear doors opened, and a guy in dungarees, a work shirt, and a baseball cap with the Sunbeam Bread logo jumped down and went around to the back. He brought out several racks of hot dog buns wrapped in plastic.

"Thanks, Slim," the vendor called to him. "I appreciate you coming out on a holiday."

"No problem. It's on my way. Going up to Lackawanna for the fireworks tonight."

"Hey." Mairin nudged Denise. "We should see if that guy'll give us a lift."

"What? Are you crazy?"

"Crazy enough to ask him. Keep watch for me and make sure the nuns aren't looking." She marched over to the deliveryman. "Hey, mister.

Think you could give me and my friends a ride to Franklin Street in Buffalo?" According to Denise, the YWCA there was cheap and didn't ask too many questions.

He scratched his head, stepped back, and looked her up and down, taking in the drab laundry uniform and her wild red curls. He had sharp eyes and an angular face with a slight shadow of a beard. "Now, why would I do that?"

"We just need a ride, is all." When she glanced over her shoulder, she noticed that the other girls were keeping their distance. Chickens, she thought.

The Sunbeam driver focused on her, then did a double take. He looked at Mairin in a way she didn't like. The way Colm looked at her when he wasn't supposed to. No, that was just her imagination, Mairin told herself. This guy was her ticket out of here.

If it feels wrong, it is wrong. Liam's words came back to her.

The man hooked a thumb into his belt loop and jerked his head toward the van. "Well now, maybe I got room for you in the truck, girlie," he said. "Climb on in."

Behind her, Mairin heard footsteps, and turned to see Helen making a beeline for her. "Oh, no, you don't." Helen grabbed her hand and hauled her back. "Never mind," she said to the driver. "My friend made a mistake."

"I'll say." The guy curled his lip and shook his head.

Mairin tried to pull away, but Helen hung on tight. "What the—"

"Bad idea," said Helen.

"I'll say," Odessa muttered behind her. "What the heck were you thinking, Mairin?"

That I'd do anything to get away, Mairin thought. *Anything.*

ON THE WAY back to the Good Shepherd, Mairin leaned her head against the window of the bus, watching the cars flow by like ripples in a river. She had scanned for chances to escape out in the air with all the noise and life and freedom—but she'd found nothing. Feeling defeated, she pressed her eyes shut, wishing she could be anywhere else. She would not survive in this place. She would not. Stewing with frustration, she opened her eyes and watched the busy traffic pushing down the expressway.

By now, she knew escape wasn't so simple. She didn't want to wind up in a situation like the one with the bread truck driver.

The others chatted away, ignoring the intermittent shushings by Sister Rotrude or Sister Theresa or one of the consecrates who didn't seem to do anything but obey orders. "Pipe down back there," roared Sister Rotrude. "And get back in your seats."

The girls scattered, flinging themselves into their seats. Mairin brooded out the window some more. As the bus exited the expressway, a panel van caught her eye. It was a tall white truck, shiny clean, with a logo featuring a still life of a cornucopia with abundant vegetables and fruits spilling out. Then she noticed the company name and slogan on the delivery van—*Flynn Gallagher Gourmet Produce. Fresh from Farm to Table.*

She sat straight up in her seat. *Flynn Gallagher.*

The truck was stopped in a line of traffic at a stoplight. She recognized Flynn in the driver's seat. He sat with his wrist draped over the steering wheel and his elbow cocked out the open window.

"Flynn," she said under her breath. "You did it, Flynn. Took over Fiorelli's truck. Just like you said you would."

Her mind shut off as a jolt of pure instinct possessed her. She lunged to the back of the bus and grabbed the red lever marked Emergency Exit. A loud bell sounded, and the bus lurched, then rumbled to a stop. Some of the startled girls screeched in confusion as Mairin wrestled with the emergency door. It was stuck. It wouldn't budge.

She pictured herself rolling into the road from the moving bus, leaving her friends behind, maybe getting run over. No. She would run for freedom, and Flynn would pick her up. Her efforts grew more frantic as Sister Rotrude charged down the aisle toward her, but the door held fast. The nun grabbed the back of her jumper and hauled her away from the door. Then she shoved Mairin toward the front of the bus.

"You get in that seat and *don't move*," she said, her voice cutting like a knife. Then she turned to encompass the other dumbfounded girls with a fierce glare. "Drive on, Sister Theresa. Ruth has made yet another grave mistake."

The whole failed incident had lasted less than a minute. Mairin knew her impulse would cost her dearly. What was she thinking? She wasn't thinking. What would she have done, anyway? Jumped into the delivery truck with Flynn Gallagher . . . and then what? He would have freaked out and made her go home and then her mom would have forced her to go back to the laundry.

What a dumb, stupid impulse. When would she ever learn?

She did learn a couple of things. One—the emergency escape of the bus didn't work, which was probably illegal. And two—Flynn's phone number was on the side of the van: FR2-3858.

MAIRIN CAME BACK from solitary at lights-out, having spent the rest of the day in darkness and without supper. She trudged up the dank iron stairs and entered the dormitory, and one of the laywomen closed and locked the gate.

When the bars to the dormitory clanged behind her, she found some of the others clustered around Angela's bed. Tired, hungry, and angry, she was surprised to see so many girls still awake, whispering and buzzing.

"What happened?" she asked, feeling a chill crawl across her skin.

"Another nightmare," Helen whispered.

Mairin rushed over to Angela. Lately, she woke up screaming or crying nearly every night. "I'm sorry I wasn't here," Mairin whispered. "I wish I knew how to help."

"I don't know how much longer I can last in this place," Angela said, rocking back and forth on the bed.

Mairin gave her friend a hug as she looked around at the girls in the dorm unit. All of them rallied around Angela. They rallied around one another. By now, they had become more than just fellow inmates. They were friends, in the truest and deepest sense. It was startling to realize how much she'd come to care about them. She wanted to help Angela try to forget the baby ordeal, and she wanted to keep her friend safe from Gilroy's attacks. Wanted Helen to find her parents again, wanted to see Odessa move to California. She hoped for a better life for Denise, Janice, and Kay.

"You guys," she said, "I want you to know—when I first got to this place, I didn't expect to make friends. But now . . . well, now I know that I couldn't have survived this long without you."

"Oh, Mairin. You were so angry when you first got here," Angela said.

"Yeah, I was kinda scared of you," Kay added softly.

"We all need each other," Odessa whispered, "and that's a fact."

"I have something to ask you guys," Mairin said, her heart pounding as she motioned them to gather close.

"Ask away," said Odessa.

"I've been trying my darnedest to find a way out of here."

"We noticed," said Janice.

"I know it's possible to escape. I just know it. But I keep getting caught. I hate myself for failing. I just hate myself. So I've been thinking. Maybe I keep failing because I've been trying to do it alone."

"You're strong," Janice said. "One of these days, you'll make it."

"It's not enough to be strong. I need a better plan. And . . ." She looked around the circle of faces. "I need your help. I need a team."

"And you want us to be the team." Denise sat back and folded her arms in front of her.

"Not just for me," Mairin said, her voice thickening with emotion. "This place is killing us. We all need to get away from here before something even worse happens." She studied Angela's thin, tense face in the dim light, then grabbed her friend's hand. "I want to help you more than I want to help myself."

A single tear slipped down Angela's cheek. "You're right," she whispered. "This place *is* killing me." Then she dashed the tear away. "I'm in."

"What are you on about?" Janice asked. "You're going to get us all in trouble."

"Don't you want to get away from this place?" Mairin asked.

"And do what, exactly?" asked Janice. "We got no place to go. Nobody to look after us."

"Haven't you been listening? The YWCA on Franklin—"

"Costs money," Denise pointed out.

"It sounds too crazy," Janice said. "It'll never work. Instead of one girl getting caught, you'll get us all caught."

"Not if we work as a team," Mairin insisted.

"Hey, maybe *you* can stomach the closet," Janice said. "But not me. I like you, Mairin, even though you're scary sometimes. But I think it's too risky."

Helen's chin jutted out in resolute fashion. "I disagree. Mairin, you've been right all along. We can't stay here any longer. We have to get out."

"Yeah, we have to go," Denise agreed, surprising Mairin. She was seated at the end of Angela's bed, gently patting the other girl's ankle.

"We have to go," Angela echoed, her voice still raspy. Maybe she'd hurt her vocal cords, screaming from nightmares.

"We'll find a way out of here, I swear," Helen whispered, joining them on the other side of the bed.

Mairin felt a rush of emotion so powerful it confused her, made her almost light-headed. Rage at what had happened to Angela. Relief that the other girls were with her at last.

"We're going," she said. "Together."

"We have to do it right this time," Helen said.

Mairin nodded. "Exactly. It's going to work this time. We'll work as a team."

"But how?" Denise asked. "How are all of us going to disappear without getting caught?"

"And once we're out, then what?" Janice asked.

"Then we're screwed," Denise said grudgingly.

"What do you mean?" Mairin bristled.

"We don't have any money. How far will we get without a penny to our name? We're not going anywhere without money. Where'll we go? Who will help us?"

Mairin leaned toward her. "I know where there's money. Maybe a lot of money."

"Aw, come on," Odessa said, cocking a skeptical eyebrow.

"No, really," Mairin said. "Remember how I told you about the cash money they keep in the office? We could take that."

"Sure, as soon as you tell us where it is," said Helen.

Mairin deflated. "All I know is it's in the office. I heard them talking. We have to figure it out. Sister Gerard acts like it's this huge secret. I heard her say she gives it to St. Apollonia. So maybe that's some kind of charity box, or—"

"What?" Angela pushed herself up onto the heels of her hands and looked at Mairin. "What did she say?"

"Pretty sure I heard her say she was giving it to St. Apollonia to keep safe."

"Well then, she just told you where the money is," Angela said.

Mairin frowned. "What? I don't get it."

"The reliquary. The one in the prioress's office. Supposedly it contains St. Apollonia's teeth."

"No way." Mairin shook her head in disbelief. "You mean that big reliquary has St. Apollonia's *teeth*? Jesus saves, wouldn't that be something."

"Why her teeth?" Denise demanded.

"Haven't you studied the Canon of the Saints?" asked Angela.

"I haven't studied a goddamn thing," Denise grumbled.

"Well, if you had, you'd know she was a virgin martyr who was tortured by having all of her teeth pulled out or shattered."

"What the hell?" Denise recoiled. "Why?"

"Because . . . well, because there were a bunch of heathen marauding sailors who wanted her to—you know." Angela shuddered. "And it gets worse. After they caught her, they made a fire and threatened to burn her unless she denied her faith. They tried to make her blaspheme and invoke their heathen gods. So instead of denying Christ, she threw herself into the fire and burned to death."

"Whoa." Odessa shuddered.

"So back then," Mairin said, "there were worse things than laundries."

"That's it?" asked Helen. "That's what happened?"

Angela shrugged. "That's how the story goes. These days, Apollonia is the patron saint of dentists."

"I never been to the dentist," Denise said.

"Well, the Catholic ones have a shrine to her in the waiting room," Angela said.

"So how did her teeth end up here?" Mairin said. "And does that mean the money's in that fancy box? The reliquary? With her teeth?"

"Could be," Helen said, leaning forward.

"You'd be stealing," Janice pointed out, her eyes wide behind the glasses.

"Is it?" Mairin shook her head. "They're making us work six days a week for no pay. So who's the thief?"

"We earned that money for them," Helen said.

Janice's eyes shifted from side to side. "Yeah, but—"

"Look, if you're having second thoughts, now's the time to let us know," said Mairin.

"And if you rat us out, I'll mess you up but good." Denise balled her fists and glared at Janice. "Don't think I won't."

"I'm not gonna rat anybody out." Janice moved closer to Kay and stared at the floor.

"Okay," said Helen. "Let's assume you find the money in the reliquary. What if it's not enough? What if it's like, five dollars? How far would we get on five dollars?"

"It's more than that," Mairin said. "It has to be. Why else would they hide it? And if it does go missing, they can't say anything, because they're hiding it from the diocese. Sister Bernadette brought that up one time, and Sister Gerard nearly took her head off." Mairin pictured the Hills Bros. coffee can her mother kept in the kitchen cupboard behind the sugar canister. Mam hid money from Colm—her emergency fund, she called it. That was as close as Mam ever came to admitting Colm was irresponsible with money.

"We still have to get over the wall, though," Denise pointed out. "And once we're out in the neighborhood, how're we gonna avoid getting nabbed?" She turned to Mairin. "Folks around here would just bring us back."

Mairin cringed, remembering her experience with the razor wire, and with the woman down the road.

"Okay, one thing I learned at the Falls is we have to lose these clothes. We're too conspicuous in these getups."

"They took all our street clothes," Helen said.

"Well, here's a thought. What the hell do you think we do in this place, all day every day?" Denise said, her voice taut with eagerness.

"We launder other people's clothes," said Angela.

"So we, what? Help ourselves? Steal the clothes? Someone's going to notice," Janice pointed out.

"Not if we're careful. How many tons of laundry go through this place?" Helen said. "Stuff goes missing all the time, and I bet the nuns just make excuses if a client complains, if they even know."

"And then what? After we're wearing street clothes, what then? Do we stow away in the delivery trucks?" asked Janice.

"We can't leave in the delivery trucks," Angela whispered. "Mairin tried that, too."

"Bookmobile," Janice said quietly.

"What?" Denise gave a snort of disbelief. "No way would they let us just ride out of here in the bookmobile."

"It comes once a month, on a Thursday, at four o'clock. And guess what else happens on Thursday at four?" Odessa folded her arms and waited.

"Sister Rotrude and Sister Bernadette go to confession," said Janice.

"While the library driver goes to the office with the list of approved books," Helen said, her eyes burning bright. "And remember, Sister Gerard goes to her diocese meeting every Thursday. Makes a big deal of it."

"The driver leaves the keys in the van," Angela said. "I've seen her do it."

"What good is the bookmobile if we don't know how to drive?" asked Odessa.

"Who says?" Mairin felt a thrill of anticipation. "My brother, Liam, taught me to drive. I'm really good at it."

"We can't take the bookmobile," Odessa said. "That's stealing for sure."

"We'll leave it as soon as we get far enough away from this place. Maybe even leave it in the library parking lot." Mairin looked around the circle of faces, then grabbed Angela's hand. "When's the next bookmobile day?"

Part Three

The Girls on the Bus

*Buffalo gals, won't you come out tonight?
Come out tonight,
Come out tonight?
Buffalo gals, won't you come out tonight,
And dance by the light of the moon?*

—Traditional, 1844

Chapter 15

One reason the laundry operation of the Good Shepherd was so successful was the unwavering schedule followed by the strict nuns. The laundry's private clients—hospitals, hotels, and uniform companies—valued the reliability of their services. This was a source of great pride for the nuns. Mairin had heard Sister Gerard boast about it more than once. But soon, routine and righteousness would be their blind spot.

Mairin was counting on this as she and her friends prepared to make their escape. She was filled with gratitude that, finally, her group of friends had come to believe that there really was a way to leave this prison of captivity and torment.

Night after night, the girls stayed up, co-conspirators whispering fervently, feeling the boldness of their shared purpose. They vacillated between excitement and fear, an unlikely sisterhood forged in suffering and silence, about to risk everything on a desperate bid for liberty. Mairin, lit by the fire of determination, sometimes felt like a battle commander, plotting each step of the way to freedom.

Everyone had a role to play. They had to sneak street clothes from the incoming laundry, collecting things piece by piece and hiding them on top of the cupboards in the shower room. They noted the precise time of Father O'Flaherty's weekly confessional rounds. They had to sign up for the monthly bookmobile visit.

"I have a question," Janice whispered one night. "What will we actually *do* when we get clear of this place? I mean, freedom's a good thing and all, but how do we go on from there?"

"When a girl is released," said Denise, "she gets her street clothes back, and that's about all. I seen it."

"We could take a Greyhound bus," Mairin said, picturing the busy, crowded station where she had said goodbye to Liam when he was going into the army.

"Or a city bus to my friend Tanya's," Angela said.

"We'll catch holy hell if we get caught," Janice said.

Mairin studied Janice's face in the pale light slanting through a dormer window. She seemed sincere, most of the time. But she could also be a snitch; they all knew that. It was important to make sure she was all in with the plan.

"Well," Mairin said, "how about we all say what we *want* to do. And then we'll figure out how to go after it. What do you want, Janice? Would your family let you come back?"

Janice traced her finger along a crack in the floor and shrugged. "Don't have nothing in the way of family," she said. "I was in foster care before they sent me here. And no way would I go back to the foster home." She shuddered. "It's actually worse than this place."

Mairin couldn't imagine anything worse than this place. "We'll get jobs."

"Doing what?" Helen asked. "Thanks to the Good Shepherd, we're not even getting a high school education."

"You're one of the smartest people I've ever met," Mairin said. "You can do anything. We can all do anything. I worked at Eisman's orchard in the Fruit Belt the last two summers. Look, anywhere's better than the Good Shepherd, right?" She reached under her thin mattress and took out the flyer she'd swiped during the outing to Niagara Falls. She smoothed it out on the floor so they could all see. "You could come with me to Heyday Farm," she said. "See, they're looking for workers. Says shelter provided."

"I don't know nothing about farms," Janice said.

"I seen you climb a ladder and pick an apple," Denise said, poking her with an elbow. "Jeez, even Kay could do that."

Kay perked up when she heard her name. "I like apples," she said.

"You like everything," Denise said.

"Suppose we get there and it's just as bad as this place? Then what?" Janice bit her lip and looked around the circle. "Seriously, then what?"

"It won't be worse," Angela said. "Nothing's worse."

"I'm gonna take the train to New York City, baby," Denise said. "That's where you can really make it."

"Make what?" asked Kay.

"*It*, doofus. Like, make some kind of life for yourself. Something better than this." Denise encompassed the room with a sweep of her arm, then turned to Angela. "What's the first thing you're gonna do when we get away from this place?"

Angela's eyes went soft and dreamy. "Go to the library and take out any book I want."

"That's the *first* thing?" Denise scoffed.

"Well, maybe not the first. But I miss reading so much. Miss Adler at the Jefferson Branch is one of the best people I ever met. I've always thought I'd like to be a librarian myself."

"Would she let you stay with her, no questions asked?" Mairin whispered.

"I think I can stay with my friend Tanya. Her folks are cool. Maybe they'll let me stay with them until I can get a job and finish school."

Helen drew her knees up to her chest and rested her chin on them. "I never thought I'd actually miss school, but I do for sure. Even gym class. So I guess I'll go see my dad's secretary at the U and see if there's been any word." Her shoulders tensed, and Mairin saw the flash of worry in her eyes. "She kept pink peppermint candies in a jar on her desk and she always let me help myself."

"And she won't turn you in?" asked Denise.

"Not when I explain what this place really is."

They sat in silence for a few minutes. Mairin was nervous, knowing there were a hundred ways the plan could fail. "What about you?" She nudged Odessa, who was sitting next to her. "You'll head straight to California, right?"

Odessa drew in a long breath that seemed to end with a shudder. "I can't go," she said, her words little more than a gust of air.

"What the hell?" Denise demanded. "We're supposed to stick together."

Mairin's stomach clenched. "Odessa?"

Odessa leaned forward, her expression fierce. "Listen, I've helped you with this plan in every way I could think of. And I'll help you get out of here. But I'm not coming. My sentence is up in six weeks. I'll be free without having to escape, and I won't have to worry about the cops coming after me. I'm sorry, but I can't risk getting caught. 'Cause if I do, they'll make me stay longer."

"So you think we're not gonna make it," Denise spat.

"I think you are, but there's no guarantee," Odessa shot back. "My release next month is a sure thing if I stay out of trouble. I've already helped you guys with the clothes and nearly got caught by Sister Theresa yesterday. Made me realize I better be super careful. Because I sure as hell can't stay here a single minute longer than I have to. I can't do it," she finally whispered, her voice barely audible as she faced each girl in turn.

Mairin placed a hand on Odessa's shoulder, even though her stomach sank with disappointment. "I get it, Odessa. I really do. You've got to look out for yourself. We don't blame you for betting on a sure thing."

"I feel bad," Odessa said, "but I just can't risk it."

"Way to be a team player," Denise grumbled.

Mairin glared at Denise. "Odessa managed to sneak more street clothes than any of us, and that's a big deal."

Odessa nodded, her lip trembling slightly. "You know I wish I could go right this very minute. I'll still help where I can. Like I can make sure they're keeping to the usual schedule with the bookmobile, and I could even set up some kind of distraction to give you more time."

"I still say we're not going to get far without a few bucks in our pockets," Denise reminded everyone. "Mairin, you sure as hell better be right about finding some cash in the office. Without funds, we'll probably end up in family court, and that would land us right back here." She grimaced, as if sensing a bad smell.

"I hear you," Mairin agreed. "Guess we'll find out soon." She hoped Angela was right about the reliquary. She had to be right. The whole operation hinged on them having enough money to get them to freedom.

Odessa picked at the blanket on her cot. "After you're gone, it's gonna be the longest six weeks of my life while I wait for my freedom."

"Don't forget. Fourth of July at the Tesla monument," Angela said.

"I hope I'll be long gone to California."

Mairin glanced toward the hallway, where a bulb in a wire cage lit the gate at the top of the stairs. "So. Are you ready?"

There were nods all around. "It's a full moon tonight," Helen said. "That's auspicious."

"You're probably the only one who knows what *auspicious* means, but it sounds good to me," said Mairin. "Think they're dead asleep now?"

Angela nodded. "Be careful, Mairin."

The girls crept back to their beds. Their wakefulness and impatience were palpable; Mairin could feel it like a wave of energy. Only Kay drifted off to sleep, blissfully unconcerned about what tomorrow would bring. Mairin waited until she couldn't stand it any longer. Hurrying soundlessly on bare feet, she sneaked out of the dormitory and hurried down the stairs.

The place was never truly quiet. She could hear the wind whistling through the complex, the thump and rattle of the distant coal furnace that never yielded adequate heat, except in the wing where the nuns stayed. She crept through the chilly, dimly lit hallways, her heart thundering against her rib cage as though it was trying to outrun the sin she was about to commit. She had never stolen a thing in her life, not even Liam's Halloween candy when he left his bag unattended.

But this was her chance. The walls of the Good Shepherd, this grim edifice of brick and iron and stone, had stifled her for nearly a year. She knew that if she could just find the cash, she and the others could escape the life that had been forced upon them.

As she passed the door to the dreaded closet, she shuddered. Never again, she thought. Ever. Yet her confinement in the closet had served a purpose. Thanks to its proximity to the office, she'd gleaned useful information by listening through the vent.

The office door creaked open with a treacherous groan, and Mairin froze, not daring to breathe. After a few minutes, she crept inside. It was dead silent and chilly. The very air of the Mother Superior's inner sanctum felt heavy with the pervasive scent of incense and stale cigarette smoke, a lingering reminder of Sister Gerard's stern presence. There was a full moon, which Helen said was auspicious, but at the moment, its light was hidden in the clouds. A watery glow emanated from the sodium vapor lights over the parking lot outside, reflecting off the silvery frame of the reliquary. Dust motes danced in the feeble light, and Mairin tried to stay calm, letting her eyes adjust. It was creepy, being alone in the dark with a dead saint, but she didn't dare switch on a lamp for fear of alerting someone.

She set down the key and went to work. Her fingers trembled as she ran her hands over the fancy reliquary, its gold leaf flaking off beneath her touch. She tried lifting the top, but it wouldn't budge. Frustrated, she considered breaking the glass. No. The crash would wake someone for sure, and the whole place would go on lockdown. Then her fingers found a latch under the back edge of the big case. She jimmied it, and it unhooked with a soft *click*.

A rush of elation filled Mairin, and she bit her lip to stifle a gasp of triumph. Here at last was a chance for deliverance. It was a sin. It was salvation. Instead of reforming her character as the nuns had promised her mother, this place had turned her into an unrepentant thief.

She took in a nervous breath. People who disturbed the remains of saints were supposedly doomed to burn in hell. She shrugged the worry away. She already lived in hell.

Inside, she found a fancy monstrance on a pedestal. It was shaped like the chalice the priest lifted during holy communion, only this one had a glass capsule inside. She lifted the thing out and set it on the desk, angling it toward the light.

Inside were some small objects. A couple of stones or pebbles. She tipped them out into her palm and studied them. The objects were nothing special. Stones. Or bones. Or ... teeth?

"Jesus," she hissed, dropping the things back into the capsule and pushing the monstrance away. Were those really some dead saint's teeth? *Gross.*

She stood on tiptoe and peered down into the box. It was completely empty, other than the desiccated carcass of a moth. She tried tapping the velvet-lined base of the container to see if it had a false bottom, but it was solid, with no seams or hidden closures.

So where was the money? Had they been wrong after all?

Desperation tightened her chest as she searched again, feeling around the outside of the coffer. She tipped it back and checked the underside—nothing. Think, she told herself. Think think think. The girls were counting on her. She'd persuaded them to join her. She couldn't fail them now. She thought about Angela, who had gone through the worst ordeal of them all. Helen, desperate to see her parents once again. Denise and Janice and Kay, all deserving of a better life than the cruelty and drudgery here.

"Help me out, Dad," she whispered, wondering what Patrick O'Hara would do in this situation. When people were counting on him, he always stepped up. It was actually his last act on earth—he stepped up to save someone. Maybe he'd known he couldn't survive the rapids, but he'd joined the rescue anyway. She wished he hadn't been a hero that day, but now she understood why he'd made that choice. The thought gave her a flicker of hope. She had to find her way back to a world filled with love and possibility, like the one she'd known with her father. He wouldn't have given up.

Mairin racked her brain, trying to piece together everything she'd overheard during her hours in the closet. She'd heard Sister Gerard clearly tell Bernadette to put the cash into St. Apollonia's keeping. Those were the exact words. Now she scowled at the reliquary, thinking hard. What a fancy container for someone's old teeth, even though they were supposedly verified by the Vatican.

What would a person sacrifice for her faith? Apollonia had sacrificed her teeth and thrown herself into the fire rather than bad-mouth her lord Jesus. Did she not realize that suicide was a sin? And how the heck did her teeth end up in Buffalo?

It all seemed pretty sketchy to Mairin. As sketchy as nuns hiding money from the diocese.

How do you imagine we pay for all the good we do?

Mother Superior's words rang hollow, because they did no good at all for the girls who were forced to live here. Under the guise of reform, they subjected girls to chilly dorms and meager meals, long hours of dreary labor, a cycle of prayer and repentance, all performed under the constant threat of humiliation and punishment. Some were forced to see the doctor who did horrible things to the girls he was entrusted to care for.

With a frustrated sigh, Mairin glared even harder at the reliquary. She had examined every detail of the stupid contraption. Or had she? Maybe she'd overlooked something. Maybe... sitting back on her heels, she studied it again. There was a martyr's palm on the front of the stand. In catechism, Mairin had learned that the palm was a symbol of the spirit over the flesh.

As she crouched there, scowling, the moon emerged from behind the clouds and cast more light through the windows. Now she saw that the palm frond was made of brass, with a small button at the center.

Mairin felt a prickle of inspiration. The relic, it seemed, had its own secrets.

Chapter 16

There were times when Sister Bernadette found the silence of the Good Shepherd unnerving. With 164 souls living here at the refuge—and young girls at that—it would seem only natural to hear plenty of chatter and noise around the place. But the rules were strict in this regard. No one was allowed to speak without permission, and this was enforced with a nun's ruler or penance stick.

Even so, the girls always seemed to find ways to skirt the rule, holding conversations and sometimes even singing in the laundry rooms until someone stifled them.

Bernadette would never dare to complain about it. She conceded that her discomfort with the enforced silence had its roots in her own flawed character. She was supposed to embrace the tenet that silent contemplation and prayer were essential for redemption of the spirit. When the nerves got the better of her, creeping around her like a choking vine from the past, it helped to remind herself that she was in a place of safety here at the Good Shepherd, and for that, nothing but gratitude was in order.

The days were regulated by the chapel bell, keeping the whole community on track with uninterrupted sameness. The predictable routines of the community were a welcome contrast to the chaos Bernadette had endured as a child. She was still haunted by memories of shouting neighbors; screeching stray cats; rumbling traffic and horns; and the oniony, old-sock smell of her mother's visitors. Most nights of her childhood were punctuated by the sounds of shattering beer bottles; creaking bedsprings; and loud, gulping snores.

After matins, she made her way to the office to see to the usual chores. Here in her austere little chamber and at her desk in the office, she heard only the whistle of the wind under the eaves and the rumble of the old coal-burning furnace in the basement.

The office was empty, as Thursday was the day Mother Gerard spent away from the refuge, attending meetings with the diocese and conducting business with suppliers and clients on behalf of the Sisters of Charity. Mother Gerard never complained about the many tasks she juggled to keep the Good Shepherd running. Bernadette considered it a privilege to do her small part.

She knelt at the prie-dieu to offer a prayer before getting to work. The light through the window fell just so across a framed picture of Jesus standing at the door, a print of a famous allegorical painting. The glowing face of the Lord was enhanced by the sunlight, and the verse at the bottom always filled Bernadette with inspiration: *I am the way, the truth and the life.*

Bernadette whispered a quick prayer of gratitude before getting to work on the laundry records, receipts, invoices, and correspondence of the day. This was where she belonged, helping with the day-to-day operations of this place of redemption. She went about her tasks with a brisk and satisfying air of efficiency, recording what came in and out of the laundry, and keeping track of the all-important host production operation. It felt so very right and proper to provide communion hosts for the diocese.

She paused in her work to peruse an unusual note from the Redcap Uniform Company. The client's operations manager mentioned that they believed there were two missing shirts from their recent bundles. This was unusual, because Sister Theresa and the laywomen in charge of intake were meticulous when it came to managing the inventory of each job. It was very likely that there had been a miscount when the items were dropped off. Bernadette set the letter aside to bring to Sister Gerard's attention later, after confession today.

Yet something niggled in the back of Bernadette's mind. Last week, a fancy hotel that provided laundry service for guests had indicated a couple of missing garments as well. In a normal week, nothing went missing. Yet this was two weeks in a row that a discrepancy had been noted. Was someone in the operations department getting careless? Sister Gerard was not going to be happy, as she prided herself on the accuracy of the laundry work.

Bernadette fed a page of Sisters of Charity letterhead into her typewriter, enjoying the crisp precision of the roller as she snapped the paper bar into place. The inky scent of the ribbon filled the air when she started typing a message to the manager of the uniform company, promising that a thorough recount and search was underway, and that any discrepancy would be promptly addressed. Bernadette knew that the Redcap account was of particular value to Sister Gerard, because the firm always paid in cash, week in and week out. This meant that the payments were kept in the cash drawer and not deposited in the bank.

In her heart of hearts, Bernadette knew this practice was a dangerously loose interpretation of diocesan bookkeeping standards. She also knew better than to question the wisdom of her superiors. But her deepest thoughts were sometimes tinged with suspicion and weighted by unspoken truths. Even so, fear of reprimand kept her from speaking up.

Perhaps, then, it was propitious that today was Thursday. Thursdays were Bernadette's favorite day of the week, since it was the day everyone went to confession—the girls to whisper their shame to the visiting priest and receive penance, and the nuns to keep their consciences clear. For Bernadette, it was a break in the silence as well as a chance to unburden herself of her judgmental thoughts about procedures that had been in place since long before she'd come to serve at the Good Shepherd.

Father O'Flaherty rarely had much to say during her sessions, but as far as she could tell, he did listen.

Bernadette's spirits lifted a little when she checked the calendar and saw that it was the third Thursday of the month, which meant a visit from the library bookmobile. The event always created a flurry of anticipation. The driver, a kind woman named Mrs. Jenkins, always brought a selection of books to be checked before distributing them to the residents, sometimes enjoying a cup of tea in the refectory while she waited for Rotrude and Bernadette to approve the selected books.

Not all the girls here enjoyed reading books. A few of them had never learned to read at all, and even though the mission statement of the Good Shepherd included "education of the mind and spirit," no one here bothered to do any instruction other than having a girl read from scripture at mealtimes.

However, a good number of the girls and nearly all the nuns craved the solace of the printed word. Bernadette knew it was a sin to yearn for the small pleasure of a book, but even the staid approved materials she borrowed often felt like a new adventure for the mind.

A book might be a small beacon of hope for the residents here, a chance to travel to worlds beyond their own through the pages. It was little enough to offer the girls, who seized on any interruption in the monotonous drudgery of laundry work and the stifling silence enforced by the nuns. Not so long ago, when she was a student here, Bernadette loved to lose herself in stories of saints, sin, and redemption.

Sister Rotrude took her role as book arbiter very seriously. It was her job to scrutinize each title for propriety, making sure the material was appropriate for young girls. To root out harmful material, she used an ancient Catholic text called *The Index of Forbidden Books*.

Bernadette looked forward to the afternoon diversion, and was always proud to assist with the process of approving the day's choices. She couldn't help being curious about some of the texts that were rejected. There was an illustrated astronomy book that mentioned Galileo Galilei, who claimed the earth revolved around the sun—which it certainly did, but the text was still forbidden. Another offending title was an illustrated book called *The Wonderful Wizard of Oz*, which had become a famous movie, but there were witches both good and bad in the story, and a little girl who didn't know her place. Bernadette had been disappointed to learn that she would never be permitted to read the ancient Greek play *Lysistrata*, because it was about a group of women who used their collective power over men in order to end a war. Ending a war was never a bad thing, Sister Rotrude had explained. But the women's method—banning intimacy from their husbands—was ungodly.

Bernadette completed her tasks for the day just as the afternoon sun painted lively shadows across the room. The chapel bell rang, signaling that Father O'Flaherty was hearing confession. The nuns went in pairs to ensure that the girls would not be unattended. Bernadette knew there was no hurry to get to the chapel, since she and Sister Rotrude were always last to be shriven—after the girls, the consecrates, and the nuns.

The autumn sunshine felt as warm as a blessing on Bernadette's face and hands. While she crossed the quadrangle to the chapel, she saw that the bookmobile had pulled up right on time, its engine humming softly and then shutting off. The senior girls would go first, selecting their books and placing them in the bin for the driver to bring to the office for Rotrude's approval. The girls were required to go directly back to work. They would not receive their book selections until after evening prayers.

The chapel was nearly empty when Bernadette entered the dimly lit sanctuary, dipping her finger in the holy water font and making the sign of the cross. She avoided eye contact with those making their exit, as absolution was a private matter. Sister Mary John was practicing the organ in the choir loft, which she did each Thursday to cover the secret whispers of the sinners in the confessional, and the murmurs of penitence. The music swelled with the haunting melody of the "Stabat Mater Dolorosa." The somber notes resonated deep in Bernadette's gut, seeming to speak of sorrow and salvation all at once.

Sister Rotrude, with her eyes like flint, entered the confessional with a sweep of her habit, the old wooden door creaking shut behind her. Bernadette slipped into the other booth, which was separated by the larger priest's chamber in between. She closed the door with a soft *click* and waited her turn, hands clasped together as if they could hold back the tide of her own conscience.

In the dim interior of the confessional, Bernadette couldn't help but wonder what Rotrude had to confess. Although only a few years older than Bernadette, Rotrude exuded confidence in all that she did. She never wavered. Bernadette tried to be a stoic, but sometimes she let out the occasional hushed sob as she poured out her sins.

While she composed herself and considered her recent transgressions—pride, envy, covetousness, carelessness—she listened to the full-throated tones from the organ. The music paused at a rest, and in that moment, Bernadette thought she heard a noise of some sort. She frowned and cocked her head. A strange *thunk* echoed through the confessional, and her frown deepened. As the music started up, Bernadette wondered what she'd heard.

It was unseemly to leave the confessional before making her confession and act of contrition, but Bernadette pressed on the handle to take a look outside. Oddly, the door wouldn't budge. She tried again, pushing with her shoulder. It seemed to be stuck, or perhaps jammed.

Feeling the heat of a blush on her cheeks, she tapped on the privacy screen that separated her booth from the priest. "Father," she said, then cleared her throat. She was going to have to speak louder to be heard over the organ. "Father, I'm so very sorry to interrupt, but the door is jammed here. I can't seem to open it."

The screen slid aside, and she could make out Father O'Flaherty's silhouette on the other side.

"What's that you say?" His voice was taut with annoyance.

"The door, Father. It won't open." Her pulse sped up, driven by nerves.

The priest murmured something, then said, "I'll come help you in a moment."

Bernadette could hear him bumping his shoulder against the middle door.

"What's happening here?" the priest demanded, his tone now edged by bafflement. "The door won't open."

"Something has blocked it." Rotrude's strident voice could be heard over the organ music. "Someone, help us!"

The music swelled, masking the cry, as Sister Mary John played on.

Bernadette's breath came in quick, shallow gasps while she pressed herself more forcibly against the door. The stout wooden structure wouldn't budge. Panic welled up inside her as seconds stretched into eternity. Her thoughts flashed on an image of the closet where students were confined as punishment, and she felt a surge of new empathy for the girls who were forced to stay locked away for hours on end. After only a few minutes, Bernadette was ready to crawl out of her skin.

There were narrow louvers on the upper part of the confessional door, and by climbing up on the kneeler, she could peer out. There was no one in the chapel that she could see within the limited view. Angling her gaze downward, she saw that a long rod of some sort had been run through the handles of all three confessional doors, effectively locking her, the priest, and Sister Rotrude inside. The stout rod was ornately carved, and she realized it was the staff of the processional cross used during mass.

"It's barred from the outside," she called to Father O'Flaherty. She couldn't get her hand through the wooden slats of the door.

Rotrude was blustering in a fury about an act of defiance or mischief. "We'll have to break it down," she declared.

The entire confessional creaked as she slammed herself against the door. But the polished oak held firm.

Finally, after what seemed like an eternity, the music died into silence.

"Help!" Rotrude shrieked. "We need help down here. We're locked in!"

"In the confessional," the priest called after her. "Someone has blocked the door."

At long last, Bernadette could hear rushing footsteps. The chapel erupted into chaos, the air now filled with clamoring voices. The processional staff was pulled from the door handles. Gasping as though she'd been starved for air, Bernadette exited the booth. Nearby, Father O'Flaherty and Sister Rotrude blinked in confusion.

Then she bustled over to the priest. "My goodness me, Father. It was a mere prank by some of the girls, I fear. When I find the culprits, they'll pay dearly, I can promise you that. Please, come with me to the refectory for a calming cup of tea."

Father O'Flaherty mopped his brow and demurred, making a hasty exit. Once he was gone, Bernadette noticed that Rotrude's face was contorted with rage and worry. Her strides were long and agitated as she whirled toward the exit. "We'll get to the bottom of this," she said.

In the foyer, they saw Mrs. Jenkins pacing back and forth, her face florid. She looked uncomfortable in the chapel, as most Protestants did when they entered a Catholic church.

"Mrs. Jenkins." Sister Rotrude bustled forward. "I'm so sorry to keep you waiting. There's been—"

"Ma'am. I mean, Sister. I'm not sure what's... Well, I'm afraid the van's gone."

Sister Rotrude exchanged a glance with Bernadette. "Sorry, what?" she asked the woman.

"My van. Er, the library van. The bookmobile. It's not where I parked it in the usual spot. D'you think... Did somebody move it?"

"I don't understand," said Sister Rotrude.

"It's just... gone. Like, stolen, maybe?" The woman knotted her fingers together.

"From our parking lot?" demanded Sister Rotrude. "That's preposterous."

"I understand, ma'am. But I did take a look around, and it's nowhere in sight."

Moving swiftly, her face taut with exasperation, Sister Rotrude instructed some of the nuns and laywomen to head off in search of the bookmobile. Her face was dark with fury. "I imagine this is the work of the same mischief-makers who caused havoc in the chapel."

Bernadette hurried across the compound to the parking lot gate and looked out onto Best Street. Even a few steps outside the refuge, the world looked different, the afternoon light deepening to gold. She saw a few people going in and out of their houses, or sitting on their front stoops, smoking and gossiping. She returned to the main building. "There's no sign of it. Perhaps some of the students took it."

"That's impossible," Sister Rotrude said. "The girls are children. Even the senior girls haven't learned to drive. They certainly couldn't drive that vehicle."

"Mrs. Jenkins, did you leave the key in the ignition?" asked Bernadette.

Her face reddened and she shrugged. "Reckon so. I always do."

"Well. I'm so very sorry for this inconvenience." Sister Rotrude's temper burned in her eyes. "Please, come to the office and we'll sort this out. In the meantime, Sister Mary John, summon the girls—all the girls—and question them until you get to the truth. Sister Theresa, organize a door-to-door search of the neighborhood. Mrs. Jenkins, someone will give you a lift back to the library."

"But the bookmobile—"

"We shall take full responsibility for it, of course." Sister Rotrude gestured for Bernadette to follow her to the office. "I would not want to have to alert the authorities," she murmured.

Bernadette suspected that she knew the reason for that. The local juvenile courts were a major source of funding for the Good Shepherd, sending girls in need to the refuge. But fear held her tongue captive. Although she'd clearly had nothing to do with the fiasco, Bernadette dreaded the idea of a reprimand. She lived in terror of finding herself ostracized or, worse, cast out.

She could tell that Rotrude had come to realize that the bookmobile was well and truly gone. And after assembling all the girls from the junior and senior classes, Sister Mary John reported that six of them were missing.

"When Mother Gerard returns," said Rotrude, "we shall have to go to the authorities and make a report. Oh, those girls will burn when we find them." She whirled to face Bernadette, and Bernadette flinched at the rage in her eyes. "Stay by the phone," she instructed.

"Yes, Sister." Bernadette dipped her head in reverence. Deep inside, she felt an unbidden flicker of admiration for the girls' boldness.

"And while you wait, pull the records of each of the missing girls. I'm confident they'll be found."

"Yes, Sister," Bernadette said again.

Footsteps rang down the hallways, but the main office seemed eerily quiet. Bernadette picked up the roster of missing girls, wondering what could have possessed them to pull such an elaborate prank.

She carefully noted the information on each of the fugitives. Their real names reverberated through Bernadette's mind. It was as if their true identities could not possibly be erased, even by the iron will of the nuns here. Mairin O'Hara, enrolled by her mother and stepfather for lascivious behavior. Angela Denny, whose pregnancy and tragic delivery were still a mystery. Helen Mei, awaiting news of her parents in China. Denise Curran, sent by the juvenile court after multiple arrests for brawling in foster homes. Janice Dunn and Kay Collins were both wards of the state.

Bernadette's gaze lingered over Angela Denny's record. Did she know that she had turned eighteen yesterday? It wasn't likely. With no clocks or calendars in the common areas, birthdays slipped by unnoticed.

Shaken by the events of the day, she went to the prie-dieu and knelt down to murmur a prayer that the missing girls would soon be safely returned.

When she finished her prayer and stood, something caught her eye. At the edge of the reliquary stand lay a key. Just an ordinary key, the sort that was kept in a special drawer in Sister Gerard's desk. But it was out of place. Both Bernadette and the Mother Superior were meticulous about keeping things in their place.

Bernadette picked up the key, turning it over in her hand. On closer inspection, she noticed that flecks of something like dried paint littered the floor under the reliquary stand. Flecks of paint from the reliquary. She looked through the glass front of the coffer at the monstrance inside. Had it always sat precisely like that, or had it somehow moved slightly off-center?

Something was not right. She felt the back of her neck prickle. Almost without forethought, she reached for the palm frond button on the drawer and slid it open.

A gust of relief burst through her when she saw the bills in place. Perhaps she'd been careless last time she'd accessed the drawer and had dislodged some of the old paint. But no. Bernadette was never careless. Even as a tiny child, she'd learned to be vigilant and precise to protect herself from the chaos of her mother's life.

Her hand shook as she checked the drawer more thoroughly and made a horrifying discovery. Some of the money had been removed. She was sure of it.

Shaking with fear, she checked the ledger sheet under the cash drawer. Her record-keeping was impeccable. Now it only verified her suspicions.

Perhaps Sister Gerard had used some of the money. Maybe she'd taken it with her to her meeting today. But no. She was always meticulous about recording withdrawals.

Bernadette returned to the prie-dieu and sank down, squeezing her hands together, her eyes shut tight. Dread was a physical pain, stabbing her with the realization that she would have to explain to Sister Gerard that the library van full of girls was not the only thing missing.

Chapter 17

As she drove the library van toward the main gate of the complex, Mairin forced herself to proceed slowly, the way the regular driver would. She glanced at the sign of the saint with the Latin phrase. She had seen it on the day she'd arrived here. She hoped to never see it again.

"I never figured out what that sign means," she said, her heart racing.

"'*Salus animarum suprema lex*' is Latin for 'the salvation of souls is the supreme law,'" Helen said.

"Yeah, fuck that," said Denise. "Step on it, Mairin."

Pulling out onto Best Street, Mairin felt dizzy with fear . . . and elation. Everything had fallen into place. She'd slipped into the chapel, her heart pounding and her palms sweaty, as Bernadette and Rotrude entered the confessional booths. With the organ music booming from the loft, Mairin had darted forward, shoving the processional staff through the handles of the confessional doors. *Take that. See how YOU like being trapped.*

Next, the girls made their way to the bookmobile. Mairin had glanced back one last time at Odessa, who lifted her hand in solidarity as they exited the building.

With a synchronized burst of courage, they rushed over to the van. Helen carried a laundry sack stuffed with street clothes and a church envelope with the money. Mairin slid into the driver's seat, turned the key, and the engine churned to life. The bookmobile felt different from the

Nash Rambler Mairin had learned to drive in. She sat up high in the driver's seat, trying to get accustomed to the feel of the van swaying along, top-heavy, the steering wheel almost too wide. One of the side-view mirrors was broken off, making it hard to see behind her.

"Get down, you guys," Mairin said. "And hang on!"

She hadn't driven in a long time, and now she was responsible for these girls. Their safety was literally in her hands, and she trembled with nerves. She reminded herself of the lessons Liam had taught her—eyes ahead, easy on the pedals. The steering wheel felt loose in her hands, the van lumbering from side to side as she drove forward.

Once they cleared the gate, pure euphoria had broken over the group like rays of sunshine.

"We're out," Denise said in a giddy whisper. "Everybody—change into your street clothes."

At a traffic light, someone tossed Mairin a shirt to put on. As they rumbled along the streets of the city, the fresh air of freedom filled their lungs, and for a few moments, the girls were quiet, paralyzed by the enormity of the world beyond their prison.

The intricate grid of Buffalo's streets surrounded them, a landscape of both hope and unknown hurdles. Then Angela reached forward and turned on the radio. "Ain't No Mountain High Enough" was playing. They all joined in, belting out the song at the top of their lungs as they left Best Street behind.

"You guys!" Denise grabbed a pack of Kools that had been tucked under the windshield visor. "Oh yeah," she said, tipping one out. "Who wants a smoke?" She pushed in the dashboard lighter.

"You shouldn't smoke," Janice said.

Denise pulled out the lighter and clumsily tried to touch the hot red center to the end of the cigarette, wobbling with the motion of the van. "Who says?"

"Well, the . . . I guess, nobody. Oh, heck, let me try one," said Janice. She managed to light one up, staring cross-eyed at the burning tip as she sucked in a drag, then erupted in a fit of coughing.

"Put that thing out," Angela said, grabbing the cigarette from her and tossing it out the window. "You don't know how to smoke."

Mairin glanced over at Janice, who looked relieved. The next song started to play—"She's So Fine"—and they all joined in again, practically yelling the chorus. If Odessa had been there, she would have cringed at the shout-singing.

"Look at us," Angela crowed, seeming happier than she'd been in months. "We are *so* fine, all of us!"

"So fucking fine," Denise said with a laugh.

"And *so* wayward," Helen chimed in.

A commercial aired, and Helen twiddled the dial, pausing when a familiar song came on on a Gospel music station—"Oh Happy Day."

"Odessa's favorite," Mairin said. "That's her signature song." She wondered how Odessa was doing, left behind to serve out her sentence. She hoped suspicion didn't fall on her friend. It would be a disaster if the nuns made Odessa spend more time in the hellhole that was the Good Shepherd.

Mairin joined in the chorus when it came around—*Oh happy day*. They all belted out the words as the big, boxy vehicle rattled and swayed, and books lurched back and forth on the racks. In the middle of the next chorus, Mairin took a corner too sharply, and the van felt like it might heave over.

Books flew everywhere, hitting the floor, one of them bonking Kay on the head and eliciting a yelp.

"You're okay," Janice said in a soothing voice. "You're fine."

"No, I ain't." Kay let out a squawk of fright. "I'm skeerd. *Skeerd*. We got to go back!"

"Don't be stupid," said Denise. "We are not going back."

Setting her jaw, Mairin slowed down, then took a right on a street she didn't recognize, hoping it would lead to a spot where they could abandon the van—not too close to the Greyhound station, but close enough to reach the terminal on foot. The idea was to trick people into thinking they had taken the bridge across to Canada. In the summer, teenagers crossed the Peace Bridge freely, heading for the amusement park at Crystal Beach.

"Hey," said Helen, looking around. "Is this the right way?"

"I don't really know how to get there," Mairin finally admitted. "Is there a map somewhere? See if there's one in the glove box."

"Maybe there's an atlas," Angela said, scanning the racks of books and magazines.

"Are we lost?" Janice asked.

"Lost? We're lost?" Kay screeched hysterically, her panic escalating. She lunged for the window and cranked it down. "Help! Somebody! We're lost!"

A few pedestrians seemed to pause and look at the van.

From the very start, Mairin had worried about Kay. She was very sweet and only wanted to please people, but she couldn't always think straight.

"Shut up, you dumbass." Denise rolled the window back up. "You're going to attract attention."

"Too late," said Helen. "Those people on the corner are pointing and waving."

"Are not," Angela said. "You're just imagining things."

"We better get rid of the van quick. It's the first thing they'll be looking for," said Denise.

Mairin glanced in the rearview mirror. She caught a glimpse of something through the dirty rear windows. A flicker of something. Flashing lights?

Everything inside her erupted in panic. "The cops," she said through gritted teeth. "Is that the cops behind us?"

Denise peered out the back window. "Shit, I think they spotted us."

Mairin's stomach sank. They'd counted on having more time to get away.

"Shit shit shit," Denise repeated.

"You said a swear." Kay eyed her reproachfully.

"We have to ditch this thing right now," said Mairin.

"That wasn't the plan," Angela said. "We are not far enough away. We'll be caught for sure."

Janice glanced from side to side. "It's not supposed to happen like this. You said—"

"I know what I said," Mairin snapped, trying to focus on her driving.

"Dammit!" said Denise. "More cops! I think they found us!"

At the end of the block, another black-and-white squad car turned and started coming toward them.

"What're we gonna do? What what what?" blurted Kay. "What what what?"

"Run like hell, that's what," said Denise.

Mairin took a hard right onto a busy commercial street. With a surge of courage, she hit the gas and drove until she spotted a parking lot near a busy intersection. Kay shrieked in terror. Mairin pulled into the lot and threw the van into park. She heard a whistle and then gruff orders bellowed through a megaphone, but she ignored them.

"Go!" she yelled, wrenching open her door and jumping down to the pavement.

The rest of the girls bolted out the back door. She saw Denise duck into a shadowy alleyway. Helen made a leap for a rusty fire escape attached to an old building. The whistle sounded closer, and the rest of them scattered in all directions like frightened mice.

Mairin ran. In all her life, she had never run so fast. She ran as if she were on fire. As if the devil himself nipped at her heels. She ran as if her life depended on it. She ran without looking back. She ran for longer than she ever thought she could.

The escape plan had imploded into utter chaos, and now the only option was to disappear into thin air.

Her breath escaped in ragged gasps as she darted down alleyways and through backyards, between warehouses and old graffiti-stained buildings by the port. She charged down a brick street, running blindly, losing herself in an unfamiliar sector of the city. The shouts and whistles and footfalls of her pursuers grew faint, but she didn't dare slow down. The whoop and wail of sirens meant that the search was still on.

She came to a busy street and wove through the surging traffic. A clamor of honking horns and groaning brakes filled the air as she darted between moving cars and trucks. She ran until she could no longer hear the sirens. When a sharp whistle split the air, she darted down an alley between two buildings, her thin-soled shoes pounding the broken and buckled pavement. At the other end of the alley, she found herself in a maze of loading docks and steel truss bridges. She didn't recognize any of her surroundings, but a heaviness in the air told her she was near the lakefront. Keeping to the shadows, she raced as fast as she could, seeking a place to hide. She ran until she couldn't run anymore on her shaky, exhausted legs. Finally, she slowed to a walk, trying not to double over from the stitch in her side.

In a narrow passageway between two buildings, she ducked into a recessed doorway that was littered with old, dry papers and empty beer cans. Leaning against a stained brick wall, gasping for breath, she used the tail of her stolen shirt to mop her brow. It was some guy's bowling shirt, a two-toned button-down with *Alley Cats* embroidered on the pocket. The shirt—purloined from the laundry—was many sizes too big, draping down almost to her knees.

As she tried to quiet the clamor in her chest, Mairin pushed her panic aside and tried to think straight. She wondered what had become of the others. Nothing had gone according to plan. They were all supposed to stick together, but when everything fell apart, they had scattered to the four winds.

Now the sun was going down, and a chill wind rolled off the lake, and Mairin found herself alone.

She had envisioned an emotional farewell with her friends. A last embrace before they split into the sprawling city. She thought there would be time for hugs all around and promises to meet every July Fourth at the Falls. In her pocket, she still had the photo booth strips they had taken at Niagara Falls. She'd planned to hand them out so everyone got one.

A terrible thought struck her. The money. *The money.* They were supposed to divvy it up so each girl would have an equal share—for bus fare, train fare, a place to sleep, something to eat... She'd taken such a risk to get the cash. Had someone grabbed the envelope from the laundry bag as they'd all spilled from the van? Oh, she hoped so. Maybe it would help at least one of them find a better life.

She had no idea where she was, and no idea where to go. She had nothing. No money, only the clothes on her back and her cheap, dusty canvas shoes. Darkness was falling fast. Shadows flickered in the alleyways and unfamiliar streets. A neon sign that read *McGavin's Bakery* cast a pinkish glow on the street corner, deserted except for a trash can, a newspaper vending box, and a phone booth.

Mairin shivered. She was hungry and thirsty and tired to the bone. A terrible sense of defeat washed over her. After everything she'd gone through to free herself from the Good Shepherd, she had failed. She'd failed herself and worse, she'd failed her friends. They were supposed to be a team. What an idiot to think she could get away with this—just a kid, leading other kids—and now she had no idea where any of them had ended up.

Maybe she was exactly what the nuns had called her and all the others, over and over again—a wayward girl. A girl with no prospects for the future, a girl who would ultimately have to surrender and serve out her time, washing away her sins as she labored over other people's laundry.

Everything inside her recoiled at the prospect of giving up. She kicked at a weed growing through a crack in the sidewalk. Be a dandelion, not an artichoke, her dad would tell her. She gave the weed another kick, then froze in mid-motion. Slipping off her shoe, she tipped out her last remaining hope.

It was the Mercury dime Flynn Gallagher had given her.

Part Four

The Age of Aquarius

It is a new age and a new change will come about.
—Peter Max, artist

BUFFALO EVENING NEWS

Six Girls Escape From Detention Facility
Four Still At Large

Ronald Charles, Staff Reporter, Police Beat
BUFFALO, Thursday, August 21, 1969

Earlier today, six youths of the Good Shepherd Refuge, located at 485 Best Street, escaped from the residential facility. The girls, aged fourteen to eighteen, fled in a stolen county library "bookmobile" van. Names are being withheld pending notification of families and Erie County social service agencies. Three of the runaways were quickly apprehended in the vicinity of Browne and Gainey and were held at the Clifton Street substation. Officer Deborah Coney, who is familiar with the Best Street facility, is in contact both with the prioress of the Good Shepherd and with juvenile department authorities.

One of the three apprehended subsequently escaped from police custody and is still at large.

Three others are also at large, and a search continues to be underway. Citizens who encounter the runaways are advised not to approach them, but to contact authorities.

The library's property was recovered undamaged in a parking lot near the area where the youths were apprehended.

Chapter 18

Although it was a warm summer evening, Mairin shivered as she slipped into the phone booth on the street corner. Under the glow of the pink neon light in the bakery window, she took the Mercury dime from her shoe and dropped it into the coin slot. She paused, weighing her options, wondering who to call. She had one dime. One shot. She didn't want to make a wrong move.

Her first impulse was to phone home. But no. Her mother would drag her back to the Good Shepherd. Besides, Mairin didn't want to be anywhere close to Colm ever again. Fiona, then. No, thought Mairin. Bad idea. Fiona might not have come back from her aunt's in Bradford. And if someone other than Fiona answered the phone, Mairin would have to hang up and the call would be wasted. If Mr. or Mrs. Gallagher picked up, they'd probably feel obliged to tell Mairin's mom.

Mairin shut her eyes, opened them, and then with determined finger strokes, she dialed the number on Flynn's truck. FR2-3858.

It rang four times. Five times. Six. She feared he might have left for the day. She was about to give up and press the coin return when he picked up.

"Gallagher's."

The sound of his voice made her melt with relief. "Um...Flynn. It's—it's me." Mairin sobbed, barely able to choke out her own name. "M-mairin."

"Hey, hey, hey now," Flynn said. "Is that Mairin? Mairin O'Hara?"

"Y-yes. I . . . I . . ." Her breath came in sobbing gasps.

"Whoa, take a breath, girl. What's going on?"

"I need help, Flynn. I didn't know who else to call. And you s-said I c-could call you anytime—"

"Are you in some kind of trouble?"

"No. But . . . yes." She sounded like a crazy person. She struggled to control her voice. "Oh, Flynn. I need help. I'm, uh, I'm lost in the city."

"Lost? You want me to call your mom?"

"*No!*" she burst out with sharp urgency. "Please don't tell her. *Please.* She sent me to the Good Shepherd, and it's terrible there, and I can't stay there anymore. I just can't."

A beat of hesitation. "Where are you?"

"I . . . um, oh gosh, Flynn. I don't know. There's a bakery called Mc-Gavin's with two three four seven over the door." She clutched the phone and tried to lean out of the booth to read a street sign, but she couldn't find one. The flurry of panic inside her intensified. "I don't know what street this is."

"Hey. McGavin's Bakery. I'll find it. Sit tight and wait for me."

The wait felt like hours, with hunger gnawing at her stomach and fear gnawing at her chest. She paced back and forth on the sidewalk, flinching at each approaching car, wincing when a passerby glanced her way. She picked up a yellowing copy of *Time* magazine from a bus stop bench. The cover showed an astronaut and the headline "Man on the Moon."

Mairin gasped. Really? Was there really a man on the moon? She'd been gone a year, and the whole world had changed. She skimmed the article, and yes, it seemed that the moon landing was real. She paged through the rest of the magazine, suddenly hungry for news of Liam. Was he in Vietnam now? Was he staying safe? She grimaced at a picture of weary-looking soldiers on the march. Please be okay, she thought, and started to pace again.

Her breath coming in anxious gasps, she waited forever. She waited a lifetime. Two lifetimes. The distant *yip* of a siren nearly sent her back into hiding, but she didn't want to miss Flynn. Finally, a tall, boxy produce truck lumbered toward her and swung over to the curb.

"Get in, kiddo," said Flynn, motioning to her through the side opening of the step van. In his denim work shirt with the sleeves rolled back, his hair curling over the collar, and his expression gentle and welcoming, he was like a dream come true.

Mairin leaped.

"Aquarius" by the 5th Dimension streamed from the radio. Flynn turned down the volume. "Now," he said, "what's going on?"

Mairin clutched the sides of the passenger seat, and for the first time in nearly a year, she felt safe. *Safe.* Then the story rushed out of her in a jumble of words and tears. She didn't give him details of how she'd managed to get away, and she didn't mention the other girls. She certainly didn't mention the money. The less he knew, the better.

The same was true for Mairin herself. She was desperate to learn what had become of the others when they'd scattered. She prayed they had all managed to get away and find help, but it was probably better not to know. That way, if she was ever questioned, she could answer honestly. In all likelihood, she would never see any of the girls from the Good Shepherd again.

Maybe it was a good idea to let go of reminders of the grinding labor and discipline meted out by the Sisters of Charity. Maybe a fresh start would open the door for all of them to move ahead with their lives, putting the nightmare of the Good Shepherd behind them.

"Whoa," Flynn said, flicking a glance at her after she got the story out. "So you're telling me you were in some kind of prison? And you escaped?"

"You have to believe me," she said, noting his doubtful tone. "Because if you don't, I'm getting out of this truck right now and you'll never see me again. And—"

"Hey, I never said—"

"You think I'm making this up?" She thrust her arm at him, displaying a livid bruise. "And what about this?" She pulled the collar of her shirt aside to show him the spot on her shoulder where she'd been strapped so hard that the fabric of her smock had made an impression in her flesh.

"You didn't let me finish," he said, his voice quieter now. "I never said I didn't believe you." He eyed her oversized bowling shirt and thin-soled shoes. "I'm real sorry that happened, Mairin. I didn't realize you'd been sent away. But I don't know how to help you. Should we report this to ... I don't know, the police or the county?"

"No," she said instantly. "The county social services and the juvenile courts *send* girls to the Good Shepherd. The nuns have everyone convinced that they're actually helping." She shuddered, reliving the torments, suddenly fearful that the nuns would be able to find her anywhere. They could walk through walls. They might show up on any given street corner.

"Well, you can't be on your own," he said. "A young kid like you."

"I'm not young," Mairin snapped. "Not after that. I'll never be young again." The truck smelled of fresh apples and herbs. She looked back at the cargo area, stacked with fruit crates and bins of fresh vegetables. "Can I have something to eat? Please?"

His gaze softened. "When was the last time you ate?"

"Breakfast."

He nodded. "Help yourself to something from the back. Anything you want."

She nearly swooned from the aroma, longing to devour everything at once. She gorged herself on ripe raspberries and blueberries and a fresh, crisp apple. How delicious it all tasted after the bland food at the Good Shepherd.

"I'm desperate to see Fiona," she told Flynn between bites. "Did she come home from Pennsylvania? Is she all right, then?"

"Back at school, same as always."

Mairin wondered if a girl who had been sent away to have a baby and place it for adoption could ever be "same as always." Angela Denny had been forever changed; that much Mairin knew. But she didn't press Flynn for details about his sister. There was no way a boy could know what it was like for a girl to have a baby and be forced to give it away.

"So what's next?" Flynn asked her. "You need to go somewhere safe. Do you have a grandma or an aunt, or ... ?"

In a family like the Gallaghers, there were relatives in abundance. But Mairin's family was smaller. Her mother's people were in Ireland, and she never spoke of them. Her dad had been an only child, and his folks had retired down in Florida. They didn't like visiting because of Colm.

"Heyday Farm," she said. "The one out past Gardenville."

"Yeah, I know the place. It's on my pickup route because they have a pretty good orchard," he said. "There's this girl I know—Haley—she lives out at Heyday. It's a . . . I guess kind of a hippie commune."

"Haley Moore. I remember her. Your girlfriend."

He offered a noncommittal shrug.

"They gave out flyers at Niagara Falls saying they're looking for help." She took it out of her pocket and showed him. In her other pocket, she had the photo strips from the Fourth of July. Angela and Helen, Janice and Kay, Denise . . . Where were they tonight? Were they safe?

"So you want to go to this farm." Flynn studied the flyer. "Look, it might not be the best—"

"I want to go anywhere but back to that prison. Anything but the nuns."

"Oh, you won't find nuns there," he assured her. He turned in the driver's seat and studied her in the yellowish light of a street lamp. "I feel so bad that you had to go to a place like that," he said.

She knew what he was asking without hearing him ask it. "I wasn't in trouble, Flynn. I swear. It was nothing like that. I didn't have a baby. I didn't break any law. It was all because of Colm. My mother's husband. My stepdad. He's . . . well, he's not very nice to me."

Flynn gave her a look that reminded her sharply of Liam's expression when he'd caught Colm in her room. Shock and just plain anger. She knew then that she didn't have to explain any further.

They drove out past Gardenville. Watching the colors of the sunset streak across the rolling landscape, Mairin felt an ache in her chest. It had been so long since she'd seen beauty like this, so long since she'd eaten an entire pint of berries, so long since she'd had a conversation without being shushed. Moment by moment, she was shaking off the horror of the Good Shepherd.

The farm consisted of a big house and a bigger barn, surrounded by a collection of lean-tos and dilapidated buildings and acres of fields surrounding a tree-lined pond. A row of derelict bunkhouses lined an old orchard. A woman in a flowing caftan came out of the main house and greeted Flynn by name. "You're later than usual for picking up our crates," she said.

"I'm not here for that," he said. "This is my... this is Mairin. She needs a place to stay. Mairin, this is Saffron."

The woman called Saffron had waist-length hair streaked with gray, and a face webbed by sunshine. She looked nothing like a nun, and that was all that mattered to Mairin.

"Welcome, little sister," she said, giving her a sandalwood-scented hug. "We're glad you're here."

"Um... thank you?" Mairin felt bashful. Maybe a tiny bit suspicious. She was not this woman's sister.

"We're all a family here," Saffron told her. "You'll live and learn together with all of us. Remember, everything that happens is there to teach you—if you pay attention."

"Yes, um... ma'am." She almost said "sister" by mistake. Then she was seized by an urge to run again. How was this different from where she was before? The nuns had made her wary of being "taught" anything. Maybe this was a bad idea. Maybe she was flinging herself into another situation where she'd be a captive.

Mairin tried to still the hammering of her heart. No. She looked around. She didn't see walls or barbed wire. No robed figures gliding around, giving orders. She saw only the orchard among the rolling hills under a sunset-painted sky.

A singular wave of feeling came over her, a sense of gratitude and relief so powerful it nearly knocked her over. She went to stand in a field of soft, waving grass and wildflowers, and she threw back her head and spread her arms and breathed deeper than she'd ever breathed in her life.

"You all right?" Flynn was behind her now.

She turned and felt a jolt of yearning when she looked at him—solid, confident, a place of safety. But she couldn't ask more of him. She had to figure out how to stand on her own. "Yes," she said. "And thank you, Flynn."

"Listen, I know you must be glad to be away from the nuns, but this"—he encompassed the fields and orchards with a gesture—"is different. Like, radically different. People come and go around here. You never know who you're going to meet. Things could get kind of rough."

She read the meaning of his words. "I appreciate that. But I survived the Good Shepherd. There's nothing here I can't handle. Really. Really and truly."

He dug in his pocket and found another dime. "Guess the last one was well-spent. Here's another, to remind you. Call me, Mairin. Swear you'll call me if you need anything."

She smiled, feeling wobbly with relief. "Of course I will, Flynn. And ... can you tell Fiona to come see me? I really want to see her."

"Sure. If this place doesn't work out, you let me know, okay?"

"Okay."

"You be safe. Never forget who you are."

"I won't."

ON HER FIRST night at the commune, and many times after that, Mairin stood in front of the rust-edged bathroom mirror and stared at her image. There had been no mirrors at the Good Shepherd. More than a year had passed since she'd had a good look at herself.

The girl in the mirror looked impossibly young, yet somehow, a hundred years older. She recognized the freckles and the green eyes. But her face was longer, leaner. Her hair shorter, a mass of curls that just brushed the tops of her shoulders and needed four barrettes to keep it out of her face.

There was a new hardness in that face. She was no longer a girl who picked apples and sang along with the radio and daydreamed about going on her first date. Now she was a fugitive, hardened by punishment, determined to do whatever it took to survive.

She thought about Flynn's words. *Never forget who you are.* Had she even known in the first place?

The past year had messed her up so bad, she didn't know who she was anymore. Her mother called her a sinner. At the Good Shepherd, she was called a wayward girl. Here, they called her "hey, babe" or "hey, man." She looked around at the people coming and going from the compound and realized there were all kinds of ways to be wayward. And all kinds of ways to be lost.

At first, Mairin had worried constantly about being found and sent back. She worried about what had become of the other girls. Did Angela get help from Tanya or her librarian friend? Did Denise make it to New York City? Had Helen's parents returned from China? And what had become of Janice and Kay?

As time went on, she relaxed her vigilance, bit by bit. Her confidence grew along with a sense of independence. Even if someone found her, she vowed that nothing would compel her to go back to that place—not her mother, not the Church, and certainly not Colm Davis. Before long she would be eighteen, and then no one could tell her what to do.

According to the commune elders, like Saffron and the owner, Jax, Heyday Farm was supposed to be a joyous center of peace and love and expanded consciousness. Mairin discovered that on any given day, it was a place of shared work, constant togetherness, free love, and lots and lots of drugs. People came and went, some toting little more than a guitar and a sleeping bag. There was a small cadre of hard workers—Mairin made sure she was one of them—but there was also a lot of sitting around, staring at the sky, and playing records by the Doors and Jimi Hendrix and Janis Joplin. People stayed up late, reading and talking about books—*Siddhartha, On the Road,* a poem called *Howl.* Half-clad couples would take a blanket out to the woods or by the pond and make out. Mairin was embarrassed about her limited knowledge of sex, so she avoided the guys who asked her if she wanted to get it on.

Someone suggested she might want to pick a new name, like Paisley or Nirvana, but she recoiled. They'd forced "Ruth" on her at the Good Shepherd. "I have a name," she said, thinking of Flynn's words again. "Call me Mairin. Mairin Patricia O'Hara."

Day by day, Mairin settled in. She wore tie-dye and sandals and beads in her hair. She ate vegetarian meals and slept in a leaky Quonset hut and took outdoor showers and listened to hard rock on a transistor radio. She encountered Haley Moore, who didn't seem to remember her, but was vaguely welcoming. Haley was as exotic as ever, her eyelids heavy behind the round lenses of her shades. She hung out with a guy who had wispy facial hair and bleary eyes, who liked to eat brown rice goulash out of a hubcap.

Mairin tried smoking pot, but it hurt her throat and made her dizzy. She turned down offers of acid. She wrote letter after letter to Liam, explaining to her brother where she'd been and where she was, hoping she would hear back from him.

She lost her virginity to a guy named Domino because she was curious and filled with yearning. She chose him because he was sweet and willing to wear a condom. Domino had soft eyes that held her gently in his gaze, an easy smile, and a patient way about him. He didn't say "let's get it on," but seemed interested in her. He read her signals, and urged her to tell him what she wanted, what she was feeling.

She didn't think what she was feeling was love, but a compelling warmth that built to a burst of physical pleasure, then a shower of relief. Finally, she understood what all the fuss was about. At that point, she knew for sure that the Catholic nonsense about burning in hell for having sex was just that. Nonsense. How would celibate priests and nuns know, anyway? And why would God make sex so much fun if he didn't want people to enjoy it?

Eventually, Domino had to go back to college in order to avoid the draft. Mairin moved into a big room in the main house and made friends with other guys, but mostly, she worked. She had a special knack—even a passion—for growing things. She knew, either by instinct or plain common sense, what it took to manage the fields. And what she didn't know, she taught herself. At night, she read the *Whole Earth Catalog* and the *Utne Reader*, studying the new practices that avoided herbicides and pesticides. She learned the serious side of produce farming and management, and she noticed that the workers who saw value in producing something of substance were the ones who found themselves. Others drifted from day to day, laconically making art and music and conversation, then getting high and falling asleep. Mairin aligned herself with the workers. There was a kind of grace in making something or growing something, and collapsing exhausted into bed after a long, productive day. Working hard helped her avoid dwelling on the dark memories of the laundry.

The cops showed up on a dope raid, sending the residents scurrying for cover. Mairin was horrified when one of them cornered her in the room she shared with a woman named Narnia. As she pressed herself against the wall, Mairin held her breath, certain they were about to drag her away.

"What's your name?" the cop asked. He was short and broad-shouldered, with a big gut.

"It's . . . Ruth, sir. Ruth Shepherd, sir." Finally, her fake name was useful.

The cop searched her room, checking out the neatly made bed, the planting charts and calendar on the wall, the books stacked on a milk crate next to a gooseneck reading lamp. In contrast to the rest of the clutter, her corner was meticulously tidy.

"Hey, Whitney," the cop's partner called from another part of the house. "Come check this out."

The cop gave her one last look, eyes flicking over her head to toe, then left the room to join his partner. They found some woman's stash of weed, took one guy in for an outstanding warrant and another for a parole violation.

And then they left. Mairin had to remind herself to breathe.

One day that first fall, Fiona came to visit, driving a pockmarked Dodge Dart, which she parked by the painted bus. The girls flew into each other's arms, gasping and sobbing and laughing all at once. The year apart had seemed longer because so much had happened.

"You look so different!" Fiona said, keeping hold of Mairin's hands but stepping back. "Just look at you! What happened to your hair? Oh, I've missed you so much. I couldn't believe your mom sent you to the Good Shepherd."

"Because of Colm, my stepfather. Flynn told you, right?"

"He did. It sounds awful."

"It was. I would have sent you letters about it, but I didn't have your address in Pennsylvania, and besides, everything is censored. They hide what really goes on there."

"I'm glad you got away," Fiona said. "And this place! Look at this place!"

"It's really nice here, mostly," Mairin said.

"What do you mean, mostly?" Fiona's eyes narrowed.

"Running a farm is a lot of work. And not everybody's into work around here." She was determined to stay optimistic. "I'm learning so much, Fiona. As soon as I turn eighteen, I'll get a regular job."

"You're not going back to school? Senior year is pretty darn fun," Fiona said.

"School's going to have to wait," said Mairin. "I can't risk it until I'm eighteen—they could send me back to the Good Shepherd. Maybe next year I could attend trade school or ag school. Now, tell me about you. How are you doing?"

"I'm going to graduate next June, that's how. My ma doesn't want me to go to college, but I scored really high on the Regents exam, and I'm going to do it."

"Good for you," Mairin said. "You were always the smartest one in the class." She paused and brought Fiona over to the porch. The house had once been grand, with a wraparound veranda and lovely pillars, but now the paint was peeling and the floorboards were sagging. "Tell me about . . . you know."

Fiona did know. She sat on the porch steps and traced her foot in the dry earth. A song by Led Zeppelin drifted from an open window, like a wail of emotion. "Oh, Mairin. It was so hard."

"I'm sorry. I thought about you constantly when I was at the Good Shepherd. A few of the girls there were pregnant. I always hoped you were in a kinder place than that."

"Aunt Cookie's wasn't bad. The bad part was that I had to go through it at all—hiding myself away, and then pretending it never happened. Why does it have to be such a secret? And why don't we hold the boy responsible?"

"I have no idea. It doesn't seem fair."

"For me, the worst part was when they took my baby."

"Oh, Fiona." Mairin could not imagine it. She gave her friend's hand a squeeze. "Tell me."

"She was beautiful," Fiona said with a faraway look in her eyes. "So tiny and sweet. They let me hold her for a few hours, and I never wanted to let her go. I called her Ruby, although I'm sure the people who adopted her gave her another name. I wanted to keep her. I wanted that so bad."

"Of course you did," Mairin said. "I'm really sorry. I know that doesn't help, but I'm sorry."

"I never even had a choice. No one asked me what I wanted. And I think about my baby all the time, even now. I just wonder, you know, where she is, what she's doing . . . She's always right here." She pressed a fist to her chest. "Here in my heart. It's a feeling that'll never go away. I suppose I'll have kids one day after I get married. But that baby—my beautiful little Ruby—will always haunt me. I'll always wonder about her."

"Can't you find out who adopted her? Maybe you could meet her."

"Impossible. It's called a sealed adoption. My mom signed away all my parental rights after she was born."

"Fiona, that must be so sad. You've got me crying, and I never even met her." Mairin could offer no words of comfort, so she just held her friend and cried with her.

"How did everything go so wrong for both of us?" Fiona asked. "Me being stupid enough to get pregnant—"

"You weren't stupid. You just did what everybody does when they first start feeling, you know, that way."

"And you," Fiona said. "You were punished for no reason at all. No good reason, anyway."

Mairin nodded her head and pulled away. "You know, this all started for me when Kevin Doyle's mom and my mom found out we went on a date. Our moms were sure I was going to get pregnant." She felt a spike of anger. "I still can't believe my mother sent me to the nuns."

Fiona shook her head. "Kevin joined the army, did you know?"

"Really? No, I didn't know." Mairin tried to picture him in uniform, his shaggy hair reduced to a buzz cut. For a brief moment, he had been her whole world. Now he was just someone she used to know. "Do you ever see Casey Costello?"

Fiona gave a half shrug. "At the CYO dances sometimes. He acts like he doesn't even know me, like he never got me pregnant." Then she brightened. "I'm going to find somebody better at college. Or maybe I won't. Maybe I'll just grow up to be a weird old lady like my aunt Cookie."

"After the year we've had, being a weird old lady doesn't sound so awful," said Mairin.

FLYNN SHOWED UP now and then, picking up produce or returning crates to the farm. At first, Mairin thought he came to see Haley, but she realized he was also checking on her. She wondered if Flynn realized

Haley was cheating on him with the wispy guy, but she concluded that it was none of her business.

Still, her heart always lifted when Flynn visited. His dark hair was always slightly tousled, as if he didn't have time to fuss over appearances. But he had a twinkle in his eyes that softened his serious demeanor. There was something compelling about his determination to build his business. Even though he usually spent most of his time with Haley, he somehow managed to make Mairin feel seen, listening closely when she told him about her garden plan and produce yield. That was definitely the mark of a good listener, because not many people cared about farm management. She couldn't help but feel drawn to Flynn—his kindness and steadiness; his work ethic; and yes, his strong, manly looks.

Mairin weathered the cold winter with a changing array of people who slept in tepees pitched on a hillside, or in VW vans or in the school bus. After the police raid, she was able to relax her vigilance, because she realized people tended to see what they expected to see. She stopped glancing over her shoulder. No one was looking for her. And if she was found, she wouldn't go back to the nuns the way she had the first time, like a lamb to the slaughter. Knowing what awaited her, she would fight for her life.

She survived on homemade bread, vegetables from the root cellar, and a generous stack of books on farming and land management and cultivation. In the spring thaw, when the sap was running, she learned to tap the maples and deliver the sap in big cans to a local producer named Mr. Barrett. Jax, who had inherited from his grandparents, was so pleased that he let her keep some of the money.

But as the seasons changed, commune life lost its glow. People lay around and had random sex and got high and made music and danced. It was miles better than the nuns, but Mairin sometimes felt restless with the urge to do something. To make something. To be something.

A small core of dedicated residents—Mairin included—did most of the work. She found herself wanting more—not just for herself, but for the farm.

It was a truly wonderful place, nestled in the valley of three hills, with a pond fed by a rushing creek and crowned by a forest of maple and larch. But it was falling into disrepair. Jax, laconic and too fond of weed, tended to sleep all day and leave the chores to others. She overheard him telling people he was behind on his property taxes.

Hearing him complain irritated her. He was letting the place waste away instead of seizing the opportunity. She could picture the farm, exactly, in every detail. At night, she would lie awake, envisioning how she would restore the old farmhouse and barn. She knew how to take care of the orchards and the fields, rotating them to get the best yield. If it were up to her, she wouldn't waste the chance to turn the place into something.

On the Fourth of July, 1970, she took the bus to Niagara Falls. The cascade had been restored to its thunderous glory, and the crowd was as big as the one the year before, when the nuns had brought them here. Mairin watched and watched, stiffening with eagerness when she saw someone who looked like one of her friends—a girl with an Afro who wasn't Odessa. A tall, slender young woman who wasn't Angela. Someone with chin-length shiny black hair who wasn't Helen. A girl with hacked-off brown hair and a big laugh who wasn't Denise. No sign of Janice or Kay. Music and speeches, protests and demonstrations against the war flowed past. Mairin kept the statue of Nikola Tesla in view, just in case.

Just in case one of the others remembered the pact they'd made.

She waited until dusk, but no one came. In her mind, Mairin relived the days at the Good Shepherd, and some of the memories made her feel physically ill. Other memories, though, filled her with tenderness for the girls who had survived the ordeal by her side. At least, she hoped they'd survived. She had led them away from that place, but then they'd all lost each other.

Riding the last bus home, Mairin struggled to keep her spirits up. Expecting someone—anyone—from their group to show up had always been a long shot. They all had their lives to live, and maybe that didn't include a yearly visit to the Falls.

LATER THAT SUMMER, Mairin approached Jax and told him she was going to move on. She had grown and healed here, gaining in confidence, and it was time.

He roused his lanky form, and his face fell into a sorrowful expression. "What'll we do without you, Sunshine? You're the one who keeps this place going."

She smiled briefly. "I need to get a job."

"Tell you what. You go make a bunch of money working for the man, and I'll sell you the whole place," said Jax. "Can't afford the upkeep and taxes anyway."

"Man, wouldn't I love that," she said, and she meant it. "Maybe I'll win the Irish Sweepstakes and come take it off your hands."

She got a job at Eisman's, back in the neighborhood where she'd grown up, taking the Gardenville bus to the Fruit Belt every day. Only instead of picking apples, she now had the knowledge and skills for a bigger role. Mr. Eisman had expanded his operation to offer Concord grape juice and cider, and maple syrup from local producers. He must have seen something in Mairin, because he paid for her to take classes through the Cornell Cooperative Extension program.

Classes. She never thought she'd study anything, except how to survive from one day to the next. The nuns had robbed her of an education, but this was a new opportunity. To her surprise, she thrived when learning about cultivation, soil health, tillage, crop management, profit and loss.

There was another surprise the day she entered a new class on berry cultivation. The room hummed with the soft murmur of voices as she found a seat and began flipping through her notes. She looked up to see Flynn Gallagher coming through the door. He paused, scanning the room, and he grinned when he saw her.

"Miss Mairin O'Hara. It's been a while. This seat taken?" he asked.

She smiled back, drawn to his rugged charm and easy smile. "Fiona said you were taking some classes."

"When I can."

"She said you've been busy."

He nodded. "Added a couple of trucks and drivers to keep up with demand."

"That's good, Flynn. Really, it's great. I'm working for Mr. Eisman now."

"Farm life didn't suit you?"

"It did, actually. I loved the farming part of it. The commune? Not so much. The owner says he wants to sell the place." She sighed. "It's a good farm, but it needs a lot of work. It's kind of a wreck, and he owes back taxes. Makes me nuts to hear him say that, because it could really be productive."

"I ought to buy it, then," said Flynn. "I'm not afraid of hard work. Are you?"

Mairin didn't know what to say. He ignited something in her, something new. Talking with him awakened a sense of possibility. A part of her that had been numb ever since her ordeal at the laundry started to tingle with feeling.

After class, they lingered by the doorway. She sensed he might be as reluctant to part ways as she was. Flynn had a new way of looking at her, his gaze warm as he took in her corkscrew curls that had finally grown out, her low-cut jeans and Pink Floyd T-shirt. Could be he regarded her as something more than his kid sister's friend.

"You're serious?" she asked softly. "About Jax's farm, I mean."

"I might be. Are you?"

"Absolutely." She offered a wistful smile. "And I'm absolutely broke. But I can dream."

MAIRIN WENT TO the house on Peach Street for the first time since being sent to the Good Shepherd. She stood on the sidewalk, gazing at the old place where the memories of her father had lived, missing him with fresh waves of grief. It occurred to her that the whole ordeal would never have happened if only Patrick O'Hara had lived.

She had come here because she needed her birth certificate in order to get a driver's license. She wasn't sure how she'd feel when she saw her mother. Did she expect an apology? Maybe, she thought, an explanation would suffice. Really, she just wanted to understand why her mother had packed her up like an unwanted parcel and delivered her to the nuns. Fiona said it was because of both their mothers' blind loyalty to the Church. Always the Church. Mairin couldn't comprehend how a mother could put the Church above her child.

There was no car in the driveway, a hopeful sign that Colm was away. Drawing a deep breath, Mairin let herself in, the snap of the screen door announcing her arrival. "It's me," she called. "You home, Mam?"

A heavy *thump* came from the kitchen. Mairin found her mother standing at the ironing board, the pillowcase she was working on starting to smoke as she stared across the room, her eyes and mouth round with shock. Just the smell of the scorching fabric awakened nightmare reminders of the laundry. She rushed forward and grabbed the iron, setting it upright.

Then she stood across from her mother, her feelings a jumble of contradictions—affection and resentment, yearning and revulsion, love and disappointment. Her mother had always been pretty, with her auburn hair and light eyes, but she looked thin and tired now, her face webbed by lines of anxiety.

"Ah, Mairin," she said. "Jesus in the garden, and here you are entirely." Her eyes filled, and then the tears slipped unchecked down her cheeks.

"I wanted to see you, Mam." Mairin's voice broke. For a long time, she had nurtured a hard ball of anger at her mother, but seeing her now only brought a wave of sadness and regret.

"Come here, my girl. *Is ceol mo chroí thú.*"

It was the soothing voice of Mairin's childhood—*You are my heart's music.* She stepped into her mother's arms and they held each other. Mairin inhaled the familiar scent of Jergens lotion and Aqua Net.

"They came looking for you," her mother said, stepping back and wiping away a tear. "What could you have been thinking, running away like that? I didn't have the first idea where you'd gone."

"What do you suppose I was thinking, Mam?" Mairin said. "It was terrible there. Do you have any idea how terrible it was? And just so you know, I'm not going back. Ever. I know how to keep myself safe."

Mam looked Mairin up and down. "You've grown. You look good." There was a note of pride in her mother's voice. "A fine, grand girl, strong and sturdy."

"I've been working." Mairin surveyed the bins of laundry stacked on the kitchen table. "What's all this?"

"This is how I've managed to support myself," her mother said.

"What about Colm?" Mairin asked.

Mam shrugged. "He was let go from the power company. Said he'd find work at the docks, but he doesn't come around anymore."

Colm. Gone. "When?" Mairin asked.

"Since last spring."

"You're better off without him," Mairin said.

"Am I, then? I can barely keep up with the bills."

"You can divorce him now, right?" Mairin said. "He's abandoned you—"

"Ah, Mairin. You know I'd never." Mam's shoulders slumped. "I would have brought you back home after he left, but you'd already run off. I had no idea where you'd gone. Why wouldn't you have called me, just to let me know you're all right?"

"I was afraid you'd make me go back. I wasn't all right at that place, Mam. I wasn't."

Mairin couldn't bring herself to commiserate with her mother. She unplugged the iron and moved the laundry bins. Then she put the kettle on. "Sit, Mam. What do you hear from Liam? I tried to send him letters from the Good Shepherd, but the nuns censored everything and I have no idea if he ever got them. Since I left, I've been writing to him, but I haven't heard back."

"He's not much for writing a letter, your brother," Mam said. "He was on patrol on some river called the Bassac, over in Vietnam. He's been sick with the malaria, and he said a Vietnamese lady doctor saved his life. He'll be discharged soon. So I've that to look forward to." She sank down into a chair and folded her arms on the table. She gazed at Mairin with a faraway expression, her eyes unfocused.

"You shouldn't have done it, Mam," Mairin said. "You shouldn't have sent me away."

"I had no choice. I was afraid for you, Mairin."

"Because of Colm," Mairin said, not bothering to suppress a shudder.

Her mother didn't respond for a moment. "A man in his cups can't be trusted," she said.

"Then you should have sent *him* away," Mairin said.

"You think that was an option? A man can't be sent from his own home."

"This is your house," Mairin said. "Yours and Dad's."

"Not according to the law. It's a man's world, Mairin. A woman can't even get a bank account or a charge card on her own."

"Mam, I was fifteen. *Fifteen.*"

"Aye, and I didn't want you to wind up like . . . Fiona, having a child that would be stolen from you."

"The worst thing I ever did was go to the movies with a boy. Why would you assume I'd get pregnant?"

Mam flinched at the forbidden word. "Because that's what happens to girls who . . ."

"Girls who what? Have sex? Girls who get raped by their stepfathers?"

Another flinch.

A sigh of exasperation blasted from Mairin. "You can't even say it, Mam. But you'd rather throw me in prison than admit you didn't trust your own husband around me."

Her mother fell quiet again. The kettle whistled. Mairin got up and filled the teapot to brew. Mam got out a box of gingersnaps and put a few on a plate.

Then she looked directly at Mairin. "'Twas for the best. Those places—the Magdalene laundries—they exist for a reason. I had my time there as well."

"You mentioned that to Sister Rotrude when you took me to that place. You knew what it was like, then," Mairin raged. "You knew how bad it was."

"Some things are worse." Mam spoke quietly. "And I'm glad you never discovered that on your own."

"Worse?" Mairin asked, incredulous. "What could possibly be worse?"

"I fell pregnant with a Protestant boy," Mam said.

"*What?*"

"I was seventeen, and he was a soldier, and it was a great scandal and a shame on the family. My da wouldn't look at me. Wouldn't let me back into the house. I had to walk all the way by myself to the Clare Street laundry in Limerick. It took me a right full day."

"Wait. You had a baby in Ireland?"

Mam rubbed her thumb at a nonexistent spot on the Formica table. "They tried to tell me the babe didn't survive, but I didn't believe them. 'Tis a fact that the agencies were not above deceiving a girl or pressuring her into adoption. One of the sisters told me the truth. She let me hold my baby one last time." She got up and went to the hall table and took something from a drawer and handed it to Mairin. It was a tiny bootie of white wool. "I had a little boy."

"*Mam.*" Mairin was rigid with shock.

"When I could get up after the birth, they sent me to church to pray. I had to go in there and light a candle, but I never did light it. They made me put my hand on the Bible and swear never to speak of it again. My very own parents said the baby wouldn't be allowed in their house. That they couldn't afford to keep it. They said I was being cruel to the child to deprive it of a loving, two-parent home."

"Oh, Mam. Really? You never told me."

"I never told anyone. Except your da."

So much misery and shame, Mairin thought. When would it end? Mairin knew she had to find a way to forgive her mother. The bitterness inside her felt like a kind of poison, and she didn't want to feel this way. Now that she finally understood what had made Mam this way, she realized her mother was a wayward girl. Like her.

"Do you know what happened to your baby?" she asked.

"An American couple took him away to Buffalo, the sister told me. There were false registrations, and I was so terribly young and alone, but I had to try to find my boy. That's why I came here, to find him."

Mairin was flabbergasted. Her mother, forced to place a baby for adoption, the way Fiona had done. "So... you didn't find him."

"I hadn't expected Buffalo to be such a big, bewildering place as this. God only knows what would have become of me if Patrick O'Hara hadn't come along."

Mairin's chest ached. She reached across the table and tucked her hand into her mother's. "I miss him," she whispered.

"Every day," her mother agreed. "Will you stay, then, Mairin?"

Mairin fell silent. She studied her mother's face, and with surprising ease, she could picture Mam as a confused teenager, wild curls framing her face, green eyes round with the kind of fright Fiona and Angela had experienced.

The girls of the Good Shepherd had shown Mairin what the human spirit could endure. Her mother had been a wayward girl like them. Like Mairin.

She wanted to hug the girl her mother had been. Wanted to tell her she didn't deserve what had happened to her. Instead, she took her mother's hand and said, "Yes, Mam. I'd like that."

In the fall of 1971, Mairin stood outside the bustling bus station, her breath visible in the autumn air, crisp and filled with the bittersweet scent of fallen leaves and the distant promise of winter. She remembered trying to find the bus station on that frantic day with a van full of girls two summers ago, wishing the escape had gone as planned. The previous summer, she'd gone to Niagara Falls again on the Fourth, only to be disappointed. But not surprised. By now she'd resigned herself to the fact that the girls of the Good Shepherd wouldn't see each other again. And that was probably all right. It was probably better to keep the past tucked away like an old ache, pretending it hadn't happened. The problem for Mairin was that it *had* happened, and a part of her lingered in that terrible place, still trying to get over it.

A group of weary travelers streamed out of the station, but she saw only one face—Liam, his uniform rumpled, his duffel bag slung over his shoulder, his eyes searching the crowd. Amid the chaos of the bus depot, time seemed to stand still. Her brother was back, at last.

She pushed through the crowd, her steps quickening until she was in his arms, enveloping his lean frame, the buttons of his uniform pressing against her cheek. The familiar warmth of his embrace felt like coming home.

Mairin's heart ached at the sight of him, changed but unmistakably Liam. She sensed immediately that he was no longer the carefree boy who had left for Vietnam, but a somber man whose eyes seemed haunted by the shadows of war. He held her tightly, as if anchoring himself to her. She smiled through her tears, whispering words of welcome. Sensing the unspoken stories, the unshed tears, Mairin made a silent vow to help him find his way back from the darkness. "Mam's got supper waiting," she said. "Let's go home."

Skinny, lanky, sallow, and all smiles, Liam swept into their mother's kitchen and wrapped her in an embrace. He was prone to long silences, and not inclined to talk about his time over there. Mairin could relate to this in her own way. It was hard to speak of things to people who hadn't experienced them.

Now that his battle had ended, Liam told their mother he just wanted to make sense of it all. He wanted to go to college. Thanks to his military service, he would have the means to do that.

"College, is it?" asked Mam, raising her eyebrows. "And what sort of trouble will you be getting into there? All the marching and shouting and waving of signs looks like nothing but trouble to me."

Liam's grin lit the whole kitchen. "Not everyone who goes to college joins the protests. I'm interested in studying medicine."

"Medicine?" asked Mam, staggering a little as she set the table with the good china for his homecoming. "You want to be a doctor?"

"I do, Mam," he said. "I spent weeks in the hospital over there. Had a lot of time to think while I was lying in bed. I want to do something good in the world. After what I saw there, I think I need to do something good."

Mairin felt a thrill of inspiration. "Oh, Liam. I think that sounds wonderful."

"Yeah?"

"Yeah. Dad would be really proud to have a son going to college. A son who's a doctor."

"He would," their mother said softly. "He would indeed."

"How about you, squirt?" Liam asked Mairin. "What's next for you?"

"Your sister's taking classes through the Cornell ag extension," said Mam. "Fancy that."

Liam nodded. "*Very* fancy."

"I hope I can do something good in the world, too," Mairin said. "Maybe nothing so grand as healing the sick."

"Whatever you do, 'twill be grand," said their mother, beaming at them both. And for a few moments, she looked like the Mam of their youth, who used to sing the old songs when she put them to bed at night, who would soothe Mairin as she teased the burrs out of her hair, who dried Liam's tears when he came home with a scraped elbow or knee.

"I have to find my old school records in the basement," Liam said.

"I'll go with you." Mairin didn't want to let him out of her sight now that he was back. By the dim light of a bare bulb, they found the records from St. Joe's. Liam noticed a dust-covered box labeled *Patrick O'Hara*. It was filled with things they'd never seen before, relics of a life cut short—

their father's high school diploma. His service record in the Second Infantry Division in World War II. He'd earned a commendation for his part in the Battle of the Bulge. There was an official death certificate in an envelope along with documents from the power company and some news clippings about the accident.

"He saved thirty lives that day," Liam said, his voice low and rough as he perused the yellowed documents. Along with the news clippings and many letters of condolence, they found a crisp, sturdy envelope with a string clasp and a printed label—*Settlement.*

Mairin took out the document and brought it over to the light. The pages were printed on thick, fancy paper laid out in intricate paragraphs in small print. She scanned the text, not comprehending all of it. Then her gaze fell on a phrase: *Beneficiaries of the Claimant are entitled to a settlement of weekly cash benefits equal to two-thirds of the deceased worker's average wage...*

"Liam," said Mairin. "Does this mean what I think it means?"

He read and reread the document. "Mam probably didn't understand what this is. She didn't realize she's entitled to compensation. We need to sort this out for her. Because what I think it means is that Dad..."

"Is still taking care of us."

Chapter 19

Mairin always remembered her promise to the girls of the Good Shepherd on the Fourth of July. The following year, she went to the Falls with her mother and Liam. Things were better for Mam now that she had the settlement. Liam got a used car and a part-time job, and he went to school and studied all the time. He didn't talk about what he'd gone through in Vietnam, but Mairin noticed that he flinched at loud noises, and he'd started smoking. He went to meetings at the VA, where he spoke with other guys who'd been in Vietnam. He said it helped to share.

Sometimes Mairin was tempted to tell people what had happened at the Good Shepherd and how it affected her, but she could never quite find the words. It was impossible to explain to someone who hadn't been there. But there was no VA program for girls who had been tormented by nuns. And so, the memories lived inside her like a cold, dark hole of nothingness.

This year on the Fourth, the war protests were louder and the music more angry. Hair was longer, skirts shorter, and the drugs more plentiful. Mairin scanned the crowd for hours, but the only familiar face she saw was one from Heyday Farm—Haley Moore. She was with a guy wearing motorcycle leathers, and she looked different—skinny, with dark circles under her eyes. She didn't seem to remember Mairin at all, but offered a brief, slack-mouthed smile. Mairin wondered if Haley would be surprised to hear that she was seeing Flynn. They weren't a couple. They weren't anything—yet. But she thought about him all the time. His dreams ran parallel to hers—a farm, a family, a purpose. A life that felt safe and secure. Even so, Mairin didn't trust herself to want more.

When she and her family got home that day, a sound of distress came from Mam in the backseat of Liam's Chevy. An old Nash Rambler was parked in the driveway.

"It's Colm," said Mam.

Liam got out first and strode up the porch steps and went into the house, Mairin and Mam at his heels.

Colm sat on the davenport as if he'd never left, smoking a cigarette and drinking a Genesee beer. He looked older, his thinning hair stretched across his head, his cheeks sagging. "Deirdre," he said, stubbing out his cigarette. "I've come back to you, Deirdre."

"Ah, Colm." Mam's face softened briefly, but at the same time, her posture stiffened with wariness. "And there ye are entirely."

Mairin's stomach twisted. She clenched her jaw to keep from screaming at her mother to throw the guy out.

"I've decided to forgive you," Colm said, steepling his fingers together. "I'm back. Folks at church said you're doing good these days."

"That's what it's about, Mam," Liam said, moving toward Colm. "He's not here to support *you*. He's not that kind of man."

Someone at church must have mentioned Patrick O'Hara's settlement, Mairin realized. Due to her father's accident, her mother was entitled to a portion of his wages—far more than Colm must be making. "Mam," she said through her teeth.

"It'll be good again, Deirdre," said Colm, ignoring Liam and Mairin and fixing his gaze on their mother. "You'll see..."

Her mother looked lost and indecisive. Her chin trembled. "Colm, I..."

"I know it's been hard without me," Colm said in a gentle tone. "I'm sorry I was gone so long. But I'm back now, and things will be better. That's a promise."

Mairin and Liam exchanged a glance. She could feel her mother's tension—the inner battle between the teachings of the Church and her yearning to be free.

"Ah, Colm," Mam said, holding his gaze with hers.

Mairin held her breath, terrified that her mother would retreat. She could see Liam, frozen, but ready to spring if triggered.

"I made you a promise," Colm urged. "I swear, everything'll be all right."

Mam's gaze moved over his face, then cut to the cigarette butt smoldering in the ashtray, and the beer bottle leaving a ring on the coffee table. Then she drew herself up, squaring her shoulders. "You're not welcome here, Colm. You can leave now."

Mairin nearly melted with relief. And with pride in her mother. She knew how hard it must be for Mam to break free of a lifetime of habit and stand up to him.

His brows crashed into a frown. "This is my home," he blustered, surging to his feet and drawing himself up to his full height.

Mairin couldn't handle it anymore. Just the sight of him dredged up memories. "You heard what my mother said. Get out, Colm. And stay out."

"None of your sass," he said, turning on her, his gaze drifting over her like an insult. "You've been nothing but trouble. Even the Sisters of Charity couldn't save you."

Mam planted her hands on her hips and faced him squarely. "'Twasn't Mairin who needed saving, Colm Davis. I wish I'd never listened to you. I'm done now. Done with you for good, and that's a fact."

"Don't you speak to me like that. You'll not put me out of my own house," Colm blustered.

"I will not." Mam glared at him with fire in her eye. "You'll walk out under your own steam, and you won't come back again."

Colm made fists with both hands. Liam stepped in front of Mam, his demeanor calm but ice-cold. "You heard her. It's time to go. Don't turn this into a fight you can't win."

Colm glared at him, seeming to size up the situation. "Useless, skinny bastard," he said. "I spent years raising you, and this is the thanks I get?"

"We'll thank you to leave," Mairin said, moving in next to Liam. "And don't come back."

For a moment, Colm didn't move. Then his shoulders rounded, and he turned on his heel, stalking out the back door and slamming it behind him.

Mam was shaking, blinking back tears.

"It'll be all right," Liam said. "I'll call a locksmith first thing in the morning."

Chapter 20

The following year, Mairin made her traditional visit to the Falls with her brother and his girlfriend, Barb. Liam had met Barb at RIT—the Rochester Institute of Technology, where they were both premed students. She knew they were serious, because Liam had decided to get an apartment close to campus—and close to Barb—in the coming year.

He and Mairin no longer worried about their mother's safety. The Church had finally done something good for Deirdre O'Hara. She had been granted an annulment based on the fact that she and Colm weren't able to have children. She didn't have to lose face with her friends in the Church. The only thing she lost was a man who didn't deserve to be her husband.

Mam seemed softer and more mellow these days, content to have her children home with her. The settlement money from Dad's accident didn't make her wealthy by any means, but it eased the burden of her worries. Mairin would never say as much to her mother, but she thought Mam was obviously much happier knowing Colm wasn't coming back.

In 1973, Mairin celebrated at the Falls with Fiona and Flynn Gallagher. Fiona knew there was a mutual attraction between them, but it was a slow burn, and she encouraged them. But Mairin knew that she needed to trust her own feelings. The Good Shepherd had messed her up so bad, she didn't know how to listen to herself. She thought about telling Flynn why she absolutely had to be at the Tesla statue precisely at noon, but decided against it. She just didn't have the words.

THE FOURTH WAS the first day Mairin had taken off in months, because Mr. Eisman had put her in charge of organic practices for some of his acreage, and it had turned into an all-consuming project. He'd also trusted her to hire workers when they were needed, and she made a project of finding girls who were lost—the ones who hung around the bus station or the lakefront docks, girls who needed a helping hand. Although Mairin herself was just twenty, she had a way of sensing when someone was in trouble.

The Paris Peace Accords removed the United States from the conflict in Vietnam. The patriotic songs were louder, the protests quieter. Mairin took pictures with her new Instamatic camera. As they watched the West Point marching band, Fiona gave Mairin a nudge. "Look who just showed up."

Mairin shaded her eyes and turned, and her heart skipped a beat. She glanced at Fiona and Flynn. "I'll be right back," she said, and wove a path through the crowd.

She stopped a few feet from him, a man with long hair curling over his collar, a mustache and goatee, a tie-dye band around his forehead, and aviator sunglasses. "Kevin Doyle," she said.

He turned to her, and a slow smile spread across his face. "Mairin O'Hara. It's been a while."

For an awkward moment, she didn't know what to do, so she stuck out her hand to shake his. More awkwardness—his right hand and forearm bore shiny scars that looked like he'd been burned.

"I heard you were in the army," she said.

He nodded. "Yep."

"Are you . . ." *Are you all right?* So many of the boys who came back were not. Her own brother waged a constant battle with nightmares and flashbacks. "How are you?" she amended.

"Glad to be home in one piece, that's how." He showed her his arm. "Had an accident while I was in country. You weren't there to put out the fire that time." He grinned to show he was joking.

"Oh, Kevin. I wish I had been. What's next for you?"

His grin turned thoughtful. "I'm going to seminary school in East Aurora."

"*Seriously?* You're going to be a *priest?*"

"That's the plan. I thought about studying law. Either way, it's all about dealing with people's sins. How about yourself, Mairin? What's next for you?"

She paused, then said the most honest thing that came to mind. "I'm still trying to work that out."

MAIRIN WAS NOT surprised when no one showed up the subsequent year. By now she knew that work and time and priorities could get in the way of the best intentions. She also allowed that maybe the others were reluctant to see each other again. Life had swept them down different paths, as life had a habit of doing. This year was particularly disappointing because Mairin was bursting with news.

She milled around the statue, listening to Dionne Warwick's "Then Came You" blaring from a set of loudspeakers. She did her usual crowd-scanning. She waved to Roy and Shirley Barrett, their little towheaded daughter swinging from their hands between them as they watched a juggling clown. The Barretts had a maple farm upstate, and they supplied Eisman's with syrup. Their daughter was a handful for the older couple, but they clearly adored her.

She was about to go over and say hello when someone spoke behind her.

"I'd know that curly red hair anywhere," the voice called over the roar of the Falls and the blaring music.

Mairin whirled around and came face-to-face with Angela Denny. She looked more beautiful than ever in a red miniskirt and white peasant top, blond hair flying like a shiny banner.

They hugged and babbled with joy, the words tumbling from them in a cascade like the Falls. "Stop," Mairin said, laughing. "I'm so happy, I can't breathe!"

"Same here."

They hugged again, then leaned back to stare at each other. Angela smelled of fresh air and sunshine.

"I brought a camera." Mairin took out her Kodak Instamatic and snapped Angela's picture. They tried to figure out how to do one together, giggling and probably failing as Mairin held the camera at arm's length.

"Hey, would you mind taking our picture?" Mairin asked Mr. Barrett, who was still nearby with his family. "This is my old friend Angela," she said. "Ang, this is Roy and Shirley Barrett, and their little girl, Everly. They're our best maple syrup producers at Eisman's."

"Lovely to meet you, dear," said Mrs. Barrett.

"Likewise." Angela looked at their little girl, a blond sprite with big blue eyes. "She's so cute."

"Thank you. We're very proud of her." Mr. Barrett took a couple of shots of Mairin and Angela together.

The little girl broke away and rushed into the picture as the shutter went off. "Everly, come to Mama!" called Mrs. Barrett.

The child offered one last cherubic smile and a giggle, then rejoined her parents. Mr. Barrett took another picture and handed back the camera. "You girls have fun today."

Breathless and animated, Mairin and Angela rushed away from the crowd, eager to catch up. "This is the first year I was able to come," Angela said. "It's been hard to get away. School and work..."

"You're here now." Mairin was practically giddy with delight. "You look wonderful. Tell me everything. Are you doing all right?"

"I'm in college, can you believe it?"

"College!"

"Over in Geneseo. I'm going to be a librarian," Angela said. "I'll be starting my first full-time job at the main branch in Buffalo."

"A librarian," Mairin said. "That's perfect."

"What about you?"

"I've been working since I got out. I was never much for school, but I've been taking courses in organic farm practices."

"And that," Angela said, her eyes sparkling, "is also perfect."

They smiled at each other and marveled at how very much the same they looked and sounded, and how utterly different they actually were.

"No word from anyone else?" Angela asked her.

Mairin shook her head. "I feel terrible about how it all fell apart that day. I'm so glad you're all right. Tell me everything, starting with us ditching the van."

"I went to my friend Tanya's house. Her parents were cool, and they let me stay awhile. I got a job working at the General Mills factory that year, making Cheerios." She caught Mairin's look. "Yep, I came home every day smelling of Cheerios."

"Better than smelling like bleach and Borax." Mairin made a face.

"True. Tanya went away to college, and I stayed with Miss Adler—Rachel Adler, the librarian at the Jefferson Branch. She made anything seem possible."

"Even college." Mairin sighed. "I keep wondering about the others. I just hope they managed to get away."

Angela shook her head. "It was in the paper. You didn't see it?"

"What? No?"

Angela nodded. "The very day of the escape, it came out in the evening paper."

"I had no idea. What did it say?"

"Almost nothing. There was a bit that said three girls were captured—"

"Three!" Mairin's heart sank. "Which three?"

"There were no names. But the report also said one of the three got away. The other two were returned to the Good Shepherd."

"And they didn't say which two." Mairin shook her head. "I'd love to know what became of the money I took from the nuns," she added. "What a fiasco. Having the cash would have made things a lot easier." She noticed a shift in Angela's expression. "What?"

Angela's face paled, and she twisted her fingers into knots. "Mairin, I took the money."

"What?"

"I grabbed the laundry bag as we were all running away. I felt like the worst kind of thief."

"*I* was the thief," Mairin said.

"You stole from thieves, but we were all supposed to share the money. I wish I could have found everyone so we could have shared it like we planned, but I was so scared of getting caught. I had to be so careful.

I knew the nuns wouldn't ask for it back because they couldn't admit they had it. But it still felt risky." Angela stared at the ground. "It's gone now, Mairin. I'm so ashamed. I used some of it to live on when my gran wouldn't have me back, and the rest was for school. Oh, Mairin."

Mairin sensed her friend's wrenching pain. "Angela. It's okay. I swear it's okay."

"It's not. I feel so guilty."

"Stop," Mairin said. "You were the one who suffered the most. We all know that. If that money helped you even a little bit, then I'm glad you ended up with it."

"Well, now that we've found each other, I'm going to pay you back," Angela said resolutely.

"Hey. Don't you dare. It wasn't my money to begin with. It was the nuns', and heaven knows, they owed you." Mairin gripped her friend's hand. "Really, Angela, let it go. I don't need anything from you except to know you're all right. Because *I'm* all right, really. I have a job. I have plans. That's all in the past. Let's keep it there, okay?"

"Oh, Mairin. You're the best."

"We're all the best. Look at us now."

Angela expelled a happy sigh. "I'm so damn glad you're one of the ones who got away."

"Same here, Angela. It's such a relief to see you. I'm back with my mam. I thought I'd never forgive her for sending me to that place, but she told me some things that happened in Ireland, and I think I understand her better."

"That's good, Mairin. I'm glad to hear it."

Mairin hesitated, then said, "Angela, my mother had a baby at a Magdalene laundry in Limerick, and it messed her up but good. Do you know, the nuns there tried to tell her the baby didn't survive? Mam found out that they gave her little boy to an American couple. That's how she ended up here in Buffalo. She came to find him, but she never did." Mairin looked out at the Falls. "She found my dad instead."

Angela squeezed her hand, then sobered. "I wish my baby had survived. Even though her father was . . . you know. None of that was her fault. I really wish she could have lived."

"Of course you do." Mairin squeezed back.

"Did the nuns lie to me?" Angela asked. "The way they did to your mother?"

Mairin grimaced. "I wouldn't put anything past them."

"My gran had the death certificate. Said she threw it away, though. Said she was erasing my sin. She won't hear a thing from me. I told her how terrible it was for me—the birth and the loss of the baby. She pretends it never happened at all." She rolled her eyes.

"Angela, I'm sorry. It's terrible what happened to you." And to her mam. And to Fiona. How many girls had been punished for a pregnancy?

"I'm doing better now."

"I try not to think about it. You know, all the stuff that happened."

Angela nodded. "Same here. But . . . Miss Adler from the library said I should get some help. You know, like counseling. There's a counselor at the college that I talk to."

"You mean, like a shrink?"

Angela grinned. "Well, not like Sigmund Freud, where I have to lie on a sofa and pour my heart out. Just . . . the counselor helps me talk through some things."

"And does it work?"

She was quiet. Her porcelain-blue eyes were distant for a moment. "Yeah. Sometimes, at least."

"That's good."

"What else, Mairin? You look so good."

"Well, at work, I've been doing something . . ." She felt a bit bashful, but she knew Angela would understand. "Sometimes when I see a girl like we were—you know, lost or in some sort of trouble—I try to convince Mr. Eisman, my boss, to hire her. So she doesn't end up in a place like the Good Shepherd. I try to find girls to help at Eisman's before the system finds them. It doesn't always work," she admitted. "But when it does, I feel as if I've actually done something."

"Of course you have, Mairin."

"Maybe I'm trying to make up for screwing up the day we ran away."

"Stop. You didn't screw up. You gave us a chance, and now we know at least two of us are doing okay."

"I think about the others, though."

"So do I. And I think they're better off because of the chance you took."

For the first time, Mairin looked back on that day and felt something other than regret. "Thank you, Angela. Thanks for saying that."

"Because I mean it. Because it's true. Now. What else?" Angela brightened. "Tell me something good."

"I'm seeing a guy I really like." She just blurted it out. "I think I've been half in love with him all my life. His name's Flynn Gallagher."

"Saying his name makes you sparkle," Angela said. "And that is a very good sign."

"We've been talking about this crazy dream together," Mairin said. "We want to move to a farm, grow things, have a family one day."

"I hope you do, Mairin. You deserve it. You deserve every happiness."

They talked for more than an hour, and ended with promises to stay in touch. "Let's not lose each other ever again," Mairin said.

"We won't," Angela said. "My God, it's good to see you. You're really the only one who knows, if you get what I mean."

"I do, Angela." She squeezed her hand. "Thanks for coming."

Now Mairin understood why her brother was so diligent about going to his VA meetings. The only ones who truly understood what they'd gone through were those who had gone through the same thing. It was both painful and gratifying to reconnect with Angela. On the one hand, they shared a powerful bond. But on the other hand, the encounter brought back memories that Mairin usually managed to relegate to the deepest, most hidden reaches of her heart.

MAIRIN WAS EXCITED to tell Flynn about finding Angela, yet the conversation was harder than she'd anticipated. She went to his apartment in town, an efficiency walk-up near his truck warehouse. "I loved seeing her," she told him. "I've been trying to find the girls every year on the Fourth of July, and finally one of them showed up. She's wonderful, Flynn. I want you to meet her one day."

"I'd like that," he said, holding her gaze with his. "I want to know everyone you know, Mairin."

The warmth of his words touched her heart. "Flynn, I don't know what

I would have done without you that day," she said. "The day I escaped. You saved me. You really did."

He slipped his arms around her, his touch easy and assured. "I tried to help. But you're the one who did the saving, Mairin."

She felt the strength and safety of his embrace. "It was . . . it's hard to explain, but it was a joyous moment when I saw Angela. And it was also really tough. It brought back a lot of memories. Like a tidal wave of memories."

"It sucks, what happened to you," he said, his lips close to her ear. "I wish it had never happened. But it did happen, and you survived, and I bet it made you stronger."

"Stronger than what?" she asked. "I wasn't strong. I was fifteen. Those memories are hard to shake. I might never shake them." She shuddered. "I guess we all have scars. Liam—he has scars, but he seems okay, you know. Goes to his meetings and stuff." Then she looked up into his eyes, and it was like looking at heaven. "I don't have scars, Flynn. I have wounds."

"Oh, baby," he said, pressing a long, soft kiss to her forehead. "I wish I could save you from that."

"I'll never be okay," she whispered, even though she felt the power of his embrace.

"I can't save you," he said. "But I see you, Mairin. I *see* you."

Somehow, that was enough. She thought of all the times he'd come to check on her at the commune, watching over her, even from a distance. She melted deeper into his embrace, and he kissed her and said, "I want to make love to you, Mairin."

"I want that, too," she said, her hands mapping the topography of his shoulders and arms. "I do." She knew it was the answer he was waiting for. "You do realize, I grew up believing sex outside of marriage was wrong."

He pulled back. "That's okay, then—"

"—but *I* was wrong. The Church is wrong. It's a bunch of Catholic nonsense." She kissed him again, savoring his taste and the softness of his lips, then whispered, "The nuns always told me if we had sex before marriage, we'd burn in hell."

"I've got a better idea," he said, kissing her back. "Let the two of us burn right now."

"Where are we going?" Mairin asked, looking over at Flynn as they drove together out past Gardenville. They often took rides on Friday after work with the radio turned up high. Their dates usually ended up in a tumble of lovemaking at Flynn's place. During her time at the commune, she'd learned about sex. But Flynn showed her what love felt like. Today, he seemed more purposeful. Energized, even.

"I had a meeting at the bank this morning." He turned down the volume, then reached for her hand, his fingers intertwining with hers.

Her pulse quickened. "You got the loan," she said.

"The bank turned me down." He stared grimly at the road ahead.

"Oh, Flynn." She squeezed his hand.

"Until Mr. Fiorelli guaranteed the loan for me." His expression changed to a grin that highlighted his incredible face, with its strong jaw and piercing eyes.

It took her a moment to realize what that meant. "You got it," she whispered. "You finally got it."

"It's crazy, right?"

"It's crazy, and exactly right." They had talked for a long time about their shared dream, but it had always been only that—a dream, glistening in some unreachable distance that was littered with in-between hurdles. "This is amazing," she said. "I can't believe it's happening." Her pulse quickened as she recognized the rise in the road and the rolling green hills under the summer sky. He turned the truck onto a rutted track marked with a *Posted—No Trespassing* sign. "Remember this place?"

"Are you kidding? Of course I do. Wow, it's even more of a wreck now than it was when I left." The painted bus was overgrown with weeds and vines, the peace signs and slogans peeling and faded. In the distance, the house and barn and outbuildings lay in a state of quiet abandonment.

She was speechless as he drove up to the house. A flood of memories came rushing back. She could still hear the echoes of bygone music and laughter, shouting and drumming. She remembered sitting for hours by the pond with a chain of wildflowers in her hair, trying to figure out who she was.

The porch sagged under the weight of neglect. The house was a skeleton of its former self, curls of paint revealing the old wooden siding, the windows gazing out like eyes lidded with torn shades. Flynn's hand trembled a little as he turned a rusted key in the lock, the *click* echoing in the stillness of the summer afternoon. The door creaked open, protesting as he pushed it aside. Mairin trailed behind him, stepping cautiously on the old floorboards.

"This is it," Flynn said. "It's not much to look at now, but I've got big plans, Mairin."

Her heart skipped a beat at the promise she heard in his voice. She herself had been making plans since the first day she'd set foot on the farmland. They moved through the old house, dappled with shadows and dusty sunlight. "It's like it's been frozen in time," Mairin said. She walked closer to him as they exited through the back door. Her gaze scanned the horizon, now streaked with the deepening colors of late afternoon. "You're right, Flynn," she said. "It's a wreck."

"Yes, but I—"

"A beautiful wreck," she said. "We used to have bonfires right over there." She pointed. "Everyone would gather around, singing and sharing stories until the stars came out." Then she turned to him. "It was a lonely time for me, Flynn. The land taught me a lot, but I always knew there was something missing."

He touched her cheek. "What was missing, Mairin?"

You, she thought. *You.* She felt as if she were balanced on a precipice, afraid to fall. She wanted to tell him. She was scared to tell him. Her vision blurred with tears. Here she stood with the one person who unknowingly held the other half of her soul, but she felt so uncertain, so damaged by the brutal year with the nuns that she couldn't imagine showing her heart to him.

"Mairin?" he prompted.

She looked up at him, remembering all the times she'd looked up to Flynn Gallagher, the boy with the gleaming dark hair and the quiet smile, the man who seemed to understand her without words.

"We can bring this place to life again," she said. "Make things grow, bring people together."

He smiled, his eyes softening with relief. "We can," he agreed.

Her gaze swept the weedy garden around the house. "Dandelions don't need any help," she said. "My dad always told me to be a dandelion, not an artichoke. They're hard to grow."

"We'll grow artichokes," Flynn said. "We'll grow anything you want. You and me together. This is where it's going to happen, Mairin. Everything we talked about. And probably things we never even dreamed about."

She slipped her arms around him, pressing her cheek against his warm chest, listening to the steady beat of his heart and inhaling his scent. This moment had been a long time coming. It was slow but steady, a gradual discovery that there really was a kind of love that was as safe and warm as a blanket in winter. A kind of love that lasted as long as life. A kind of love that could save her.

"I totally and completely love you," she said in a small, shaking voice.

He leaned down and brushed his lips over her temple. Then he lifted her up off the ground and hugged her against him. "Did you just whisper that? Say it again, Mairin. I want to hear you say it again."

MAIRIN AND FLYNN were married at their farm in the summer of '75. The orchard was their canopy, and their mothers and friends prepared a banquet with produce grown on the property. Mairin's own mother sang a traditional wedding song in Gaelic. The honeymoon had to wait for winter, because in addition to being their shared passion, the farm was an uncompromising tyrant. They brought the place back to life, refurbishing the farmhouse and reviving its patchwork of vibrant greens and lush reds in the orchards and fields.

In the shadow of the trees, on the edge of the main orchard, nestled a row of weathered cottages that had once housed the fruit pickers during harvest season.

Mairin made a special project of restoring the cottages, breathing new life into the worn walls and creaky floorboards, adding fresh coats of paint in cheerful colors, new roofs, and simple furnishings. Flynn's huge extended family, along with friends and neighbors, pitched in as the once-abandoned buildings were transformed into cozy sanctuaries, and word spread that there was a place for girls in need of shelter. Young women came and went, helping in the orchards and fields, manning the roadside farm stand, filling crates for the delivery trucks, most of them grateful for the dignity of work and a safe haven.

She wrote a letter to Angela Denny in Geneseo, telling her about the project. Since their meeting at the Falls, the elation of finding each other had mellowed. That initial burst of camaraderie had been genuine, but fleeting. They had exchanged phone numbers and addresses, but then the calls and letters gradually dwindled in frequency. Though Angela had declined the wedding invitation, she'd sent a heartfelt card of congratulations and a set of Belleek porcelain bookends. Angela explained that she wouldn't know anyone at the wedding, and didn't want to have to explain how she and Mairin had met. Something about their shared trauma at the Good Shepherd made them cautious, perhaps. They remained friends—from a distance. It was enough to know that they could find each other again if they needed to.

FLYNN AND MAIRIN worked themselves into exhaustion some days, but they were replete with satisfaction, because they were building their dream, cultivating it with patience and love. Each sprout that broke through the soil, each flower that blossomed into fruit, marked their progress. Each harvest was a celebration of their tenacity and dedication. In the winter, the land rested beneath a blanket of snow, and they planned and struggled to manage the budget. They made love by the warmth of a wood stove, and waited for spring to beckon.

One autumn evening near the end of the apple harvest, Flynn brought Mairin down to the orchard to watch the sun go down and listen to the whispering trees. Lights were coming on in the workers' cottages, turning the windows to gold.

"Look what we did," Mairin said, leaning back against the broad wall of his chest. "What we're doing."

He brought his arms around her from behind. "We're just getting started," he said. Then he took her hand. "I made you something. Come see."

They walked over to the orchard gate, which used to have a shabby hand-lettered *Heyday Farm* plaque. "I replaced the old one," he said.

Mairin stared at the new sign, her heart bursting with pride. The new sign read *Wayward Farm*.

BOOK TWO

Now

Part Five

I always thought, this will go away. I'm not going to feel this anymore.
—*Bonnie A., survivor*

Chapter 21

Lily Gallagher's eyes shone as she held up the poster she'd just finished decorating, a masterpiece of glitter with the message *Happy 50th Anniversary!* How's that, Grandma?" she asked. "What do you think?"

Mairin beamed at her youngest granddaughter, a sprightly chatterbox who had her father's dark hair and her mother's freckled, milk-pale skin. "Isn't that lovely," she said. "We can't go wrong with gold glitter, can we? Let's display it on the easel in the foyer."

A black lab named Seal, whose sweet face was sugared with age and calm wisdom, lay at Mairin's feet, thumping her tail as if in approval. Mairin always had to have a dog. For the comfort. For the companionship. For the knowledge that, despite what had happened in the past, everything was all right. Through the years, there had been many dogs at Wayward Farm, and Seal was the best of them all, an angel dog.

"Tell us again how you met Granddad," Lily said, setting aside the poster and getting out scissors and glue for a paper chain. The light-filled banquet hall of Wayward Farm had been the backdrop for elegant weddings in recent years, but the golden anniversary celebration was to be a homemade affair.

The place had changed over the past half century. After Mairin and Flynn retired, their daughter Colleen had reimagined the vast property as a destination event venue. The stunning banquet hall and catering kitchen had once been a working barn. Now its understated rustic chic had made it a premier setting for weddings, reunions, and farm-to-table culinary events with renowned chefs and sommeliers who came from far and wide.

Mairin couldn't think of a more appropriate place to celebrate her fifty years with Flynn.

The early years had been hard, and sometimes Mairin wished she could forget the rough patches and move on. But the memories that had brought her to this point were indelible, as much a part of her as her wavy white hair and stubborn will.

"Earth to Grandma," Lily prodded.

"Ah, you know the story." Mairin looked up from the guest list on her yellow legal pad and smiled at her granddaughter. The list was growing by leaps and bounds, but Mairin had anticipated that, given the size of her family. "It's not even a story, is it? He is Fiona's brother, so there was no meeting him, was there?"

Fiona, who sat at the long banquet table where she was helping address the invitations, caught Mairin's eye. "When your gran and I were starting kindergarten, my mother made Flynn walk us to school. A big sixth-grader he was, and so resentful at having to babysit two wee girls that he told us we'd have to get our ears pierced on the first day. We were wild with terror!"

"You mean you believed him?" Mairin's daughter Colleen shook her head. Colleen had her computer attached to a scanner. She was working on digitizing old photos for the anniversary slide show.

"Back then, we believed everything Flynn told us," Fiona said with a wink. She was a wonderful artist, putting her flourishes on the invitation she was designing for the event.

"Still do, for better or worse," Mairin said, feeling a soft wave of contentment. Fifty years, she thought. Sometimes, that felt like forever—an entire lifetime. Other times, 1975 felt as if it were only yesterday.

"But weren't you just completely mad with romance?" Lily stood up, clutching her chest and reeling with a swoon.

"Go on with you," Mairin said. "Your granddad and I were so busy putting our life together, there was hardly time to go mad."

"Always so practical," Fiona said. "Maybe it's time to go a little mad."

The scene in the banquet hall brought a smile to Mairin's face—her granddaughter, daughter, and best friend all pitching in for the celebration. And outside, spring had arrived in full force at Wayward Farm, the place she and Flynn had built together, renovating the grand old farmhouse, barn, and workers' cottages, and cultivating the terrain, acre by acre. Now the orchards were bursting into bloom, the fields tilled and seeded, the vineyards just starting to bud.

She remembered planting each section, expanding whenever they had the resources to do so, always looking to hire workers like the girl she had once been—teenagers who needed a boost in life. Mairin hoped she'd done enough. Sometimes she ruminated about it on sleepless nights. Her brother, Liam, was a doctor at Roswell Park, helping cancer patients. Mairin was never sure she'd been brave enough, smart enough, grateful enough for the life she had.

"WHAT DO YOU think of this for the opening image of the slide show?" Colleen turned her screen toward the group. "The wedding portrait? Or this one—the two of you cutting the cake?"

"What kind of cake was it?" Lily asked. "I'm hungry."

"A pink champagne cake from McGavin's Bakery," Mairin said, regarding the picture of her beaming self from fifty years ago. Her hair fell like flames down her back, and the gown was a ridiculous seventies concoction, with pointy shoulders and cascading flounces. Fashion crimes aside, she'd been sublimely happy that day, certain her dreams were finally coming true.

"McGavin's ... Oh, that takes me back," she said. She could still picture herself in a panic near the bakery on the night of the escape. Adulthood had been forced upon her the moment she'd run away from the Good Shepherd. Despite the daily joy of her family life, there was a place in the past that was still an unhealed wound. Mairin didn't speak of it, but the pain lingered. She was usually able to ignore the shadows, but sometimes she would take out the memories in private and ask herself why. Why had she been subjected to the Good Shepherd? Why did that one year have the power to haunt her, even decades later?

She had the love of a good man. They'd raised four excellent humans—

Patricia, Colleen, Patrick, and Declan. They had built something together. They had weathered their share of joys and sorrows, triumphs and losses. When Mairin had laid her mother to rest ten years before, the sadness had mingled with forgiveness. Mam had fully embraced her role as Irish granny to Mairin's children, knitting Aran wool sweaters and singing the old songs to them, baking endless apple pies and filling their heads with stories of their long-gone grandfather, the hero of the Falls.

When gathering a bouquet of life's blessings, Mairin was grateful for the sweetness of a family she adored and friends to keep her company. But few of them knew about the Good Shepherd. That part of herself was private. And it still hurt.

Now she looked across the worktable at Fiona. Their eyes met, and Mairin could tell her friend had old memories of that year, too. Different ones. After the state had unsealed all adoption records in 2019, Fiona had been found by her daughter—the baby she'd named Ruby before being forced to surrender her. Now Fiona delighted in knowing her grown daughter, but she had confessed to Mairin that she was full of regrets at having missed out on Ruby's life.

Mairin's elder girl, Patricia, and her daughter, Irene, came bustling into the banquet hall, armed with sample menus and a tray of cookies that smelled like heaven. Patricia was an award-winning catering chef, famous for her locally sourced specialties involving maple syrup, New York apples and berries, and cheese from Cuba Lake.

"Time for a union break," Patricia declared, taking off her apron. She inspected Lily's poster and gave her a thumbs-up.

Irene sat down at the table, her attention caught by the stack of old photos waiting to be scanned. "Looks like a trip down memory lane," she said.

"That it is." Mairin exchanged another glance with Fiona.

"We're going to want to hear all the stories." Irene gazed fondly at a picture of Flynn posing with a new tractor, the one he'd bought the year the price of Concord grapes hit a record high. "Granddad was so handsome," she said. "He could have been a movie star." She found a shot of Mairin in shorts wearing a middie blouse and eating an ice cream cone. "Both of you could have."

Mairin shook her head. "Go on with yourself."

"I mean it. People spend hours in the gym to get in shape like that."

"We didn't have a gym. We had the farm."

"A farm with a roller coaster?" Lily asked, pointing out the background of the photo.

"That was taken at the Comet at Crystal Beach—an amusement park across the Peace Bridge. The Comet was a super tall, scary roller coaster. Crystal Beach used to be our one annual getaway," Mairin said.

"I remember when you didn't need a passport, and the border checkpoints were manned by schoolteachers on summer break," Fiona recalled. "Loblaws used to give out free ride tickets as a reward for good grades."

"I guess that's why I never got a free ride," Mairin said. "You were always the smart one."

Irene pulled four black-and-white photo strips from the bottom of the pile. "Look how young you were in these, Grandma. And with short hair, like Raggedy Ann. Who are these other people? And what are you all wearing?"

Mairin adjusted her glasses and took the old photos from her. She hadn't seen the pictures in ages and thought they were lost. They had been stored in a shoebox with all the other unsorted pictures she kept meaning to get to. "We were at Niagara Falls. This is from one of those old photo booth machines," she said. "You insert a coin, and everybody piles into the booth and makes faces, and voilà—the machine spits out the picture. Back then, we thought it was magic."

She would always remember the day she and the girls from the laundry had taken turns cramming into the booth at Niagara Falls. They had been so young. So beautiful. So hopeful, even in the face of their confinement. Their goofy, laughing faces were forever frozen in time.

"Do you remember any of those girls?"

"Angela Denny," Mairin said. "Helen Mei. Denise Curran, Janice ... gosh, I forgot her last name. And Kay. I can't remember her last name, either. And Odessa Bailey."

"And what's with the getup?" Lily asked, leaning on the table.

"That was a ... school uniform."

"Not a good look for you," Lily said.

Mairin shrugged. She felt Fiona's eyes on her. She'd never told her kids or grandchildren about the Good Shepherd. She didn't like to speak of it, although her mind returned over and over to the laundry in a seemingly endless loop, even as she fought to keep the images out of her head. It was as if her brain tried to make sense of the experience, or figure out if she could have responded differently. Sometimes there were nightmares of danger, dread, being chased. Sometimes there were flashbacks when something triggered her and she felt the trauma all over again. She had stopped going to church long ago, because it was full of triggers.

"Have you kept in touch with those people? Where are they now?"

"We lost touch, for the most part." After that momentous day so long ago, they'd scattered like seeds in the wind. She pointed to one of the girls. "Well, Angela and I are friends. She's over in Brockport. We text every now and then."

"Wait a minute." Patricia nudged in next to Mairin. "You said this girl's name is Odessa Bailey?" Patricia pointed to the laughing, bright-eyed girl in the picture. "I've heard of her."

Mairin frowned. "What do you mean, heard of her?"

"I mean, just the other day. Could be her, or someone with the same name. I wrote it down because she sounded so interesting in this interview I heard. It was on Fresh Air—you know that's my favorite podcast." Patricia listened to endless podcasts and radio shows while she cooked. "Anyway, there was an interview with an author named Odessa Bailey."

"She has a book?"

"About music. It was just published, and she was talking about it on the radio." Patricia took out her phone and tapped the screen. "The book sounded really good, so I put a hold on it at the library."

"Wait, what?" Mairin felt a beat of curiosity. "You're saying Odessa Bailey has a book?"

"Just listen. Maybe it's the same person." Patricia connected her phone to the Bluetooth speaker, and the host introduced her guest—college instructor and writer Odessa Bailey, author of the newly published music retrospective *Oh Happy Day: The Gospel Roots of Rock*.

Mairin didn't move a muscle as she listened to the lively voiced author chatting about her book and playing clips of old familiar songs—"Chain Gang," "Bring It On Home to Me," and "A Change Is Gonna Come."

Odessa Bailey sounded so strange and yet so familiar. "I grew up in Buffalo," she said when asked about her background. "Had a rough year in the 1960s when I was a teenager. I was sent to a reform school run by nuns. When I got out, I made my way to San Francisco. That reform school is long gone now, I imagine. At least, I hope it is. I haven't been back east since the old days. But with this book . . . well, the next stop on my book tour is Zawadi Books in Buffalo. Maybe I should look back. Sometimes you have to look back in order to find your way forward."

"What are you working on now?" asked the host.

"Well, there's a question," the author said. "I'm looking for my next idea. I have to find a topic I'm passionate about. Or maybe I'm waiting for it to find me."

Colleen tapped in a search on her laptop and looked up the author's photo—a vibrant, pretty woman who looked to be about the same age as Mairin. She held it next to the photo strip from 1969. "That's her. Oh, look at her, at that smile. Those eyes."

"She looks the same as she did in that picture of yours, Mom," said Patricia.

"Yes," said Mairin, feeling an unexpected surge of emotion. "Yes, she certainly does. That's quite . . . extraordinary." Her hands shook as she grabbed her phone and sent a quick text: I FOUND ODESSA.

Chapter 22

Angela Denny heard a text notification tone and looked up from the book she was reading to glance at her phone screen. Then she frowned and picked it up.

"What's that look, hon?" asked Jean, pausing at the front door. She was on her way to her Spanish conversation group. "Somehow, you're managing to scowl and raise your eyebrows at the same time."

Angela tried to compose her face into a smile. "Oh, a text from an old friend. Kind of a long story."

"I like long stories," Jean said. "You know that."

Angela waved a dismissive hand. "It's not much of a story. Just a note from a friend I haven't heard from in a while. Hey, while you're out, can you pick up some white port and tonic water?"

Jean didn't know much about the old days. They had been together for only two years, and they tended to talk about their future together, not the past. This suited Angela just fine. She had been through too many beautiful, damaged relationships to count. Something had ruined her. Something had made it impossible for her to let people close. Well, not exactly *something*. She knew what had ruined her.

When she first met Jean and their bond was new and very special, Angela made a conscious decision to keep the past where it belonged. In the past. This was contrary to everything she'd learned through years of therapy, but she kept finding partners who couldn't handle the honesty.

Jean was different, though. Jean, with her sharp mind and loving heart, could read Angela down to the last blink of her eye.

"Don't you have somewhere to be?" Angela said, feeling a prickle of apprehension.

Jean took off her jacket and hung it on the hall tree. "It'll wait."

"This could take a while."

"To explain a text message?"

Angela turned the phone screen toward her.

Jean read the message aloud: "'I found Odessa.' Isn't that a city in Ukraine?"

"It's the name of a girl I knew back when I was a teenager."

"Girlfriend?"

Angela shook her head. "Just someone I knew. For a bit."

"And Mairin? The one who sent the text?"

"Same."

Jean held out her hand. "Let's go make tea."

That was code. Early on in their relationship, they'd agreed that whenever one of them needed a long talk, they would make tea and sit on the sunporch overlooking the backyard and spend as much time as it took to sort themselves out. Angela wondered if Jean realized what a miraculous thing that was for her—a safe place to sit and talk.

They curled up together on a white-painted wicker sofa with cabbage rose cushions. It was not a stylish room, but it was filled with plants and books, graced by Gertrude and Alice purring contentedly in their basket in the sun.

"There's something I haven't mentioned. Something that happened to me when I was seventeen." Angela stirred the sugar in her tea.

"Something bad?"

"About as bad as it gets."

"And it has something to do with Odessa?"

"No. Yes. Not exactly. We were both sent to a place over in Buffalo—a home for girls run by nuns."

"A home? I thought you were raised by your grandmother."

Angela nodded. "I was. But one year, when I was in high school, Gran sent me to this place called the Good Shepherd. Ever hear of a Magdalene laundry?"

Jean, raised by loving agnostic parents in Westchester County, shook her head, clearly mystified.

"Picture a Catholic prison where girls branded as 'wayward' were forced to work in a laundry factory."

"What?" Jean's eyes bugged out.

"Seriously. Girls were sent there for all sorts of reasons. My gran made me go to the place because she found me kissing another girl and thought the nuns could straighten me out."

"Oh, shit. Oh, honey." Despite her indulgent family, Jean was familiar with the bumps along the way faced by girls like them. "Was it like a pray-the-gay-away camp?"

"Worse, if you can imagine that."

"You never told me. Why did you never tell me?"

"Because it was such a long time ago. Because it's bad. Because it screwed me up all my life. I was always troubled romantically," Angela said. "Until you. Everything's been so good with us, Jean. I didn't want anything to screw *us* up."

"We're stronger than anything that happened to either of us in the past. Keep talking." Jean's unwavering certainty was one of the things Angela loved most about her.

Angela inhaled slowly, practicing her breathing technique. "We might need something stronger than tea."

"Just tell me. I'm listening."

Angela had spoken of her ordeal to therapists and professionals. To friends and lovers. But never to someone who cared about her the way Jean cared. She'd always intended to open up about the year that had defined the rest of her life, but she had not yet found the right moment. The message from Mairin was the nudge she needed.

She spoke haltingly at first, but with increasing confidence, and Jean listened with an open, gentle expression. Angela described the doctor and his "treatments," leading up to the shock of discovering her pregnancy.

"Oh, dear God." The color drained from Jean's face.

"I confronted the nuns and Gran about the pregnancy. Told them I was not pregnant when Gran sent me to that place. How did they suppose it happened? Was it an immaculate conception? But they all stonewalled. Wouldn't hear the truth. They speculated about deliverymen and visitors to the refuge. Accused me of being a seductress. That was the word they used—*seductress*. They all ganged up on me and said I had to place the baby for adoption. I refused to sign anything, though. I was so scared, but I didn't want to make such a huge decision . . . I kept refusing to agree to anything. But since I was an underage minor, I was forced to place my baby for adoption."

"Back then, they could do that." Jean recoiled at her own words.

"Whether they could or not, they did lots of shady things. Gran couldn't read, but she signed some papers. I believe it was a letter of intent to release all parental rights."

"Oh, Angela. What happened to the child?"

"My baby was stillborn."

"*No.* I'm so sorry. That must have been terrible for you." Jean's eyes, the softest shade of brown, turned softer with sorrow.

"I was under some kind of deep sedation during the birth, and then kept constantly sedated for days afterward," Angela said. "By the time I finally learned what happened, Gran had signed other papers. The nuns told her the baby was buried in consecrated ground—even with original sin on its soul—and that was good enough for Gran, I suppose. After she died, I didn't find any records at all. The hospital's gone now. There's no record of a birth or a death of a baby girl on that day in 1969."

Angela shut her eyes, reaching for the memory of the ordeal, but it was all a blur. Still, she never stopped dreaming of her baby. The dreams had started when her body had first quickened with the pregnancy, and she was tortured by fright. The birth itself would always be a vast, blank nothingness in her mind, commencing with a mask coming down over her nose and mouth. The entire experience—including the pain and the fear—was lost to her. Then she'd awakened to the grim news that the baby had not survived. Her breasts were bound and she was given an injection to stop her milk production.

"I've always thought there was something particularly horrible about the birth of my child," she told Jean. "Maybe other girls had the same experience. All I know is that it was brutal, the way they hauled me off in the night to give birth. When I finally came to, I told my grandmother I wanted to know where the baby was laid to rest. She said the sisters took care of it, and a good thing, too." Angela mimicked her grandmother's accent. "'We've no money for a burial and Lord knows it was a shame entirely. Their help was a blessing.' And then she sent me back to the Good Shepherd because I wasn't 'cured' yet of my affliction."

"I'm sorry," Jean whispered. "I'm so sorry. I wish I could go back and protect that poor girl from those nightmares."

"I was utterly betrayed," Angela said. "My own grandmother—the only stable person in my life—turned on me and sent me to that place. And... after I escaped—"

"Wait, escaped? You mean like a prison break?"

"Well, kind of like that, I suppose. You're going to love this part. A group of girls and I got away in the library bookmobile."

"You're right. I love that."

"We didn't make it far. We had to ditch the van and make a run for it. I laid low and got a job. I stayed with a friend, and then a woman named Rachel Adler gave me a room in her house."

"Rachel the librarian," Jean said. "You've told me about her. You were really fond of her."

"She saved my life, and that's the honest truth. I was a hot mess, and I don't know what I would have done without her. I opened up to Rachel. I mean, really opened up. I told her everything—the doctor, the baby, the punishments, everything. Her reaction was fierce. I have a feeling it triggered her own memories of being in a concentration camp. She contacted the county child protection department and filed a report."

"Was anything done about that doctor?"

"I can't be sure. I guess she probably knew it was a painful subject for me. She did convince some state or county agency to initiate an investigation into the Good Shepherd and perform financial reviews. Later we heard there was a 'change in leadership' at the place, and they closed down almost overnight. I don't remember the details of how it all worked out. Chances are, nothing was done. Back then, almost every single city official was Catholic—mostly Irish Catholic—and the diocese was all-powerful. This was back in the era when the Church would simply cover up a scandal by reassigning clergy. I was just so traumatized, I ran away from anything to do with that place. Rachel set me on a new path. That's when I got a scholarship to SUNY Geneseo."

"Okay, thank you, Rachel." Jean pressed a hand to her heart.

"Right?" Angela felt a wave of fond remembrance. "I wish you could have known her. She passed away a few years back at the age of ninety."

"And your gran?"

Angela sighed. "Things were never right between me and Gran. I confronted her about forcing me to go to the Good Shepherd. I tried to understand how she could have done that to me. I really did. But she was from the old country and her beliefs were bigger than me in her eyes. She wanted to make me go back, but I was eighteen by then and I refused."

The tea had gone cold. Angela said, "So, a few years after the escape, I met up with Mairin. She was a fellow escapee."

"Mairin who just sent you a text."

Angela nodded. "She has a big family place outside Buffalo, in the hills to the east of the city. A farm she started with her husband. It's a beautiful place. I'll take you to visit one day." Angela smiled. "It's still a working farm, but it's also an event venue called Wayward Farm."

"I like it. So your friend Mairin found someone named Odessa. Another girl who was trapped at that place?"

Another nod.

Jean took her hand. "Call your friend Mairin."

"You think I should?"

"I think it's important."

Angela scrolled through her contacts. "That was an amazing text," she said when Mairin picked up. They chatted briefly, and Mairin sent her a link to a recent book review in the *New York Times*.

"Imagine Odessa, with a bestselling book," Angela said, marveling.

"I wish I could get in touch with her," Mairin said. "She's coming to Buffalo for a book signing at Zawadi Books. I think it'd be really something to see her again."

Angela glanced at Jean. "Yes. It would. Absolutely."

"Think she'd remember us?"

"Absolutely," Angela said again. "Let's do it. Let's get in touch with Odessa."

"She's a famous writer now. How would we even do that? Do we just show up at her book signing?"

"We can find her before that," Angela said, "through her publisher."

"You can do that? Just call a publisher out of the blue?"

"I'm a librarian. Retired now, but still. Book publishers love me."

Chapter 23

Mairin parked in front of the Mansion on Delaware. The grand property, with its tall windows and mansard roof and lavish gardens, had once been the home of a long-ago industrialist. More recently, it had been rescued from dereliction and transformed into a luxury hotel.

"Odessa has great taste in hotels," Angela said, peering at the graceful building.

Mairin nodded. "I'll say."

"Have you read the book yet?" Angela asked.

"Cover to cover. I loved it. Made me want to listen to all the old songs. You?"

"I read it in one sitting as soon as you told me. That was the first I've heard of Odessa's book. Gosh, that's one thing I miss about my library career—getting advance copies of any book I wanted. That used to be one of my favorite perks of the job."

"I listened to the audiobook, too. Unabridged, read by the author. Got a whole section of the garden done while I listened. I could still hear our old friend's voice."

They got out of the car. Mairin tipped back her head, looking around. "My dad and I used to walk up and down this street when I was little. He'd tell me stories about the rich folk who lived in the fancy houses. But I think he made things up just to entertain me. Damn. I miss him to this day."

"I never knew my father," Angela said. "According to my gran, he met my mother in a dance hall. After she had me, she took off after him and never came back."

"That sounds tough, Angela. I'm sorry."

"I try not to dwell on the sorry things that happened to me. Hard, though," Angela admitted.

Mairin knew it was because of the baby. A wound that would never heal. She took Angela's hand in hers. "Let's go in and celebrate our old friend."

Odessa met them in the lobby, her arms and her smile wide and open. "Oh happy day," she practically sang, swaying her hips. "Get in here, my girls. I can't wait to catch up."

They went to a grand salon where quiet music played and servers moved discreetly among the elegant tables, pouring cocktails and French tea. Odessa ordered a kir royale for each of them.

"Look at you," said Mairin. "Look at this place."

"Pretty cool, huh?" Odessa looked around at the opulent room, with its tall windows and fringed draperies. "Time was, they'd've made me come in the servants' entrance."

"Time was, we all had to do their laundry," said Angela.

Odessa fell quiet for a few moments. "Are y'all doing all right?"

"We're good," Angela said softly. "I mean, I have my moments, but life is good."

"Tell us about you," Mairin said. "About your book, for heaven's sake. You wrote a damn book, and it's a bestseller. I heard about it from my daughter, and I read it immediately. It's wonderful, Odessa."

"Thank you. I swear, it was a long road to get myself here," Odessa said. "After the Good Shepherd, I worked my way west, just like I said I would. I did every sort of odd job along the way—Avon lady, shoe salesgirl, waitress, you name it. Once I got to the Bay Area, I found my ma's cousin, Bobby Freeman."

"The rock star. He's in your book," said Mairin. Odessa's memoir had braided together her family history with music, connecting Freeman with Sylvester Stewart—later known as Sly Stone. "Odessa, that's really cool. And you were a college teacher."

"I loved school. Studied journalism and worked as a freelance writer. I always knew I would teach."

"We want to hear everything," Angela said.

"Well, let's see. I live on a street with some old historic buildings in the heart of San Francisco. Oh, you would love Perdita Street. It's got a world-class bookshop, and a barbecue joint called Salt next to a bakery called Sugar. What more do you need? Life is good, my girls. I've been married twice—first time I had two great kids and a lousy husband. Second time, I ended up with two spoiled dogs and married the love of my life. I took a sabbatical and wrote this thing I've been thinking of ever since my church days at Humboldt Parkway right here in Buffalo."

"Well, I thought it was fantastic," said Angela. "I can see why it became a bestseller."

"Really?" Odessa grinned and shook her head. "It just seems surreal. Who knew the world wanted to hear from me? And now the publisher wants another book. All I have to do is find a subject I'm crazy enough to spend a couple of years writing about." She sighed. "I'm so glad you got in touch with me. I think about y'all—that year—more than you know."

"It's . . . Right now it feels like no time has passed," Mairin said, feeling a sense of wonderment. In the company of Angela and Odessa, she felt curiously at ease in a way she didn't around anyone else. With these women, she didn't have to try to explain about the year of darkness. They just knew. "We haven't seen each other in decades and here we are talking like we did when we were kids."

"Shared trauma," Odessa said. "I hope we've all had counseling about it."

Both Mairin and Angela raised their hands. "Of course," said Angela. "And it helped, but talking to someone who lived those days is different. I'm glad we're together again."

"I worried about you, Odessa, when we first left," Mairin said. "I was afraid you'd get in trouble once we got away, but I was scared to try to make contact."

"Ooh, I remember that day as if it were yesterday. The day you escaped. The nuns were sure I was in on the plan." Odessa took a shuddering breath, then sipped her drink.

"What made them think that?" asked Angela.

"They were mean, not stupid, remember? They could tell we were friends. Rotrude questioned me for a couple of hours, and I got the paddle. Sister Gerard did the same, and sent me to the closet."

"I'm so sorry, Odessa," said Mairin, shivering at the memory. "The whole point was to keep you out of trouble."

"It was bad. I can't believe you survived the closet so many times, Mairin. Although I did overhear things, being stuck in there for so long."

"What things?"

"You should have heard them when they realized their money had gone missing. Total meltdown. Complete and total meltdown. They blamed Bernadette for being careless. Beat the crap out of her and made her do penance for days. But they couldn't report it missing for obvious reasons."

"Because they were hiding the cash from the diocese."

"I sure hope you girls put that money to good use," said Odessa.

Mairin and Angela traded glances.

"Our plan kind of fell apart," Mairin admitted. "The cops came, and we had to ditch the van and make a run for it. We all rushed off in different directions."

"It was me," Angela said, the words rushing from her. "I grabbed the bag with the money. I still feel ashamed about that."

"Stop it," Mairin said. She turned to Odessa. "Angela used it to survive and to pay for school."

"We were supposed to share it," Angela persisted. "I felt so guilty, but God forgive me, I used it all on myself."

"Girl," Odessa said. "Survival and school after all you went through? I can't think of a better use of their damn money. It's poetic justice. The bookmobile never came to the Good Shepherd again after that." Odessa let out a wistful sigh. "Not while I was there, anyway. They blamed the driver and discontinued the program. Rotrude and the priest were fit to be tied, being locked in the confessional like that. Lord Almighty, you should have heard them."

"All these years later, it's still one of my proudest accomplishments," said Mairin.

"If we'd had smartphones back then, it would have gone viral," said Angela.

"Oh, they were viral all right," Odessa assured her.

"They didn't extend your sentence, I hope," Mairin said.

"Threatened to," said Odessa. "I was terrified they might. They moved me to a different unit. It was just as terrible, and the girls there were mean, and racist. But my parents showed up the day my sentence was up, and they refused to take no for an answer. I remember my daddy counting out a good sum of money—in cash—for some sort of 'discharge fee.' I bet it was another grift the nuns pulled. But my folks were so relieved to get me out that they didn't question it."

"It's nice that your family actually wanted you to come home," Mairin said. "I was afraid my mother would march me straight back to the Good Shepherd. She was Irish Catholic to the core, but eventually the two of us made our peace with each other."

"Sometimes I wonder what became of that place," Odessa said.

"The laundry was shut down and the nuns moved to Hamburg, a few miles south of here," Angela said. "No more laundry."

"Well, that's something, at least."

"You can thank a librarian for starting the investigation," Mairin said.

Odessa turned to Angela. "You?"

Angela shook her head. "Her name was Rachel Adler."

"I hope she knew what an impact she had on the girls back then," Mairin said.

"Oh, I think she did. We named a women's studies collection in her honor at the branch where she worked."

"Do you suppose we could find out what became of the others?" asked Odessa. "This is really the first time I've felt the urge to look back at that period of my life."

Mairin took out the photo booth shots and laid them on the white linen tablecloth. They were quiet for a while, looking at their youthful, shining faces. "Maybe we should try. Whatever became of them—Helen and Denise and Janice and Kay?"

"We should." Angela snapped her fingers. "I'm a librarian. Research is my superpower."

Chapter 24

A roadside sign along the narrow, twisting mountain road warned travelers to proceed *Slowly and Quietly*.

"A timely reminder," said Angela, who was in the backseat of Mairin's Subaru. "Why aren't there any guardrails?"

"After all these years, and you still don't like my driving," Mairin said, flexing her hands on the steering wheel. "I did the best I could in that van."

"You did," Angela conceded. "Why'd she want to meet here, anyway?"

Mairin shrugged. "She said it's close to where she and her husband retired."

"Good choice. This view is absolutely amazing," said Odessa. They passed a scenic overlook with a magnificent view of the small village far below, and the craggy Shawangunks in the distance. "This is not the New York most people picture when they think of New York."

Their anticipation built around every hairpin turn in the road. When the Mohonk Mountain House came into view through an old stone archway, Mairin slowed way down, hearing gasps from Angela and Odessa.

Perched at the edge of Mohonk Lake, the imposing residence was a breathtaking, rambling fortress, a masterpiece of stone and brick spires. Mairin parked and they went inside, through the lobby with its soaring ornate woodwork, fireplaces, and nooks and crannies filled with comfortable Victorian furniture. Staircases with wooden balusters went upward forever. Someone in the reception area directed them to a salon overlooking the lake.

A couple of groups—all women—were gathered around tables, hard at their games of mahjong. "I get it now," Odessa murmured. "This is why she wanted to meet here."

Mairin looked around the room, filled with women like her, women of a certain age, women of all shapes and sizes. "I don't see Helen," she said. "Maybe she's not here yet."

"Maybe she looks totally different," Angela said.

"Or maybe—" Mairin spotted a woman with smooth, white-streaked hair who seemed to be dozing by a window overlooking the lake and the Shawangunks towering in the distance. "Oh my gosh," she whispered, feeling a rush of emotion as she recognized a certain tilt of the woman's head from years ago. Mairin moved closer and leaned forward to make sure she was awake.

Then she said, "*Lún dào ni zhuā le*," the phrase of invitation Helen had taught her fifty years before. She'd never forgotten it.

The woman blinked, then looked up, and reared back with a gasp. "You came!" she said.

"Of course we did," Mairin said, her heart filling up.

Helen stood quickly, assuming that flawless posture with which she'd always carried herself.

"Mairin," she said. "Angela and Odessa. I don't believe my eyes. I'm so glad you found me."

"Seems like we're getting the band back together again," said Angela.

"It's wonderful to see you." Odessa gave her a hug, and they all had a turn. "Let's sit. We want to hear what you've been up to all these years."

They gathered around, and for a surreal moment, Mairin had a flashback to the four of them at one of their secret meetings in the chilly dorm. Although they had only known each other for a brief season of their lives, these women knew her in a way no one else did, or ever could.

Now they spent a few minutes filling Helen in about Odessa's book, and marveling over the way it had awakened so many memories.

"The last time I saw you," Mairin said, "you were climbing a rusty fire escape up the side of a building."

Helen gave a shudder. "The day of the escape. Yes, that actually didn't work out so well for me. Some woman in an office saw me through the window, and she yelled for the police. She was screeching something about the communists invading."

"You're kidding. So did you get away, or . . . ?"

With a doleful look, Helen shook her head. "I was nabbed by the police that very day."

"What? *No,*" Mairin said.

"Yes. And I mean nabbed. I got to the roof of the building and was looking for a place to hide when one of them grabbed me."

"Ah, Helen. You must've been so scared," said Angela.

"Startled, I suppose. Disappointed in myself. But scared? I don't remember feeling like that. The nuns got me used to being scared."

"Did they take you back to the Good Shepherd?" asked Mairin.

"They took us to a substation. Or maybe it was the main police station."

"Us?" Odessa leaned forward. "You weren't the only one?"

"Me, Janice, and Kay," Helen said. "Kay was hysterical, and only Janice seemed to be able to calm her down. Kay was begging to go back to the Good Shepherd. She was just so afraid of the outside world."

A server came with a pot of tea and a tiered platter of tiny sandwiches and sweets. Mairin took it all in, feeling a wave of gratitude that they were together again after all these years. In her life, she'd made many friends who were precious to her, but she'd never had friends like these.

"So did they . . . what? Arrest you?" Angela asked.

"No. We were just kids, remember. And I got lucky. One of the arresting officers was a woman whose sister had once been at the Good Shepherd. She said something like 'I know that place; my sister hated it there.' I could tell she knew it was pretty grim."

"She knew, but she let them send you back there?" Odessa shook her head.

"It probably wasn't up to her. They put us in a room," Helen said. "It wasn't a cell, and the door wasn't locked. Maybe it was some kind of holding room or interrogation room. The three of us were whispering, wondering what we should do next. I said we should try to leave. Kay couldn't handle it. She couldn't handle anything except a promise that she'd get to go back to the Good Shepherd. And then Janice said she'd go back, too."

"What?" Odessa frowned. "Why would Janice want to go back?"

"I was appalled, too, but Janice said something like she had nowhere to go anyway. Said at least at the Good Shepherd, she'd have food and a place to sleep."

Mairin would have preferred to starve in the cold.

"Poor Janice. She never said much about her background, but I always had the sense it was pretty bad," Odessa said.

"Janice told me I should go," Helen said. "She said she'd keep my secret. Promised not to snitch. Remember what a snitch she used to be?"

"That was her thing," Mairin said.

"I just assumed she wanted to get away as much as we did," said Angela.

"Did the cops let you go, then?" asked Odessa.

"Not right away. Sister Gerard showed up, all flustered and nun-like," Helen said. "She swooped in like she'd come to save our souls. The police were falling all over themselves."

"Uh-oh." Mairin shuddered, picturing the woman's mask of piety.

"They gave her the room with us, and that *Sound of Music* mask dropped, as you can imagine."

"Sister Gerard was awful," said Mairin.

"She was. She tried to get me to say where you and Angela and Denise went. I had no idea, but she didn't believe me. She threatened to drag me back and throw me in the closet."

"I'd've welcomed the company," Odessa said wryly.

Helen pursed her lips, then said, "I looked her in the eye—I don't know where I got the courage to do it, but I looked her in the eye and said, 'You're going to let me go, because you don't want to have to explain to the diocese about the money you've been hiding.' I nearly wet myself. I bet she did, too, come to think of it. But she didn't back down. Called me a liar and said I had to go back and pray for forgiveness."

"Oh, Helen. What a nightmare." Mairin had never shed the memories of the fierce nuns and their iron rule. Even now, she could clearly picture Sister Gerard's ice-cold glare, the persistent sprouts of hair on her chin, the odor of her smoker's breath—and the way she could magically transform into an angel in front of outsiders.

"But you got away, right?" Odessa said.

"Yes. I asked the policewoman if I could use the restroom and when I finished, I simply walked down the hall out the front door. No one seemed to notice, or maybe no one cared. Maybe that female cop had some sympathy for me and didn't say anything. I went outside and kept walking, and I walked all the way to the university. Blocks and blocks. My father's department secretary was always good to me. Miss Rudolph knew my parents would never have placed me at the Good Shepherd if they'd known what it was. I stayed with her until my parents were released in 1971 after Kissinger went to China to improve relations. Meanwhile, I refused to go back to my old school—Archbishop Walsh—for obvious reasons."

"Good call," said Angela. "I'm sorry you were separated from your parents for so long."

"Oh, they were livid when I told them what the Good Shepherd was really like. My father made a formal complaint to the diocese, but by that time, the nuns had gone. Turns out the diocese has a habit of deflecting blame and covering things up. I went to a public high school. Got into sports in a big way. That's thanks to you, Mairin."

"What? Me?" Mairin was flattered, but confused.

"I never really did anything physical until you started those kickball games at the Good Shepherd, and taught us the self-defense moves. Physical strength gave me confidence, something I didn't get at parochial school. I never forgot that, and I tried everything the school had to offer—martial arts, track and field, swimming. It changed my life. I was always good at academics, but the athletics opened a door I never knew was available."

"What door is that?"

Helen leaned back in her chair and smiled. "The military."

"Seriously?" said Odessa. "Wow, how did that come about?"

"President Ford signed a bill allowing women to attend the military academies. After high school, I went to military prep school, and as soon as I was eligible, I applied to West Point and was offered an appointment. Got a nomination from Governor Hugh Carey himself, in fact."

"You went to West Point," Angela said, regarding her with wide eyes.

"That's just incredible," said Odessa.

Mairin regarded her mild-faced, diminutive friend with a surge of pride. "Wow, Helen, what an accomplishment."

Helen sighed. "It was hard, and gratifying, and challenging, and frustrating, and rewarding... and everything in between. But after the Good Shepherd, nothing else ever felt that hard. Sometimes I think I found the strength to do it because of what I endured at that place. They gave us all the gift of physical and mental toughness, didn't they? The Sisters of Charity hardened me to any ordeal I might encounter in my life."

"You were a trailblazer," Mairin said, feeling a beam of pride. "West Point, Helen."

"More than a hundred women started that first year—1976. Sixty-two of us finished. Sometimes I'm amazed any of us survived, because we didn't exactly get a warm welcome. The Academy was not quite prepared for us. There were urinals in the girls' bathrooms. The superintendent was still resisting us. And don't get me started on General Westmoreland. To him, any woman who could succeed at West Point was a freak, and he used to say, 'We're not running the military academy for freaks.' All these years later, I still remember him saying that."

"Yet another reason history was not kind to the man," said Odessa. "I'm glad you stuck it out, you freak."

Helen laughed. "You should have seen the uniforms. They didn't fit any woman's body. And the men hazed us mercilessly, me more than most. I was called gook, yellowface, hojo, commie. We were all harassed. Some were assaulted—including me."

"Oh, Helen." Angela touched her arm.

"I kicked that guy's ass," Helen said. "And then I served for thirty years as an intelligence officer and translator. I was awarded a lot of plum assignments because I'm bilingual."

"I love that," said Odessa.

"It all sounds so fantastic, Helen," said Mairin. "West Point. That blows my mind."

"Serving in the military was never a space on my bingo card when I was a kid, but it turned out to be a wonderful choice. We were stationed at posts all around the world. Mostly Asia."

"We. You married? Had a family?"

She smiled. "I got married at the Peninsula Hotel in Hong Kong, 1984."

"That sounds so fancy. Are you still married?"

"Oh, yes. I'm one of the lucky ones."

"No, that would be your *husband*. Who's the lucky guy? Was he in the army, too?"

Helen shook her head. "Oh, no. Far from it. He was in the entertainment business. I have some old pictures on my phone. Want to see a few?"

"Are you kidding? Of course!"

She took out her phone and tapped the screen, then turned it to show them the image. There was a young, radiant Helen—the Helen they all recognized, only this was a Helen who exuded presence and confidence. A handsome, beaming man stood at her side. She scrolled through a few more pictures of the young couple, including one of them posing in evening wear in front of a step-and-repeat logo backdrop.

"Wait a second," Odessa said, expanding the photo with her fingers. "Is that... I know that guy. I mean, I don't *know* him, but I recognize him. He's famous, right? Like, Bruce Lee famous."

Helen's eyes twinkled. "Maybe not *that* famous, but he was in quite a few films back in the eighties. Ever heard of the *Iron Tiger of Fury*?" She showed them a movie poster on her phone.

"Oh my gosh, he was the Iron Tiger? I loved those movies, the whole series." Odessa clasped her hands together. "Evan Ling, right? You're married to Evan Ling! That's so cool!"

"He was also the *Lonely Dragon of Death*," Helen said with a laugh. "I don't know if that series ever made it to the States."

"How did you meet him?" asked Mairin.

"He was filming an action sequence on the Peak Tram, which is right by the U.S. Consulate General, where I was working. I did what any fangirl would do. I rushed him for an autograph—which he gave me, along with his phone number."

"Girl." Odessa shook her head.

"I know," said Helen. "Anyway, he retired a long time ago, and we settled here to be close to my parents and to our son, Brandon."

She swiped to another picture. "I hope Evan gets to meet you one of these days. He's on a trip with Brandon. They're exploring the Galapagos Islands."

"Well, here's to your wonderful, huge life," said Mairin.

"To all our wonderful lives," Helen said. "Let's have a game for old times' sake, shall we?"

As they set up the mahjong tiles, Odessa picked one up and turned it over in her hand. "These are a lot different from your homemade set in the laundry," she told Helen.

"This set was a gift from Evan's family in Hong Kong," Helen said.

"It's absolutely gorgeous."

"I wonder what became of your homemade tiles. You made them out of priest collar tabs, didn't you?"

"I did. What a strange and awful chapter of our lives," Helen said.

Mairin clung to the idea that it was just a chapter in a long life. Yet she still carried the wounds that had been inflicted at the Good Shepherd. No matter how far she had come, she had never confronted or examined what had happened to her. The emotional pain had never really left her. She didn't talk about it much. She didn't dwell on it. There was nothing to be done, and she saw no point in wallowing. But something that traumatic didn't simply disappear. It lived deep inside her blood and bones. Maybe the healing would have started fifty years ago if they'd known how to talk about it.

She wondered if she had done enough, reached high enough, in her life. She had not lived a life of consequence the way these women had. She was not like Angela, with her decades of service as a librarian. Or like Helen, a military trailblazer. Or Odessa—a teacher and now a bestselling author. Mairin was just... ordinary. She had a lovely husband and family. Yet her life was full, her satisfactions many, and it seemed petty to fret about the past. This life is enough, she told herself.

While the others arranged their tiles on the ornate racks, Odessa sat very still, staring at the other three. Her eyes seemed lit from behind.

"What?" asked Mairin. "Are you okay?"

"Oh. Oh, yes. More than okay." Odessa's eyes shone. "I think I know what my next book's going to be about."

Chapter 25

"Welcome to my world," Angela said, leading the way into the Merriweather Branch Library. Mairin, Helen, and Odessa followed her through the bright, welcoming space. "I was head librarian at the Jefferson Branch—that old building across the way." Looking like a queen and turning heads as she passed, she waved to a woman behind the main circulation desk.

"It's a joy to see you in your element," said Helen.

"Thanks." She stopped at a corner seating area. "My happy place," she said, gesturing at a collection of polished wooden barrister bookcases with glass doors.

"Rainbow Reads: The Angela Denny Collection." Mairin read the plaque on the wall. "Angela, it's wonderful. Curated by a human, not suggested by an algorithm."

Angela beamed at them. "The Friends of the Library fundraised to create it. I figured out who I was in the library, and this is the honor of my life."

"It's fantastic," said Odessa. "What a wonderful contribution."

"And can I just say, you *look* incredible? As usual." Mairin eyed her with admiration. "I love your clothes. You definitely have a presence."

Angela beamed at her. "From the moment I could afford nice clothes, I always dressed up instead of down. My therapist applauds it as a means of self-care. Or maybe she wants to make sure I don't feel guilty for splurging."

"Totally worth it," said Odessa, eyeing her slim dark trousers and flowing silk top.

"Thanks. Means a lot, coming from a famous author. Let's go to the research room." Angela headed into a paneled room with a long table. "I pulled together some documents to get us started," she told Odessa. "I really hope you'll find the story you want to tell about the Good Shepherd."

There was a large screen computer and a stack of documents on the table. "We always knew the place on Best Street was haunted. Turns out we weren't wrong."

Mairin and Helen exchanged a glance. They all sat down and looked at the screen.

Angela walked them through a brief history of the forbidding hulk on Best Street. Built in 1880, it was founded as a place for wayward girls, and it served that function for most of its existence. It became a repository for girls who lacked stable homes and families, unwed mothers, girls who were lost or guilty of petty crimes. Throwaway girls.

"By 1970, the Sisters of Charity had closed up shop and moved on," Angela said. "Currently, they're operating out of an address in Astoria. Not operating as a laundry, of course."

"I bet they found some other grift to wash away their sins," said Mairin.

"They claim to offer family services. Mother Gerard left her post in a hurry, probably over the financial records. Some of the Sisters of Charity went to a more modern facility in Hamburg, and rebranded themselves as something called Hopevale. It's a county agency now."

"What happened to Best Street?" asked Helen. "Did they turn it into a maximum-security prison, then?"

"I pulled all the records I could find," Angela told them. "County and state agencies kept trying to make use of the space. It used to be the Masten Park Secure Center, a juvenile prison. Prior to that, it was a drug treatment center. Then it was vacant for a while. It was never a happy place." Angela showed them some old notices from the paper and public records, along with articles and posts from social media sites. "I found only a few testimonials from people who say they were helped. Most had nothing good to say."

"Even just looking at the pictures gives me the creeps." Helen shuddered.

"Do you have flashbacks?" Mairin asked her. "Or weird moments like that?"

Helen shrugged. "Sure. Hard to escape."

They sat together in silence for a moment. "No one else in my life truly knows what it was like," Mairin said. "I'm grateful that we're together again."

"It's pretty horrible that even a short time at that place messed with us as bad as it did," said Odessa.

"I'm usually able to put it all behind me," Helen declared. "Life is too busy to dwell on that time."

"We don't have to go down this road if it's too upsetting," Odessa reminded them.

Angela brought up another screen. "It'll always be upsetting. But maybe it's time. We're not getting any younger. Check this out. Obituaries of Sister Mary John and Sister Theresa. Remember them?"

"Ugh. Yes," said Odessa. "I googled a bit once, but it was too upsetting, so I didn't pursue it."

"Don't blame you," said Mairin. "But we're okay doing it now?"

"We're together now," Helen said. "This is different. It *feels* different."

"Think any of the nuns are still around?" Mairin asked.

"Actually, yes," said Angela. "So get this—Sister Rotrude and Sister Bernadette are living in a Catholic-run retirement home called Holy Cross Haven over in Tonawanda."

"Tonawanda. Wow. Just a stone's throw from here, right?" Odessa sat back in her chair. "How can that be? Those nasty old biddies."

"Remember that time I learned how old they were and we were all amazed?" said Mairin. "We all thought they were a hundred years old, and it turned out they were only a few years older than us."

"You're right," said Helen. "Bernadette wasn't even twenty when we were there. Even Rotrude was young. My God, I thought she was ancient."

"We all did," said Angela. "Being evil ages you. Or maybe it was just those dumb habits. The nuns were so much younger than they looked in those horrible outfits."

"I'm going to find them," said Odessa, her voice crisp and decisive. "Pay them a visit. See what I can learn from them." She looked around the table. "Y'all don't have to come. I wouldn't blame you if you don't want to head down memory lane with me."

"I was a lieutenant colonel in the U.S. army," said Helen. "They don't scare me."

"I raised four kids," said Mairin. "Nothing scares me."

"And I'm an angry lesbian librarian," said Angela. "Nothing scares me, either."

Chapter 26

The Holy Cross Haven smelled like pee. Everything looked clean enough, all the neutral-toned surfaces scrubbed and shined, but the pervasive odor was unmistakable, slithering invisibly through the hallways, which were lined with doors to the residents' rooms.

A few of the doors were decorated with cheerful sprays of flowers or wreaths, cards, or children's art. For the retirees who had no family and few visitors, the doors were left plain. The door to the room Sister Bernadette shared with Sister Rotrude had no ornament. Several years ago, a volunteer from the Church had brought them a St. Benedict door hanger from Medjugorje, where the Holy Virgin had appeared to six children back in the eighties. But the heavy beads and cross banged whenever the door was opened or shut, and someone complained about the noise, so now the memento hung above Rotrude's bed.

Bernadette preferred to while away her time in the dayroom, which was bright and busy and didn't smell as strongly of pee. It was also farther from the dining room, thus avoiding the oniony odors of the bland but heart-healthy food from the kitchen. The sunlight spilled through stained glass windows, casting a kaleidoscope of colors upon the walls.

There was a TV on one side and on the other, tables and chairs set up café style. Some of the residents enjoyed sitting and chatting. Not Bernadette. She spent most of her days in one of the floral wing chairs, reading or immersing herself in silent prayer, and ignoring the relentless noise of the ancient, inane shows some of the residents craved—*The Price Is Right* or *Davey and Goliath*—which aired on some rerun station. At the moment, the room was blessedly silent, leaving space to think and reflect.

When not engaged in reading scripture, Bernadette tried to stay active, attending yoga and taking part in a walking group. According to the activities director, walking and yoga helped with bladder control. Rotrude claimed that yoga was for pagans, but Bernadette did not see anything wrong with using the body the Lord gave her. She hoped that staying in shape would help her avoid the need for the disposable underthings so many of the older residents used. She dressed as she had all her life, in her black tunic and practical oxford shoes. The habits had changed over the years, though. The veils were short these days, just a nod to tradition.

Today, Bernadette and Sister Rotrude sat together near the window, working a thousand-piece jigsaw puzzle depicting the classic image of Jesus knocking at the door. His glowing face was incomplete, but the verse at the bottom from the Book of Matthew was coming together. Bernadette had found the letters to spell out *I am the w__ and the ____h and the life*, and she was hunting through the tiny pieces for the rest of the phrase.

Rotrude was focused on piecing together the top edge of the door, draped with a thorny vine. Privately, Bernadette thought she looked like an old crow sitting there in her wheelchair, scowling and idly running her thumb over a couple of wiry chin hairs.

Rotrude seemed undiminished despite her age, though. Her face was webbed by fine wrinkles, each line drawn by years of unwavering belief and service, and her eyes held the steady flame of conviction. Bernadette wondered if she, too, looked undiminished by life. Whenever she looked in the tiny rectangular mirror over her sink, she saw a face that looked ordinary in every way. That was all she had ever seen, an unremarkable person who had led an unremarkable life. When it was her time to go, she assumed her exit would be unremarkable as well.

It was so quiet here. So little to do. Like many of the residents, Bernadette lived in the past, when the days had been filled with duties that never seemed to end. She and Rotrude had little to say to each other these days. Their bond was forged of common experience more than deep regard. They had spent their lives in service, from the Good Shepherd Refuge where they'd helped so many girls, to the later years when they had dedicated themselves in other ways. That was Rotrude's point of view, anyway. That they had been called by God to help.

Bernadette had less certainty. She had traveled to far places in the world, always seeking to find her true purpose in the service of the Lord. Even after her pilgrimage and long stay in Beit Jala in the Middle East, enlightenment eluded her. Now she had reached a place in her life where she was sometimes inclined to look back and question it. She still bore the weight of secrets that had haunted her for decades. Her spirit, once lit with the unwavering faith of youth, now held a conflict that too often kept her awake long into the night.

She tried to focus on the jigsaw puzzle. She found a piece that completed the pale, slender hand of the Lord, raised against the door's rough planks. The piece made a satisfying *click* as she set it into place.

"Hellooo!" The director's chirpy voice intruded into the silence.

Rotrude lifted her nose like a hound on the scent, because Mrs. Bates always sounded animated and upbeat when visitors came. Sometimes she was showing prospective residents around the place; other times it might be a family member or a health department inspector looking for infractions.

". . . you for coming," Mrs. Bates was saying as she led a group into the dayroom. "It's such a blessing to have visitors. I'm sure they'll be delighted to see you. Sister Bernadette! Sister Rotrude! You have visitors."

Bernadette was certain she'd heard wrong. She moved to tuck the snowy wisps of her hair under her headpiece, a gesture of vanity that was automatic. Then she surreptitiously turned up the volume of her hearing aids. "Visitors," she whispered, her voice hushed with wonder. She locked eyes with Sister Rotrude. "Are you expecting someone?"

"Certainly not," Rotrude said, narrowing her eyes behind her wire-rimmed glasses. She still spoke with the brogue of her native Ireland. "And who would we be expecting, after all?"

"Some of your former students have come to see you," said Mrs. Bates, officious in her matching sweater set and green-rimmed glasses perched on her nose.

Students? That must be some kind of mistake. Bernadette and Rotrude had never had students, not in that sense. But of course there had been the fiction that the girls at the Good Shepherd were being taught something other than laundry, mending, and host-making chores.

Feeling an eruption of nerves, Bernadette stood up and turned to greet the newcomers—four women flanking Mrs. Bates. As they approached the table, Bernadette felt a momentary confusion. Students? The visitors were older, like her, although in their street clothes they all looked vibrant and young. She studied each one—an Asian woman standing with perfect posture. A round-faced matron with a shock of white hair; flashy, fancy eyeglasses; and a confident stride. A tall Black woman with her head tilted in curiosity, a notebook and pen under one arm. And a willowy, fashionably dressed woman with long, still-blond hair and electric-blue eyes.

Bernadette felt a twinge of recognition. And then... her heart dropped to the floor. It was as if the years peeled away, and she was young again, a newly fledged member of the order. There was something sharply familiar about these women. The blond one in particular awakened memories. Except for the lines of maturity on her face, she looked virtually the same as she had long ago. Those disconcerting blue eyes seemed to stare deep into Bernadette's soul.

"Oh," she said. "Oh, Sister Rotrude, look who has come to see us."

"I don't know these people," Rotrude said with her customary brusqueness. "I have no idea who they are."

"In that case, we'll refresh your memory," said the Black woman.

"Lovely!" Mrs. Bates clasped her hands. "I'll leave you to reacquaint yourselves, then. Oh, and don't forget to sign the guest book on your way out."

"Thank you," said the Asian woman.

They each brought a chair close to the puzzle table. Bernadette's heart hammered in her chest, but she tried to remain calm. This was simply a social visit, she told herself. Perhaps these women were paying them a kindness.

"Do you remember us?" asked the Asian woman. The question sounded blunt, but not unpleasant.

"Should we?" asked Sister Rotrude, her hands touching the beads of her rosary belt. "Sister Bernadette and I helped so many girls over the years..."

"We were held at the Good Shepherd on Best Street," said the Black woman. "We were there in 1968 and 1969." She introduced herself as Odessa Bailey, and the others as Mairin O'Hara, Angela Denny, and Helen Mei. "Of course, back then, you forced the inmates to be referred to by a number and by the names you assigned to us."

"Yes, we were very dedicated to protecting your privacy, and that of your families," said Rotrude with a sage nod.

The visitors exchanged glances. Bernadette sensed their tension, but they seemed calm and polite. Odessa Bailey took out a mobile phone and placed it on the puzzle table. "I've been gathering information for a book I plan to write—a memoir about my girlhood in Buffalo. Do you mind if I record our conversation?"

Bernadette darted a look at Rotrude, expecting her to erupt with anger. Instead, Sister Rotrude made a steeple of her fingers. "We don't mind reminiscing about all the good we did. Now, who are you again?"

"Perhaps these will refresh your memory." Mairin showed them some black-and-white photo strips, the sort people used to make in a photo booth machine. "These were taken at Niagara Falls on July Fourth, 1969."

Bernadette remembered the excitement of that day, the sunshine and music, the crowds and the scent of funnel cakes and corn dogs and cotton candy. "Oh, the miracle at the Falls."

Mairin O'Hara rolled her eyes. "If you say so."

Rotrude sat forward in her chair, features sharpened like a ferret. "Ah, so you were the gang of truants who tried to escape that summer," she said. "We suffered no end of turmoil because of what you did."

There was a tense beat of silence. Bernadette had to remind herself to breathe.

"We'd like to find more information about the Good Shepherd," said Odessa. She seemed polite and professional. Reasonable, yet firm, like a journalist or scholar. "We learned from county records that it ceased to operate around 1970. Can you let us know what became of the residents there? And the community?"

"We were bidden to another calling," Rotrude said coldly. "The county social service agency took charge of the students and they were reassigned to other facilities."

"What about the records at the Good Shepherd?" asked Angela.

Rotrude frowned. "What sort of records? I'm sure they all were sent along with the residents."

Bernadette froze inside. Not all the records were sent. Prior to the move, Sister Gerard had put her in charge of forwarding or disposing of certain records.

Angela Denny studied Rotrude and then Bernadette with a measuring look. "I gave birth on March twenty-third, 1969. The baby was stillborn. I'd like to find a record of the birth."

Bernadette almost stopped breathing. The events of that terrible night and its aftermath were seared in her memory. She had never spoken of it to anyone. But she could never forget.

"I can't imagine why you'd think we could help you with that," said Rotrude, her eyes on the table in front of her.

Bernadette tried to say something, but the words stuck in her throat. Not long after the girls had run away, there were visits from diocese and county officials. Sister Gerard had been apoplectic, and only Bernadette knew the reason. The prioress was terrified that her trail of corruption would be found out. Her command to Bernadette had been fierce and urgent. She was to destroy the records of private adoptions that had been facilitated while Sister Gerard was prioress. Bernadette clearly remembered how her fingers, cold with nerves, had fumbled as she carried a stack of manila file folders down to the old cast-iron incinerator in the basement.

And she clearly remembered the disobedient impulse that had led her to preserve certain records, a decision that had caused her to live in fear for decades.

And now here was a woman, asking the question Bernadette dreaded.

"I've tried to find information—hospital records, a death certificate, a burial record, anything," said Angela. "But I've found nothing."

Bernadette took a deep, steadying breath. This was her chance. Her moment to unburden herself. "Perhaps we—"

"Well, I'm sure we're not expected to know what to do about that," Rotrude huffed.

Angela focused on Bernadette, her face bright with interest. "Perhaps... you were saying?"

Bernadette's courage shriveled up. "Perhaps... everything was lost once the county agency took over the property."

Angela's expression dimmed. She seemed tightly wound, brittle with anger. "I've checked. The county also reports that no records were found. How can there be no record of a birth that definitely happened?"

"That is not for us to say," Rotrude stated. "We were in charge of your spiritual education, not public records."

Odessa sent Angela a quelling look and gently touched her arm. "Has anyone else from our days at the Good Shepherd been in contact with you?" She indicated one of the photo strips. "That girl is Janice Dunn. And that one is named Kay. I'm afraid we can't recall her last name."

"Collins," Bernadette blurted out. "Kay Collins." Kay had been simple, Bernadette recalled, and very sweet and compliant.

"And I'm proud to say that Janice Dunn joined our faith community," Rotrude said with a sniff of self-importance.

"She... Sorry, what?" Mairin frowned. "She *joined* you?"

Those green eyes. Bernadette flashed on another memory—curly red hair, bright green eyes, freckles, and fearless defiance.

"She took vows?" asked Helen. "Is that what you mean?"

"Yes, indeed she did," Bernadette said, relieved to move on to a more pleasant topic. She'd been pleased to welcome the girl called Janice, who took the name Johanna and became very devout. "She was extremely devoted to Kay. Sister Johanna had a special gift for looking after people. I believe she served at Mount St. Vincent, so perhaps you might find her there."

"And this girl?" Odessa pointed. "Denise Curran."

"Ah, she was a trial, that one," said Sister Rotrude, glaring at the image. "Nothing but trouble since the day her own pa delivered her to us. She wasn't but eleven or twelve years old, and there was no getting past her mean streak. The devil was in that one, for sure. Never saw nor heard from her again after that day you terrible girls ran off."

Bernadette saw the color rise in Mairin O'Hara's cheeks like the mercury in a thermometer. She always did have equal measures of Irish temper and Irish charm. She noticed Odessa catching Mairin's eye and giving a slight shake of her head.

"We're done here," Odessa said. "For now. Here's a card with my number and email address."

Rotrude snatched it with lightning speed and drew it into her tunic pocket. "We've no more to tell you," she said.

Bernadette knew she'd never see the card again.

At that moment, a chime sounded over the PA system, and Mrs. Bates announced that dinner service would begin in fifteen minutes.

Bernadette forced a smile. Tell them, she urged herself. *Tell them.* But just as quickly, the urge disappeared like a wisp of vapor. "It's very nice of you to visit," she said. "I'm glad you're all doing so well."

"I WANTED TO strangle them both," said Mairin as they walked down the hall toward the lobby.

"Me, too," Helen agreed. "And thanks to my training, I actually know how to do that."

"It took every bit of restraint to be civil with the old harpies," said Angela.

"Thanks for holding back," Odessa said. "It must have been so hard not to rip into them."

"It was," Angela said. "But if and when I actually address that topic, it won't be a casual conversation."

"Understood. And I do hope you'll address it one day."

"My partner, Jean, and I have been talking about it," Angela said. "Just in a very general sense, since we all got in touch again. She's very supportive."

Odessa looked her in the eye. "Angela, if any of this bothers you—"

"It all bothers me," Angela admitted. "And that's okay. I absolutely do want to help you, Odessa. This is an important story, and people need to know what happened."

"You've all been so great," Odessa said. "Especially today. I learned a long time ago in journalism school that if you need information from a source, you're more likely to succeed if you're nice to them and let them have their say. They didn't give us much, but it's a start, anyway."

In the lobby, they took turns signing the guest book, as the director requested. Mairin signed her full name—Mairin Patricia O'Hara Gallagher—and added her mobile number.

"Wait for me," said Helen. "I need the restroom."

They chatted a bit more while they waited, sharing remembrances of Janice and Kay and Denise. "Can you believe Janice took vows?" Mairin asked.

"Maybe she stayed because she had no other option," Angela said. "And she was fond of Kay. Poor Kay probably couldn't have lived independently in the outside world."

"I hope Janice was different," Odessa said. "It would be great to hear that she had some compassion. Maybe she tried to be a force for reform."

"We should try to find her," Mairin agreed. She glanced back at the hallway, now filling with residents on the way to the dining hall. "I can't shake the feeling that there's something they're not saying."

Odessa turned to her. "I felt it, too. Rotrude isn't about to give an inch, but Bernadette looked ready to jump out of her skin. I might try to come back and visit her without Rotrude hovering around like a damn buzzard."

Angela stood near the door. Mairin could tell from her posture that Angela was not okay. "Hey," she said, "hey, girlfriend. How are you doing?"

Angela dabbed at her cheeks. "Sorry," she said. "This ... today. It took me back to some dark places. It was such a long time ago, but sometimes I think I'm losing my mind. Do you know, I still dream about my baby?"

AFTER THE VISITORS left, the two nuns remained in the dayroom, the weight of their shared history heavy in the air between them. For a few minutes, Bernadette toyed with the jigsaw puzzle, just to give her hands something to do. A twisted vine here. A cobblestone there. Another letter in the Lord's words—the *ay* to complete the word *way*.

Finally, she couldn't bear the silence any longer, and she broke it, her voice trembling with the weight of her confession. "Sister Rotrude, do you ever think about the work we did at the Good Shepherd Refuge?"

"Of course I do. We lifted those girls out of the gutter of evil and helped them find their way to redemption. That's the work we did, and were pride not a sin, I would take pride in our accomplishments."

"But some of them, they were innocent. They came to us broken and abandoned, in need of help. We accused them of transgressions they didn't commit, punished them for things they couldn't control. We beat them, pulled their hair, locked them away. We forced them to work in the laundry, and they never earned a penny from their own labor."

"Hard work has never done anyone any harm. Why, the very judges in the family courts entrusted us with the children. And as for pay, they were given food and shelter, and the grace of a religious community." Rotrude's gaze hardened as she snatched a puzzle piece and pressed it in place. "We did what we knew was right, guided by our faith and by the Church's teachings."

Bernadette lowered her head and studied her hands, flecked with age spots, the nails yellowing, an old woman's hands. "I can't help but wonder, Sister Rotrude, if we ever truly helped them or if we only added to their suffering."

She couldn't quell the memories of the girls' sorrows, their tears, and their fragile hopes, and the cruel way they'd been treated at the laundry. As the passing of the years brought her closer to eternity, questions and doubts clouded her vision. She could not embrace certainty the way Rotrude did. Brutal punishment, harsh rules, and iron discipline mangled the very souls they sought to save. Even now, decades later, she could hear the echoes of the girls' cries with haunting clarity.

"Suffering?" Rotrude burst out. "Those women who came today are alive thanks to us. If we hadn't saved their souls, they would have fallen into perdition long ago."

The dinner chime sounded again, but neither of them moved. Bernadette didn't feel the least bit hungry. She, with her burden of doubt, and Rotrude, with her armor of conviction, both sat lonely in the twilight of their lives, guarding the memories of a time long past, and waiting for grace, which seemed slow in coming.

Bernadette toyed with another puzzle piece. The *tr* of *truth*. "There," she whispered, not bothering to look at Rotrude. "It's finished." She stared at the puzzle for a moment longer.

Then, spurred by a fresh impulse, she practically jumped out of her chair and bustled down the hall, power walking toward the lobby.

"Sister Bernadette," called Rotrude. "Sister Bernadette! What are you after? Have you lost your mind entirely? Stop!"

Bernadette set her jaw and rushed into the lobby. Only the receptionist was present, staring at her computer screen with a bored expression. Bernadette darted through the automatic doors as they swished open. She heard the receptionist call something about signing out, but Bernadette ignored the order. All her life, she had adhered strictly to the rules. It was the only way she knew how to function. But even a lifetime of obedience couldn't stop her now.

The four women were walking toward the parking lot.

"Wait," Bernadette called to them. "Wait!" She was nearly out of breath from running. She approached Angela Denny. Bernadette gasped as she pressed her folded hands against her chest and tried to force herself to speak. "You were called Agnes at the Good Shepherd."

Angela tossed her long, wavy hair and set her hand on her waist. "I was. I never cared for being called someone else's name."

"None of us did," said Odessa.

"I'm . . . it was customary," Bernadette said, still trying to catch her breath. "There were rules. But some rules were . . . Oh, in retrospect, perhaps they created unintended . . . issues."

"What are you trying to say?" Angela glared at her.

"It's difficult, but . . . I'm afraid . . ." She glanced over her shoulder, seeing that one of the attendants was coming toward her. Residents' comings and goings were strictly monitored at Holy Cross Haven. Behind the attendant, Rotrude was in hot pursuit, pumping away at her wheelchair.

Bernadette's pulse was racing. "There's something you should know about what happened back in 1969."

Angela glanced around at her friends as they moved in close. Then she folded her arms. "Is that so?"

Bernadette took a deep breath and exhaled a silent prayer. Then she found her voice. "It's about the night of March twenty-third." She paused, her heart beating fast.

"What about that night?" Angela drew herself up and held very still, not blinking, not breathing, a statue of ice.

Mairin stepped closer to her, assuming a protective stance.

Say it, Bernadette urged herself. Just say it. "That night, when you . . . gave birth, and you were told your baby was stillborn." She pressed her hands against her chest. "It's been eating away at me for far too long. But there's a very hard truth you deserve to know. Your baby didn't die."

Chapter 27

"Are you sure you want to go back to that place?" asked Flynn, stepping up behind Mairin and nuzzling her neck. She'd been standing at the back door, organizing her bag for the day.

She smiled and turned in his arms. "I can't believe I'm saying this, but yes. I don't expect a return visit to the Good Shepherd to be fun for any of us. But that place didn't destroy us when we were young, and it won't destroy us now."

"Want me to come?"

"You're sweet to offer." She pressed her hand against his soft denim work shirt. She knew he'd been planning to help with the pruning of the orchard today, with spring right around the corner. He was supposed to be retired—they both were—but there was always something to do around the farm. "This is a girls' thing," she told him. "And if we do find what Sister Bernadette swears we'll find, it might get emotional for Angela."

"I guess she'll need her privacy, not some old guy hanging around." He kissed her forehead. "You're a good friend, Mairin."

"Am I? Sometimes I wish there was more I could have done for Angela through the years. Supported her more. Been a better friend. It was bad for me at the Good Shepherd, but her experience was much worse."

"The two of you have a special bond," Flynn said. "I'm glad you have each other. But I worry about you, darlin'. To this day, there are things you hold inside you."

He knew her so well. Sometimes better than she knew herself. He was—he had always been—the one person who truly saw her. It was a miracle that he loved what he saw. "You're probably right. I keep them in the past, where they belong." But were they in the past if she still had nightmares? The pain didn't go away just because it happened a long time ago.

"I love your sense of determination," said Flynn. "I always have."

"I like to think it started with my father," Mairin said. "He was what I held on to during the dark times. He was my guiding light. Even now, when I think of him, I can remember his words of encouragement."

She pressed her cheek to her husband's chest. She reminded herself that she'd lived a full life. She'd had ups and downs. But there was something missing, some element that seemed to hover just out of reach. Although her ordeal at the Good Shepherd had happened so long ago, she carried ghosts from that time. She could still hear the cries of the girls in the dormitories at night. She could feel the aching hunger and discomfort of the closet. The painful punishments she'd endured still felt like fresh wounds.

"You're right about me and Angela." She stepped back and looked up at him, drinking in the warmth in his eyes. "Why is it that some people who survive a trauma together have a lifelong bond, while others avoid each other? Ah, Flynn. We both experienced so much shame and embarrassment . . . and now all those memories are flooding back."

"I've been trying to figure out if there's something I can do." He hooked his thumbs into his jeans pockets and gazed out the window. Their daughter Colleen drove up and parked in front of the banquet barn, and Seal loped across the yard to greet her.

Mairin smiled and kissed his cheek. "You've been doing it for fifty years, my love. And now this opportunity has come up. We have a mystery to solve. It's like we're a team again, only we're not scared little girls anymore."

"You never were," he whispered against her temple. "You were never scared."

She lingered in his embrace for a moment longer, then stepped away. She dropped her phone into her backpack and zipped it up. "But we were powerless."

"And now you're not." He walked downstairs with her, passing the photo display wall covered in memories of the cornerstone of their lives—kids, grandchildren, and pets. "To be honest, the four of you together are kind of scary."

"Who's scary?" Colleen came in through the kitchen door, Seal trotting by her side.

"Your mom and the wayward girls."

Colleen checked out Mairin's outfit and nodded approvingly. "You look fantastic."

"But scary." Flynn gave her a teasing grin, then headed outside with Seal the dog.

"I brought this in case you need it after visiting the dungeon." Colleen set her bag on the counter and took out a tall bottle of tequila. "I still can't believe you were in a reform school, Mom. Run by evil nuns. It's bonkers."

"It was worse than bonkers. Did you know, there was a similar one in Albany? And Philadelphia? Turns out there were Magdalene laundries all over the place. Your grandmother was sent to one in Ireland. I bet she never told you that."

"Granny Deirdre?"

"Come sit." Mairin poured them each a cup of coffee and they sat together in the sunny breakfast nook. Facing her daughter, who had the O'Hara red hair and freckles, she explained the reason Deirdre had come to Buffalo as a girl of eighteen.

"She had a baby, and she never found him," Colleen said softly. "That's so sad."

"I'm afraid it might have happened more than we'll ever know," said Mairin.

"You never told me," Colleen said. "Why haven't you told me until now?"

Mairin paused, watching the emotions play across Colleen's face. "When my mother was alive, she didn't want you to know. Back then, there was so much shame associated with it. But now, seeing all of this happen, I realize that history is part of who we are, and secrets can be toxic. I grew up never knowing my older brother, never even knowing *about* him until I was much older. I didn't mean to keep things from you.

It's time to break the silence and let go of the fear that has kept this hidden for so long."

"Have you ever thought about tracking down Granny's boy? You and Uncle Liam have a brother, out in the world somewhere. With DNA searches, you might find a match."

"I might at that. Maybe I'll try it one day."

Colleen brushed away a tear. "I'm sorry that happened to Granny."

"As am I. But back then—in Ireland, and here, and all over the world—unmarried girls were expected to surrender the baby and move on with their lives as if it had never happened."

"They lied to her," Colleen said. "The nuns at the Good Shepherd lied to your friend Angela, too."

"Yes. I can't imagine what she's feeling now. If Bernadette is telling the truth, there's a person who's been in the world since 1969, and Angela never knew it."

"Is it worse that Granny Deirdre knew her child was alive and never found him?" Colleen asked. "Would it have been better to never have known he survived?"

"I don't know," Mairin replied slowly. She'd thought about this so many times over the years. "It makes me grateful that I got to keep all the kids I had."

"Even when there were days that you wanted to sell us at the farmers market?"

"Oh, I guess I had a few days like that." Mairin sighed, and her smile disappeared. "Knowing there was a child of hers in the world but never knowing what happened to him was a defining piece of my mother. She was so angry, even if she stuffed away that anger most of the time."

"She knew how bad those places were. Why did she send you to one?"

I survived, and I knew you would, too. Decades later, Mairin could still hear her mother's voice. "Unresolved trauma, misguided beliefs instilled by the Church. Her own insecurity. Plus, her creepy husband, Colm. I suppose she was the best mother she knew how to be." Mairin sighed again, and took their mugs to the sink. "I sure wish you'd known my dad."

"Me, too. He'd be proud of you, Mom. I'm proud of you," said Colleen.

"We're all proud of you." Her husband came back into the kitchen and kissed her temple. "You look ready for anything."

"Aw, Flynn." She pulled him close, inhaling his warm scent and feeling a surge of gratitude. "I'm taking the Sprinter van, okay? It's got enough space for four old ladies and a nun."

"Sounds like the start of a joke," he said.

"It's no joke."

"I know, my love. Be careful."

"Always."

MAIRIN, ODESSA, ANGELA, and Helen waited in the van in front of the retirement home while Sister Bernadette stopped in the lobby to sign herself out for the day. Mairin glanced over at Odessa, in the passenger seat. "Last time we were in a van together, we were driving *away* from the Good Shepherd."

"The legendary prison break," Angela said.

"I always wished I could've gone with y'all that day," Odessa said.

"No, you don't," Helen said.

"I wasn't the best driver back then," Mairin admitted.

"Oh, but it was magic," Angela said. "I still remember how it smelled—books and motor oil and menthol cigarettes. We turned the radio on loud and sang along. You would have loved that part."

"Until the cops showed up." Helen shuddered.

Mairin turned on the radio and tuned it to Big WECK, the oldies station from Buffalo. A hearing aid commercial played, and she cringed. "Hearing aids. God, we're old."

"Hey, don't knock 'em." Helen grinned, indicating a tiny translucent wire by her ear.

A Tony Bennett song played, and Mairin shook her head. "Now, that one's probably even older than we are."

Angela looked anxiously out the window. After being told that her baby had survived, Angela had been dealing with a lot. Mairin had introduced her to Fiona, who had endured a similar experience, but with a different outcome. As soon as the state had allowed adoption records to be unsealed, Fiona had been reunited with the baby that had been placed in the arms of another woman. Fiona had shared her insights with Angela. Mairin hoped it had helped, even a little.

"Okay, here she comes," said Angela.

In her plain cloth coat, clutching a square pocketbook, her wimple and veil fluttering in the breeze, Bernadette exited the building, walking quickly. A shadow lumbered behind her—Sister Rotrude in her wheelchair.

"*That* one's not coming, is she?" asked Helen.

Even from a distance, they could hear Rotrude hurling dire warnings at Bernadette. "Absolutely not," said Mairin.

Angela climbed out and opened the sliding door for Sister Bernadette. Tension thrummed in the air as Mairin headed for Best Street.

"Rotrude didn't want you to come," Angela said to Bernadette.

"Sister Rotrude believes there is nothing to be gained by opening old wounds and raising difficult questions."

"And you? What do you believe?"

"The truth matters," Bernadette said. "Truth, and accountability."

Mairin wished the nun had embraced that back when they were girls in need of an ally. She reminded herself that Bernadette had probably been just as fearful of Sister Gerard and Rotrude as the rest of them. During the drive to the city, Odessa interviewed Bernadette. After the closure of the Good Shepherd, she'd served in places near and far, from Buffalo and Albany to the Middle East, claiming she had been seeking grace and enlightenment. She never said whether or not she found it.

They all fell quiet as they approached the old place. Mairin stopped the van in front of the complex. She rolled down the window and stared at the main entry gate.

"It's hardly changed at all," Odessa said, her eyes wide as she scanned the old brick wall, its height extended by chain-link fencing at the top. The gray stone buildings still had their sharp, peaked rooftops and barred windows. The rusty iron exoskeletons of the fire escapes hung from the buildings, reminding Mairin of the hiding places in the attic. Also unchanged was the quality of the light and the air—heavy with humidity from the lake, and an atmosphere of desolation from the exhausted surrounding neighborhood, with its vacant lots and broken houses.

"Let's go," Mairin said, driving slowly through the main entrance. It looked every bit as intimidating as it had the first time she'd been brought here.

A small welcome sign did not look terribly welcoming, but pointed the way to the office.

"What's Darul Uloom Al-Madania?" Odessa asked, reading the sign. "And what's Masjid Zakariya?"

"A mosque and a Muslim school for boys."

"So they're just going to let us into the Mother Superior's office and... what? Poke around?" asked Angela.

"I called ahead and told the director we're here to do some historical research. Mr. Rizek was a little hesitant, but he said he'd allow it." Odessa handed out some plain scarves. "We're going to need to cover our heads," she said.

The architectural clash of the buildings was striking. The compound resembled a prison complex with sally ports surrounding Gothic structures, administrative offices, and quadrangles. Signs in Arabic were posted in front of the chapel and the old laundry buildings. The orchard had been razed, and the yard with the clotheslines was now a sports court.

Mairin looked around at her friends. As they secured their head coverings, their faces reflected the jumble of emotions she was feeling—apprehension and curiosity, anger and fear.

The office was located not in the massive main building, which looked abandoned, but in a newer space in front of it constructed of modern blocks. Angela opened the door and stepped inside. She and Odessa introduced themselves and the others to a bearded older man in a skullcap. Standing behind a desk, he kept his eyes trained on Angela as he called out something in a foreign language. Two more men, similarly dressed, came through a side door.

The three of them spoke rapidly together, and then one of them made a call, speaking briefly and rapidly into a smartphone. Then the tallest of the three said, "There has been a mistake. I am sorry. It's not possible to allow you on the premises."

"I was told we were welcome to tour the old buildings." Angela handed him a card from her head-librarian days. "They're significant structures in Buffalo's history."

He inspected the card and pursed his lips. "It is not possible," he repeated.

"Mr. Rizek, you said we'd be permitted to visit," Odessa reminded him, presenting her own press card. "Of course, we'll respect the private areas—"

He spoke to the other men again, his voice low and tense. Then he turned back. "I was mistaken when I invited you here. My colleagues are objecting to the visit."

Angela's face fell. "But—"

"If I may." With unexpected firmness, Sister Bernadette stepped forward. She kept her head lowered in deference and said something in a foreign language.

The men listened, then exchanged a few more words with Bernadette. She spoke the language slowly, but with crisp conviction. Then she turned to the women. "We'll be allowed to tour the original building, the one that housed the office of the prioress. It hasn't been renovated so they're concerned for our safety."

There was more chatter, and then Mr. Rizek led the way to a small construction trailer, where he gave them each a plastic hard hat. Mairin turned to Bernadette. "You speak Arabic?" she asked.

"A little, yes." The nun looked almost comical in the oversized orange helmet. "I made a pilgrimage to Beit Jala—that's a town near Bethlehem. I stayed for several years and studied Arabic. It was necessary for our ministry."

"And what did you say to those men?" asked Odessa.

"I let them know that we are not so different. We're members of a faith community, accepting surrender to the will of God. I promised we would be quiet and respectful. And that we'd wear their safety helmets. That was their main concern, since the building hasn't been renovated yet."

Mairin could tell the others were as surprised as she was. She felt slightly mollified by the idea that Bernadette had not spent her entire career in a "faith community" that tormented young girls the way the nuns had at the Good Shepherd.

Mr. Rizek led them to the original main building, the brooding hulk where they had all been forced to submit themselves for intake so long ago. All the paint had peeled off the heavy door, and it creaked when it swung open. Rizek flipped a switch, and a series of fluorescent lights behind wire cages blinked and buzzed to life. The walls, which had once displayed icons and portraits of past prioresses, were dingy and scarred with age and neglect.

Mairin felt a chill roll over her, and she looked around to see if the others felt it. She still remembered the forbidding shadows in the long, arched hall, with its "classrooms" where the girls had been forced to labor. They passed the door marked *Clinic*, and she took Angela's hand. It was ice-cold.

"The office of the prioress was here," Angela said, indicating the double doors. Most of the leaded glass in the doors was missing. Inside, there was an air of swift abandonment. A few items of shabby office furniture were stacked, upended, and draped in cobwebs. There was a tall built-in bookcase, empty except for a few dusty periodicals. They stepped past some broken chairs and a prie-dieu with cushions that had been chewed by rodents. More than one desiccated mouse carcass could be seen. The grand desk of the prioress and the reliquary were gone. At the far end of the office was a hallway, pitchdark, but Mairin remembered it fresh as yesterday. The closet. The place she'd been confined for hours on end.

Rizek's mobile phone rang. He looked at the screen, and then dismissed them with a wave of his hand and hastened away.

"So what are we looking for?" asked Odessa, turning to Bernadette. "You said there were records. What happened?"

The nun paused, scanning the dimly lit room. "We were told by the diocese that the place was closing. We should have anticipated the change. Laundry services were no longer productive, what with the innovation of automatic washing and drying machines."

"No more demand for free child labor," Helen murmured.

"Sister Gerard put me in charge of the records," Bernadette said. "There were certain confidential papers she wanted me to get rid of. I was told to dispose of them in the incinerator in the basement."

"She said to destroy records? Of us? Of the girls who were incarcerated here?" asked Mairin.

"She claimed it would protect certain girls and their families from shame. People's private lives were at stake. We had been entrusted to guard their privacy with all vigilance."

"That's the rationale?" Helen scoffed. "Did you also destroy records of the funds Mother Gerard stole?"

"The funds disappeared the day you girls did," said Bernadette. "It was never spoken of again." She sighed. "I was young and weak, though I know it's no excuse." She went to the built-in bookcase and inspected the dusty shelves. "I was supposed to follow orders to the letter, but there were certain records that I simply didn't feel right about destroying. I didn't want to be the one to burn the truth about someone's existence. So—God forgive me—I left them be."

"And you think there are still records stored here?" Angela looked around the room.

Bernadette nodded. "Did you discover the secret of this wall?" she asked, pointing it out. "Ruth, I know you found out many secrets when you were here."

"Mairin, not Ruth. And this was supposed to be a facility to care for young girls. Secrets should have had no place here."

Bernadette looked away. "I left this stack of issues of *Catholic Fireside* on the shelf here," she said, indicating the bookcase. "Not likely anyone would be interested in reading them, and I was right. They're still here." Lifting up on tiptoe, she moved the pile of dusty, yellowed periodicals, which dated back to 1967. "There's a latch, see?" She showed them what appeared to be a small gate hook.

"Whoa," said Helen. "There's something behind it."

With some pushing and pulling, the bookcase swung outward like a door. Puffs of ancient dust rose, and someone sneezed. Behind the bookcase was a dark recess.

Angela shone her phone flashlight into the space. "It's a safe," she said.

Dust and rodent droppings covered the large, heavy safe, which looked like a relic from the 1800s, heavy and ornate with a dial on the front.

There was some kind of writing engraved on the top, now encrusted with dust and cobwebs.

"The records are in there?" asked Angela, her voice taut.

"This was used only for the most sensitive documents, such as birth, death, and adoption records. Sister Gerard said the hidden safe was meant to protect the records from the elements and from prying eyes, and from being destroyed or lost."

"There's a record of my baby's birth?" Angela seemed to have trouble breathing, and Mairin moved close to her. "You remember that specifically?"

"I do. It was so very tragic . . . and . . . I recall seeing the tiny footprints done in ink. That struck me as unusual. I didn't think . . . it didn't seem to make sense that there would be footprints of a babe that didn't survive."

"And it never occurred to you to question this?" Helen asked.

"I was very young, and new to the novitiate. Unquestioning obedience is the first thing we're taught." She shut her eyes briefly, and her lips seemed to move in a silent prayer. "The hospital trusted Mother Gerard to register the birth, but she never did. She claimed it was a matter of privacy."

"Well, open it," Angela said, her voice trembling with strain, "and let's have a look."

Bernadette frowned. She leaned forward and rotated the dial. Then she stepped back, her forehead knit in a frown.

"You don't know the combination," Helen said.

"I'm sorry. Only the prioress had the combination."

"It didn't occur to you that we'd need that?" Mairin asked.

"I thought . . . perhaps you could find a way to open it."

"Well, did she write it down? Stash it away somewhere?"

Bernadette's brow knit in distress. "Not that I know of. She assumed the safe was empty, so the combination wouldn't matter. I . . . I recall that one of the numbers was a seven. I saw it when she added Angela's records to the safe."

"And you didn't burn these records."

"I . . . No. They seemed too important. Too consequential. So I left them here. Closed it and spun the dial."

"Could we hire a—what? Like, a safecracker?" asked Mairin. "Is there such a thing?"

"We need to get it open," Odessa said. "But how? It probably wouldn't be a good look to bring in a locksmith. The guys in the front office are already super suspicious."

Helen brushed past Bernadette. "Let me have a look." She blew the dust from the top of the safe, then used her headscarf to wipe away the dirt. "There's some kind of writing here."

Angela shone her light. They leaned in, and Helen read the engraved words aloud. "*I prayed for this child, and the Lord has granted me what I asked of Him.*"

"Lovely," Mairin said with a bitter edge to her voice.

"It's a verse from the first book of Samuel," Bernadette said softly.

Helen knelt down and spun the dial. "Sometimes with older locks, you can feel your way through the combination." She tried a few times. "Not this one. And this safe is huge. It must weigh a ton."

"Let's find a locksmith who makes house calls," Mairin suggested. Then she shook her head. "Duh. I guess they all make house calls."

"That might be a problem. Mr. Rizek will think we're up to no good," Odessa pointed out.

"Hang on a sec." Helen held up her hand. She scrubbed her scarf over the verse at the top and stared at the words. "First book of Samuel?" she asked Bernadette.

The nun nodded. "From the Jerusalem Bible. The approved edition."

"Do you know the chapter and verse?" Helen persisted. She was like a hound on the scent.

"Of course," Bernadette replied. "Chapter one, verse twenty-seven."

"So, one-one-two-seven," Helen guessed.

Mairin nudged Odessa. "She was a lieutenant colonel in the army, remember."

"If this works . . ." Helen bent down and turned the dial.

"We'll give you a medal," Angela said.

"We'll give you a lifetime supply of chocolate," said Odessa.

Helen tried the combination and let out a sigh. "Nothing."

Disheartened, they all looked at one another.

"No, you're on the right track." Bernadette brightened. "I think... Try those numbers in reverse."

Helen spun the dial, rotating to the digits in reverse. At the last turn, they heard a soft *click*. A quiet gasp from Angela. And the door of the safe swung open.

Chapter 28

Everly Lasko went to check the mailbox, taking pleasure in the scent of lilacs along the garden path. She found the usual assortment of bills, coupons and marketing mail, a couple of catalogs, including one she'd done some modeling work for, touting "Flirty, age-appropriate party dresses." She rolled her eyes and consigned it to the recycle bin.

She set aside a couple of pieces for her husband—Nathan's annual fly-fishing tournament and a postcard about the firemen's fundraiser for which he was co-chair this year. Then she came across something unusual—a hand-addressed note on nice cardstock. She felt an odd nudge of familiarity. There was something about the handwriting that resembled her own precise, Palmer Method script, the style that used to be taught to third-graders. The return address label was from a stranger—A. Denny, Brockport, NY. Frowning slightly, she slit open the envelope to find a letter in that same script.

To Everly Barrett Lasko,

My name is Angela Denny. At the age of seventeen, I gave birth on March 23, 1969, at St. Francis Hospital in Buffalo. When I recovered from the anesthesia, I was told the baby was stillborn. A recently discovered record from the Good Shepherd Refuge, the home where I was confined, indicates that the healthy baby girl was adopted by Roy and Shirley Barrett...

A single photo had been tucked into the envelope. Everly had to sit down as she studied the image of a slender blond woman, her face composed as she gazed straight at the camera.

Everly might have been looking at a picture of herself.

She gripped the edge of the kitchen table, bombarded by a barrage of emotions as her breath came in quick, panicked gasps.

She'd always known she was adopted. That was never in question. Roy and Shirley Barrett called Everly their chosen child. They had become parents through adoption when they were in their forties. By that time, they had finally given up trying to conceive a baby. They had applied to several agencies, but were deemed too old to adopt a newborn.

Then one day, when they had all but given up hope, the nuns of Our Lady of Charity and the Good Shepherd Refuge had matched the Barretts with a baby girl. Everly grew up happy and healthy, an indulged only child doted on by her aging parents. But through the years, she had often questioned her origin. She had always wondered. Due to the nonstandard nature of her adoption—something she learned was all too common in the 1960s—she was never able to learn anything about her birth parents.

As she got older, more questions burned inside her. She wondered each day who she really was. She asked why there was so little information about her birth parents. Her mom and dad had no answers. They were simple, working-class people, and the only record they had was a birth certificate with their names on it. All Everly's parents had known was what the nuns had told them—that the birth mother was an indigent girl, sound of mind and body. When the girl went astray, her family knew it would be best to choose adoption to give her child a better life.

Better than what? Everly pondered this now. Her parents were gone, and any other answers with them. As the mother of two, she tried to imagine what it was like for a girl to give birth, and then place the baby with strangers. What she knew from her own experience of giving birth to Oliver, and then Violet two years later, was that her love for them was so instantaneous and profound that it felt like a physical bond, too powerful to ever be broken. The thought of surrendering a baby at birth was almost inconceivable.

In grade school, Everly had fielded all the usual questions from her schoolmates. *Who are your real parents? Why did they give you away? The Barretts aren't your real parents. They're old, like as old as my grandparents.*

Stung by the blunt, hurtful questions and comments from the other children, Everly would sometimes stare at her reflection in the mirror and wonder who she looked like. Her adoptive parents were nice-looking people, but Shirley Barrett was short and slight, dark-haired and gray-eyed. Her husband had a solid, stocky build and ruddy skin. Everly never knew where her wavy blond hair had come from. And what about the light blue eyes that had been so easy to match with the trendy blue eyeshadow that was popular when she was a teenager in the eighties? The unusual height and slender build that had landed her modeling jobs? Did she get her height from her mother? Or from her father?

As a dreamy young girl, she would sometimes fantasize that they were enchanted people in a fairy tale, forced by an evil spell to leave their beloved daughter to the Barretts for safekeeping. One day they would come back for her, sweeping away all the feelings of rejection and abandonment and whisking her off to a lifetime of adventure.

She had always envied those adoptees who found their birth moms at some point in their lives. After New York State had unsealed all birth records, she had combed the registries obsessively. She'd even made several in-person inquiries with various agencies, but in time she gave up. The girls' home in Buffalo no longer existed. She had traced the Sisters of Charity to a location in Astoria, Queens, but they had no records. There had been no pre-placement home study or investigation.

Everly didn't really know why she yearned to learn more. She just did. She had never been able to quell the need for a connection to a hidden past. Yet as she grew older, she had to accept the fact that perhaps the person she sought didn't want to be found. Judging by the adoptee message boards she subscribed to, the process was complicated. Some were happy reunions. Others, not so much. But at least there was a sense of *knowing*.

Some people were finally given letters from their birth mothers. There were explanations. Rationalizations. Sometimes, revelations.

There was no letter for Everly.

Until today.

Her hand shook as she reached for her phone and dialed Angela Denny's number.

Two days later, Everly prepared to meet her birth mother face-to-face. Since that first phone call, Everly had thought of little else. As the years had slipped by, her hope of finding the woman who had given her away had faded. And now, finally, fate had opened a door. The thoughts of betrayal and abandonment she'd harbored all her life had been dispelled by the truth. In its place was a much bigger, more complicated story.

Angela Denny. Her birth mother had a name—Angela Denny. Would seeing her in person finally answer Everly's questions about herself? Would she finally understand her own origin story? Would she be able to see her face in someone else's?

Maybe she and Angela shared personality traits or mannerisms, tastes or habits. Her own children, especially her daughter, took after her in so many ways.

Soon, she would know. Maybe not everything, but so many blanks would be filled in.

In the hours after receiving the letter, Everly just had to sit with the revelation and digest it in her own way until she could share it with those who mattered most. When she told her husband, Nathan had held her close, and he hadn't asked her why she was crying. She couldn't have explained it, anyway. It was just an overwhelming feeling.

Nathan had offered to come with her to the meeting, but Everly told him to go to work as usual. As fire chief, he navigated a packed schedule from dawn to dusk when he was on shift. Everly assured him it would be enough to have Violet with her today.

Her daughter lived in the city, close to the courthouse where she worked. Violet must have been tracking her on their shared map app, because she came out of the vintage townhouse where she lived with her fiancé. Violet and Matt had become parents the year before, and they were planning to get married in the fall.

Violet was her usual gorgeous self, in wide-leg jeans and a light jacket over a striped top. Subtle makeup and pink lipstick. When she jumped into the car, her features were taut with anxiety. "Hey," she said, studying Everly's face, then her outfit.

"Hey," said Everly. "Look at us."

The tension broke a little as they laughed at themselves. Everly was wearing wide-leg jeans and a knit jacket over a top that was not, fortunately, striped.

"I wasn't sure what to wear to meet my birth mother," she said. *Birth mother.* Spoken aloud, the words sounded surreal. "Millie's with Matt?"

Violet nodded. "They're watching *Peppa Pig.* And, Mom, I'm reeling. I mean *reeling.* How are you not just a total basket case?"

"You think I'm not? I'm a wreck. Excited, but a wreck." Everly could feel her daughter's eyes on her as she pulled away from the curb and headed for the expressway.

"Okay," said Violet. "Tell me everything."

"I don't know everything. We—Angela Denny and I—wanted to meet in person right away. There's just too much to cover in a phone conversation."

"Well, tell me what you know so far."

Everly knew her daughter would already have done a thorough search for Angela Denny. As a prosecutor, she had access to all kinds of records and databases that normal civilians didn't. "Tell me what *you* know," she said.

"You knew I'd check. She's a retired librarian living in Brockport," Violet said. "No criminal record, no red flags. I don't think she's a fraudster. There's a driver's license photo from the DMV that looks . . . Did you bring the letter she sent you?"

Everly nodded, easing onto the main route and heading east. "It's here, in my bag. Take it out and have a look."

Violet dug in the bag and took out the envelope. She stared at it for a moment, then removed the card. "It's letter-pressed," she said. "On nice stationery. Nice handwriting." Ever since becoming engaged, Violet had been obsessed with paper goods. She fell silent as she read the letter and studied the photograph. Then she looked up. "Holy effing shit, Mom."

"She has a long story to tell, so we both agreed to meet at Wayward Farm, which is owned by her friend."

"I looked that up, too," Violet said. "It's out by Gardenville. It's known for culinary dinners, banquets, and weddings. Belongs to the Gallagher family. Stellar reviews."

"She promised we could have a private meeting there, free from noise and interruptions. I knew you'd want to be with me."

"Of course." Violet's voice squeaked with excitement. "Have you told Dad? And Oliver?"

"Dad knows. I haven't said anything to your brother yet. He's been so busy with his workload at the firm."

"Yes, dealing with all the criminals he defends." Violet sniffed.

Everly's children were both lawyers—and professional rivals. Violet was an assistant district attorney. Her brother was a criminal defense lawyer. Brother and sister had never faced each other in court, but they liked to tease one another about it. Everly was equally proud of them both.

"Oh, Violet. I think she's the one. I'm as sure as I can be at this point. Everything she's told me so far lines up with what little information I have."

"Well, if her claim is true—that she was lied to and never consented to surrendering her baby—it's totally illegal."

Everly nodded. "I thought I'd be like other adoptees, with a way to find the facts about my origin once the records were opened."

"But you didn't find any record to open."

"Because I never existed until my adoptive parents were given a birth certificate with their names on it. They were never aware there was supposed to be a pre-adoption birth certificate. The document was never registered with the health department at all."

"That's human trafficking," Violet huffed. "We need to do something."

"Not today," Everly said. "Let's take this one step at a time." She felt a ball of stress form in her chest.

"You're right. Sorry. How are you feeling about all this, Mom? Really."

"Unsettled. Nervous. Curious. And probably everything in between. My origin story has always been a mystery, and suddenly, it's not."

"It just seems so huge. Does it seem that way to you?"

"Oh my gosh, *yes*. It's so much to take in. I've barely been able to sleep. I can barely get my head around the idea that I'm about to meet my birth mother. I think I always harbored some kind of bitterness about the woman who gave me away at birth. Not soul-shriveling bitterness, but a kind of judgy resentment. I just thought, how can a mother abandon her baby like that? And now I know why. She didn't abandon me. She was lied to, led to believe I didn't survive."

She turned down a winding, rural road at a sign for Wayward Farm. The driveway was long and lined with rough-hewn fencing, shaded by sugar maples that were beginning to unfurl for the season. There were distant fields and orchards and vineyards, a row of beehives, and a riot of flowers in bloom in hedges and garden beds.

"Wow, it's gorgeous here," Violet said. "Angela Denny said it's her friend's place? Did she say how she knows the Gallaghers?"

"She and the friend were in a home in the city for wayward girls."

"A *what?*"

"Back in the sixties, that's what some of the homes were called. Especially the ones that were Catholic run."

"I'm glad it's not the sixties," said Violet. "My daughter will be, too."

"I'm sure it was pretty awful for young girls."

"Wayward Farm," Violet said. "I guess we know where the name comes from. Wow, it's really pretty. I love the converted barn." She perked up. "Maybe it's a contender for our wedding venue."

"Let's get through this meeting first."

"Of course, Mom."

Everly parked in front of a beautiful Victorian farmhouse painted white with black accents. Its wraparound porch was decked with hanging baskets and aspidistra plants. Lavish gardens surrounded the home.

On the front lawn was a massive shagbark hickory tree with painted chandeliers hanging from its limbs. One long branch had a swing suspended on stout ropes. Everly felt a strange flash of familiarity, but shook it off. She'd never been here before.

"All righty, then." She flexed her hands on the steering wheel. "Do I look okay?"

"Always," Violet said. "I've always said I have the most beautiful mother in the world, and right now, you're *glowing*."

"That," said Everly, "is the sweat of anxiety."

"Take a breath, Mom. I'm going to wait here for a minute, okay?"

Everly nodded. Her daughter knew her well, instinctively giving her a private moment with the stranger who'd birthed her. She got out of the car, bringing along a tote bag with a photo album. She hadn't known what on earth to bring with her. She had so little to go on.

She approached the house, her heart pounding with anticipation, hope, and apprehension. The years of searching, the countless dead ends, and a lifetime of yearning had led to this moment, which felt laden with heaviness. Her age-old curiosity was about to be satisfied.

The front door opened, and a woman stepped out onto the porch. She was tall and blond, wearing jeans and white sneakers and a soft white sweater with the sleeves pushed up to the elbows. She looked younger than expected. Everly reminded herself that they were only seventeen years apart in age.

At the top of the porch steps, Angela hung on to the railing as if to steady herself. Then she stepped down to the yard. Her soft, willowy movements made her seem fragile, perhaps hesitant.

The moment they locked eyes, the connection was palpable, a bond that somehow existed despite being invisible to them both. Her gaze met Angela's, whose features held a lifetime of untold stories.

Tears danced in Everly's eyes as the magnitude of this long-awaited reunion sank in. Words were choked by waves of joy and sorrow that had been suppressed for decades.

Angela's trembling hands reached out to clasp hers. Then, in a movement that was wholly unplanned but felt completely natural, Everly embraced the woman who had always been a part of her, even in absence. In that unspoken gesture, understanding and acceptance flowed between them, bridging the expanse of lost time.

Angela felt delicate, and her scent was delicate, vaguely floral. The years of longing and questions melted away in that moment, replaced by a profound, unspoken understanding that bridged the space between them.

The palpable silence grew heavier with each passing second. Then Angela began to speak, her voice trembling with wonder. "It's really you," she whispered, her voice breaking. "You're Everly."

"You're Angela." Everly's voice cracked over the name.

"Alice," she whispered, tears streaming down her face.

"Sorry, what?"

"When I was pregnant, I called you Alice. I wanted to give you a name, something that was mine alone to give, even if I couldn't keep you."

The world broke open with a torrent of emotions as the weight of Angela's confession settled over Everly. Angela's story intertwined with the fragments she had crafted into her own identity, finally weaving together an unexpected truth.

The name *Alice* resonated with a profound sense of belonging, but also a deep sadness for the years that had slipped away. The name bound her to a past that didn't belong to her, and yet it did. In that moment, two lives collided, bridging the gap between past and present, and Everly could finally exhale the longing that had consumed her.

Her nerves felt raw with vulnerability. She was floored by the idea that she was this stranger's daughter. A lifetime of searching and longing converged at this point, lifting her higher than she had ever dreamed possible.

She hadn't expected the rush of emotion to hit her so fast and so hard. Angela. Her mother's name was Angela. She turned and beckoned to Violet. "My daughter. I told you about her on the phone."

Violet practically floated across the lawn, her face blooming with joy.

Angela Denny's blue eyes swam with tears. She smiled—a shy, uneasy smile that opened her face like a flower. "Can I . . ." Angela held out her hands. "Can I hug you?"

Violet gasped with a sob. Angela opened her arms, and the three of them held on tight for long moments.

"Shall we sit?" Angela pointed to the beautiful porch furniture. There was a low table set with a pitcher of iced tea, a plate of cookies, and a box of tissues. "We have the place all to ourselves. And it's a lovely day."

"It is," said Everly, "a lovely day."

"I can join you . . . or not," Violet said. "Up to you, Mom."

"Oh, please stay," Everly said. "You know I'm going to tell you everything anyway. This will save some time." She turned to Angela. "My daughter and I tell each other everything. Well, practically. As far as I know."

"Everything," Violet agreed, and gave Angela another hug.

"That's wonderful," said Angela. She inhaled and released a steadying breath. "I don't know where to start. I've thought so much about this day. Barely slept a wink last night. The main thing is, I want to be completely open and honest with you about everything."

"Of course. I wouldn't want it any other way."

Angela looked from one to the other. "Sorry—I keep staring. Do you mind if I just take a minute and . . . gaze at you? I can't seem to stop . . . I hope you don't mind."

"It's mutual," Everly said. Angela had a regal face, with high cheekbones and wide-set eyes that were as blue as Everly's own. She was amazed to finally find someone she looked like. At last, the complete picture of who she was began to fill in.

"You're both so beautiful." Angela's voice faltered.

Violet plucked a tissue from the box. "I was thinking the same thing about you."

Everly could only stare in wonderment. "And wait until you meet my grandchildren. Violet has a daughter, and my son, Oliver, has a little boy."

"I would love that so much," Angela said. "*Grandchildren*. That makes me a great-grandmother. How can I be a great-grandmother? Just a week ago, I had no living family."

"I can only imagine what's going on in your head," Everly said. "To learn you have a daughter, and a granddaughter and grandson, and two adorable great-grandchildren."

"What's going on in my head is like every holiday on the calendar all at once," Angela said. "I can't . . . It's hard to describe. Maybe I believe in miracles after all."

She really did emanate a glow, thought Everly. All the times she'd imagined her birth mother, she had never pictured her quite like this, a flesh-and-blood person, not a dream. "I'm glad this makes you happy."

"It absolutely does, but... like I said on the phone, there's a lot to cover. Some parts of my story might be hard to hear."

"All we need to do today is talk," Everly said. "Get to know each other."

"I don't know what to call you." Violet filled their glasses.

"Angela works just fine. I would love to know everything about you. Everything you're willing to tell."

Everly could feel the nerves emanating from Angela, so she started off with the simple facts. "I'll begin with what I know. My parents were named Roy and Shirley Barrett. They had a farm not far from here, where they produced Concord grapes and maple syrup. A doctor referred them to Our Lady of Victory in Lackawanna, but the waiting list was long. Then they heard about the Good Shepherd. My folks were not Catholic, but they were told it didn't matter if they came up with some kind of special fee, like a tribute to the Church. They also had to pay all the expenses of the birth mother."

Angela's face stiffened. "I'm guessing it was a cash transaction."

"You're probably right. Look, my parents were... not sophisticated. My mother never finished high school, and Dad was a farmer like his father before him. I had a wonderful childhood. I appreciate the good life they gave me. But there's a part of me that always wanted to know you. To appreciate you for giving me life."

Angela's eyes filled with fresh tears. "And for that, I'm grateful, Everly. Truly."

"They were given minimal information—that the birth mother was underage, and the family wanted the records to be permanently sealed. A long time ago, I registered with Catholic Charities and other search organizations, but there were no leads."

She told Angela about her repeated—and fruitless—requests to the long-gone hospital where she'd been delivered. "I even tried a DNA kit, but no matches came up."

"If you'd like a sample from me," Angela said, "I don't have a problem with that."

Everly studied Angela's hands, the turn of her ankle, the way she crossed them. She pondered the sound of Angela's voice. So very strange, yet so very familiar. "A DNA test is probably not necessary."

Angela smiled and took a sip of iced tea. Then the smile faded. Her hand shook as she set down her glass. "I'm sorry it was frustrating for you," she said. "So. The hard part. A lot of this is hard. I suppose I should start with the reason I was sent to the Good Shepherd."

"I thought it was because you were pregnant," Everly said.

"Actually, no. Girls were sent there for many reasons. Some were sentenced by juvenile courts. Some were placed there by families facing financial hardship. There were any number of reasons. Yet we were all categorized as wayward girls."

Everly braced herself. Had her mother been a criminal? Was that the *hard to hear* part?

"When I was about fifteen or sixteen," Angela said, "I fell in love with another girl." She paused.

Everly and Violet waited. "And?" Everly prompted.

"These days, it's not so unusual. At least, I hope it's not."

"Of course not," Everly said.

"Not even a little," Violet agreed.

Angela's smile flashed briefly, soft with relief. "But back then, I had no idea what was going on inside me. I thought I was losing my mind. The only thing that kept me sane was reading certain books from the library. A librarian introduced me to novels about a young gay woman. The books are from the fifties—really outdated now, but it was comforting to read something that kind of normalized the feelings I was having."

"Thank heaven for librarians."

"Right? It's no accident that I spent my whole career in libraries. Unfortunately, my grandmother didn't think it was normal at all. She was very Irish, very Catholic, and functionally illiterate. She truly believed the nuns would straighten me out. I thought I was supposed to *want* to be straightened out. At first, I thought they would have a way to fix me."

"Oh, Angela." Everly took her hands. They were slender hands, with oval-shaped nails and delicate wrists, and they looked remarkably like Everly's own. "You were never broken. You didn't need fixing."

"Thank you for saying that. But back then, I couldn't have known."

"Well," said Everly, "if that was the hard part, then I think we survived it." Then she noticed a shadow in Angela's eyes. "That wasn't the hard part, was it?"

Angela darted a look at Violet. "It was not."

"I'm used to hearing things," Violet said. "I work in the county prosecutor's office. Please go on."

"It's about the way I got pregnant." Angela pursed her lips. "Back then, we weren't even allowed to say *pregnant*. Most girls didn't know how it happened. I certainly didn't. There was no such thing as sex education in Catholic school, that's for sure. I came from a culture of profound ignorance about these things. My grandmother forbade me to even look at a boy." She shook her head. "Avoiding boys was not much of a challenge for me."

Everly shifted in her chair. She felt the breeze on her face, and saw it lift the wisps of hair around Angela's face. Her mother didn't like boys, but she ended up pregnant. Everly's stomach knotted. "So my... the man who fathered me..."

"Was not a good person." A look of terror darkened Angela's eyes.

"I'm listening." Everly looked at her daughter, who nodded.

"Whenever a new girl arrived at the Good Shepherd, she was sent to the clinic for a health exam—that was what we were told. Each inmate was taken there by one of the nuns. The nun waited outside while the doctor..." Her breath quickened, and she closed her eyes for a moment. "Sorry," she whispered.

Everly gently laid her hand over Angela's. "Take your time. Please. Take all the time you need." Inside she was screaming the unthinkable words. My father was a rapist. My father was a rapist.

Angela opened her eyes. "His name was Seamus Gilroy."

Everly took in the name like a noxious poison. The person who had fathered her had a name. Seamus Gilroy.

"He was a volunteer physician at the facility," Angela said, her voice cracking. "Under the pretense of examining me and 'treating' me for my 'affliction,' he raped me. It happened over a number of weeks. Finally, one of the other girls came with me to the clinic and made him stop. That was my friend Mairin. Mairin O'Hara. She wasn't timid, like me. She was brave, and she knew how to fight. Thanks to her, I didn't have to go back. But by that time, it was too late. I was already pregnant."

Everly gasped. "Angela, I'm so sorry. That's the worst thing I . . . oh, God." She felt a wave of nausea. "The . . . he's a rapist."

"Yes."

She recoiled from the images rapidly forming in her own head. "Is he . . . do you know where he is? What became of him?"

"Records from the state board of health indicate that he lost his license to practice in 1970. Beyond that, I don't know anything more. I suppose I could have dug deeper, but it took many years—lots of therapy—for me to deal with what happened. I didn't really want to spend time looking for him."

"Digging into the man's criminality wasn't your job," Violet said firmly.

Everly looked down at the floor, then at Angela's face. She could too easily picture that beautiful young girl, terrorized by a predatory doctor. "That never should have happened to you," she whispered. "I wish it never had. And I do realize what I'm saying. I'm here—I exist—because you were raped. And I still wish with all my heart that it hadn't happened."

"You had no control over how you got here," Angela said. "I'm just glad you're here." Her hand drifted down over her stomach in an unconscious gesture. "When I discovered I was pregnant, the nuns and my grandmother accused me of being a seductress."

"Blaming you for being raped," Violet said. "Great."

"As far as I know, no one held Seamus Gilroy to account," Angela said. "These days, we know that the Church was much more concerned about protecting its reputation than protecting children. And as for the baby, I was never given a choice. I was so scared and confused, I didn't push back against the idea of adoption—at first. And then, as the pregnancy progressed, I felt a bond forming with the baby—with you."

Angela's mouth softened with a small, fleeting smile. "I got it into my head that I would like to keep my child. I was filled with the urge to love you and raise you myself. Heavens, when I brought up the idea, all hell broke loose. I had to go to confession every day for a week. I did hours and hours of penance. I was lectured about being covered in sin. They said I'd be subjecting an innocent child to eternal damnation, because a baby born out of wedlock could not be baptized. They said if I intended to keep the baby, I'd have to pay all the fees to the Good Shepherd and to the hospital, hundreds of dollars they knew I didn't have. Still, I fantasized about running off. I concocted all these crazy plans."

Everly pictured her as a frightened teenager, alone against the world, a child trying to raise a child. Would they have had a chance? What would their lives have become?

"And then one night," Angela said, "my water broke. I thought I had wet myself. They took me away, and the nuns at the hospital were awful, too. Zero compassion for a frightened girl. They gave me a general anesthetic that I probably didn't need. I came to hours and hours later, alone in a hospital bed." She gazed at Everly's face. "That's when they told me the baby had been stillborn."

"You were lied to." Violet's voice was low and unsteady with rage.

"What do you call it these days—gaslighting," Angela agreed. "Yet I believed them. They kept me in the hospital for an entire week, maybe longer. I'd been given an episiotomy, and I was still actively bleeding, and my breasts were leaking, and I was probably swimming in hormones, about to lose my mind. They gave me so many sedatives, I lost track. I had no idea what to feel. Grief for a baby I'd never known? Relief that I wasn't pregnant anymore? Fear that it could happen again? I was not okay for a long time. I mean, I'd created this life inside my body, but I never once saw you, or held you." She paused. "Eventually, they sent me back to the Good Shepherd, and I was supposed to carry on as if nothing had happened."

Everly didn't know what to say. She looked over at Violet, who sat very still, tears slipping down her cheeks.

"I did ask about a burial," Angela said, "and all they would tell me was that the child had been laid to rest in consecrated ground. It's hard to describe the fog I was in. Could have been the drugs they gave me. So maybe I asked where this 'consecrated ground' might be, maybe I didn't. Either way, we now know I would have been lied to even if I'd asked. Later—after I escaped from the Good Shepherd—"

"Wait a minute. You *escaped?*" Violet sat forward, her eyes wide.

"I did, a few months after I was discharged from the hospital. They tried to keep me there, because they didn't believe they'd cured my 'affliction.'" She knotted her hands in her lap. "I simply couldn't take it anymore. A group of us escaped together, and we all went our separate ways."

Everly sat in silence. Her heart hurt as if it had been dealt a physical blow.

"It's a lot to take in, I know," Angela said.

Everly nodded. She took a tissue from the box on the table. She finally understood why there were no records to find. No letter for her in the archives, because her birth mother didn't know she had survived. Then she cleared her throat and said, "It's horrific. I hate that you were attacked by a monster. I hate that my birth was so traumatic for you. I'd do anything to change that."

"It's not your fault," said Angela. "None of this was your fault. Or mine."

The three of them sat listening to the sounds of springtime—chirping birds and a whispering breeze. The scent of lilac and hyacinth filled the air. Everly felt overwhelmed by awe and tender emotions.

"It wasn't your fault, obviously," she said to Angela, "but it's been your burden to bear. I can't tell you how sorry I am about that. I could say I wish I'd never been born, but... well—" She gestured at Violet.

Angela managed a wobbly smile. "We don't always get to choose the things that life hands out to us, do we? I can tell you that I found some measure of healing with years of therapy. Decades." She took Everly's hands. "I've had a lovely career, and I have a few close friends. I'm in a loving relationship now. I met Jean a couple of years ago, and we have a sweet little house in Brockport with a garden and two cats."

"That's wonderful," Everly said. "I would love to meet her sometime, if that's all right."

"I know Jean would like that," Angela said.

Somehow, they relaxed into conversation. They spoke of their lives—mundane matters, important matters. It didn't feel like an ordinary friendship. It felt more consequential in ways Everly had never experienced before. She opened her photo album to the old pictures of her life. It was an unremarkable but happy life—school plays, basketball games, piano recitals, holidays, her wedding and honeymoon, her kids through the years. Yet Angela gazed at them as if they were the Dead Sea Scrolls.

"I don't have much to show you," Angela said, taking out an album with just a handful of pictures. Some of the captions were carefully written in that curiously familiar script.

"Are you left-handed?" Everly asked.

"I am indeed," Angela said.

"We both are," Violet said. "All three of us are."

A negligible detail, but to Everly, who had grown up with two right-handed parents, it seemed significant.

"These pictures of you when you were younger," she said to Angela. She couldn't finish as a wave of sentiment rolled over her.

The similarities were remarkable. They marveled, laughed, and cried together. Finally, a missing piece of Everly's lifelong puzzle settled into place.

She was intrigued by an old-fashioned photo booth strip, showing a group of laughing girls all crammed together in the booth.

"I can't get over how much you and Violet look alike," Everly said.

"That's from Niagara Falls, summer of 1969," Angela said. "The summer we escaped from the Good Shepherd in a library bookmobile."

"Wait... the *bookmobile?* You have to tell us," Violet insisted.

Angela regarded the photo with a distant gaze. "Maybe you'd like to meet my friends. The ones who were with me at the Good Shepherd."

Chapter 29

"And here I thought I was going to kick back in my old age," Mairin said to Colleen and Patricia as they carried things to Mairin's car. Colleen had a bankers box of files, and Patricia brought a catering tray of little sandwiches and crumpets and sweets—records for the lawyers and refreshments for the meeting.

"You're not old, Mom," said Patricia. "You're just getting started."

"I'll remember that next time I get stuck in yoga class." Mairin opened the trunk and they put the boxes and the tray in. She wasn't sure the materials—odds and ends of the past that had lain in boxes and folders for years—would help with the legal proceeding Angela was building against the Good Shepherd Institute, but they'd been told to assume any small thing might be significant.

She turned and gave each of her daughters a hug. Her grown girls were her best friends—bossy Colleen with her red hair and fiery spirit to match, and the ever thoughtful, inventive Patricia, whose culinary skills had made her a local legend. "You know, I'm not going to pretend this won't be hard—not just for me and the girls. For you and your families, too."

The controversy in the local media and online was already gaining momentum. Much had happened since the discovery of the hidden records at the Good Shepherd. More irregular and illegal adoptions came to light, and the scandal made its way into the local papers and media, then the national news. Calls went out seeking survivors of the Good

Shepherd, and women came forward, finally finding their voices after decades of silence. There were multiple causes of action, including the potential for a class action against the diocese.

"We're a well-known family in the area," Mairin said, "and not everyone is going to love us for stirring up trouble with the Church. Sometimes I wonder what it will do—"

"Mom," said Patricia, "what would it do to us if you kept silent and did nothing?"

Mairin gave her hand a squeeze, feeling a wave of relief and gratitude for her daughters, these excellent women who filled her with strength. "I raised you right. And now I'm off to the big city," she said, her comment tinged with irony. Buffalo, just a short drive away, was a city that felt like a small town, a patchwork of neighborhoods that held the past in their tired old bones. As she drove away, she thought about the joyous celebration of the past weekend. A rowdy crew of family and friends had come to honor her and Flynn on their fiftieth wedding anniversary.

Mairin and Flynn had planned a private "fifty-moon" celebration, just the two of them on a luxury Mediterranean cruise. But the trip was months away. In the meantime, Mairin had other things on her mind.

The girls of the Good Shepherd—they would always be the girls despite their ages—had all agreed to go on record with their experiences. Although Angela had suffered the most egregious offenses, each one of them had been damaged by their time at the laundry. Each one had been the victim of criminal abuse. There was more healing to be done.

Angela's granddaughter and grandson, both lawyers, had introduced them to the legal team that specialized in seeking justice for survivors of church and institutional abuse. The state of New York had opened a window, lifting the statute of limitations for crimes against child victims and adult survivors.

The law offices of Roberta and Richard Sherman were located in the shadow of the Erie County Courthouse. Mairin had only been to court for jury duty a few times. She stepped out of the car to look up at the imposing neo-Gothic structure.

Angela arrived with her daughter, Everly, and granddaughter, Violet, and they crossed the parking lot to help Mairin with what she'd brought.

"You three, I swear," Mairin said, regarding them with admiration. "I feel like a theme song should start playing when you ladies show up."

"Go on with your bad self," Angela said. "We're early. I couldn't sleep a wink."

"It's a beautiful day. We can wait over there." Violet gestured at a bench in the shade of a stately tree in the Niagara Square park.

"Let me get a picture." Mairin set down her box and took out her phone. "And then I have something to show you."

The three of them posed together near a cherry tree that was bursting with blossoms. Everly, a professional model, organized the shot. It was almost like a time-lapse photo, they were so much alike. The slender height. The blond waves. The huge, expressive eyes. The effect was magnified because there were three of them, all so similar. Mairin was struck by a wave of sentiment for her friend, this woman she had known most of her life, this woman who had faced so many struggles alone. At last, Angela had found her missing pieces.

"What is it you wanted to show me?" she asked.

Mairin lifted the lid of the bankers box. "I spent hours hunting for this," she said. "Remember when we first found each other at the Tesla statue?"

"Of course," Angela said. "Summer of 1974. It was such a thrill to see you again."

"More than you know." Mairin handed her a vintage Kodak processing envelope. The photos they'd taken that day with her old Instamatic were faded, but the images were clear enough—two young women with the misty veil of the Falls behind them, their brilliant smiles masking the scars of the ordeal they'd survived. In the pictures, they seem balanced on the precipice of time, ready for a new beginning, naively willing to embrace whatever life had in store for them.

"Those outfits," Violet murmured, pointing out Angela's red miniskirt and Mairin's denim shift dress, lavishly accessorized with cheap, chunky jewelry. "They're awesome."

"I asked a guy to take our picture, remember?" Mairin said.

Angela nodded as she studied the photos with a thoughtful smile.

"The guy was one of our maple syrup suppliers." Mairin fixed her eyes on Angela's daughter. "Everly, check it out. The man's name was Roy Barrett, and he was there with his wife and little girl. And when he was taking our picture, his kid photobombed us." She indicated one of the prints, which showed two smiling young women and a laughing, towheaded child posing in front of them.

Both Everly and Angela leaned in, and almost on cue, their eyes filled with tears.

"We're both in this picture." Everly's voice broke as she pressed a hand to her chest. "It's . . . it's . . ."

"It's kind of a miracle," said Angela in a low, unsteady whisper. "You and I were in the same spot at the same time."

Mairin moved back, giving them a moment to recover. Violet handed out tissues. "You were both there," she said. "You were there together, and you didn't know. None of us knew."

"I wish I'd known," Angela whispered. "Why didn't I recognize my own flesh and blood?"

"Because the nuns took her from you," Violet said.

"I wish I could remember," Everly said. "I'd give anything to remember that moment."

"You would have been five years old," Angela said, dabbing at her cheeks with a tissue. "I do remember that you were very cute, and full of energy." She turned to Mairin. "Thank you for finding these amazing photos. You've been a wonderful friend to me all my life. I don't think I tell you that enough."

"Keep the pictures," Mairin said. "I scanned them all."

"The lawyers are going to think we're basket cases," Everly said. "Here, give me something to carry." She dried her eyes, then picked up one of the boxes. "Is that baked goods I smell?"

"My daughter Patricia is a chef. It's going to be a long day, and she knew we'd need sustenance." Mairin saw Angela stiffen slightly. They might need more than finger sandwiches before the day was out.

Helen and Odessa arrived together, exiting a sleek rented navy blue

Tesla. Mairin felt a wave of satisfaction in the company of these women. She had plenty of friends—her bestie, Fiona, and so many others she'd been blessed with in her life. But the friends she'd made at the Good Shepherd shared a special bond. She could feel it now in her bones, and it steeled her nerves for the coming ordeal.

For Mairin, revisiting the past was like reopening a wound that had never healed properly. But there was also a measure of relief in knowing that she wasn't the only one still experiencing symptoms of trauma decades later. Finally, there was context for the unspecified distress they had all experienced in some form or other, all their lives. It had a name—Post-Traumatic Stress Disorder. The flashbacks, nightmares, hypervigilance, and triggers of trauma were not figments of their imagination. Simply being able to talk about it validated the experience.

"Y'all ready for this?" asked Odessa as they waited in the lobby to be led to the conference room.

"We'll have to air all our guilty secrets," said Helen.

"We're not guilty," Odessa pointed out. "We were never guilty."

"And there are no more secrets," Mairin said. "Secrets are what you keep when you're ashamed of the truth. We have no reason to be ashamed ever again." As they stepped into the lobby together, Mairin felt the weight of what they were about to do. She touched Angela's arm, held her back a little. Angela's trauma was in a class by itself.

"Are you sure?" she whispered. "It's going to be hard."

"I can do hard things," Angela told her. "Jean and I have talked about it at length. I have to pursue this, not only for me but for all the girls like us, and for future girls. So people will know what happened. It's been years, but we were all haunted, weren't we?" Her gaze moved around the group. "This will set us free. The more we get out, the smaller it becomes."

Mairin bit her lip, then said what had been on her mind, what had been keeping her awake at night. "Angela, I wish I'd protected you more. I wish I'd done more."

Angela squeezed her hand. "Listen. You were the friend I needed when I needed someone. For fifty years, that's what you've been to me. I had to be able to stand up for myself. I learned that from you. From that feisty little corkscrew-curled redhead I met in the worst place in the world."

"She's not wrong," Helen said. "You showed us what it was like to have a spine, and grit, and even humor in that place."

"Not to mention a mean left hook," Odessa added.

Mairin couldn't speak as they followed a receptionist through an open door to the conference room. Her friends' words had fallen over her like a balm. Maybe living a life of consequence didn't mean awards and accolades, but simply being a source of true friendship.

Everyone found a seat around a table furnished with yellow legal pads and pens, and a printed meeting agenda. At the head of the table, Angela stood tall and resolute. Her hands trembled slightly, betraying the pain and trauma she had carried all her life. "I'm truly indebted to you girls," she said. "Having your support makes anything seem possible."

"We're going to see this through with you," said Everly. "That's what family is for. And friends, too."

Angela's eyes glistened. "I'm still getting used to the idea of family."

Mr. Sherman, the lead attorney, arrived with two assistants. The silver threads in his hair caught the muted light, and he wore rimless glasses that seemed to magnify his gaze. His suit bore the gentle creases of countless hours spent at a desk. As he arranged some documents before him, his fingers betrayed a brief tremor that he acknowledged with a self-deprecating smile that quickly vanished under the practiced steadiness of his resolve. While his assistants connected everyone to a shared screen at one end of the room, Mr. Sherman explained how the options for victims had expanded so claims that otherwise would have been barred by the statute of limitations could still be pursued.

"You say we can file a suit," Angela said. "But against whom? They're like ghosts. Most of the nuns who harmed us are gone. The entire operation closed up shop decades ago."

"But the institution didn't disappear," said Mr. Sherman. "Nor did the cause of action." An assistant distributed a document that named all the defendants, from the Sisters of Charity as an entity all the way up to the diocese of Buffalo and the bishop himself. "Now. I'm obliged to tell you that the diocese has a reconciliation and compensation program. Some survivors choose this because remuneration can be awarded in a much shorter period of time than if you file a lawsuit. However, you'd have to waive the right to further action if you accept the terms of the settlement." He handed out another document explaining the program.

"Reconciliation?" asked Angela, frowning at the information. "How can we possibly have a reconciliation process if the truth doesn't come out? Who would we even be reconciling with? I have no wish to be reconciled to the Catholic Church or anyone in it."

"Reconcile is just a legal term, referring to a settlement offer. You don't have to reconcile with anyone, just accept the terms of the settlement."

"We'll support whatever you decide," Everly said.

"I've already decided," said Angela. "I won't settle before the story comes out."

"I have further information on the doctor." Violet passed out more paperwork. "Seamus Gilroy was married, and he had at least six children that I could find records for. He lost his license in 1970. He died a couple years later of an apparent drug overdose."

Mairin felt a prickle at the nape of her neck. Just hearing about the doctor took her back to her first day at the Good Shepherd. She still remembered his weirdly flat eyes, his damp lips, the antiseptic smell of him. Then she remembered the fire that had driven her to fight back, even using a plaster cross to defend herself. You did good, she told her younger self. You did good.

"Six children?" Odessa shivered. "Wonder if any of them mourned him?"

"I have to warn you," said Mr. Sherman, "it's going to be an uphill climb. The Church will do everything in its power to deny responsibility. They will try to contradict your claims. They'll contend that written records no longer exist. They love to challenge claims in which alleged victims can't recall specific dates, places, and times—"

"I have dates," said Helen. "And specifics. I kept a log of each day I was there. I wrote down everything." She brought up a digital presentation on the shared screen—columns of Chinese characters made with a laundry marker on old, creased paper. "I brought the notes with me the day we escaped. Rolled up and stuffed down my shirt." She displayed each page in the original form, and next to it, the translation in English. "My parents tried to lodge a complaint against the Good Shepherd back in the seventies, but it went nowhere."

"It wouldn't have," said Mr. Sherman. "Especially not back then. The diocese was all-powerful, and the key city officials were Catholic—administrators, the DA, most of the judges."

"This is gold." Violet studied the document on the screen. "Dates, times, names..."

"It's going to be very helpful," said Mr. Sherman. "Still, I have to warn you again—these things don't always go well. The defendants will push back. They might say that witnesses are gone or too old to remember. They could say you have false memories."

"They can't say that about me," Angela declared, locking eyes with her daughter. "My 'false memory' is sitting across the table from me, eating a crumpet."

ANGELA WAS TOLD to expect resistance from Gilroy's family. The legal team had warned her to anticipate shock, confusion, and denial from people who might have known a different man from the monster who had attacked young girls at the Good Shepherd. She and Everly were determined to try, however. Although not mandatory to the case, a DNA test proving that Everly Barrett Lasko was indeed the biological daughter of Seamus Gilroy would be a powerful, irrefutable piece of evidence.

Besides proving that the man had impregnated Angela, the data would verify that Everly's adoption had been fraudulent. The Sisters of Charity had misrepresented and concealed the truth of her birth. They had denied Angela her rights as Everly's mother.

"People can't be compelled to allow a DNA test," Violet explained. "They're likely to see it as an invasion of privacy."

Angela and her legal team encountered refusals from one Gilroy son and a daughter. There had been no replies from a couple of others.

It was Mairin who finally found a way in. A lifelong resident of Buffalo, she had a way of finding connections between people. An old friend, a priest named Kevin Doyle, had a number of Gilroys in his parish. Father Doyle had a quiet but urgent word with a certain one of his parishioners, and persuaded him to meet with Angela.

Now Angela, Everly, and Violet had a meeting scheduled with Thomas

Gilroy, born in 1962. A Frank Lloyd Wright scholar who had worked on the restoration of the Darwin Martin House, Thomas Gilroy was the father of two, grandfather of one, and a volunteer with the Buffalo City Mission. He agreed to meet Angela, Everly, and Violet in the library of the Martin House, a stunning complex that had been the architect's personal favorite, filled with soaring, light-filled spaces and surrounded by a beautiful park.

The library—always Angela's safe space—was furnished with prairie-style tables and chairs, and lavish volumes about the artist's work. As a member of the museum board, Mr. Gilroy had arranged for the meeting to take place after hours.

Angela's stomach churned when she looked at the man. He was older than Seamus Gilroy had been, but something about him reminded her of the doctor—a certain set of the shoulders. The shape of his jaw. The long-lashed, watchful eyes. She must have given some indication of her discomfort, because Violet moved closer to her and squeezed her hand.

"I read the report you sent through Father Doyle," the younger Gilroy said. "That man doesn't sound like the person I knew as my father. He was a gifted physician. A devout Catholic. We went to church every Sunday."

Violet consulted her notes. "You were six when Angela Denny became pregnant while an inmate at the Good Shepherd—the place where Seamus Gilroy served as physician."

The room was silent. Angela stared at the surface of the table, struck by the knowledge that the man sitting across from her was Everly's half brother. He kept staring at Everly and Violet with a probing gaze, as though trying to detect any similarities they might have to his family. She wondered if they bore a resemblance to his own sisters, or perhaps his daughter.

Now Everly faced him with a sturdy conviction that made Angela proud. "The nuns who arranged the adoption gave my parents fraudulent information, so there was never any way for me to learn who I am. It was not until this year that I found Angela, my birth mother. I'm sure you've seen the news reports of the hidden records of the Good Shepherd coming to light."

"I have," he said, shifting in his seat.

"There's an easy way to know if Seamus Gilroy was my biological father. A DNA test."

"I don't need a test to prove what I already know," Mr. Gilroy shot back. He pushed his chair away from the table. "I'm not sure why I agreed to this meeting in the first place." He got up and went to the door.

"Imagine not knowing your identity," Everly said to him. "Do you know what a pre-adoption birth certificate is?"

He turned back. "I do not," he said.

"Do you know I've never been out of the country?" Everly told him. "In order to get a passport, a pre-adoption birth certificate is required to prove an adoption is legitimate. I've applied for one several times, but I keep being told it doesn't exist. But I exist, don't I?"

"I fail to see how this is relevant." His voice was sharp.

"I never knew fully who I am," Everly explained. "What happened to me when I was born is not a victimless crime. It's human trafficking. I don't feel like an adoptee. I feel like stolen goods."

"I'm sorry you feel that way, but I can't help you." He shrugged, but seemed to hesitate.

"Even if you don't want to help us, you can help your family," Violet pointed out. She leaned forward and pinned the man with her gaze. The temperature in the room seemed to drop a few degrees. "This story's only made the local news so far, and your father's name hasn't been mentioned yet. But it will be, and the story won't just be local—it'll make national headlines. It will come out. And when it does, for the sake of your family, you'll want to be able to say you were cooperative."

Gilroy's eyes narrowed in hostility. Angela thought for a moment that they'd wasted their time once again.

But then Thomas Gilroy came back to the table and slowly sat down. Now those eyes glimmered with uncertainty. "What do you need from me?"

"Who would have thought we'd get help from a *priest?*" Odessa said, stepping with the others into the meeting room of the rectory where Father Kevin Doyle lived.

"I've known him almost all my life," Mairin said. "Back then, he was the coolest kid. He was my first crush. My first date."

"Wonder what made him want to join the priesthood," said Helen. "That date, maybe?"

"Very funny. He served in the army," Mairin pointed out. "He went to law school *and* seminary. I suppose, like all of us, he was looking for something. They're not all . . . like that. He is as horrified as everyone else about clergy abuse. When he worked in the chancery as canon lawyer, he found out the diocese had withheld the names of dozens of priests accused of abuse and was keeping them in the ministry, and he went to the press about it."

"In that case, we could use a few more like him," said Odessa.

Mairin was glad she'd stayed in touch with Kevin, who had officiated at several weddings at Wayward Farm.

"Father Doyle gave me the nudge I needed," said a voice from the doorway.

Mairin and the others turned as one toward the door. "Janice," she whispered. "Oh my gosh, *Janice.*" Her appearance was both a shock and completely unsurprising. "Janice Dunn, as I live and breathe."

Though lined by the passing of years, her small, sharp-featured face and pointy glasses were utterly familiar. But now she wore a modern nun's habit—a calf-length navy skirt with white stockings and a white blouse. A matching headpiece fell gracefully down her shoulders. She was one of the last remaining nuns in the Sisters of Charity motherhouse in the Riverdale section of the Bronx.

She teared up as she greeted each woman. "The wayward sisterhood," she said.

"That's us," Angela said. "I appreciate you coming. I know you were reluctant at first."

"I didn't want anything to do with this . . . situation. Which is not like me, is it? I was the worst tattletale, wasn't I? But I prayed on it, and I couldn't in good conscience stay away."

"Nothing about this is easy," Odessa said, ushering her to a chair. "The only thing harder is staying quiet about the things that happened at the Good Shepherd. How was the train?"

"Long," Janice said, and then her old sly humor slipped out. "How were the last fifty years?"

"Also long," Odessa said with a grin.

The women spent some time getting reacquainted. "I owe you an apology," Mairin said to Janice. "For screwing up the day we ran away from the Good Shepherd. Nothing worked out the way we'd planned."

"No, it didn't," Janice agreed. "Kay and I didn't even try to run. What would be the point? Kay was in full-on meltdown. The lights and whistles were too much for her. It was all I could do to keep her calm."

"That was incredibly loyal of you to stick by her," Odessa said.

"When they took us to the police station, you were the only one who could calm her down. Were they horrible to you when they took you back?" asked Helen.

"About like you'd expect," Janice admitted.

"And yet you took vows." Angela regarded her with a mystified expression. "You became one of them."

"I became a nun, but I was never one of them," Janice said. "I felt called. Not just to help Kay, but girls like me, girls who grew up in foster homes that weren't very nice. I had this idea that I could be a force for reform, and I dedicated my service to that. I spent most of my life as a caseworker for people with developmental disabilities."

Mairin felt a beat of emotion as she regarded Janice. By now Mairin was old enough to know how very complicated people could be. A person was never just one thing, and choices were based on factors that others might not be aware of. Mairin's own mother had been proof of that.

"Whatever became of Kay, do you know?" asked Odessa.

Janice sighed and reached for a tissue. "Ah, Kay. She had nothing but love in her heart. I still remember that little mouse she used to feed in the dorm. She became a ward of the state when she came of age, and she was sent to a group home. By then, I was a novice in Morristown." Janice braided her fingers together. "We'll never know what she suffered, because I never saw her again. She wasn't able to tell me what happened to her in that home. I learned that she died of sepsis when she was in her twenties."

"So young," Odessa said. "That's heartbreaking. That group home must have been a nightmare."

"Denise Curran is gone, too," Angela said. "My granddaughter tracked down records showing that she died of alcohol-related illness in her forties. No record of a marriage or children."

"Ah, Denise," Mairin said softly. "She was tough. But she showed us her heart. I don't think she ever recovered from the abuses at the Good Shepherd."

"That place ruined her," Odessa said. "And so many others. We're only beginning to find out. We were survivors . . . but just think of what Denise and girls like her could have been if they hadn't been thrown away by the system."

"That's what's at stake here," Mairin said. "That's why we're doing something."

Janice nodded solemnly. "Too many girls were destroyed by that place. But I've learned that not all sisters in Christ are the same. And I won't be afraid to say so when I sit for the deposition tomorrow."

IN A CONFERENCE room of the courthouse, Angela sat doubled over in a wooden chair, her head between her knees as she struggled with a barrage of anxiety. After months of preparation, she was finally about to give her testimony in open court.

She had prepared for this like an athlete in training, yet now that the moment had arrived, she felt crushed by the weight of old memories. Beside her, Jean rested a hand on the small of her back, moving it in light, soothing circles. Angela gritted her teeth and lifted her head. She didn't need a soothing touch. She didn't need to be touched at all.

Jean must have sensed something, because she stopped and stood up, strong and beautiful in a knit suit, her silver hair polished to a sheen. "I can only imagine what you're feeling right now. But don't make me guess what you need."

Angela managed a brief smile. "You're the love of my life," she said. "But . . . could you go find Mairin?"

"Be right back." Jean gave her shoulder a squeeze and hurried out.

She slipped out the door, but not before Angela caught a glimpse and heard the babble of the crowd in the foyer. The sensational aspects of the case had attracted all manner of attention—traditional media, online influencers, bloggers, vloggers, trolls, and general rubberneckers. Much of the case involved stultifying procedural matters and paperwork, lawyers wrangling over what seemed like minutiae, requests and rulings. Still, the crux of the case was an all-too-human story—the abuses she had suffered while in the care of the Good Shepherd.

Mairin slipped into the room and took a seat next to her. For a moment, neither of them spoke. Then Angela said, "You were like a breath of fresh air, that first day I met you at the Good Shepherd."

"I was scared shitless," Mairin said.

"Well, it came off as bravado. All those escape attempts—"

"All those failures," Mairin pointed out.

"But we finally got away, didn't we? Seriously, I felt braver just being around you."

"Thanks for saying that. I'm just proud to be your friend."

Angela squeezed her hand. Mairin's testimony, Helen's detailed diary, statements from Odessa and Janice and other women who had endured the Good Shepherd had painted a devastating picture of the abuses that went on at the institution. Sister Bernadette had submitted responses to an interrogatory, verifying the complicity of the nuns. The diocese had no defense against the irrefutable fact that DNA evidence proved Seamus Gilroy had fathered Angela's child, although the lawyers had warned Angela that there might be an attempt to characterize the rape as consensual.

The Gilroy family had been divided over the issue, and the rift was apparent in the courtroom. Some of the doctor's older children were convinced that their father was no rapist, merely the target of a seductive teenage girl. Thomas and his two younger sisters had reluctantly accepted the truth and awkwardly extended their sympathy to Angela. Thomas had said, *I guess a part of me knew the moment I laid eyes on your daughter.* They'd introduced themselves to Everly—their half sister. Everly was hesitant yet understandably curious. She wasn't ready to forge ahead with a relationship, but was keeping an open mind.

A soft knock came at the door. Mairin gave Angela's hand a final, firm squeeze. "Listen, Ang. You've been amazing through all of this. But you don't have to be brave today. You just have to tell your story, exactly as you lived it."

"Yes," Angela said, getting to her feet. "This day has been a long time coming. I'm ready."

Chapter 30

Mairin dressed for court with care. Morning light streamed through the lace curtains of the bedroom, falling across the old plank floor and braided rug. She checked her reflection, satisfied that the navy dress and tasseled pumps projected understated confidence. Or so she hoped.

"You're different." Flynn eyed her warmly in the mirror from behind, his hands resting on her shoulders.

"How so?"

"You've been sleeping better, for one thing."

"Have I?" She tilted her head, putting on a small gold earring in the shape of a Celtic knot. "Maybe it's because it's all out there now. There's nothing left to hold in, and the past has lost its grip. Oh, Flynn, Angela was magnificent, like a queen, sitting there, telling all the world what happened. It's got to be enough. It has to be." She leaned down and put an old Mercury dime in her shoe. "For luck," she said. "No matter what happens today, at least we brought things to light."

It had been a long road for them all, and most especially for Angela. The constant back-and-forth between the lawyers and the diocese legal team had dragged on forever. As expected, other victims of the Good Shepherd had come forward, and other suits were in process. But Angela's was the first, and her success or failure would affect many others.

"You did," he said. "I'm proud of you. I should tell you that more often."

"Flynn," she said, "sometimes I wonder... when I was a girl, just a Buffalo girl picking apples in the summer, I always thought I'd do something big. A big dream. A big life. Now I wonder—did I? Did I put enough good in the world?"

"Don't you see? You've done all those things. You've done them your way, standing by your friends, raising your family, sheltering workers, building the farm into a legacy. Mairin, you've done enough. More than enough."

"Flynn Gallagher, I totally and completely love you," she said. "And I should tell you *that* more often."

She held his hand during the drive to the city, so very grateful for this man. She had loved him in countless ways over countless days, in the quiet moments and the spaces between words. Now she drew strength from him, vowing to face the uncertainty that lay ahead with determination.

The news and social media had erupted into a firestorm around not just Angela, but everyone involved. Mairin had all but shut down her presence online, because there were those who were still convinced the Church could do no wrong. She and the others were aware of the cost of speaking up—yet they didn't back down. As a family, the Gallaghers had been on the receiving end of some online hate—bombed with negative reviews of Wayward Farm, of Patricia's cooking, even of Dr. Liam O'Hara's medical practice. But the voices of support were much louder and more authentic. Ultimately, they'd all agreed that shining light on the truth was worth the cost.

En route to the courthouse, they passed the district still known as the Fruit Belt, although it was no longer a region of orchards and farms, but a sprawling medical complex bisected by the expressway. A few of the older homes stood as reminders of times past. Mairin still remembered racing with Fiona from block to block, chasing the ice cream truck or playing a game of hide-and-seek. She'd had a crush on a boy named Kevin, and she'd dreamed of a life of adventure. That time of innocence was long past, yet something of it had always lived inside her, giving her hope.

In the shadow of the granite edifice of the courthouse, she met up with the others. There was a flurry of family and friends around them. With pride in his voice, Odessa's husband told everyone she had nearly finished writing her new memoir. The girls who had been silenced would finally have a voice.

Accompanied by her action-star husband and handsome son, Helen bore herself with military precision, even though rules prohibited her from wearing her dress uniform to a court appearance. Angela and Jean, newlyweds now, were surrounded by Everly and family.

The four of them came together and moved as one up the courthouse steps. Their nerves seemed to jangle in unison even as they drew strength from one another. They'd survived an ordeal few people knew about—beaten, locked in a closet, forced into labor, a baby whisked away by criminals—and they had shared their demons with the world, remembering out loud the suffering they'd endured. They had done their best, reconstructing their experiences at the Good Shepherd. Bringing the truth to light had been a painful cleansing.

The packed courtroom was alive with spectators in the upper and lower galleries. The air was filled with the burble of murmuring voices and electronic beeps, the shuffling of papers, and the occasional cough.

Officials from the diocese, along with their lawyers and spokespeople, filled the gallery behind the defendants' table. In a wheelchair in the aisle sat Rotrude, righteous and impenitent, glaring in defiance through wire-rimmed glasses that magnified her fierce eyes, always the steadfast defender of the Church.

A small, dark figure sat next to her—Bernadette, her gaze darting anxiously between the people from the diocese and Angela's team. Father Kevin Doyle pointedly took a seat near the front of the room—on the plaintiffs' side.

Mairin was surprised when Bernadette stood abruptly and muttered something to Rotrude. Odessa nudged Helen and Angela, and they all watched the elderly nun as she stood at her full height, her cheeks flushed. With slow, deliberate movements, Bernadette removed her wimple and veil. The layers of stiffened linen fell away, and she let them drop to the wooden bench. Her cropped gray hair was matted every which way, spiky and downy like that of a baby bird.

Rotrude glared up at her, eyes smoldering, a gaze Mairin recognized even now. The older nun hissed an order—*Sit down*. Mairin expected Bernadette to melt into submission the way she always did, but Bernadette took a step back, her gaze sweeping over the diocesan officials and their defense team. Then she took the rosary from around her waist, dropped it in Rotrude's lap, and turned away, crossing the aisle and taking a seat next to Father Kevin.

"I hope the judgment goes your way," she said to Angela. "My role in your ordeal is an unforgivable offense. I wish you well."

"You did your part," said Angela. "You finally told the truth."

Then a bailiff arrived, commanding all to rise as the judge entered the courtroom.

As the doors of the courthouse swung open, sunlight spilled onto the steps, casting a glow over the gathered crowd. The women exited the courthouse the same way they'd entered, four abreast, heads held high, hands clasped in solidarity. They were shadowed by their legal team as they moved to the podium that had been set up for the press. Microphones bristled from the lectern, and cables snaked down the stone steps.

"Finally, after decades of suffering and silence, we have a moment of accountability," said the lead attorney. Mr. Sherman summed up the proceeding, which found that the Sisters of Charity, under the diocese of Buffalo, were negligent and complicit in the abuse suffered by Angela Denny. Although there was no real way to compensate for the soul-deep damage inflicted, the matter would be resolved at a number that recognized the magnitude of the culpability and harm caused by the Good Shepherd.

"It's not a victory," Angela said, taking a moment at the microphones. In her posture and steady voice, she personified resilience and an unyielding spirit that refused to be silenced. "But it's a defeat for institutions like the Good Shepherd, and the shameful conduct and complicity of the diocese."

Mairin swelled with pride in her beautiful friend. She gripped hands with Helen and Odessa, who stood by her side.

"I am not the winner here," Angela continued. "There is nothing to be won from the ordeal I survived. Money is not at the heart of what I need most. But there will be justice. What happened, happened. My story has been told."

Chapter 31

At Wayward Farm, the apple harvest was underway. A few workers balanced on the orchard ladders, their long burlap sacks slung from their shoulders. The tinny sound of a radio played, reminding Mairin of the days of her youth. The aroma of cider wafted from the big wooden press. She waved to the workers, inviting them to help themselves to a drink.

Flynn and Seal were waiting for her at the end of the orchard. He took her hand and they stood together, streaked in sunset colors, watching as the workday ended and people went to their cottages or trucks. "Look what you made here, Mairin," he said.

"We did it together," she said. Seal's tail thumped against her leg.

He nodded, smiling down at Mairin. "We did good."

She felt cherished and rapt, filled with wonder as she took in the beauty of the moment. She had learned over the years to notice even the smallest moment, because sometimes that was all there was. Her heart filled with gratitude for him, and for the home where they'd raised their family, and made a place for broken girls to find shelter and purpose.

They could see a few cars arriving from the road, passing the spot where the old hippie bus used to sit. "Time to go," she said to Flynn. "I hope you're hungry. Patricia and her team have been working all day."

They walked together to greet their guests—friends and family coming to mark the conclusion of the court case. It wasn't a celebration—

never that—but a gathering. Tonight's event would offer a chance for people to talk and reflect, or maybe to simply sit in silence together and enjoy a glass of wine. Angela and Jean and their newfound family were surrounded by Odessa and Helen and their loved ones, chatting away as everyone moved to the banquet table set up under the outdoor chandeliers that hung from the old hickory tree. Servers circulated with trays of champagne and hors d'oeuvres, and "Runaway" by Del Shannon drifted from the garden speakers.

"Give me a minute," Mairin whispered to Flynn. Suddenly, every breath felt saturated by the weight of what she was feeling. He stopped walking and kept hold of her hand.

"Take all the time you need," he said.

Mairin drew in a breath, steadying herself. She knew that healing would not come all at once, and they were only at the beginning. But the world was new and fresh, she thought. She looked at the others, sipping their welcome drinks and chatting together. They were light and shining, like her. They were old. Like her. They were confident and beautiful. Like her. They would forever be wayward girls. Like her.

A Note from the Author

When I posted a photo of a historic walled complex in Buffalo to a large Facebook group called "Buffalore," I didn't expect the deluge of comments that flooded in. I knew then that there were stories to be told, so I got to work on *Wayward Girls*.

Although most of the incidents in this novel are fictional, they are inspired by true events. The systemic abuses perpetrated by the Magdalene laundries have been documented in Ireland. In the nineteenth and twentieth centuries, the practice spread to many countries around the world, including the United States, where there were at least thirty-eight such institutions. Women and girls, most from poor homes, were regularly confined to these religious-run, state-sanctioned prison systems of slave labor and abuse.

The Good Shepherd Institute (also known as Our Lady of Charity for the order of Roman Catholic nuns who ran it) at 485 Best Street in Buffalo operated as a home for girls from the 1880s to the 1970s. Although the characters in this novel are purely fictional, the storylines were informed by the lived experiences of real victims at this location and similar institutions across the country. The abuses suffered by girls as young as twelve included harsh corporal punishment, shaming, and isolation in dark closets. A former inmate of the Best Street location described being locked inside a broom closet so small that she had to draw her knees to her chest to sit down. There was also a shower room referred to as the Dungeon Room, where women were confined in darkness, and they could hear the sound of scurrying rodents.

These and other atrocities have been verified by accounts in scholarly and court documents, and by testimony from former inmates. Currently there are multiple lawsuits involving the Good Shepherd, brought by individuals who suffered harm at the hands of the Catholic organizations responsible for operating them.

The library bookmobile did in fact pay regular visits to the Good Shepherd on Best Street, although the escape using the library van is pure invention on my part.

The Magdalene laundry on Clare Street in Limerick, Ireland—referenced in Deirdre's backstory—was still in operation until 1990 and is now the site of the Limerick School of Art and Design. The local government there is attempting to seal the records of the mother and baby homes, obstructing access to information that could help families know where they came from.

According to the *New York Times* and other sources, there is evidence of falsely recorded adoptions arranged between 1946 and 1969 by the St. Patrick's Guild, an adoption society run by the Sisters of Charity. The same practice also occurred in the United States and other countries. Many girls were pressured against their will to surrender their parental rights. Others were told falsely that their babies didn't survive. Between 1945 and 1973, an estimated 1.5 million to 4 million women in the United States lost their children to unauthorized, irregular, or forced adoption.

The Catholic League and other church organizations continue to deny, gaslight, and lie about the role of the Church in these abuses—even as they disingenuously establish funds to compensate and silence survivors. In 2019, Bishop Richard Malone resigned from the diocese of Buffalo. In 2020, the diocese filed for bankruptcy, and in 2024 its headquarters in downtown Buffalo and other properties went up for sale. Diocesan officials announced that the diocese would be putting forth $100 million to settle the numerous abuse claims lodged against it. However, the diocese also filed a motion to block plaintiffs from pursuing civil claims.

Regarding the specific dates and time frames associated with the Child Victims Act and the Adult Survivors Act, I took some liberties for dramatic purposes. Currently in New York State, the age for taking action under the Child Victims Act is capped at fifty-five, and the Adult Survivors Act lookback period ended in November 2023. But there can be exceptions, and help is still available for victims.

If you suffered abuse of any kind, it was not your fault. You have the right to contact a local child protection agency, a private attorney, a support group, an abuse hotline, or a mental health professional. Victims can also reach out to organizations devoted to helping victims of clergy abuse such as SNAP (Survivors Network of Those Abused by Priests) or RAINN (Rape, Abuse and Sexual Exploitation National Network). If you believe someone is in imminent danger or this is a situation of current abuse involving a minor, please call 911.

Acknowledgments

A novelist works alone to bring her stories to life, but if she's lucky, she is graced with plenty of help along the way. Thank you for research help from Geri Krotow—a talented author and Buffalo native who went above and beyond for a writer friend. To Cynthia Van Ness, librarian of the Buffalo History Museum, to the multilingual Dave Richter, to attorney Richard Serbin and his assistant Marianne, and to author and lawyer Robert Dugoni for input on legal details. A very special thank-you to participants in the Facebook groups "Buffalore" and "Survivors of Good Shepherd/Magdalene Laundries in North America" for their informative and sometimes wrenching posts about the Good Shepherd in Buffalo.

My writing group—Warren Read, Maureen McQuerry, Lois Faye Dyer, and Anjali Banerjee—offered feedback and encouragement through draft after draft of this story. I'm especially grateful to Diane Shanley, keen-eyed copy editor, and to Anne Caroline Drake for her excellent proofreading skills and insightful comments.

Thanks to my editor, Rachel Kahan, who has a magic touch when it comes to bringing a book to life. I so appreciate your trust and respect, insightful feedback, and your creativity and patience. Thank you for believing in this project and for helping to shape it into something truly special.

Thanks and love to my agent, Meg Ruley, who has been in my corner since the previous century. You and Annelise Robey have been my steadfast partners, and through many years and many books I've grown and benefited immeasurably thanks to your industry knowledge, smart instincts, determination, humor, encouragement, caring, and love.

Special thanks and heartfelt gratitude to Mary Odermat for always encouraging the love and support of the Odermat and Angel family and all of their animals—Claire and Lance, Jake and Charlie, and their furry friends: Seal, Ares, The Bear, Buckle, Juice Newton, Ranger, Trestles. This family's unwavering support and dedication to pet rescue is making a profound difference in the lives of countless animals in need.

I can't believe I'm lucky enough to have a husband like Jerry Gundersen, who listened to me read the *entire first draft* of this book during a cross-country drive. Payment will be made in the coin of the realm.

Finally, I would like to thank *you*, the reader, for taking the time to read this novel. There are many steps between my first inspiration for a story and the book finding its way into your hands—my lone self, laboring in isolation for months, followed by a flurry of activity from literary and rights agents, editor and publisher, art director, marketing and publicity team. But in the end, it all comes down to a reader like you, who probably has a million things going on and a million books to choose from, but you picked this one. It's incredibly humbling, and it's a privilege I'll never take for granted.

My first novel was published in 1987. I wrote it longhand in bound notebooks and typed it up on a borrowed Selectric typewriter. Seeing it published was a dream come true for me, and it was you, the reader, who made that dream come true. Sustaining a writing career that spans decades takes more than hard work and dedication from the writer. It requires readers like you, who spend your precious time reading my novels, year in and year out. Your curiosity and engagement with my stories mean the world to me. Your support is a cherished gift, and I am deeply grateful for each and every one of you.

Susan Wiggs is the author of more than fifty novels, including the beloved Lakeshore Chronicles series and the recent *New York Times* bestsellers *The Lost and Found Bookshop*, *The Oysterville Sewing Circle*, and *Family Tree*. Her award-winning books have been translated into two dozen languages. She lives with her husband on an island in Washington State's Puget Sound.